DEADLY

REDEMPTIONS

By Elizabeth Munro

The Chronicles of Anna

Book 3

Blue Swell Books
Nanaimo, B.C.
Canada

Second Print Edition: March 2016
ISBN: 978-1-988257-07-5

Visit www.elizabethmunro.ca

By Elizabeth Munro

Four Months Earlier...

When we arrived at Jack's immense family home in Connecticut, Soros led us through the large kitchen and into a private dining room. Decades of cigar and cigarette smoke yellowed the plaster walls.

Mister Gerald Walker sat at the head of the heavy old wood table. He appeared as I expected. Mid-thirties and well dressed.

Smelly.

A tidy pony tail, low on the back of his head, bound his long prematurely grey hair. Piercing dark eyes closely studied us from behind wire frame glasses. He was in good shape and had the bearing I'd come to associate with command; straighter in stature and more relaxed yet subtly wound somewhere inside like an explosive spring. He stood and embraced Soros then Jack. He shook Harvey's hand then took mine and kissed it.

"Welcome, Precious," he said as he ran my knuckles under his nose.

"Thank you, Mister Walker," I replied. Jack's hand tensed on my back as I tried to stay calm. As long as Walker paid attention to me he wasn't hurting Jack.

"You have no idea how my brother RJ tantalized me with hints about you," he said. He leaned so close I made out a few still dark hairs in his eyebrows then he put the skin above his top lip almost right on top of mine and inhaled. His hands stroked my cheeks. "She is so full of your scent, Jack."

I held still and waited until he turned aside and sneezed, curious what he'd read which made him clear it from under his nose.

"Mm," he said. "RJ says I wasn't imagining things when you disappeared from my sight a few weeks ago. Where did you go?"

"Richards' compound, Mister Walker," I answered. Jack said co-operate so I would.

"And what else did my brother learn?"

"I can only travel where there is a road. I'll react instinctively if me or my mate is in trouble."

The back of Walker's hand stung my cheek.

"My mate and I, Precious," he corrected.

"I will react instinctively if I am in trouble or my mate is in trouble, Mister Walker," I said, correcting my self without giving in by copying him. After two tiring days bouncing in Soros' truck I would have to be careful. Jack's hand reached a little further around my side so he could strengthen his grip but otherwise he didn't move. I knew what Jack meant by hurt and in comparison a slap didn't hurt.

"And what did you not tell my brother?" He asked.

"I can control the time of arrival within an hour or two before or after departure, Mister Walker."

"Did you see her react, RJ?"

"Yes, dear Gerald," Soros replied as Walker took a couple of steps back and pulled out his knife. "But we must not, my sweet brother. I know how much you want to see it. Father's grandsons have damaged her line. The travel would tear it from her, killing them."

Walker's broad face showed rage for a few seconds as he contemplated the consequences of trying anyway. His fingers shook on the handle of his blade before he put it away.

"Unimportant. You will tell me what it was like, RJ."

"Of course."

Sig hadn't warned me against travel. I guessed he told Soros during their chat at Jack's the day we fled. The day Paul died. As my breathing returned to normal I felt Jack loosen his grip.

"Precious? My brother says you can read family lines."

"Yes, Mister Walker."

"You will show me another time," Walker said.

"Yes, Mister Walker."

He moved to the head of the table and picked up his coffee, looking me over as he sipped. Harvey remained silent behind me at Jack's side and I could feel Soros' eyes imagining me wearing less.

"I will read you, Precious. Then you will tell me all about the amazing thing you can do which RJ says is my surprise." He licked his lips as he approached, standing much too close. "I love surprises, Precious. You will not love disappointing me."

I didn't know what to say so I kept my mouth shut.

Walker leaned in closer as his nose slowly moved over my right cheek. "Yes, Mister Walker," he whispered.

"Yes, Mister Walker."

"Mm, good," he said then his nose paused over my right ear, where the man who raped me hit me with his gun. "Attention from Mister Stanton, I believe." His tongue felt its way through my hair. "Yes, Mister Stanton. I found him with his pants down, chest full of holes like a peg board," he gestured to his head. "Something wrong here. Did you do that, Precious?"

"Yes, Mister Walker," I answered. Jack's hand moved up and he took hold of my bra. Walker didn't scare me but the thought of what he'd do to Jack if he interrupted him did.

"And what did you give Mister Stanton in return?"

"Everything he wanted, Mister Walker," I whispered. Those had been Jack's words when he'd forced me to tell Paul about it.

"I see," Walker said. I flinched when he bit my ear.

His nose moved along my throat to my shoulder as if following a trail. It stopped where I'd been cut by one of Damian's men in February. "One of Father's dumb grunts," he muttered as he kept going, working down my back as he turned me in place. Jack's hand brushed across my skin as I turned to face him.

"Ah, RJ. The man you lost in Calgary," he said. My shirt came up in the back. "Where did you find him Precious?"

"Last December in Edmonton, Mister Walker."

He lowered my shirt and worked his way to my thigh, dropping to his knees before he paused at the other scar from the fight in my home with Damian's men just five months earlier. He didn't comment then he turned me to face him and paused at my crotch.

"Mister Stanton hurt you here," he whispered then started his way up my stomach.

"Yes, Mister Walker," I whispered in reply, blinking away tears. Grateful my back was to Jack. I didn't want to see his face.

"Mm, Father," Walker said when he got to the scar above my belly button. I expected more questions but he straightened up instead.

"And now, Precious. What did you show my brother that is so glorious?"

"I can read the line of any man loyal to Mister Howard like a home movie, Mister Walker. Forward, rewind... past, future," I said, hoping it was okay to call Damian Mister Howard. I'd always called him Damian and suspected another backhand if I tried.

"Really? What did you not tell my brother, Precious?"

I took a deep breath. "I can show you what I see, Mister Walker. He only has to be within my range. I don't have to touch him."

Soros growled beside me. I'd made him think I had to have my hands on him to do it.

"Show me," Walker said. "Show me RJ."

"Yes, Mister Walker," I answered then I pointed under my nose. "Read me here, please. Follow."

I pulled my top lip between my teeth as his smell tried to overwhelm me then sent my sense to Soros' line and locked on. Walker stood close, watching my eyes as I looked into his. After a few seconds we watched ourselves through Soros' eyes.

I led him backwards.

Soros followed Jack and me into the room then the door from the parking lot. He watched my butt as Jack pulled me from the truck then my bare back as Jack's hand reached under my shirt. He greeted the man at the gate then his hand on my thigh.

"Forward," I whispered as I skipped ahead, emphasizing Soros' hands on me though I didn't think Walker would care.

Walker at the table. He picked up his mug then on his knees in front of me. Held my elbows as he intently watched my face. He spoke. Soros turned around and walked to the door. I flew out of Jack's reach, blood already pouring from my mouth. Soros took a step in my direction as my nails dug into my chest. Jack grabbed me and put his hand on my skin. He froze and held me still as Walker looked in my mouth. I skipped ahead. I sat in Jack's lap, facing him and trying to get something around his arm. My face hidden behind his head. Blood on the floor.

"Stop, Precious," Walker said.

I let Soros' line go and stood nose to nose with Walker.

"Not a word," he said. "You'll spoil the ending."

I swallowed hard, feeling sick to my stomach. "Yes, Mister Walker."

"She sent Father to the other side?"

"Yes, Gerald," Soros said as he walked to the door. Bastard knew something was coming and didn't want his clothes messed.

"How? Gun? Knife?"

He slapped me again when I didn't answer. I thought he was asking Soros.

"Both, Mister Walker," I said, refusing to put my hands up.

"How many, Precious," he asked, coming closer. I realized there was whiskey on his breath along with the coffee.

"Five rounds," I whispered as my lungs started to fail. "The knife twice, Mister Walker."

Jack got his other hand on my waist and tried to pull me toward him but I didn't budge. I put my hand on his and took it off as I raised my chin to try and stare down at Walker.

"Do you like numbers, Precious?"

"I like numbers, Mister Walker."

"Mm," he said. His top lip went between his teeth and he moaned. I didn't think anyone else heard.

"How many is that... five and two?"

"Seven, Mister Walker."

He took two steps back, his hand loosely swinging at the end of his right arm. Before I saw him move his fist hit my mouth. I felt a crunch as Soros flew past me. My hands jumped to my chest to try and free the lancing pain instead of my crushed face. My line tearing as Jack's children tried to get away hurt more. My fingers slipped on my skin as the warm wetness on my chin spread.

Jack got his hands to my skin, steadying me on my feet and the pain in my chest lifted as quickly as it had come. My tongue found a hard piece of tooth underneath it then the jagged other half still in place.

"Hold her, Jack," Soros said. "Gently."

Jack kept one hand on my side and the other went around me. Soros had control of him. I smelled him in Jack. The broken tooth felt like a nail jammed up in my gums and my lips were both split inside and bled. I tried not to swallow and let it run freely down my chin.

Walker used a cloth napkin to push my lips out of the way. I held still, again refusing to let my courage fail. It would quickly slip away once it started to go.

"Just one?" Walker asked. "Bad luck."

Since we played numbers I expected to be hit again. He wanted seven.

"How many is that Precious... seven less one?"

"Thix, Nither Balker," I said.

"Thix? Bad luck, Jack," Walker said. "I can't think what Jack has thix of and we've already done teeth."

He opened a drawer in the table and pulled out a pair of clippers. Heavier ones for small branches. My mother used the same ones in her garden. "We'll have to be creative."

"Bleath, Nither Balker... hith me again," I begged.

"I can, Precious," he replied. "But it won't count. Have a seat, Jack."

Jack sat.

"You'll need both hands."

Jack pulled me down on his lap, facing him. Then he pushed up my shirt so his arms touched my skin and his hands were free.

"No, Baby," I whispered in his ear as I wrapped my arms around his head. I pictured the clippers in his hand, four fingers and a thumb. That was only five. Walker wanted six. "Not your thingers."

"Not fingers, Precious," Walker patiently said like he spoke to a child. He put the clippers in Jack's right hand. "I want knuckles... that should take care of the two smallest fingers on your left hand."

I reached between us to undo Jack's belt, his body already tensing. He grunted and shuddered as something small and soft landed on the floor. Any other time it would be erotic, Jack grunting and shaking underneath me, but it was horrible. The blood from my mouth ran on his shirt and his head felt cold next to mine. I finally got the belt off after the last two pieces of his smallest finger hit the floor. I wrapped it around his upper arm and pulled it tight as he moaned and shook with the fourth.

"Ith okay, Jack," I forced out past my fat lips. I felt stupid for saying something so useless but couldn't think of anything else. He constantly trembled. I held his belt as tight as I could with one hand and held his head up with the other. With nothing to do, I heard the joint tear apart. Jack's stomach heaved and sour coffee from the night before mixed with the blood on our shirts as the final piece came off.

The clippers fell. Jack's colour was gone and his glassy eyes looked past me. I heard Walker's chair slide out and his cutlery on his plate.

"Good to see you again, Jack," he cheerfully said. "Nice to meet you, Precious."

"Nithe to meet you, Nither Balker," I said. Jack kept hold of me so I tightened the belt even more as Soros put a cloth on Jack's hand. The fragile new skin under my bandage shifted with the pressure as I pulled. The burn Soros gave me at Jack's kitchen stove was barely a week old.

"Hold it tight," Soros told me and I pressed it on Jack's brutalized hand. "Get up, kids."

I stood, leaning over staying as close to Jack as I could. Then I pulled on the belt.

"Stand up, Baby," I said. Walker chewed with his mouth open and Harvey already had the door. Soros waited in the hall. Jack made it to his feet, leaning on me, his chin on my shoulder as we made our awkward waltz across the floor. His hand slipped. "Thick ith in my bra Jack," I said and he did.

We followed Soros out and down the hall then struggled up several flights of stairs to what I assumed was the top floor. Jack's stomach started to go again.

"Breathe, Baby," I said. "Keep ith down."

He didn't say anything but I could hear his lungs filling more than before. We passed several doors on each side before we turned to find Travis waiting outside one. He opened it and let us in, clicking it shut behind. A first aid bag waited on the floor in front of a wooden chair. Soros pointed. "Sit."

I pushed Jack down as Soros pulled up the other chair and sat next to him.

"Let's look," he said as he pulled the cloth off. Jack's hand oozed where his two fingers had been. I took a deep breath to keep my stomach under control and with two free hands I was able to pull the belt even tighter. I wrapped it around his upper arm a couple of times and managed to secure the end under itself. The first aid bag held a pair of scissors on top so I cut Jack's shirt off as Soros dug around in the bag.

Soros took a syringe and injected it into Jack's hand. I put my burned hand on Jack's shoulder to keep him up and reached into the bag. I'd recognized the morphine so I took it and a syringe. Soros glanced at what I was doing and didn't comment. I read the vial and remembered how much then I cleaned the top and drew out what I thought was the right amount.

"How much are you giving him?" Soros finally spoke. I moved my hand out of the way so he could see. "Double it."

I paused.

"Jack had a problem with morphine. That won't do a thing for him."

I nodded and drew more then cleaned a spot on Jack's arm and emptied it into the muscle. Soros grabbed another vial and told me how much to give him so I did. He sewed as Jack's breathing eased and his head tipped back on the tall chair. I breathed easier, too. His colour seemed to improve. May have been my imagination.

Cautiously, I took my hand from Jack's shoulder and he stayed upright so I undid his bloody pants so they would be easy to pull off when he stood. My bloody clothes went on top of Jack's shirt. No point in spreading blood and vomit across the bedroom.

I knelt next to Jack as Soros worked. He was quick with the stitches. I took a few vials of morphine and more syringes and stuffed them in my bra. When he was done, I took Jack's belt off his arm and Soros watched Jack's hand for a minute until he was satisfied nothing leaked. Then I held it up as Soros put a thick dressing on.

"Get him to the bed."

I pulled Jack up and kicked the blankets out of the way before pushing him in. The morphine and needles went on the table.

"Let's look at you."

Jack lay on his side so I sat on the edge of the bed as Soros moved the chair closer. He pulled my lips back with his latex gloves, still covered in Jack's blood. Then he took the syringe he used to freeze Jack's hand and froze my mouth including my gums where the tooth broke. He put in a couple of stitches top and bottom and got out the pliers.

"Can't fix your tooth."

I nodded and tipped my head back. The pliers lost their grip the first try and slipped off the raw nerve but he pulled it out the second try. He shoved a piece of gauze in the hole.

"Bite."

I bit then Soros cleaned my burned hand and wrapped it up. He picked up the garbage and left without a word. I turned off the lamp and climbed over Jack. The sun was up outside, blue sky and bright light. I reached over Jack and put his hand on his chest so it was up as high as I could get it then I pressed my chest into his side and carefully took his hand out of my bra. There was no pain so I stayed close and listened to his breathing. I worried I gave him too much morphine and eventually I decided if he was going to stop breathing he would have. We slept in the big bed, inhaling the air scented with vomit and blood.

For the next few days I took care of Jack. He didn't speak though he followed instructions and didn't come out of his stupor. I thought it might be the morphine or depression. Embarrassment perhaps; humiliation for having to cut his own fingers off in front of me. I wondered if he might even be angry about being punished for something I did. I kept him clean on the toilet and tried to feed him. Between the two of us we had one useful hand since he wouldn't do anymore than keep his right hand on me. We showered once and I put clean clothes on us but it took forever and I was nervous about having him on his feet for so long.

Soros was in and out and a Mister Someone brought us food three times a day. Jack wouldn't open his mouth to eat no matter what I tried. Someone took our bloody clothes and returned everything but Jack's cut up shirt. It was all surprisingly clean.

On the fourth day, Jack stared at the ceiling when I woke. I put my hand on his chest and to my relief felt it rise and fall. He was so still. I lay on the side of the bed by the table to avoid climbing over him and I sat, tucking his injured arm under mine against my bare side then I readied his morphine. After the shower, I kept us in underwear to avoid the hassle of dressing. Before I pulled the cap from the syringe, he rolled over and held my hands still.

"No more," he said.

I turned to face him and nodded.

"Smile for me?" he asked.

That would hurt so I shook my head.

Jack sighed. "I'm so sorry, Baby."

"I'm sorry I have strong teeth," I said, lisping as air snuck out the gap in my teeth.

Jack put his fingers on my top lip and pushed it up.

"Damn."

"It broke off. Mister Soros had to pull it. It felt better."

He pulled me closer and kissed my half swollen mouth. "You sound adorable when you talk," he whispered.

"I didn't sound adorable before?"

"I didn't think you could sound more adorable but you do." He was smooth.

"You're good, Jack," I said and gave him the smile he asked for. "I'm glad you came back. It's been lonely."

My breath heated in my throat as I tried not to cry. Jack still needed looking after.

"Sshhh," he whispered. "Do you need to fall apart now?"

"No," I said as I did anyway. Jack moved over, giving me a little more room and I curled up with him as I started to bawl.

"I'm sorry for everything," Jack said. "I'm sorry about what RJ did to you, and Stanton and the rape. I'm sorry you had to bury all that to protect your baby. I'm so sorry you've lost Paul. And for Gerald. Thank you for looking after me. If I didn't have you to come back to I wouldn't have come back."

After a while, breakfast arrived and I held it together while it was put on the little table then I wound it up again for a bit. We ate and showered. Jack paled and shook even though he said he felt fine. He didn't argue about returning to bed. There wasn't much else to do when we had to be connected together.

Tombs

Chapter 1

"I think they're done," I told Jack. His sons' soft lines in my chest felt anxious. Every week they could go a little longer without contact from him but anxious was only a minute away from agony for me when they tried to tear free of my line to get to him.

"In bed then, Baby," he said, lifting the blanket and patting the pillow.

I nodded and climbed in. My line was still healing from the damage they'd done in the first few days after fertilization, before we knew why it hurt so much, and they still wouldn't go without Jack for very long. If we tried again with his hand off me the pain would be instant. It would be a few days before we could spend another half hour detached. The sun had already fallen behind the hill to the west and the sky was long dark. Fall was well under way.

Jack told me before we arrived his father's house was like a castle. I'd never been in a castle so to me it felt more like a big old hotel. No elevators or phone-in room service but it was fully equipped with security cameras and armed guards. The big three storey square surrounded a private courtyard. Meals had been served there in the summer when the weather permitted but now the tables and chairs sat stacked out of the way.

Jack's top floor room occupied the end of the house furthest from the main doors and overlooked the parking lot and the back door we used to enter the morning we arrived. His room had its own bathroom, a privilege since he was Damian Howard's son and was big enough for a small sofa, chair and a desk in addition to the king sized bed. We had to be so close all the time we only ever used half of it. No fridge or anywhere to cook so three times a day Jack took me downstairs to the dining room. I wasn't allowed there when the men took their meals for a number of reasons I could guess at from offending them with a glimpse of my full sleeve tattoos which sometimes peeked out from under my cuff, unwanted attention as Richards' woman or the possibility I might count faces to get a handle on their numbers. That would have been too easy if I hadn't been forbidden to read them.

In truth I was Roberts' woman. The traitor's woman. And I didn't care how offensive they found my body art or how many smelly followers of Damian were still around. I carried Jack's sons to make sure my daughter wasn't harmed and Jack lived because if his sons' lines tore themselves free they would die.

Jack's room had become my stable. Only three women lived in the house. All 'bred' to men on Jack's side of the family. Their men with them off and on. They ate with Jack and me and when their men were around they joined us. At first I couldn't understand why they'd stay in a place so strange. Their reasons seemed so different. As I got to know them, I found they weren't. Trust, loyalty and obedience. My trust and loyalty were placed differently than theirs and I was in no way obedient. My dead husband Paul at one time explained to Jack that if I couldn't back up my decisions with trust and loyalty he needed to stay out of my way.

Jack spent the majority of his half hour running since he could get away instead of nervously waiting for me to start hurting. I had a bath like I did every evening except Jack didn't have to sit on the floor with his hand on me. I stepped out in time for him to get a quick shower. Neither of us had dressed. After more than four months of near constant contact, nudity wasn't a big deal.

"You usually spend your break crying," he said as he brushed my puffy eyes with his fingers.

"Because I miss you."

"Your line is blushing," he said. He could tell when I lied.

"I missed you, too," I amended. "And my baby."

"My brother says they're doing okay."

Jack's brother RJ Soros tracked her. Our bargain was to give Jack and Soros' father's line a strong reader like Jack and I. They'd get two and in exchange Soros would make sure my daughter and the children with her were left alone.

"And Paul?" Jack asked.

"I love him, as much as I love you. I miss him."

"You know I still love my first. Desiring you doesn't give me any guilt at all."

"I know."

Jack had never told me about her but he called her name at night and never with passion. Fear and anguish soaked him like his sweat sticking us together. He would tremble and I'd hold him tighter until he calmed down. I'd wake sometimes with him holding me the same way and knew my memories had woken him.

I leaned on him and he put his hands behind his head. We'd learned as long as my torso touched him he could have his hands free.

"You're lucky my will power is strong or I'd be begging for you every night."

"Not just hinting like you are now?"

"Yes," he laughed.

"What if it cures me? They won't want you around."

"What if it doesn't? Then you're denying yourself of Jack for no reason at all."

He knew my objections and gave me the same answers. We both knew what wouldn't happen before we fell asleep. Between the rape being months in the past and moving into the second third of the pregnancy, I was interested again and too stubborn to let him know how ready I was to give in. Jack pulled himself out from under me and rested his head on my stomach; his damaged hand on his sons. I was as big now at four months as I'd been with Camille at six. The two remaining fingers on his left hand felt around for them.

"It's still too soon to feel them move," I said. "Give it a couple of weeks."

"You said that a couple of weeks ago..."

"Didn't."

"I know."

As his hand kept moving I pushed my tongue through the gap in my front teeth. I would have rather spent an entire evening getting to know Soros than the mere twenty minutes we'd spent with Walker.

"Jack?" I said, remembering getting through that night and the following weeks.

"Mm?" he answered, his mouth on my stomach.

"I love you, Jack."

"I love you, Baby," he mumbled. His touch distracted and made it hard to keep telling him no.

"You want to read?" I asked. Jack's room had shelves of ancient books. Many of them he couldn't stand and would tell me about the man he was when he brought them here as if to apologize for their presence.

"No."

I sighed and rubbed my feet together as his hand ran up my side then down my leg.

"You know you want to say it," Jack whispered.

"Mm, yes," I answered as I started to lose myself. Jack pushed himself up so his head was by mine. His blue eyes sparkled as his nose teased my lower lip.

"Just say so if you want to stop. I promise I will. You just have to tell me it's okay now."

We moved closer as he stroked my cheek and I turned to face him, putting my leg up over his.

"No," he said, pushing it back down. "That's not fair. You have to tell me you want to."

I rolled away in frustration, refusing to say the words and he laughed. Jack reached over to turn off the light and lay on his back, keeping a hand on my side.

"Night, Baby," he said.

"Night, Jack."

His breathing quickly quieted while I stayed awake. As my eyes adjusted to the dark room, I made out the cold stars through the uncovered window. The house was never silent but at least down the end on the third floor where we were it was quiet.

I fingered my wedding ring. The burn healed and even with the bit of weight gain it moved around. Maybe it was time. My connection to Paul was long gone since he turned up at Jack's. Left behind dead in Jack's yard; a round from his own gun in his head.

I decided if it came off I'd ask Jack to sleep with me. If it didn't then he'd have to wait another night. I gently started working it off my finger, pressing it up into the underside to get it over my knuckle. It resisted but eventually it came. Smooth skin circled my finger where it had been for the past year. I made out the rough edge of the scar which followed it around then I put the ring to my lips and kissed it. I love you, Paul, I thought, but it's time to say good-bye.

The ring went on the little table beside the bed.

I turned to Jack and put his arm under me before I slid closer, keeping in contact until I had my elbow in the pillow beside his head and my face right above his. He slept like a stone. I let my nose touch his and still nothing so I put my hand on his cheek and waited. If he didn't wake up he'd never believe I'd even tried. The smallest unusual sound at the other end of the house would have him sitting even though I could jump on the bed without getting a reaction. I ran my thumb along his bottom lip. He pressed it up into his top one and let it relax.

My tongue came out and moistened my lips before I sealed them on his and pulled away making a tiny popping sound. Then again. I figured I could make love to him and he'd have no idea why he was smiling in the morning.

"Jack," I whispered.

"Anna," he answered.

He'd been awake the whole time. That was fair. I'd done the same thing to him more than once to eavesdrop. I didn't say anything for a few seconds and kissed him again instead.

"Is something wrong?"

I sighed. The longer I took to say it the more likely I was to say no and roll over to go to sleep.

"Jack," I whispered again.

"Anna..."

"I want you to be my lover now."

"Okay, Baby," he whispered as his arms came up around me.

Chapter 2

Jack's stomach rumbled, waking me. I giggled and turned to him realizing there shouldn't be sufficient daylight to see his face. He hadn't cut his hair or shaved since we'd arrived and it had grown quickly for four and a half months. His bone straight bangs came down to brush his nose. At least he trimmed the moustache. It would have driven me buggy if he hadn't. The beard came in red, gold and curly with the exception of where the scar ran down the left side of his face.

The sun was up which meant we'd missed breakfast. It wasn't up far enough to mean we'd miss lunch. He threw a leg over my thigh and slid his hand down from my side to the lump of boys between us.

"Hi, Jack," I whispered.

"Morning, Baby."

"Did I make up for last time?"

"Nothing to make up for. Neither one of us wanted it like that," Jack replied.

"Mm," I agreed. "I know it's not how you wanted your sons to get their start."

It was what it was. Jack ignoring my tears to give me something just a week after the rape. Awful for both of us. Not like hours ago. Looking into each others eyes, in love, getting something we both wanted.

"It wasn't. Last night was."

"Yes."

"You always call them my sons."

"Yes," I said again. He turned me to him, wanting to know why without saying the words. "I feel their connection to you but not to me like I did with Camille. I feel them a bit, more today. Maybe that's why we get our breaks now."

Jack looked sad.

"They'll feel like mine. I'm their mother," I reassured him. "I love them, Jack, like any mother loves the lives inside her. I just don't feel connected to them yet. Their strong connection is to you. It's what gave their lines life."

"Okay, I understand."

"I love you, Jack..."

"Mm. You too, Baby," he whispered, wrapping his arms around me and holding me tight. After a few minutes my eyes closed.

"I've never seen you sleep so well," he said.

I startled. I'd started to drift off.

"My hand was off you for two hours," he mouthed in my ear. "When I got a few feet from you I saw you get anxious but when I got close again you relaxed. They'll know if we're too far apart. You know they can read where we are."

I nodded, understanding. We had to keep pretending he was close enough to touch me. Seconds later there was a knock. I pulled the blanket over my head.

"Come in," Jack called. There was no point in telling them not to, they would come in anyway. The door opened and I heard the footsteps of several men.

"Jack! Good morning and good morning, Sweet Thing."

"Good morning, Mister Soros," I cheerfully said, my voice muffled by Jack's chest. I'd learned the best way to keep Soros and Walker in a good mood with me was to act as suffocatingly cheerful as they did. I nuzzled my nose in the small hairs and gently kissed him as Soros went on.

"I hear you've redeemed yourself with your mate, Top Gun."

Jack didn't say anything. I wasn't surprised. He rarely spoke to his brothers. I'd found life here much easier once I stopped expecting privacy. Jack pretended he had privacy by pretending they weren't there which seemed a lot harder on him than acceptance would be. Until we started taking our little breaks a month earlier, I spent three months in constant contact with Jack which gave me no privacy whatsoever.

Any time out of our room, two armed guards followed us. Not because they thought we'd try anything but for the protection of the traitor Jack Roberts and Richards' woman. The men guarding us were considered deeply loyal to Damian and either Soros or Walker. I hadn't risked reading them myself. It was just safer to keep my nose out of things as Jack had warned me. Walker memorized my scent that first day and Jack explained he could tell quite accurately who read what when he put his mind to it. Our guard would follow orders and protect us. Not everyone in the house would.

"Let's see the smile Jack's put on your face, Sweet Thing."

I rolled my eyes and stuck my tongue out under cover of the blanket before I sat up with a big grin on my face. I kept the blanket part way up so my tattooed arms and shoulders were visible. Soros stared but Harvey and the other man looked away in obvious discomfort at my shameless inked display. I reached under the blanket and squeezed Jack's free hand.

"Get dressed, kids. Mister Walker expects you for lunch. It's time to earn your keep, Sweet Thing."

I turned to Jack. "Did you hear, Jack? We get to eat at the big kids' table. Doesn't that sound delicious?"

"Delicious," Jack muttered, knowing exactly what I was doing and not liking it at all.

"Make pronto," Soros said and sat down to wait. We must have slept later than I thought if we had to hurry for lunch. Jack pulled me from the bed, keeping himself between me and Soros. Then he dragged me into the bathroom. While the shower warmed, he took his hand off me.

"See?" He whispered.

I put his hand back. "I don't like it. They'll hurt you if they find out we've been keeping it from them."

"The sooner there is less risk of me hurting your line if I make a mistake the better."

We stepped under the water and even though there was no need he kept his hand on me. After a moment though he took my left hand and tried to put my ring back on.

"Please, no."

"Why did you take it off?"

He was genuinely upset and I was upset about him trying to put it on me. Even more upset he didn't simply understand. I crossed my arms, pulling my hand free and keeping it from him at the same time.

"Are we going to fight, Jack?" He stared a moment, considering then he put the hand holding the ring on my hip and grabbed the soap with the other. I relaxed my arms and got to washing. If Soros waited then we shouldn't delay. Jack stiffly participated in our well practised routine and when I turned to the running water he tightened his arm around my ribs.

"Why?" He hissed in my ear.

"Because he's dead. How do I have a future with you if I'm pulling him along with me?"

"You have no future with me," he said. "Maybe a few months. Why do you disgrace yourself further?"

I glared at him, tears starting. Sleeping with him felt like a terrible mistake. I put my hands on his angry face and pulled him close to passively feel his loyalty.

"You're still loyal to me but I taste your brothers in you now," I said. "Is it my disgrace you're upset about or your own?"

Jack pulled away and moved under the water. I stayed pressed up against him out of habit so he had both hands free.

"I took it off because I would wear yours but I guess you don't want me like that. I couldn't sleep with you again still married to him."

He sighed and put his hand to his face as he lowered his head to get it under the water.

"He disgraced me before I did anything to disgrace myself. He never knew I found out and with the exception of what we did to protect my daughter I never indulged in payback."

Jack straightened up and turned, hitting his head. "I didn't know."

I glared at him, feeling humiliated all over again.

"Now you do," I said, putting my hand out. "If last night was a mistake put it back."

Jack shook his head and reached around the curtain to put the ring on the counter.

"I'm sorry," he said.

I didn't trust myself to fairly answer so I kept my mouth shut and reached around him to turn off the water. Jack passed me a towel and I dried off before I stopped and looked up at him. Jack knew I wanted to speak and turned on the water in the sink.

"I'm sorry for what I said about your loyalty," I said as I moved my hand under the running water to make it sound like we used it for something other than hiding our whispers. "I know it's because we're here and what they did to us. If you taste of them then I do too."

"Yes," he paused. He wasn't done talking. "Will you keep it on for now, please? The women here are all married to their men except you. My brothers know we're not but the rest assume we are." He held up his left hand. "They think mine got swept up when this happened. The ring makes you somewhat less despicable."

I watched him another second.

"Okay, Jack."

"Thank you, Baby," he whispered as he turned the water off and pulled a towel around me. I took the ring from the counter and pushed it on. It didn't feel right, or I didn't. I felt like I'd taken something which wasn't mine and I wasn't sure if it was the ring I'd taken or Jack.

When we left the bathroom, Soros and the other two hadn't moved though new clothes lay out on the bed. With my stomach growing, Soros shopped for me. Tan pants with a maternity panel in the front and a soft deep pink two piece sweater comprised today's outfit. A short sleeve scoop neck top, long and loose in the front, nestled in a cardigan with a single button low where the top scooped.

"Oh my, Mister Soros. Are those for me?" I exclaimed while I peered around Jack. He hid me as I pulled my underwear on then I stayed near the dresser and helped him.

"Yes, Sweet Thing," Soros replied.

"Thank you," I said. Soros looked pleased. I knew they would be expensive and a perfect fit He pinched me once for taking something from one outfit and wearing it with another so I only mixed and matched at his direction. Otherwise his gifts only went on in complete sets. As soon as I could, I approached the clothes and picked up the sweater, feeling the light knit in my fingers.

"What a colour," I commented then I put the sweater to my cheeks. "Mm, so soft. Thank you."

"You are most welcome, Sweet Thing," Soros said. I knew he'd enjoy watching me touch it. I quickly put the pants on and pulled the short sleeved top over my head. Then the cardigan.

"Oh dear, which shoes?" I asked. Shoes hadn't been supplied so it was safer to ask for his advice.

"Those," he said, pointing to a pair of open toed brown flats. The leather showed off three rich shades.

"Yes, Mister Soros," I said as I slipped them on then toted Jack to the mirror. Soros also liked looking at me looking at myself. "As usual, Mister Soros, you have outdone yourself."

Soros beamed as we left the room. But beaming was only a second or two away from a smack for me or stitches for Jack if I messed something else up. The cuts on his thigh were evidence of that. Jack's left hand held its usual place up under the back of my sweaters. He preferred to hide it and it left him with a hand which could do pretty much everything on its own.

I followed Harvey and the other man ahead of us as we went down the hall. Soros dropped back and took Jack's elbow so Jack leaned toward him.

"I have other business tomorrow," Soros whispered. "You will take her to her doctor appointment in your Nissan. I have a room booked for the two of you in town. I expect you to return by noon the next day unless you hear from me otherwise. Pack extra just in case."

I picked up Jack's nod in the corner of my eye as we reached the stairs. Something was up if we were going alone, staying away and packing for a longer absence. He took the railing and tightened his arm around me because I couldn't reach it. Once at the bottom, he led us past Walker's private dining room before we stopped. I heard voices further down the hall around the corner.

"You will wait here," Soros said, leaving us with our guard.

I turned to face Jack and put my arms around him. He pulled my head to his shoulder and kissed my forehead. He seemed nervous. Soros said I would earn my keep and I wasn't entirely sure what he meant. It was almost twenty minutes before he returned.

"You will sit to Mister Walker's right, Sweet Thing. Jack will sit on your other side. Do not listen to anyone but Mister Walker and follow his instructions explicitly."

"Yes, Mister Soros," I answered.

"Lunch time."

Our guard led us down the hall and around the corner then into the dining room. Perhaps twenty men sat in groups around several long tables, more seats empty than taken. Walker sat alone at his table, directly facing the door and we walked through an aisle between tables to his. I stared in front of me at a spot on the wall above his head as Jack took me to my seat. Walker wiped his hands and stood.

"Precious..." he softly said as we approached then tapped a finger on his cheek so I lifted my chin and kissed him where he indicated as he chewed in my ear.

"Thank you for inviting me to lunch, Mister Walker," I quietly said. Very quietly. The room started to go silent when Jack and I entered and quieted further until completely devoid of sound. Several chairs moved on the floor and a few men stood up to leave.

"Sit, my dear."

Jack and I sat and waited, watching three backs go through the door we'd come in.

"Perhaps Precious is offended those gentlemen do not wish to dine with her?" Walker asked.

"No, Mister Walker. I sincerely apologize for offending them," I answered as I dropped my eyes to appear submissive.

Walker nodded. "Eat."

Jack and I ate. I felt relieved I'd given the right answer. After a few minutes, conversation resumed but I kept my eyes down and didn't look up at them.

Walker leaned toward me. "If you were offended, Precious, how would you recommend I mend your hurt feelings."

I felt Jack's hand move on my back with what I'd come to recognize as nervousness. His two fingers and thumb spread as he reached a little further around me.

"With Mister Walker's permission may I make some assumptions?"

"Absolutely, Precious."

Jack's thumb moved up against his first finger then back before his hand relaxed. Careful.

"I assume it will be cold tomorrow," I started. Walker nodded. "And those gentlemen are hard working and valuable."

Walker nodded again so I continued.

"Because the road from the highway to the house is so long I assume this property is grand in its scale."

"That it is, Precious," Walker said as I contemplated a quick bite of food then decided against it.

"In that case, I might suggest some work they can do around the perimeter. Perhaps a fence or other repairs?"

Walker remained silent so I went on.

"I might send them out on foot to a spot quite a distance from the comforts of the house on a task that would take the bulk of the day."

"Such a simple thing would alleviate any hurt feelings you may have suffered?"

"Not in itself. First I would invite them for breakfast. Make sure they were well fortified with a hot meal sufficiently laced with laxative."

Jack coughed as Soros and Walker laughed.

"Elegant, Precious, very elegant," Walker said.

"Thank you, Mister Walker."

He let us eat a few more minutes before he spoke again, leaning his boozy mouth right up to my ear. "How does it work, Precious? The future?"

I turned to him, keeping my eyes down.

"It changes, Mister Walker. An hour from now could be very different when it's only five minutes away. Being aware of what will happen affects it when we are surprised by what is coming. Our behaviour changes the path."

"Precious, there is a man at the table to the left by the door. Red hair and a brown shirt."

I glanced up.

"This morning I believe he took something. We do not steal here, Precious. This man knows it yet he did anyway. You will show me so I am sure then you will show me what he will do with the item he stole."

"Yes, Mister Walker," I whispered. Jack's hand slipped down to seize the waistband of my pants. Defensive.

"Please," I said gesturing under my nose and Walker quickly put his sense there. I sent my sense to the man and found his line but couldn't latch on. Again I tried, almost getting it before it slipped from my grip.

"Precious..." Walker warned.

"I can only read men who are loyal to Mister Howard. I'll get it, Mister Walker, but his loyalty to Mister Howard is so weak."

Walker's nostrils flared against my ear.

"I can read loyalties, Mister Walker," I quickly said, something cold and unwelcome settled in my stomach as I scrambled for more time. "Come back and I will show you to whom he is most loyal. I don't know the man."

I put the fingerprint of him under my nose and pulled back a bit so I faced Walker.

"I know him," Walker muttered. "Read."

"Yes, Mister Walker."

I sent my sense back to the man at the table and held it quietly to the man's line then I moved my fingers in front of my face like I tried to capture his scent and send it to my nose.

"I'll getcha..." I whispered. Walker started to speak and I put my fingers on his mouth. Then I found the bit of Damian loyalty and took hold.

"I see," Walker murmured.

I rewound, skipping bit by bit until Walker breathed in my ear. "Forward."

The man stood at a heavy door, something thin slipped in the lock and his fingers only needed a few seconds. Once inside, he took a rifle like one I'd shot with back at Paul's. Good distance, powerful. A sniper's rifle. He put it in a long bag with some rounds and walks out. Down a hall and outside where he stashed it in some bushes.

"Now what is he going to do with it, Precious?"

We watched him leave the table, talking with a couple of others. Then to a room like Jack's only smaller where he changed into light coloured clothing before heading outside. He looked to make sure nobody was around and retrieved the rifle and ran into the trees.

"Skip ahead..."

Then he lay prone, looking through the scope. I saw myself and Jack with Harvey and the other man who escorted us to lunch. We're on our daily walk; the tan pants from Mister Soros stuck out from under my jacket. Jack's fingers reached down the back collar of my jacket to keep them on my skin and as the man watched us, Jack closed in behind me to kiss my neck before he switched hands. The man's knuckle moved, barely visible in the corner of his eye and Harvey fell, a red smear on the snow behind him. The other guard uselessly stood by as Jack pulled me off the path toward the trees. Before we made it, Jack dropped. I struggled to keep his hand on me and pick him up as our escort disappeared out of sight. Then I went down.

"Stop, Precious."

I'd reached under the table and dug my fingers into Jack's leg. He had my hand, trying to loosen them.

"The man who ran down the path, to whom is he loyal, Precious?"

I read him. "The same as the man I showed you, Mister Walker."

"Any others in this room?"

It took a few minutes and I found two more, pointing them out.

23

"Finish your meal, Precious. The ones you have found will tell me if there are any others. As always, not a word."

"Yes, Mister Walker."

Jack pried my hand off his leg and I took a drink to test my stomach before trying to shove more food in. I would apologize for the bruises to his thigh later.

Before excusing himself, Walker put his hand on my cheek and kissed my neck. "You've been a very good girl, Precious…"

Chapter 3

Mister Harvey and the guard who would turn his back on us led us from the great dining room and returned us to Jack's room. Jack wanted to talk. I could tell by the urgent movement of his hand as he hurried me along the dim hall and up the stairs; Harvey in front and the other man behind. Given Walker's instructions, Jack took a risk by asking.

Jack pulled me in and tried to push the door shut but Harvey stopped it with his foot.

"Your Missus will be exercised this afternoon, you missed this morning," Harvey said.

As I looked up at Jack, my lips cooled and my cheeks whitened. Jack saw my fear and nodded at Harvey.

"Half an hour," Harvey said.

I grabbed Jack as soon as I heard the door click. Mainly for comfort but also to avoid the questions in his eyes. It didn't work for long.

"What happened?" he whispered.

I started to open my mouth and changed my mind. My hand shook when I brought it up to stop myself from talking.

"I'm sorry I pinched your leg," I said between my fingers.

He raised an eyebrow.

"I'm sick. I can't go today," I added.

"You know that's not going to get you out of it," Jack said. I nodded and looked up at the roof to keep my tears from rolling out. "Jesus, you're scared. What the hell did you see?"

"I can't say, Jack." I took a few deep breaths and tried to convince myself Walker had everything under control and Harvey said we're going out for exercise because Walker hadn't had a chance to call it off yet.

"Shit," he muttered. "I'm so tired of hearing that."

"It'll be okay," I said, hoping to sound convincing. He wasn't reassured.

"You don't believe that," he said, meaning 'you're lying, Anna.'

"I want to believe it."

"Hm."

Fear found a corner in my gut, chilling my insides and joining the helplessness and resignation I struggled with every day. Jack had me half way to the bed before I realized we'd even moved. He wrapped himself around me and knocked my shoes off my feet and over the edge onto the floor.

"Was she family?"

There were other topics he could have distracted me with. None as effectively as Paul's infidelity.

"I forgave him, Jack. Taking a second or claiming an inheritance isn't as courteous and clean cut as I was led to believe. For the men at least. Maybe because your lines are stronger the depth of your new attachment can be overwhelming. Or just takes longer to fade."

"So which was his?" I couldn't tell if Jack sounded angry with Paul or not. Jack and I crossed the same line, granted for a noble purpose and not for pleasure. And only once, not three times. I guessed Jack felt a little smug knowing the saintly Paul had fallen, too.

I sighed and looked away.

"And you say you love me." I pictured the sneer on his lips.

"I do love you."

"Whatever it is, Anna, you think it's love. You believe it is, but it's more like what you feel for a child or a pet. If you want to then keep it up. Leaving things out, acting like I'm too stupid to understand so you can pretend everything is great and there's nothing I can do about it. One day soon they're going to haul me away to take my last step and you're going to stand up here and watch."

Jack's voice broke as I saw the first tears I'd ever seen from him. He sat and pulled me up by my elbows. I got my knees under myself as he pulled my nose to his.

"Do you know what we do to traitors here? We hang them. Right outside that window."

His hands took my cheeks and turned me toward it.

"Will you stand there watching? They won't cover my head. I'll be looking into your eyes when Gerald pulls the lever. And what will you do? You'll be up here thinking you were good to me. Thinking we'll see each other again.

"Do you understand we won't?" His mouth pressed my ear as his angry whisper cut deep.

"That man and woman on the other side will remember Anna and Jack but they won't be Anna and Jack. We won't pick up where we left off. That man and woman will start off with a clean slate. Jack will be dead and the only thing keeping Anna from being close behind him are the little favours she's going to keep doing for the man who dropped Jack through the floor.

"Will you stay with my body? Waiting the hours it will take for my line to fade as the pain of our connection being gradually torn from your chest becomes more than you can bear? It'll fill you up slowly like you're sipping down a gallon of acid you can't stop putting to your lips. Will you try and remember my face when they take me away? Hoping you'll see it in our sons as you live out your days as Gerald's precious pet?

"So how about this? You keep treating me like a child and I'll get my hand off you as soon as I can. You need to treat me like the man I am and accept the fact you're the child."

Jack's anger boiled, not letting go as he finished telling me off. How dare he? Everything I did was to protect him as long as I could. I did everything I was told because anything they couldn't do to punish a pregnant woman they wouldn't hesitate to do to Jack.

"You don't know me at all," I spat. "Now that you're getting it again you have no reason to be good to me. It's only lust you feel for me anyway. I'm nothing more than the machine that keeps your children alive. Nobody is more sorry we're stuck together than I am."

Jack pushed me back on to my butt; his hands off but still close enough anyone reading us wouldn't know.

"You're a stupid, selfish bitch," he hissed.

"And you sound just like your father, Mister Roberts," I replied using the formal title I only used to address his brothers. His old family name from before he turned traitor and came to Paul and me for help.

He flinched as if I hit him. As soon as the words passed my lips I was sorry. So sorry. I crossed the line and slapped my hands over my mouth before any more damage could come out. I couldn't take them back. Jack bit his lip and tried to hold himself together then he turned his back on me and dropped his head, arms fiercely crossed around his ribs.

I realized what bothered him. Too late, of course. My tongue was sharp like a knife when my fuse ran out and I'd used it to wound the one person I had left. Slowly, I reached for his shaking shoulder but he pulled away.

"You're right, Jack," I whispered. "I'm arrogant and mean. I was trying to hurt myself by hurting you. I'm sorry I succeeded."

He roughly inhaled through his nose as he kept holding himself with his arms.

"I can't imagine what it's like for you, watching me suck up to them. Letting them touch me and kiss me. Staring at my body like it's theirs and not yours. I'm ashamed when I have to do it and I have to keep telling myself I'm being good and when I'm good you're not punished for me being bad. I'm sorry I waited so long to tell you I want you. I think that made it worse for you. I'm sorry."

Jack nodded and his arms relaxed as he put his hands on his legs.

"I go to bed every night thinking I did a good job protecting you and I've earned eight hours where I can't fuck up something so badly you'll have to pay for it. In my mind I'm shielding you like my child when all I've done is get through another difficult day at the side of my mate.

"I'm sorry for what I called you, Jack. I know I can't take it back. I can only ask you to forgive me."

Jack leaned on me and I put my arms around him. He felt bigger in my embrace, more substantial. I marvelled I could feel so much more to him than I allowed myself to see. My hand passed over his wet cheek and up to the side of his head as I pressed my nose into his hair.

"Can you believe I'm such an ass?" I asked.

"Yes," he whispered.

"Yeah," I agreed.

"I should have said what was on my mind a long time ago. Having you know how I feel won't keep them from doing it. I feel better now you know," Jack sighed. "I'm not very good at this. I've been getting more and more upset and after last night it was more than I could take."

We were quiet for a minute then Jack rolled over, pushing me down underneath him as his hand went up my shirt.

"We don't have time."

"No we don't. It's been half an hour," he whispered, putting his hand on our babies then helping me up. We got our boots and coats on and waited.

"I'm sorry, Baby. I wanted to hear you tell me something nobody else knew. I had no idea what it was like for the women here until I started going through it with you. All your decisions are taken from you. Your privacy."

I nodded, trying to stay distracted.

"Do I have to say I want you every time or was that a one off?"

"Only if you want it that way."

"I don't."

We waited five minutes, then another five. I looked at the small dark patches on the old carpet where Jack bled our first day in this room. The chairs were back at the little table so nothing concealed them in the middle of the floor. Jack rubbed my shoulder as I fidgeted.

Another ten minutes passed.

"Something's wrong," Jack said. He worried more as I felt better.

"You're right, but not for us."

Jack didn't comment.

We'd been waiting in our room for an hour when the door opened. Harvey came in alone and he wasn't dressed for the cold outside.

"Leave your coats here. Get your boots off," Harvey said.

Jack and I left the coats on the bed and the boots on the floor, pulling on the shoes we had on before.

"Follow me," he said and led us to Walker's private dining room. "Wait."

Jack and I tightened our hold on each other. We'd only been in this room once and I had a fair idea what was happening on the other side of the wall. I lifted my chin and put my nose to his bearded throat and closed my eyes. If the men from the dining room were in there I didn't want to see what was happening to them. Then as I thought about what they would have done to us if the man with the red beard had gotten away with the rifle I wanted to make sure they got everything coming to them.

"Jack, I don't like what I feel inside," I whispered as more dark thoughts filled me. They weren't loyal to Damian. They were just a split off group like Jack's had been but Jack's group only wanted to separate. This group had a very different agenda. I very much wanted to find out what kind of trouble they were planning before they took their last steps.

A sharp pained shout accompanied by a thud made it through the thick walls. I covered my ears and moaned as Jack pressed the side of my head to his shoulder and added his own hand to mine over my other ear. In spite of my stomach curdling, I wondered if they would walk up on the scaffold one at a time or together. I wanted to be very far away and right at the front of the crowd at the same time.

"I'm thinking about getting away tomorrow for the night," Jack whispered. "Just us."

I took a deep breath and thought about it, too. Every other doctor trip had been a quick there and back with Soros driving. We'd never been trusted to go alone and hadn't been alone since the day I first told Jack I loved him. We would see Sig again for a check-up of my line and the doctor would check everything else out. He considered me high risk because of the twins just as Sig did.

Jack swayed me side to side in his arms and as he did I found the strength to get through whatever waited on the other side of the door so we would have tomorrow together.

"Come," Harvey told us when the door finally opened. Jack kept a firm grip on me and I tried to keep my eyes off the table but they wandered then I turned to face Mister Steele. His eyes weren't seeing anything since it appeared he used control to manage several captives.

The man with the red hair had his back to the table and to us. Soros sang to himself as he worked on the end of the man's arm. A bloody towel covered a lump on the table beside an axe. The other three sat very still; their hands on the table.

Walker stopped us halfway between the door and the man standing against the opposite wall. I lifted my head, meeting the man's eyes, and caught a brief moment of disgust on his face. Feeling is mutual, I thought. Jack snugly hugged me and I forced myself around to face him before Walker could kiss me. Walker put his hand on my shoulder and I watched Jack's face as he gently pulled me around and kissed my cheek anyway.

"Precious," he said. "I would like you to meet Mister Tombs."

"Good afternoon, Mister Tombs," I politely said.

Tombs nodded and mumbled something. I wasn't sure it was entirely polite.

"Do you remember him, Precious?"

"May I, Mister Walker?" I gestured under my nose. I didn't know Tombs' face and wanted to read him.

"Absolutely."

"Thank you, Mister Walker," I said as I sent my sense into the man. The four at the table were loyal to him. My breathing sped up as apprehension and anger competed in me. Before fear could win I stepped past Walker and dragged Jack closer to Tombs then I intently watched him. His eyes darted from me to the door and back. He was afraid of something. Obviously of Walker and I guessed something else.

"Is it me you're afraid of, Mister Tombs?" I asked. "Do you want to get away? Why do you keep looking at the door?"

As I moved closer he glanced at the door again.

"If I was afraid of something in here I'd be looking at it... or him. You want out. Whatever you're afraid of isn't in this room."

His brown eyes widened as he struggled to keep them on me.

"I've figured it out. What is it you're afraid of?"

"Do you want to answer her, Mister Tombs?" Walker asked.

Tombs imperceptibly shook his head and glanced at the door again. I put my nose close to his chest. From that close all I could smell was Mister Steele. I couldn't read his loyalty at all.

"Release him, Mister Steele," I said. "If I read him now, I'll just read you."

I waited and he didn't so I looked at Walker.

"Please," I added and he turned to Mister Steele and nodded.

Tombs pressed himself away from me, hard into the wall then tried a step toward the door. I put my hand up, blocking his path, and he froze. He didn't want to touch me.

"Just because you can move now doesn't mean you will," I whispered. "Mister Steele will have you before you pass me."

I kept my hand over his chest and tried to find something in his line I could grab onto. Walker wouldn't have me here for anything other than this.

The singing behind me paused.

"Sweet Thing?" Soros said. "Like at Jack's, Sweet Thing."

The singing started up again. *I Fought the Law.*

"Yes, Mister Soros."

At Jack's I read Soros with my hands on his skin. It was so intense and overwhelming Jack had to pull me away when I stopped breathing. I unbuttoned Tombs' shirt. Under my hands, his breathing sped up and his chest felt tacky with sweat.

"Sshhh," I whispered to him. "It won't hurt. You won't even know I'm here. You're going to show me why you stood me up at lunch."

Jack's arm went around my middle as the other held me around my shoulders.

"Watch my breathing, Jack," I whispered and I felt his lips on my head then I looked at Walker. He quickly put his sense under my nose. My hands turned to face each other as the sides rested on Tombs' skin. I could feel his line between them; no Damian in him at all.

"What is it you don't like about me, Mister Tombs?" I whispered as I explored his line.

Tombs shook his head. Without Steele crushing his line he had no motivation to speak.

"Did a blonde woman treat you poorly once?"

He didn't react as I pressed my nose to his chest. From the corner of my eye, I watched his hands flex and Jack tightened his grip around my shoulders. Sympathy wasn't going to work with this fellow. He disliked me a lot and I needed to make him more uncomfortable than I already did, not less.

"Perhaps you find me attractive?" I whispered as my fingertips absently brushed his chest. I gently scratched a fingernail over his nipple and he shuddered. The texture of his line subtly changed, granting me a hint of something I could grab hold of if I could even get a tiny grip. Like the smallest finger hold on a cliff face it would bear my weight if I held it just right.

"Mmm," I mumbled. "You want me, desire me."

As I looked up at him his nose wrinkled.

"Perhaps you wish to ask for me? My mate is here, just say the words."

"Aaah," he started and stopped himself. I disgusted him, I knew that, and the more upset he got the closer I came to getting hold of him.

"Yes, Mister Tombs?" I asked. "Don't pull me away, Jack. I'm so close. Mister Tombs will ask for me. He wants to come to our room, undress me when you're not there. He wants to taste my skin and hear exactly how I want to have him."

Tombs growled deep in his throat.

"Aaa... abomination," he spat, hitting both Jack and I. For a brief moment I wondered how a man who was so scared could produce any spit at all. As he did, I felt his line move and I brought my knee up hard between his legs. Jack tightened his grip on me and I jammed my elbow up into Tombs' windpipe, lifting his chin as he shouted in pain. His line was unguarded so I took control, pressing my nose to his skin close enough to latch on. Tombs stomach struggled as I felt myself weakening with the close contact. I focused and found myself staring through his eyes into Jack's angry face.

"Ah..." Walker said.

"Keep it down, Mister Tombs," I whispered. "Don't shame yourself further by throwing up."

I skipped back along his line until he carried a duffel bag. Walker sensibly didn't offer any instructions; I went too fast for him to be of any help navigating Tombs' past. Tombs was cautious, checking around corners, listening for voices, making sure he was unseen. A small jump forward had him in the dark connecting wires in the light from a flashlight. The light showed the time on his watch and red numbers on whatever the wires connected to said three zero zero. The other end of the wires connected to the explosives in the bag.

Walker spoke but I couldn't make it out and Jack's arms felt so light around me. I started to lose consciousness like what happened when I read Soros with my hands on his skin. I pushed quickly through the next few minutes. Seeing Tombs in the dark wouldn't tell me where the bomb was. I had to see him leave the room. He listened at a small door and stepped out blinking in the brighter light. Walker shouted and I felt myself flying until something hit my head.

Chapter 4

I woke with a headache in the back seat of a truck. Jack held me up as we bumped along the road.

"Ow," I moaned as I put my hand to my head.

"Sshhh, Anna," it was one of the other women. Sounded like Karen but I couldn't be sure over the fading ringing in my ears.

"Here, Ma'am," I heard Soros say then the truck corrected itself. Soros called the other women Ma'am or Missus. He called me Missus Roberts when they were around. Sweet Thing when they weren't.

"What's all the excitement?" Karen asked. I pictured her brown curls bouncing about her round face.

"Gas leak, Missus Carter," Soros said. "They'll call when everything is aired out."

I felt someone lean against my leg and then coldness on my head.

"Oh dear," she said. "I hope they're careful. That stuff sneaks up on you like winter back home."

Debbie laughed from the front seat. I was sure it was her. That woman's laugh started about a yard beneath her feet so her baby felt it on its way past. She was almost six months pregnant and was always comparing notes with Karen who was five months, just a couple of weeks ahead of me. I pushed worry for them from my mind; I had a good idea what they had coming when their sons were born. I reached up and put a hand over Karen's, holding the cold pack to my head.

"She wasn't looking where she was going in the hurry to get out," Jack said.

"Stupid pregnant brain," I muttered.

Debbie laughed again but Karen sounded more concerned.

"Mister Soros, she knocked herself out cold."

"Help Mister Roberts keep an eye on her, Missus Carter," Soros said. He knew as well as Jack and I did I was out cold from touching Tombs when I read him but Karen fussed and worried. Soros gave her something to do involving me so he wouldn't have to interact with her. Karen held my wrist like she was taking my pulse then peered into my eyes.

"I'm okay, Karen," I reassured her. "Just a little bump."

"Course you are, Baby," Jack said. I reached an arm around his middle. Jack had an arm around my shoulders and his other under my sweater on my tummy. Yesterday, it kept his sons calm. Today he didn't have to have his hand on me at all. The bumpy driveway changed to pavement and Soros turned right to Hartford.

"Missus Carter? I'll send you and Missus Davis in to pick us up some dinner if they haven't called when we get to town."

"Okay, Mister Soros," Karen said. "Maybe she shouldn't eat... if she has a concussion she shouldn't eat."

"Can I get something to sip, Karen? I'm thirsty."

"I suppose..."

After a while I sat up on my own. I took the ice off and felt my head. There wasn't even a bump and the headache had faded.

We quietly ate in the truck and Karen gathered up the garbage when Soros' phone rang.

"Soros," he said when he answered it.

He listened for half a minute before he stepped out of the truck and closed the door, walking toward the other side of the parking lot to finish his conversation with his back to us.

"Jack, I feel sick."

"Okay," Jack said as he opened the door. Cold air came in. Neither of us had coats; we must have left in a hurry.

"I think it's the ketchup and onions this time." The burgers were covered in them. I had a bit of morning sickness. Random things off and on. This time it was ketchup and onions.

Soros was still on the phone on the other side of the truck when we got out. I huddled close to Jack to stay warm and felt better away from the smell.

"If I'd known it would be ketchup and onions I wouldn't have eaten them," Jack said as he tried to keep his mouth pointed away from me.

"Mm," I whispered, keeping an eye on Soros. "The red headed man stole a rifle, Jack, I watched him shoot Harvey then you. He shot me as I struggled to pull you off the trail. Our other guard walked away letting it happen. I was scared Walker would let us go out anyway, knowing what was coming. I couldn't get what I saw out of my head."

"They're traitors, Baby. I'll be excused from what will happen to them because you'll be excused. Carter and Davis will be with their women. They won't know about it. I expect we'll be gone for a few days. They have to build it... do it. Take it down."

I nodded. Thinking about the hangings made me feel sicker than the food.

"You saved a lot of lives today," Jack said.

"Nobody would have been in danger if I wasn't here."

"What's going to happen to them isn't your fault."

I tried to think about something other than onions and nooses for a few minutes until I shivered. The pink sweaters didn't hold the wind back. Karen had the windows open and took the wrappers to the garbage when Soros came around to our side of the truck. He stood close to Jack, speaking only to him as if I wasn't there. He did that when he had business. Jack would ignore him. Listening while refusing to acknowledge him.

"You and your Missus are leaving tonight. I'll have your room arranged by the time you get there. Steele compelled Tombs to recover his bag but it went off behind the house. A lot of broken windows. Tombs all over the place. The other women will spend the night in the house. They're on the other side and won't know. There's glass all over your room and it'll be a couple of days before it's usable again. You'll have two nights there, appointment at ten. Sig will see you in the hotel the next day."

Jack nodded. It was good news. Two nights away, maybe more. If they didn't get to building until tomorrow and had cleanup and repairs we could be away a lot longer.

"Sweet Thing," Soros breathed in my ear.

"Yes, Mister Soros?"

"Mister Walker will have a word with you before you leave."

"Yes, Mister Soros."

"She needs a minute, RJ," Jack said. "Morning sickness from the burgers."

Soros glanced at me before climbing in the truck to finish his dinner.

"Gerald will offer you a reward," Jack quietly said. "Don't pick what you want most. Don't pick me or Camille or anything like that. Don't tell him what's most important to you."

I couldn't save Jack by asking Walker for him. The life of a traitor wasn't a fair trade for what I'd done.

Mister Harvey met us at the front door when we reached the house. Karen and Debbie went to their rooms and Soros and Harvey took Jack and me upstairs. Soros was right. Glass covered the floor and bed. Icy wind blew in the holes where the windows had been. There were broken bits in our dresser drawers and on the bathroom floor.

We packed for several days. Jack's mood lightened with every passing minute until Walker let himself in without knocking. He took me by my elbows and pulled me close and Jack had to move quickly to keep his hand on me.

"Precious," Walker started. "You were very, very good today. Protected many lives."

"Yes, Mister Walker."

Including my own, I thought. He smelled more strongly of whiskey than usual.

"I couldn't live with myself if your loyalty went unrewarded, my dear. You would be at my right hand if I felt I could trust you there."

"Thank you, Mister Walker," I replied. He misunderstood my loyalty. Any good I'd done him was coincidental.

"You will tell me what would be a fair exchange for your loyalty today. I will not go to bed in your debt."

I stared at him for a moment as if thinking even though I'd already made up my mind.

"We will have our weapons back, Mister Walker."

Surprise flashed on his face. I also felt it in Jack's hand. It was the last thing they expected me to say. Guns could be taken away later without hurting anyone and gave him little sway to manipulate me further.

"I will not count on catching the next assassin stealing. If we are to be in your care we will have every bit of security you can offer. Including our weapons. I will stay here and hold up my promise to Mister Soros. My life is forfeit. I'm not fooling myself it isn't. Jack and I love our sons, Mister Walker, and I will not have them jeopardized by any further failure of security in this house."

Walker looked past me at Jack for an uncomfortably long time. Something dark passed between them. I'd never made a demand in the house and this one was made with confidence. I completely expected to have it honoured.

"Done," he said and walked out.

Chapter 5

Jack carried our bags as Soros led us to the first floor then past Walker's dining room and toward the front of the house. Halfway there, he turned down a short hall and used a key to open a door. Then narrow stairs, Jack's arm around my waist and we waited at the bottom as Soros locked the door behind us. Around the corner was the room from which Tombs' man stole the rifle.

"Put the bags on the counter, Jack," he ordered and Jack did. Soros unlocked a large metal cabinet and removed our guns. We watched as he opened our bags and hid them under layers of clothes. "You have balls the size of the man in charge, Sweet Thing," he said as he eyed me with disapproval. "I'm not convinced it's an attractive look for you."

"Yes, Mister Soros," I answered as Jack shouldered our bags. It was just a warning and I shivered inside, grateful Jack hadn't paid for the brazenness of my demand.

Soros pulled an envelope from under the counter and emptied it before us. A cell phone, car and wall chargers, credit cards and a large wad of cash appeared as well as our wallets.

"I'm returning your ID to you," he said. "I will know where you are through the locator in the phone. If I call and you don't answer I'll call again ten minutes later. If I don't hear from you then I hunt you down."

Jack grunted with disinterest though he grabbed his wallet and stuffed it in his back pocket. Soros didn't have to say he'd hunt the children down as well.

"Your hotel is paid for," Soros went on. "Don't assume you're unsupervised, yes?"

"Yes, Mister Soros," I answered and Jack squeezed my side in agitation. He'd been excited about the trip all the way down stairs and grew impatient with Soros' self-important briefing.

"Mister Harvey has your Nissan warmed up out front for you."

"Thank you, Mister Soros."

He put everything in the envelope and handed it to me, leading us as far as the front door. An old faded red sports car noisily idled at the bottom of the stairs.

"A Pulsar, Jack?" I laughed in surprise. The thing looked as shabby as he did with the unkempt beard.

"Oh dear God thank you. You have no idea how much I love the leg room," he exclaimed as he pulled me down the stairs to the driver's door, opened it and popped the hatch. Our bags went inside before he slammed it and twirled with me, setting off more laughter.

"I love this car," he whispered, planting a fuzzy warm kiss on my lips as my mouth opened with laughter so loud I couldn't coordinate them to kiss him back. The axe and broken glass and the vision of the shooting melted from me under the merciless onslaught of his sudden elation.

"It's a five-speed. You're gonna shift," he said as he opened my door. He stepped in before I could ask how exactly he was getting around to his door and pulled me in. He grabbed the steering wheel and found his seat as I landed in mine. His elbow honked the horn and he turned toward the front. "Father hated this car. I had to park it way across the back field. Other than the truck we took for burgers it's probably the only vehicle with all its windows."

"First," he ordered as I closed my door.

"Jeez, Jack," I said. "I'm no good with my left hand."

"Most women aren't. First."

I pushed the stick toward him all the way then at the dash wondering if his remark was a cut at female drivers or something else. The transmission felt stiff from cold and old age but at least I didn't grind the damn thing.

"Musn't mess Father's gravel," Jack said as he slowly let the clutch out. The gravel was as solidly frozen as the ground beneath and I didn't think he could have stirred it up if he tried. He eased the car around the front circle until it joined the main drive to the trees. I kept my hand on the shifter until he called second and then I did grind it as I pulled it back more towards me than the rear seat.

"Easy," Jack muttered as I found second. "Shifting isn't a test of wills. You're working with the transmission, learning what it likes and what it loves."

"I'm trying."

As the driveway entered the trees, Jack slowed, steering with one hand as he hummed to himself before he took his hand off me to turn on the radio. I gasped with worry the pain would return but he smiled and ignored me as he found a country station. I watched him tap his thigh in time with the music until just before we reached the gate. It was only then he tucked his fingers inside my collar.

"First," he said after putting his feet on the pedals. One of the guards shone a flashlight in without comment, both front seat and back before waving us past. Jack moved his hand up and my head gently swayed as he massaged my neck with his fingertips.

"Second."

Second went more smoothly than it had the first time and we bounced along a few more minutes until we reached the road. Jack could have taken over the shifter but seemed to prefer contact with me over changing gears. He rolled out without stopping before calling out third. I pulled it toward me and felt for third, grinding again as I missed it completely.

"We're gonna be slow enough for first if you don't hurry up," he laughed as we coasted then he covered my hand with his and got it in gear. The engine accusingly lugged as he eased us faster and shifted into fourth.

"You're holding it too stiffly," Jack said as he squeezed my hand, urging it to relax. His voice softened more as he traced the creases between my fingers. "And not so high, move down just a bit so you can see it in your hand."

As soon as I softened my grip he slid my hand down to the torn fake leather sleeve around the base of the shaft then back up to the knob at the top.

"See? Can you hear the idle smooth out? You're making it happy."

"Jack," I whispered at his thinly veiled banter.

He shifted in his seat. "Keep saying my name like that and I'm going to pull over and show you the back seat."

I laughed but only for a moment before I remembered we were tracked. There was no light from any vehicle behind us but I turned and looked anyway to make sure we weren't followed. If we pulled over Soros might think we were up to something.

"I know, you're wondering if we'll fit," he said but he'd felt me tense. He glanced at me then at my right hand, urgently trying to soothe the boys' lines as they responded to my anxiety. "What's the matter, Baby?"

Jack took his hand off the stick and put it under my chin, pulling me close for a quick kiss before he got his eyes back on the road.

"I want to go back," I admitted.

"Back?"

"I mean, there's got to be another um, room," I scrambled to explain. "And I'm sure someone can take us to see Doctor Targuer tomorrow."

Jack pulled over on the shoulder, his hand on mine as he geared down and left it in neutral.

"And the boys can't hurt me more now so we don't have to see Sig, right?"

"We're not going back," he said. I knew how much he needed a few normal days considering he never expected to experience another. What I recognized as my own overwhelming insecurity was embarrassing for a woman who'd always been able to take care of herself.

"No," I agreed, thinking of him. "We're not going back."

"But we're not going any further just yet." He turned the radio off then finger hooked under my chin as he tugged me closer. I glanced behind us again and he followed my stare back the way we came.

"I suppose this is what it feels like getting out of prison."

"Yes," he answered.

"I mean, what if I don't know what to order for breakfast?" I asked, thinking more out loud to myself than actually expecting an answer. "Maybe I won't pay attention when I get dressed or fall asleep when I'm supposed to be exercising."

He was silent. I'd dropped my eyes as I mused and his lips stayed still.

"What if I figure that out and get some really bad habits and screw up when we get back? Or they find out what I did while we're away? I can't bear to see them hurt you again," I said as I took a hard breath to pull back a sob. Jack's fingers slid to the sweet spot behind my ear and circled it as he put his lips to mine, gently at first then pressing me to relax.

"Jack hasn't been to prison," he whispered. "But I remember being there. I remember getting out. It doesn't feel that way to me because I still resist them in my heart. You've given up so much of Anna to survive that you gave up your will."

I nodded, knowing he said the truth. I knew I'd left those pieces of Anna behind with his brothers. Jack unzipped my coat before rubbing my stomach. He took the sleeves and pulled my arms free then tossed it in the back seat with his and turned down the heater.

"When I met you," he said as we pulled out. "You were softer and still had this little tummy, some of what you needed to carry Camille. I didn't think anything of it until you took me to the hotel but damn girl, that night it was the sexiest thing I'd ever seen. You gave one of us a child and you loved her father and you took me to bed because it would give your child another protector."

I took his hand and rested it on my leg and smiled at his awe. I had similar thoughts about it. Like it was a badge of honour. Since I didn't feel pregnant with her anymore at least I had a reminder of the time she was just mine.

"Two months later," Jack interrupted my thoughts. "You came to my room to save her again. Your body had been transformed, lean and fit. You'd become a soldier, your spirit too.

"We've killed together twice, Baby. There's fierceness in you Stanton couldn't touch. I've seen it, felt it and I know you've put it away for now because if you let it out your baby is in trouble. That's okay, you understand that right?"

"Yeah, Jack," I answered, believing it because I trusted Jack to tell me the truth. I remembered the woman I talked about and wasn't so reassured by his suggestion I'd see her again. She was as much of my past as the woman in the mirror except she kept me out of trouble. The old Anna only got me in to it.

"Ray sent me to the hotel gym every day and ran my ass off. I couldn't have fought off Stanton without Ray getting me into shape," I explained. I also remembered getting shot as Jack's man Mason and I pretended to slip away for some time alone. Before Ray slit the throat of the man who pulled the trigger and Halford clubbed the other. Yeah, the old Anna thought nothing of being at the wrong end of an ass-kicking. Or the right end for that matter.

Jack passed me the envelope and asked where we were going. I dug through its contents and pulled out a sheet of heavy paper neatly folded into thirds. Soros' elaborately sloped left-handed script only covered the top half of the page.

"The Hilton," I said. "Do you know where it is?"

"Yeah."

"He says the reservation is in your name. Use the cash for meals."

I pulled out the wad of bills and fanned through the fifties. A full bundle of a hundred made five thousand. That was a lot of cheeseburgers. I put it all away and put the envelope in the back seat.

"Look, I'm here for you when you think you're falling short. You don't have to ask and I won't talk about it again. I want you to relax and try and enjoy yourself."

"Okay," I answered, feeling a little better. "I'm glad you know me so well."

Chapter 6

Jack walked naked to the bar fridge. After checking us in, feeding me a very late dinner and sharing a bath we had uncharacteristically slow, gentle sex interrupted only once by my crying as another chunk of the day's stress left me. He squatted in front of the open door and pulled out a small bottle of Crown then poured half in a plastic glass before topping it up with Pepsi.

"Anything?"

"Maybe there's some tea left," I answered and he served me the last of the lukewarm camomile. Waste not, I thought. The bottle of pineapple juice made my mouth water but to me it belonged to the hotel and I wasn't going to take it. Still pink scars on Jack's thigh reminded me what happened when I helped myself. And I'd never liked the stuff much anyway even though I craved it.

Jack sat, back to me and stretched so I brushed my fingers along the scars running diagonally from shoulder blade to hip bone, making him shiver.

"So what's wrong?" I asked.

"Why?"

"Well, you were unusually subdued," I answered as I felt my cheeks pinken.

"Subdued? That's a terrible thing to say about a man."

Jack leaned back and rested his head on my hip. When he turned to face me, I put my tea to my lips hoping to hide my blush.

"No, I meant you didn't really say anything and you just weren't yourself," I tried to explain as I realized I might have insulted him but he laughed.

"I've slept with her a whopping three times before tonight and she thinks she knows my entire repertoire," he took my empty cup and put it on the table as I darkened even more. "You weren't so shy ten minutes ago."

"True," I agreed.

Jack watched me for a moment. "We've had a rotten day. You're emotionally finished and you're exhausted. I feel the same. I thought you wanted closeness after our fight like I did. If I misread you and you want a workout give me twenty minutes and I'll see what I can do."

"No, you're right of course," I smiled. "Absolutely, perfectly right."

Talking about sex with Jack felt natural and foreign at the same time. It was ironic the ultimate consummation of our necessary contact ended the need for it all together. The bar fridge was a lot farther away than the few feet apart he'd described earlier.

"Subdued didn't stop you from scratching me," he said, raising an arm to show me his flank.

"Sorry," I mumbled but Jack didn't look sorry.

"I like to make you scratch me," he laughed as he went back to the fridge to top up the last of his drink with straight whiskey. He picked up the remote and put it down before turning off all but the bedside light and climbing in with me.

"Can you stay closer please? Soros said we were being watched."

"That wasn't what he said," Jack lay back, standing his drink on his chest. I rested my head on his shoulder and felt better than when he wandered around the room. "The only one of them who reads farther than me is Harvey but he doesn't see too well. From just outside my range all he could tell is we're in the same general direction, nothing more, so relax. I won't get far enough away where if he shows up we can't get closer."

I rubbed my forehead where his beard tickled it then rolled away to sneeze. The light went out as Jack wrapped himself around behind me.

"There's nothing better than this," he whispered. "Getting my girl tired out and mending her broken mood. I'm quite the guy."

I giggled and pushed in closer, hearing him growl as he smoothed my hair down and tucked his head in beside mine.

"I love you, Jack."

I was asleep before he answered.

"Baby," Jack whispered from somewhere. The soft bed felt unfamiliar and the gentle hum of an elevator stopped as I startled, forgetting for the moment where we were. Jack's arm went around me and I sat up.

"We're in the hotel," he said.

"Okay," I leaned back and closed my eyes. We hadn't been asleep more than a couple of hours.

"I need to tell you something."

"Anything," I answered.

"Are you sure you won't be mad?"

"You used my toothbrush, didn't you? You forgot yours and used mine."

"Nothing so unforgivable," he laughed. Whatever it was, he felt he needed to tell me more than he wanted to.

I lifted his shoulder so he rolled away from me and I curled up behind him, my arm under his head. "Then I won't be mad," I promised.

It took him a few minutes to get started. He spoke so quietly I knew if I was facing him he'd be looking away.

"When I was a few years younger than you are I met someone. I moved in with her. I think I loved her. She said she loved me and it felt like the truth when I told her I felt the same way. We had a lot of really bad days and really good nights. I guess we could both overlook a lot when loving each other was so easy. After a few months she wanted to get married. We did. It kept her coming to my bed every night. Without her I had nowhere to go but Father's. Then she wanted a kid. I knew I was being unfair to her but I agreed. She wasn't family so it wouldn't happen.

"She was meticulous about the calendar, when to try. More frustrated and angry each time we failed. After a year and a half she came home so excited. She was pregnant. I knew it wasn't mine. There was no way it could be. I could only guess who she'd been with or how long it had been going on. I pulled off being happy about it for a week. Then when she was at work I changed all the locks including the bathroom so when the locksmith got her in the house she would have to call him back so she could use the can. It was petty, I know. I put my stuff in my car, hers on the lawn, and drove off for good.

"I left my pregnant wife and went back to Father's. Never saw her again. When I found my first I got a lawyer but before we could serve my wife Father caught us together and killed her."

I held Jack a little tighter.

"After you accepted me I left you my house. You and Paul. If I wasn't around you could sell it at least to pay for college for Camille or something. Since we went to Father's I left the house to you and Ray. If neither one of us makes it he'll have it to do whatever is best for her.

"If by some miracle we get through this I'll get a divorce. I would marry you but I'm still married to her. I'm sorry, Baby. I did something terrible a long time ago and never dealt with it."

"It's okay, Jack," I said. "Have you forgiven yourself?"

"Not really." I felt him shake his head. "The women are so young this time. I got married at twenty-one because I thought I wouldn't find my first. Everything is so out of whack with the women."

I agreed. I didn't think Karen and Debbie were even twenty. As far as the women went Alina and I were old.

"I don't know what will happen, Jack."

"I'm happy."

"Me too," I said. "I don't think anyone lives up to the rules of courtesy as much as they say. I bet there are one night stands, affairs, hook-ups and quickies more often than anyone admits. Courtesy isn't the idealistic rules to live by I was led to believe."

Jack turned to face me.

"I think I missed something. How did we get from what I told you to that?"

"I guess it doesn't matter now. He's dead. Clean slate on the other side, right?"

"Yeah."

His hand touched my cheek as I thought about what to tell him.

"I told you in January I attacked Paul, made sure he would be out of the way in Edmonton waiting for me to come for Marie."

He didn't say anything as I felt his fingers move on my face.

"Why wouldn't he? I was nuts. Forever nuts if I failed. He didn't know I'd take your father's line. Even if I succeeded I'd be just like Alina on the other side. Oblivious to the family and not remembering a damn thing."

"He asked for her, didn't he?" Jack asked.

He felt the tears on my cheek say yes.

"When we dropped off Dana she wanted to talk. I'd been gone so long she thought something bad happened to me and she never got a chance to clear her conscience. Something about Keith kicked her out, staying in a hotel, Paul showed up. She didn't know what she was thinking but they slept together.

"I tried to be a grownup about it. Like he'd been for me and your inheritance. I thought about how being with you was the most important thing in my life at the time. More important than Camille or

Paul and how little it meant after. How Paul would have felt the same way. He's a good and generous mate. More than enough to help look after which ever one of us he finds second.

"I told her we'd talk about it. We learned a lot about each other as we pulled things together after I ran out on him in January. We weren't together then and it sounded like it was the same for her and Keith. It happened, she couldn't undo it anymore than Paul could and we'd put it in the right place behind us. I'd try and understand why he never told me. I'd almost convinced myself I could do it. Until she said he came back to her bed the next night and again two nights later. He left her bed to come to me.

"I forgave him, Jack. After seeing the feelings you were left with after I accepted you I understand how it could have happened. When we jumped to Reno I hadn't. I was set on doing something about it. I started planning on blowing up at him but it wasn't enough. I loved him so much, I was terrified one of the men would find out and send him to the other side... take him away from Camille and me because of it. I was furious with him for risking his life like that. Then I decided on payback. Rub it in his face so he knew how I felt. I was going to get my payback with you."

"When I found you behind the bar you were so drunk," Jack whispered. "If you felt that way sober I wouldn't have told you no."

"I know," I said. "Before I ran out the woman in the mirror called me out of the shower. She told me Paul would kill you and it would be disgusting for me to use you like that. I would regret it and it would only make it harder to confront Paul. She was so angry with me, protective of you. She already had the feelings I have for you now. She reminded me I knew how to get it out of my system so I took off to get drunk and pick a fight.

"I hoped once I settled down he and I could talk but we never got the chance."

Targuer

Chapter 7

Doctor Targuer was a prick.

My sister Alina called men like him douche-bags and she'd be horrified such a pig earned a living putting his hands on pregnant women. He was self-important and arrogant to the point of being mean. My first visit with him left me in tears, struggling to defend myself from what turned out to be the standard rant launched in my direction. I'd since learned to keep my mouth shut and let his insults fizzle out but it had only been two weeks since the last visit and I wasn't so sure I could deal with him again. Monthly dressing-downs had been far enough apart but with every two weeks to look forward to I needed to toughen my armour.

It was easier said than done.

My strategy had been to avoid thinking about my appointment until the day of then not until we left. Last visit, I didn't think about it until we entered his office but today I couldn't avoid it. Targuer would do another scan so I had to drink up and deal with the discomfort of a full bladder until he said I could go to the bathroom.

I knew he'd make me wait longer than necessary so I delayed the water until just before we headed to Jack's car. Targuer's office was only a twenty minute drive, ten minutes of circling the block and a five minute walk. Then the waiting started. I'd been weighed and sent back to the waiting room. Jack's hand on the back of my neck as I stood on the scale and got the usual funny look from the nurse. She probably suspected I was battered in some fashion based on my silence, lowered eyes and seemingly possessive partner and she was right, though not by the man she suspected.

After another fifteen minutes I stood with Jack, he put his arms around me and let me sway like he gave me a long hug. Targuer called us in several minutes after I broke into a sweat and took his time with questions as he filled out his chart. Finally he got me up on the table for the scan.

"No Mister Soros?" He asked like he'd just noticed there were only three of us in the room.

"No, Doctor Targuer," I answered as my nose wrinkled. As family went, this old bastard had grown smellier with age. He was in his sixties, white haired and still well over six feet tall even though he'd started to stoop. Angry frown lines cleaved the centre of his face, driving down between his eyes and past the corners of his mouth.

Targuer gestured with his hand for me to pull up my shirt then fussed with the Doppler as I quickly complied and shoved the maternity panel of my pants out of the way. He put the device down and stuffed his big hands into two pairs of exam gloves; such was his disgust with me.

"I've been delivering the family's sons for centuries," he muttered as he began his great description of how I ruined his day. "Beautiful children to be sure, sired by strong fathers to worthy women. It isn't these boys' fault they were conceived in dirt."

He glared at me until I looked away and he was sure I knew exactly who the dirt was. Jack's fingers moved where they rested on my chest just inside my shirt. Small reassurance; any more would egg Targuer on. After my first visit, we horribly fought when we returned to our room. I was vicious in my opinion of his failure to stand up for me but he'd kept his mouth shut when he saw how it only encouraged Targuer. Jack was equally articulate about me not seeing what I was doing and shutting my mouth before Targuer's insults became so specific and vulgar I was sick to my stomach. We desperately needed time apart after and our forced proximity kept us both angry much longer than if he could have stormed out.

"Baby A," Targuer muttered as he felt low for him then to the side and a little higher he found Baby B. He'd been able to sense their locations accurately since about twelve weeks and Jack explained he could read readers even though their lines were in my chest. Or something. Jack suspected he could pick up where the little sense organ under their noses was once it began to form. Targuer himself bragged the high rate of readers in Jack's side of the family was due in part to his ability to help weed out inferior children. His pride in his skill was atrocious.

I pressed my knees together to keep my underwear dry as he finally squeezed cold gel on the end of the wand and picked up A's heart. I watched Jack's hand rise with my chest as I sighed with relief. Since we hadn't felt movement yet it was the only interaction we had with them.

"And you," he muttered to me as he moved to find B. "What do you have to say for yourself?"

It wasn't like him to directly engage me in conversation. I'd answer for Jack because Jack wouldn't speak to him but that was it.

"Smugly soaking up this traitor's seed?" he spat. "But I suppose it's the only way you're worth anything."

B started to thump-thump from the speaker.

"Not quite where I thought you were, little fellow," he softly said. The boys, he adored. Jack and I, not so much.

The Doppler disappeared, ending our brief moment of connection with them as Targuer walked out. Jack gave me a smile and I nodded as I struggled with discomfort. He traced his fingers down the center of my stomach then felt where Targuer said they were; his tongue in the corner of his mouth. At the sound of Targuer's heavy cart coming toward the door he wiped his hand on the paper beneath me and got it out of sight.

"I had a quick and dirty C-section planned for the moment their lines dropped," Targuer continued. The screen partly faced us and we did our best to see the images since he wouldn't do any more than get the shots he needed for their file. Parents' involvement be damned. "I wasn't going to bring sedation or sutures. Misters Soros and Walker are very anxious to get on with raising Mister Howard's brilliant grandsons.

"But now there's talk of keeping you around," he shook his head. "I might have your foul womb back in my office sooner than you think."

He angrily pressed the wand into my stomach, low on my bladder and I felt my bottom soak with urine. Even worse was how good it felt to have some of the pressure relieved. After a few seconds I stopped the flow but warmth already spread down my thighs, puddling where I pressed the vinyl mattress down.

Jack twitched in his chair and a brief look at him showed him red with anger. Then he sneezed as I dared to connect with him, the first time since we'd been at his home months before.

Kill him, I sent.

Yes, was his curt reply before I disconnected. But he didn't move. Doctor Asshole was on the A list if we ever got away.

Targuer finished up and walked out.

Jack swiped a couple of paper towels to wipe the gel from my stomach and I pulled my clothes back into place before he helped me sit, glad my coat was long and I kept my eyes lowered as I pulled it on. Jack paid attention to Targuer's location as he zipped his jacket up. I ripped up the soggy paper from the exam table and shoved it in the trash before he could see it.

"Let's go," he stiffly said as he tucked his two left fingers down the back of my coat and led me to the restroom.

"Turn around," I said as we closed the door, ashamed of my accident. "Please?"

Jack did without question. Regaining small moments of privacy had been important for him during the past day as well. When I was done, I put the lid on the bottle and shut it in the pass through to the nurse's office. The label said *Irena Walker*; my middle name. Soros' idea of keeping my identity under wraps. As far as the insurance company paying for my care was concerned I was Gerald Walker's wife. Loyal as Targuer was to Damian Howard, he wasn't going to look after my sons for free. By the time I stood, my wet pants were cold and I palmed my eyes dry before Jack turned.

"We'll get an early lunch, okay?" he said. It seemed like he had his temper under control. "Maybe drive around a bit?"

I didn't answer as we stopped at reception to book an appointment for the same day and time, just two weeks away. Soros could change it if he wanted. By the time we reached the elevator, stray rivulets of pee made their way down the insides of my calves and I spaced my feet apart hoping they would make it to my socks before my jeans soaked them up. At the car, I realized I'd ruin either my coat or Jack's passenger seat.

When I hesitated to get in Jack raised an eyebrow.

"Is there something I can sit on?" I asked.

Jack laughed. "I didn't notice you hurt your butt," he said as he got a hand up the back of my coat to grab it, pausing when he felt the wetness.

"I'm sorry," I forced out through chattering teeth. The walk to the car in wet pants chilled me and chafed my thighs. "It's my fault. I drank too much."

Jack set his jaw and focused on my line. I lied and even though he could tell and he knew I knew it still pissed him off. He was like Paul that way; the truth, always the truth. I wasn't sure until he spoke if he was mad at me for trying to get away with the lie or with what he knew right away was the truth.

"Bastard," Jack nearly shouted and I tried to bury my chin in my coat to hide. We caught the attention of a couple walking across the frozen street. He lowered his voice and moved to the left, putting me between him and them. "That's not your fault. He makes you wait too long."

He took an old blanket from the hatch and put it on the seat so I pulled the coat out of the way and shivered all the way to the hotel.

Chapter 8

"RJ will call if it's urgent or to be an ass," Jack whispered as we entered the hotel lobby. "Sorry, I know you want to get to our room. He'll leave us a message otherwise. We have to check."

I slipped my arm around his waist as he kissed my forehead. When we stopped at the front desk I became acutely aware of the smell coming from my jeans.

"Roberts, seven oh one," Jack announced to the same young man who checked us in the evening before.

"Good morning, Mister and Missus Roberts," he bravely gave us a friendly smile. Jack looked scary enough with the hairline to chin scar. The 'woke up on the wrong side of the cave' beard didn't do anything to make him look friendly and Jack knew it. "A package has arrived for you."

He opened a cupboard below the desk and pulled out a department store bag.

"And a Mister Sigmund left a message," he put the note beside the bag.

I thanked him as I picked both up and turned to go but Jack held on to me and pulled a twenty from his pocket, sliding it across the counter. "Laundry pickup, ten minutes."

The young man wasn't even finished his nod as Jack whisked me to the elevator. He took the bag as I read the note.

"Sig will be here tomorrow after lunch sometime," I said as the elevator door closed. Jack didn't say anything, though his colour darkened as his temper started to get the better of him again.

"Not your fault," he muttered and I didn't argue. "He was too rough and made you wait too long. That fucker doesn't know how to treat a lady."

I pulled up my collar to hide my face as I reddened like Jack only not with anger. I felt only shame; not like the lady Jack spoke of. The only thing about Targuer for which I felt gratitude was he found me too disgusting for the usual internal exams so I went without.

Thank God.

Once inside, I stripped and threw everything on the floor.

"Hey," Jack said softly but I turned my back on him and ran for the shower. I let it run too hot and scrubbed until the little hotel soap bar was nothing more than a sliver the water carried down the drain. Then I stepped out and roughly dried myself as punishment for letting Targuer get the better of me.

"Don't look," Jack said as I left the bathroom. I stuffed the corner of a clean towel down between my breasts to secure it as I turned to face the occupancy terms posted on the door. My dirty clothes were gone and I assumed in the laundry bag already on its way to the basement. "The phone rang about ten minutes ago but I didn't want to rush you."

He'd barely finished the sentence before it rang again.

"Stay there," Jack said then answered it. "Yell-oh."

I cringed. Soros was all about formality and Jack answered like a goof just to rub him the wrong way. I waited and listened to Jack's grunted replies for a couple of minutes before he pressed the phone to my ear. I quickly pulled out my fake friendly voice.

"Good morning, Mister Soros," I nearly sang into the phone. I heard a little poof sound and the side of my neck grew cool as the light smell of freesia and other delicious things I couldn't name reached my nose.

"Good morning, Sweet Thing," he answered. I picked up the sound of hammering in the background. "I do hope the room is to your liking."

"The Hilton, Mister Soros," I breathed with an appropriate amount of wide-eyed excitement. "Everything is absolutely first class and the staff is so kind!"

Soros loved double complements sandwiching an 'and.'

"The perfume is from RJ," Jack whispered, his nose to my neck as his fingers ran around the edge of my towel. "Numb-nuts has good taste."

"We're just opening the parcel you sent," I added. "I can't believe there is a more heavenly scent anywhere on the East Coast and it's perfect."

I winced. Everything after that 'and' was lame but Soros didn't seem to notice.

"I do hope you'll make good use of the remaining items," Soros said. "You can tell me all about it later, Sweet Thing. Now let me speak to your mate."

I started to turn to give Jack the phone but he put a hand on my shoulder to hold me still as he took the phone with the other.

"Yeah," he said to his brother. Jack sighed loudly as Soros went on. "Look, RJ. We're going to the pool and we're not taking the fucking phone with us."

I cleared my throat with surprise. More with the thought of the pool than the unusually long sentence he'd dumped on Soros. After another minute Jack hung up without saying good-bye.

"Pool?" I swallowed hard.

"Yeah, Baby. Turn around."

I did and was faced with Jack wearing nothing but a black Speedo.

"Dear God," I gasped as Jack rolled his eyes.

Then he chewed his lip and nodded. "Laugh it up. Yours isn't much better."

He pointed out the black two-piece on the bed. Combined there wasn't much more fabric than his.

"Public humiliation à la Soros?" I asked.

Jack shrugged.

"I'd wear one just like yours for a chance to show you off in it," his tongue teased his lip for a moment, making his smile slightly lopsided. "Because it means I get to see you fill it out. Please?"

Jack didn't seem to care what he wore; not enough for me to talk him out of the pool so I let him dress me in the swimsuit. At least I got a little silky black robe to pull over for the trip down to the main floor, if you could call it a robe. It was sleeveless and didn't cover my belly. Jack wore our towels around his shoulders.

I hadn't thought much of what we looked like until we entered the pool room and it fell silent. We took in the open mouths and for a moment I forgot about the big dangerous deep chlorinated puddle in front of us.

Male: six-six, shaggy hair, lumberjack beard and looking for all the world like he'd lost a fight with his chainsaw *and* his pet bear considering the deep scars and missing fingers.

Female: six foot even, two full sleeves of flame tattoos, scarred stomach, missing tooth and very obviously pregnant with her caveman's spawn.

Yeah, then there was the skimpy matching swimwear.

As the eyes found their manners and started to look away I began to giggle and Jack slipped my robe off and tossed it aside with our towels. He picked me up and cannon-balled us right into the deep end, my terrified shriek cut short as we submerged. I came up gagging nearly to the point of throwing up, barely aware of several other guests either moving to the shallow end or getting ready to leave.

The shocked look on Jack's face scared me even more and I screamed again as I tried to climb on top of him like a life raft, sure he knew something was wrong and I just hadn't picked up on it yet. He took a deep breath as I drove him under and I sunk, pulling in more unwanted water as he came up behind me. Once his arm was around my middle we were to the side as quickly as he'd dunked me in the first place.

"Damn it!" I sputtered as water came up. Jack's arms surrounded me, holding me against the pool wall. "I'm dying!"

"You're not dying. You're swimming," he whispered. Two pairs of bare feet hurried past, barely missing my nose.

"Anna doesn't swim," I coughed and spat out what I hoped was the last of the water. I hooked my elbows up on the edge and held on for dear life.

"Apparently," he soothingly said. He put an elbow on the edge with mine and his arm around my waist. "Why didn't you say something? I thought you were getting off on it."

I looked at him in astonishment. "Wasn't my screaming a good enough clue?"

"Like I said. Getting off on it. Is there something you want to admit you're not good at?"

I tipped my head over on Jack's shoulder as I got my bearings. The ladder was just a few feet to my right, the surface still disturbed at its base as the last of the other swimmers had just fled. I turned and looked.

"Yeah, they're all gone," Jack laughed. "You can't swim, can you?"

"Of course I can swim," I muttered.

"Okay," he said and pushed off, leaving me alone at the edge of the pool. I forced myself to remain calm as I held on but I imagined the deceptively clear water hid something which could pull me under. My feet brushed together and I yelped. Before I knew what I was doing I'd failed to reach the ladder and looked up at the rippled surface. Then up at Jack as my bare belly brushed down the wall and he took my hands and pulled me up.

"This won't do," he said as I gagged up more water. My nose ran freely and I turned away as I tried to wipe it without letting go again. Jack moved us hand over hand along the side until we had our feet on the bottom. I kept going to the curved set of tiled steps in one corner of the shallow end and sat sulking at the top. He pushed my sodden hair from my eyes and sat beside me.

"How the hell are my boys going to learn to swim if you're afraid of the water?"

I grabbed Jack's arm and shoved him forward. He cooperated, going in head first as if I'd tossed him.

"I'm not afraid," I said when he came back up. Whined was more like it. "I don't float."

He laughed and sank to the bottom. I waited and waited until I burst into tears, terrified he'd drown and I was too scared to help. He was right. How could I raise a couple of rowdy boys sobbing in the shallow end? When he finally came up, he pushed his bangs aside and regarded me; his eyes said the ribbing was over. Jack swam up and put his hands on the steps.

"I don't want my sons learning to swim from some summer job kid wearing red trunks and a whistle while their mother wrings her hands at the side," he whispered. "Or at least if they get lessons I don't want you having to get drunk after."

"But Targuer said—

"You ignore what he said," Jack insisted.

"Which part?" I demanded. "The part where I bleed out or the Missus Walker rides again part."

"Both, Baby. Both," he whispered and I gave in to the earnest compassion in his eyes. "I'll find a way to get you out of there, I promise."

I glanced at my feet. They were still there, both wrinkled and thankfully uneaten by whatever pool monster I still half believed lurked below. We kept to the shallow end, Jack's arms in a U around me and my hands on top of his. I'd stopped squishing his fingers to my ribs at least which was a start as we continued to float around in a lazy circle.

"I'm gonna get laid after this, right?" He whispered in my ear and I laughed with embarrassment. A couple of guests had arrived and stuck around unaware we'd scared the previous group off. I felt certain his low voice carried across the water straight into their ears. "Like if I took you to a scary movie, you'd be all over me later for protecting you."

"You tried to drown me and we're getting lunch after this."

"Then I'm getting laid, right?" Jack got his arms around my tummy. "RJ said they're um, doing it tomorrow."

I shuddered as he pulled me over to the steps. His fingers felt pruny on my stomach. I sat a step below, folded in his arms.

"Anyone not needed to build The Last Step is repairing the house. RJ said there's water damage at the back. Mould in the walls. It's a lot worse than some broken windows. You're not going back until they clean it up. It's too unhealthy.

"A couple of weeks at least."

I straightened with surprise.

"RJ is joining us for a late lunch. He's in town renting a truck and a scaffold for the exterior work," Jack whispered as he pulled me in again. "I'm going to teach you to swim. I've got two weeks. At least I can give you one less thing to fear."

I didn't notice the stares as we left. Maybe since we'd been there for an hour we felt less like the invaders we were when we arrived.

Chapter 9

"Are you going to tell me?"

The big red number changed from three to four. We rode alone in the elevator and Jack's beard still dripped in spite of a vigorous towelling.

"It's not a big deal," I avoided his stare and looked at the ceiling instead. Jack slid his hand under the back of my little black cover up just before we stepped out to see Soros and Travis waiting outside our room. I stifled a gasp and glared at Jack. He would have read them there but he shrugged to say he had everything under control. More upsetting than seeing them was relief I'd experience an hour or two of order while I spent a few pieces of dignity meeting expectations.

"Jack!" Soros called.

Jack ground his teeth in reply but I waved knowing he'd greet me directly when he could put his hands on me.

"I'll tell you," I whispered as we approached. Jack tugged me closer, only pausing to take the back of my head with his free hand and gently pull me in for a kiss. He looked pained. His admission of jealousy the day before still touched me and I came to a stop, my back to Soros. I intended to make it much more obvious to everyone I belonged to Jack.

"I'm sorry," I whispered.

Jack glanced over my head at his brother.

"I haven't shown you any affection when they're around. I wore you like some fleshy jewellery. I ignored you so if I messed up I hoped they'd ignore you, too."

His eyes widened for just a moment before he gave me a tiny nod and a coy smile. Apology accepted.

"No more," I whispered as I tugged in his beard and pulled his mouth to mine. "You're mine, Jack Roberts."

He nudged me backward down the hall with his kiss as Soros called to him, only breaking from me when Soros took my elbow and turned me to kiss his cheek.

"Mister Soros," I greeted him. "Mister Travis."

Travis only nodded.

"Thank you so much!" I exclaimed as I put an arm around Jack's waist and held him tight. "I haven't been to a pool in years and we had so much fun!"

Soros winked in reply and tipped his head at the door. Jack groaned and let us in as Travis shoved a garment bag in his hands. Soros passed me clean clothes from the closet and Jack and I stepped into the bathroom to change. I rinsed the pool chemicals from our swimsuits and hung them over the shower curtain rail, something my mother had been big on. The only thing worse than being afraid of the water would be having my swimsuit disintegrate around me trapping me in the pool.

Jack left the water running as he brushed his teeth.

"There's not much to tell," I whispered. There was no way I would share my only phobia in front of Soros. "My folks used to take us to the Colliery Dam up the hill from our house or the beach all summer long. Then when mom got sick we didn't go at all that summer. She just wasn't well enough. Fall came and she died and the only water we saw was rain."

He wiped some stray foam from his mouth and I leaned back on the counter as he listened.

"The next summer Kenny the neighbour kid took Alina and me up to the Dam. Dad said it would be good for us."

"Neighbour kid?"

I rolled my eyes. "He wanted to be my boyfriend and I only ever kissed him twice."

Jack guffawed, sobering when I shot him a nasty look. Kenny may have turned into an ass but he came through for Paul, Denis, Ray and me before Camille was born. He gave us the heads up Damian and his men were looking for me.

"Winter had been unusually dry and we were rationing water already. The lake seemed lower somehow, dirtier. So murky if you pulled your knees up you couldn't see them through the water. We didn't care. It was hot as hell.

"Part way through the afternoon we were all out on the raft. I swam out past it to avoid the boys jumping in. Kenny yelled so I turned and when I dropped my legs down something brushed my foot then wrapped around my ankle."

I flinched when Jack got his arms around me as I realized I trembled.

"I reached down to try and brush it off, had to put my face under to do it but it danced around my foot. I lifted my head up for another breath to try again but all I could get above the surface was my hands. When I tried to kick I couldn't get any higher and the thing on my foot seemed to get heavier, holding me down. My lungs hurt and I kept trying to swim up, splashing from below as much as I could.

"Then Kenny had me and whatever was on my foot disappeared but I threw up water as he hauled me to the raft. I tried to explain what happened and Alina, Little Miss Empirical Evidence jumped in to explore. I'd already caused enough of a scene but when she didn't come right back up I started screaming and people came running from everywhere. She came up with a branch, an old strip of plastic wrapped around it. Waving it like a flag and laughing her ass off at me."

"Reservation," Soros called as he banged on the door. My hands shook so badly Jack sat me down to pull my socks on for me.

"It was nearly dark before Kenny was able to get me to shore. Alina had been ribbing me about the raft monster, then the ghost of a gun shot suicide on the raft we'd only ever heard rumours about. I got stubborn."

Jack knowingly laughed, tucking a grey dress shirt into soft dark green slacks.

"The more stubborn I got the more convinced I was something really bad waited in the water. I never went back in. I thought it was nothing more than a running joke with my sister but it really scared me. I swim fine, Jack. I just had a bad moment."

I dressed in the stretchy brown pants and buttoned up the long sleeved cotton salmon coloured top Soros picked out. When we stepped out, Soros passed me a beaded hair clip so I put my hair back and stepped into the same brown boots I wore to the doctor.

Jack and I shared the back seat of Soros' truck for the ride to the restaurant, a casual place without booths, so Jack and I nudged our seats close enough he could tuck his hand under the back of my top. The waiters wore white dress shirts with black pants and aprons. Wood-slatted blinds covered the wall-to-wall windows, the bar had novelty sized pulls for serving beer and the massive TV aired a Rangers game.

"What would you like, Sweet Thing?" Soros asked.

"Pardon, Mister Soros?"

"Menu," he pointed. Jack smacked his lips as he read. I opened mine and buried my nose in it. So much for the comfort of rules for a couple of hours. I was used to getting what I got which was the same thing everyone else was served from the big kitchen.

"Well," I thought. I elbowed Jack and looked at him, pleading for help. "What are you getting?"

"RJ's buying. I'm getting the most expensive thing on the menu. I don't give a shit what it is."

I was thinking cheapest.

"Any cravings, Sweet Thing?" Soros asked. "Hurry up, the waiter is coming."

Nothing on the menu jumped out at me and Soros booted toe hit my shin more than firmly.

"Pineapple," I blurted out.

"Alright," Soros answered.

I hoped I'd get more than pineapple and fortunately I did. Soros ordered teriyaki and pineapple chicken with wild rice and a salad. A Shirley Temple to drink. Jack ordered a massive steak I had to cut up with a lobster I had to crack open and a ten dollar beer, then a twenty dollar glass of scotch.

"Business," Soros announced before we were half finished. "You're not due for a break until tomorrow."

He passed me an iPod and I pushed the little buds into my ears to find myself listening to opera. It would go on and on without a break so there was no chance of me picking up even a few words. I kept my eyes down as I finished eating then closed them and listened to the music as Jack's thumb traced slow, relaxed circles on my back. Whatever they talked about didn't seem to bother him. I think I was nearly asleep when he took my elbow to rouse me and we left for the truck.

On the way to the hotel Jack nibbled my ear and quietly sang *The Grievous Angel* to me. He changed Annie Rich to Anna Richards, making it fit in spite of the extra syllable. Soros dropped us off at the lobby and Jack and I went straight upstairs to bed.

Chapter 10

Here again.

My dream-self stared into a bathroom mirror from a year and a half earlier; the night Paul and I met. My hair had been longer and when I pulled my lips back I saw all my teeth. I wondered how quickly the amazing memory of our first night together would turn into the horror which was our last. This crazy mix of happiness, pain and my near death experience the previous summer would wake Jack as I called Paul's name in my sleep. For now, my dream-Paul lay in the room either drifting off at the end of the evening or sleeping in the next morning.

I clearly remembered Jack and me turning in after a long afternoon nap and a very late dinner.

Then the dream-hotel bathroom.

Again.

I studied the corners around the ceiling for the cracks which would appear as thunder above tore away the roof. There was no damage yet so I opened the door and smelled fresh coffee. Morning, I decided, and stepped out, my limbs still enjoying their first post-coital looseness.

I slipped in behind Paul and watched his back and shoulders move up and down. Then I reached out and carefully traced his spine with one finger, then two, and as his breathing changed I pressed up with my whole palm until I could wrap my fingers around his shoulder. I knew he was awake and when he didn't move I kissed his shoulder blade and slid my arm around him until my hand was in the centre of his chest.

I kissed him again and leaned away to look at the tattoos on his back.

"She looks just like me," I whispered.

"Who?" Paul asked.

"Her," I said as I ran my fingers over the blonde pin up girl wearing nothing but a smile.

"Except for her figure," I added.

Paul laughed. Her jaunty oversized breasts pointed in two different directions and her butt was enormous. Otherwise her face was mine. The old ink had spread so the lines weren't as clean as they would have been when it was new.

"Who's Katrina?" I asked of the other one; simple capital letters in a ribbon.

"Oh," he said, a little embarrassed. "That lasted about as long as it took to get her name on me. She left to spend the rest of the night with a friend of mine and ran out on him long before dawn. I never saw her again. I wasn't much past seventeen when I got them... actually I forgot I had them back there.

"She was an older woman, maybe your age," he teased.

I laughed then held my breath as I decided if the rumble I heard in the distance was thunder or simply one of the ten thousand motorcycles tucked in every corner around us. Within seconds it grew louder than the rumble of a thousand motorcycles. The framing screamed as the blackness above crashed in like a wave. Paul was in my arms for only a moment then he disappeared and I flew into the small sofa, hitting hard enough to knock the wind from my lungs.

As the concussion passed, I rolled naked to the floor and scrambled to my feet. The sky churned black and blue accented with blinding lightning. Over the angry rumble I heard a man's scream and knew I had to climb higher. Ice below chilled the floor and if I stuck around too long Paul and his men would freeze in place as Damian's closed in. Only entering the storm above would save them and make the ice recede.

It took a firm shoulder to get the door open and in spite of the fact I was on the second floor of the two storey motel, stairs led higher. I sprinted past numbered doors and took the first flight two at a time, then another, slowing as the storm above began to devour me from the inside out. My nails dug in deep like they did when the boys tore and I fell to my knees on the fourth floor. Through the railings, lightning lit the cornfield below and showed me faces both familiar and strange. They had a chance to fight though they were unarmed against Damian's men, free of the ice which would hold them when the storm above became too much for me to resist and I had to descend to escape.

I crawled up to the fifth floor but found myself pinned face first on the landing by the heavy weight of a man.

"Precious," Walker whispered. The raging pressure above didn't trouble him, or perhaps he himself was the storm.

"Gerald," I whispered, hoping I could strip some of his power by stripping him of his formal name.

He growled as he flipped me on my back, pinning my hands above my head. After a moment he released them as the clouds above spasmed and the pressure grew so much I couldn't move. My shoulders strained as the force above pushed my elbows into an unnatural position deep in the floor.

Gerald got his knees under him and straddled my thighs. Wind blew his long grey hair about in all directions.

From a pocket on the thigh of his pants he withdrew a folded leather case. I knew what it contained. Gerald untied the leather strap binding it and unrolled it on my stomach. I couldn't see the stainless steel pins but I heard them brush together. They were six inches long and varying thicknesses though each had a heavy ball on the end so Gerald wouldn't hurt his own hand pushing them in.

I cried out and tried to kick my way out from under him but Gerald ignored me as he stroked each fat head with his fingers. Lightening struck, illuminating his hair in a dark halo. His hand appeared before my face holding a giant pin with a shaft half an inch thick.

"This should slow you down, Precious," his voice rumbled, stopping my breath with even deeper pain in my chest. "And give me a chance to get ready. Let's see if you can save him."

He palmed the round head as two fingers of his other hand explored my left shoulder. When he found his mark he placed the point where the pin could pass through me doing as little damage as possible.

I screamed, barely registering Gerald's impassive face as the pin sunk on its way to biting into the floor.

Then warm arms held me. The thunder faded and I pushed them away as I fought to sit, clawing at my shoulder where I still imagined it impaled through.

"Sshhh, Baby," Jack whispered as I barked out a few tearful syllables neither one of us could understand. He let me back away only a little before taking my hands and putting them to his lips. The lamp came on as he moved closer and I dropped my head to his bare chest as I caught my trembling breath.

"Okay?"

"Mm," I grunted. Dreaming through being nailed to the floor would be worth it if I'd had a chance to save Paul but going through it only to wake up so close left me frustrated and angry.

"Damn it," I managed. "I'm sorry."

Jack only held me tighter. I wasn't so much sorry for waking him. It felt like I'd failed Paul again for which I was truly sorry. I shivered from the icy dream in spite of the warm room and the heat from Jack's sleepy body. He pulled the blanket up over my shoulders. He would know my dream was of Paul. He didn't have to ask.

"It's after six," he eventually said.

I pulled my lips into my mouth and bit them between my teeth to steady them, grateful I didn't have to try and go back to sleep.

"Just a sec." Jack stood and fixed me a glass of pineapple juice and Seven-Up. He sipped it before he handed it to me. "Not bad. Any other cravings I can accommodate?"

That earned a tired smile.

"Not just yet," I whispered then sighed as the cold, sweet drink whetted my dry mouth and soothed my throat. I wondered how long I'd carried on for it to hurt.

The cell phone rang from the top of the TV and Jack rolled his eyes, picking it up before climbing back into bed with me.

"I was going to order up breakfast," he grumbled as he answered it. Now he had to wait as Soros went on about being Soros. "Yell-oh."

Jack's eyes widened and he sat a little straighter.

"Good morning, Colonel," he said, wincing. Sig would remind him it was simply Sig and I gave Jack a 'you know better than that' look.

"Of course," Jack said. "That's correct. We're in the Hartford Hilton for a couple of weeks."

I pulled back a little more juice as Jack listened.

"Yes, Sir," he said and passed me the phone before he could be admonished for the three lettered term of deference.

"Morning, Sig," I said.

Careful, Jack mouthed and I nodded. RJ would have given Sig the number and who knew if he had a way of listening in.

"Anna," Sig got down to business. "I'm sorry but something urgent has come up and I won't be able to see you today. Possibly next time you're in the city."

"That's alright," I said. He still worked for the Army and I was surprised he hadn't rescheduled anything with me before.

"How are you feeling?"

"I'm okay," I said as I kept an eye on Jack.

"Any new pain?"

"There hasn't been any pain since the last time I saw you, Sig," I answered. Jack made an OK sign with his left hand and I silently giggled. It looked funny with the missing fingers. Jack poked his tongue out at me.

"It's easier to tell when our breaks are coming to an end," I added an outright lie. Jack picked up the hotel phone and started ordering up breakfast.

"That's good news then, Little One," he said. "As I said last time, you're nearly healed. I'm always concerned if there's been pain there could be more damage. I don't feel so bad about missing my visit though I do miss seeing you."

"Thanks, Sig," I answered. "I miss you, too. Whatever you're getting yourself into make sure everyone is safe, okay?"

"Until next time," he said and the call disconnected before I could say good-bye. Jack raised an eyebrow.

"He's not coming. Maybe next time."

We looked at each other. I was concerned for no reason I could put my finger on. Maybe because after today they wouldn't need The Last Step and would take it down. The hangings sat uneasily causing me to feel worry where I probably shouldn't. Jack looked like he understood, or at least he was less phased than I was.

"Today?" I asked even though I knew the answer.

He nodded.

They're hanging four men because of me, I thought. They made Tombs blow himself up with his bomb. One actually stole something but the other three were going to die for something which would never happen.

Still shaken from my dream, I excused myself and went to the shower.

Chapter 11

Jack served lunch at the little coffee table in our room after a long cold walk interrupted by a hot drink in a warm coffee shop. He promised a trip to the pool before dinner and I pretended not to hear him. We were just a mouthful in and the cell phone rang again.

"Fuck me sideways," Jack cursed around a ketchup covered French fry. His language was colourful as usual. I wondered what he'd have to say if we'd been having sex when it rang. I rinsed my mouth with tea in case I had to talk to Soros. The phone snapped open. "Yeah?"

Jack stopped chewing as he listened. I stood, surprised by his active attention on his brother. By the time I reached him, he bent over the desk with a pen and paper, scribbling down an address. Building sounds popped from the small speaker by his ear.

"Pack," he ordered as he hung up.

"Did they do it?" I whispered.

"What?" He snapped. I took a step away, confused by his mood. I hadn't seen the patriarch in him in a long time and it scared me he needed it to get something done without being questioned.

"I heard hammering," I stammered as I held my ground. "Did they do it?"

"Yes," he said as he turned to the desk for the paper he'd written on. I turned the other way and ran to the bathroom to throw up. Jack followed and rubbed my back with one hand while the other soaked a small towel.

"We're moving to a safe-house," he quickly said as I wiped my mouth. He kept talking as I brushed my teeth.

"Baltimore," he said from the other room. "Six hour drive."

I packed up our bathroom things and checked the drawers before grabbing our swimsuits from the shower rod. When I stepped out, Jack checked our guns then they disappeared into the bottom of our duffle bags. He took the toiletries from me and turned to the closet.

"We shouldn't be unprotected here in the hotel," Jack spoke with his back to me as he pulled things off the hangers. "It must be RJ's safe-house. I don't know the address."

I took the clothes from him before he could stuff them in like a ball and tried to take care folding but my hands shook. Jack went through the dressers then several hundred in cash went in his pocket before the envelope went in his bag.

"Coat, shoes," he ordered then he noticed me standing there, still holding the jeans I'd worn to Targuer's.

"There are two ways this can go," Jack impatiently said. "I can go full on grown-up with you and get you moving or you can put your pants in the bag and put your coat on. One way we're gonna fight, the other we won't. Either way we're checking out in three minutes."

I moved. Nothing would get my back up quicker than being talked down to like a family child and it would make the long road trip unbearable. Jack caught my elbow and sat me on the bed before kneeling at my feet.

"Good girl," he whispered, hands on my stomach. "Gerald learned Tombs has a couple of men we can't account for. We don't have time for questions and you know as much as I do."

He pulled me on my feet and before I could say anything, our bags were on his shoulder and we were out the door.

Jack stopped at the first mall we came to and handed me the phone then I sneezed as he connected to me.

Trust, loyalty and obedience right? He sent.

I nodded, eyes wide. One hand over my mouth and the other scratching at the boys' anxiety. He pulled my hand from my chest and put it over my mouth.

As big a girl as you think you are, you're in no shape to defend yourself. That's my job. If the phone rings, he tapped his nose to say 'tell me' as he got out and slammed the door, setting a brisk pace to the mall. *Don't answer it. I'll be here long before he calls again.*

I was too scared to even send him a message to say I understood so I looked around at the other cars to make sure I wasn't being watched then crawled into the back seat and curled up to hide.

When the driver's door opened, a couple of full plastic bags landed on the passenger seat then Jack's seat tipped forward and he got in the back with me.

"It's okay," he said. He seemed calmer but I thought he'd been calmer when we left the room and he got worked up again. He pulled my coat off and passed me a big off-white fleece jacket from the bags.

"It's not ladies wear but it'll be more comfortable for the drive than that bulky coat. Do you want to stay back here?"

I said I didn't and moved up front with him for the short drive across the street to a gas station. Jack filled the old sports car and checked the oil before we drove around back to the air hose and the restrooms. I got the keys while he put some air in the front right and he was in the men's when I stepped out of the ladies.

The clock on the dash counted up nearly ten minutes.

Jack?

I'm okay, he answered.

I hardly recognized him when he stepped out. The hair was gone as was the beard. He'd given himself a decent cut with the electric clipper dangling from his hand. His other hand held a smaller plastic bag containing what I guessed was shaving gear. It all went in the trunk and he went to return the key.

Want anything?

Something to drink please and a sandwich maybe?

Jack handed out the food without looking at me, his brow furrowed with stress. Whatever went on he either wasn't coping well or it was a lot worse than I thought and he did an admirable job of keeping it together.

I gently ran my fingers over his smooth cheek to get his attention.

"I only grew it to annoy RJ," he explained as he sipped his coffee. "It was itchy as hell and I'm not putting up with it if I don't have to put up with him."

"I liked it, Jack."

Chapter 12

"Hey, Baby," Jack softly said. "We're here."

I didn't remember anything since the last gas station before I fell asleep with Jack's coat mashed between the window and my head. We'd pulled over so I could use the restroom while Jack refilled his mug. My stomach rumbled. The sandwich at noon hadn't been much. It was after six and dark. The streetlight directly overhead showed a skiff of fresh snow on the street and sidewalk.

"I know this neighbourhood. I grew up near here. If you want I can show you where I stole the Pulsar."

"That sounds like fun, Jack," I laughed, part cut-off by another yawn. "How long are we here?"

"RJ called an hour ago," Jack answered. "I guess to make sure we're on track. He said expect to drive back in a week at the earliest. Sit tight."

Jack hopped out and walked around to open my door.

"Come on," he said. I couldn't lean far enough over my stomach to tip myself out of the low car. He leaned over to give me a kiss as he pulled his coat on. It had to be ten degrees colder here in Baltimore than back at the hotel. The fleece jacket would be fine until we got inside. I rocked back and forth on my feet to loosen up my back then followed Jack to the hatch to get our bags. "RJ said the house would be open."

I nodded. Safe house or not I didn't think it should be left unlocked. Jack explained it would be well stocked with food. We'd go to the store later for produce.

"I got 'em," he said as he put one bag over his shoulder and the other in his hand. I got caught staring at his bare cheeks and he winked.

"Jason?" A woman's voice behind me called. I looked up at Jack. Even in the limited light I could see the colour drain from his face as his mouth snapped shut.

"Son-of-a—" Jack muttered. "God damn you, RJ."

"Jack!?" her voice called out behind me, much louder.

"What's going on, Jack?"

"Fuckin' RJ sent me to my parents' house," he sighed. "Don't suppose you want to get back in the car and drive off?"

I shook my head. "We'll be in trouble if we go anywhere else."

Jack's arm went around me as I turned. The woman looked a lot like Jack, except with a grey perm. She held a big holiday wreath in one hand and a hammer in the other.

"Jason?" she asked again. A moment later she was joined by a big balding man who looked even more like Jack than she did. He wore an Oriole's jersey and pulled his glasses off to stare at us down on the curb. He seemed to occupy most of the small front porch.

"I told you I stole the Pulsar when I was sixteen, right?" Jack whispered behind me and I nodded. "I drove to Father's and never came back. I haven't seen them in twenty-two years."

"Shit, Jack," I whistled.

"Jason," he answered. "My Dad is Jack."

"You're Jack," I said as I took his hand and pulled him to the gate. His mother held on to Jack Sr.'s arm and they made their way down the stairs to the walk.

"Hi Mom, Dad," Jack quietly said.

"My God, Jason," she said then she glanced at my stomach sticking out of my unzipped jacket. I opened the latch and stepped out of the way as Jack's mother embraced him. Jack's father appeared to be in shock. I could only imagine how they felt to see their runaway teenage son after two decades.

"What are you? I mean, why?" she asked as she let him go.

"I," Jack started, seemingly as overcome as she did. He shook his dad's hand and hid his damaged one behind me. "My wife insisted it's never too late to let you know I'm okay."

At first the word 'wife' surprised me but after a moment decided to let them believe we were married rather than think he shared a room with someone else's wife since I wore Paul's ring.

"Anna Roberts," I said, holding out my hand. She handed the hammer off to Jack's father and started to shake mine then she hugged me.

"My Mom, Sheryl," Jack said. "My Dad, Jack."

"Hi, Sheryl," I breathed as she squeezed me. His Dad seemed a little cooler. He took my hand in both of his big ones and murmured my name.

"How long are you in Baltimore?" Jack Sr. asked.

My Jack insisted I call him Jason in front of his parents. He seemed relieved to see them again and proud of his 'wife' and her growing stomach. Sheryl and Jack hadn't asked yet. Maybe they worried if they questioned too much the spell would break and we would disappear.

"Not sure, Dad," Jack said. He held a bottle of beer in his good hand and Sheryl pulled a roast from the oven like she'd been expecting company. He'd held the bottle with his left as he twisted off the cap, getting a curious glance from his father. "Things are sort of on hold at the moment."

Sheryl put a salad on the table and a glass pitcher of water both full of and decorated with painted lemons.

"Between jobs?" His father asked.

"No," Jack said. "Assignments. I'm a Captain in the Army, mostly working out of the country."

Really? I sent to Jack.

Follow my lead. We'll stick as close to the truth as we can.

"Thanks," I said as I accepted a glass from Sheryl. She and Jack Sr. exchanged glances.

"We woke up one day and you were gone," Sheryl said. "Bob Henderson next door asked if we'd heard anything. His Pulsar was gone. When you didn't come back we thought you stole it and were too scared to come home."

"I dumped it," Jack uncomfortably said. "That Pulsar is mine." *Not quite*, he sent to me. *Father fixed the registration a few years later.*

"After you turned nineteen a man from the military called and said he was conducting a background check. All we could tell him was we hadn't seen you in a while. It was the last we heard."

Jack looked away. His dad was silent.

"A few years later we had a fire and lost the house. We moved here and kept listed in the book in case you ever needed us."

"Ah, I'm sorry," Jack mumbled. "How's my sister?"

I stifled my surprise.

"Cindy went to college in New York. She's married and you have a niece."

"Wow," Jack sighed and leaned back on his chair. His father had cut the roast and served. Sheryl pushed the salad toward us.

Forgetting his hand, Jack served me. Sheryl looked at his missing fingers again and started to cry. Jack's father got his arm around her. Jack and I quietly sat then he took my right with his left and tilted his head, gesturing for me to take his mother's so I did. She wiped her eyes on her napkin before taking it then Jack Sr. took the hands of his wife and son.

"Dear Lord," Jack started. "Thank you for the food on my parents' table. Thank you for my brave and generous girl Anna. Her kindness and persistence have brought me here. Thank you for letting me find my parents healthy and happy. Thank you for my unborn sons and for each day I have with their mother. Amen."

"Amen."

Chapter 13

"Two boys," Sheryl whispered as we sat in their living room. Jack and his father each had another bottle of beer. She gestured at the photos on the wall. "After the fire we called every school photographer, friends and family. Even the parents of every kid who ever invited Jason and Cindy to a birthday party. We have more pictures of them than we lost. If you're not sure how long you're staying I want to hear how you met."

Like the kitchen where we'd eaten, the living room contained comfortable older furniture. A basket of kids' toys and books sat tucked in beside Sheryl's chair.

I don't remember ever spending much time with any of my parents after taking off for Father's. Never wanted to. With the boys coming it feels good to be here, Jack sent. *The boys are their blood relatives, too.*

I realized this was likely the first time he'd had a beer with his dad.

"There's only so much I can tell you," Jack said. "The assignment we're on is ongoing."

His dad nodded in understanding.

"My team has been involved in a joint project with the Canadians, sharing resources, men, that sort of thing. One of my snipers rotated back state-side so the CO says I'm getting Corporal Creed on loan from the Canadians for a while, they have a permanent replacement with sufficient clearances but he's a couple of months away from joining us. My man leaving was a surprise. He'd been talking another tour right up until he left."

Jack shrugged.

"So we took over a corner of the hanger to prep and this tall tattooed blonde squats down with us and starts going through her kit. She doesn't say a word for a few minutes but my guys are checking her out. This can't be Corporal Creed. It's right around my birthday so I think it's a setup and they're elbowing each other trying to figure out who gets the credit and how long this little girl is going to keep a straight face.

"She says 'Captain Roberts, I know why you're giving me the silent treatment.' I kept my mouth shut as she gets rougher with her stuff. The madder she gets the more I'm thinking with my heart and not my head. I kept looking at her when her eyes were down 'cause she's getting this little bit of angry pink to her cheeks and she finally stands up and says 'can I have a word, Sir?'"

I giggled.

"She stomps about twenty feet away and stands there, arms crossed like her mom just said she can't have a puppy so I sigh and follow her. Up close she's even prettier."

Jack put his arm around me and I felt myself blush.

"'Look,' she says, real quiet. 'I get it. You don't want me here. I think it's bullshit but whatever. I'll do my job and then I'm out and you can have a good old American boy watching your ass instead of Miss Canada.'

"I still don't say a word because if I open my mouth I'm going to ask her out."

His parents laughed.

"I have a chip on my shoulder a mile wide," I explained. "Guys see me and think model, not jarhead."

"Then she goes white," Jack went on. "She says 'Oh my God, now I've done it. I just assumed you didn't want a woman with a Timberwolf backing you up. Ah, shit.'

"I give her this stupid smile and shake my head," Jack said. "She smells so good and she's so close. I hear snickering behind me and she glances at them.

"She thanks me. I raised my eyebrows to say why 'cause I still don't trust myself to speak. 'Well,' she says. 'I just thought you'd run for your CO to promise him your first born or something if that's what it took to scrub me from the roster. So thanks for letting me do my job.

"'I know they're laughing at you for not giving me a hard time,' she says. 'Maybe I can get you out of it.'"

"So what did you do?" Sheryl asked.

"His men were roaring by that point so I pulled his hands from his pockets and held them. Now we could hear a pin drop. I took a step closer and looked in his eyes. 'Jason,' I said just loud enough for them to hear. 'I'm sorry for before. What happened between us was all my fault. When we get back maybe you can give me another chance.'"

Jack threw his head back, tears of laughter in his eyes like he actually remembered.

"Then," I said loudly to get the attention back on me. "He takes my cheek in the palm of his hand and kisses me."

"No," Sheryl gasped. "You never said a word to her and you got away with it?"

Jack grinned. Then in his defence he exclaimed "she kissed me back!"

His dad held his nearly empty bottle out and Jack loudly knocked his into it. Jack finished the last of his and his dad took his empty, quickly returning with a couple of fresh ones.

"That assignment went sideways on us just a few days in. Anna got roughed up and I lost my other sniper. By the time she'd," he hesitated and glanced at his mom, "dealt with the enemy and got her gun back up we'd only lost two. We'd have lost a lot more if she hadn't gotten control of the situation."

"I should have heard him," I shuddered, thinking of the rape; of what really happened. Then I rubbed my mouth so they'd think that's when I lost my tooth. Jack got his arms around me and hid me in his shoulder.

"I didn't want to leave her alone after that," Jack said. "We had separate assignments for a while and it was really rough but I spent every minute with her I could.

"Then we were sent out together again," he lowered his voice. His parents seemed captivated. "We were compromised. The men who weren't killed were captured and split up. I didn't know if they had her or if she was dead."

Jack held up his half-hand.

"They got us out, sent me home for reconstructive surgery. I'd been back a few days. She shows up at the hospital and tells me she's pregnant."

Sheryl's hand was on her mouth and his dad looked at his knees.

"I married him the same day. We're not sure when Jack's leaving me," I said as I rubbed my stomach. "I'm not going back to the field now and they're still trying to find out who warned them we were coming."

The Last Step

Chapter 14

Jack and I felt the boys move for the first time that night at his parents' house. They'd insisted we take the spare room on the main floor to keep me off the stairs and Sheryl would offer the two empty upstairs rooms to Cindy, Darren, and Emily for their annual pre-Christmas weekend visit.

Soros called early the next day. The sketchy cell reception at his end forced me to repeat myself several times as I recounted the tale we gave his parents. Jack refused to speak to him other than to confirm he was there with me. He called again two days later then nothing.

On our third day, Jack Sr. removed himself from his stunned amicable silence and had the first of several strongly worded conversations with his son. He started with 'how could you do that to your mother' and continued with 'I adore your wife but you shouldn't have been fraternizing with a subordinate' and 'why didn't you go into landscaping like me.' To the last one Jack replied he'd have been just as likely to lose a finger.

His father conceded the point.

Cindy Turnbull and her family arrived late our first Friday night in Baltimore. Sheryl told her we'd turned up and Jack's reunion with her was a little awkward. Cindy's husband Darren was protective of his wife and it was clear Jack's disappearance had been traumatic for his little sister. It didn't take long for Darren's initial reaction to warm up and Jack and his sister talked in the kitchen until well past midnight.

The next morning little Emily wouldn't take a seat at the table, obviously frightened by the seven inch scar down Jack's face. Jack hid his upset about scaring her but his hand worked my back as he tried to think of a way to smooth things over. Inspired, I mentioned in passing that Jack was a pirate. Her eyes opened a little wider when she heard and she slowly made her way around the table so I was between her and Jack.

Eventually she leaned over my stomach for a good long look.

"Where's your eye-patch, Uncle Jason?" Emily whispered when Sheryl stood to clear the table.

"I only wear it when I'm expecting trouble," Jack answered. "It helps me see in the dark."

"Oh," Emily breathed, eyes completely round. I was surprised how much a six-year-old still smelled like a baby and I put my arm around her and thought of my own daughter.

"Yup," Jack said, still not testing her timid conversation with eye contact. "You know how the lights go out and you can't see for a minute? My eye patch makes sure one eye is always used to the dark so if there's trouble I put it on my other eye."

"Then you can see in the dark," she squeaked and Jack looked at her and smiled. "Mommy! Uncle Jason is a *real* pirate."

Jack and Darren spent the cold afternoon on ladders putting up the Christmas lights as Cindy, Sheryl and I stood on the lawn, pointing and shouting instructions. Emily helped her Grandpa put together the wooden sleigh and reindeer for the front lawn, safely out of the way if one of the ladders went over. After breakfast the next day, they drove back to New York.

"Anna-honey?" Sheryl called. I blinked and found myself alone in the bed. Not surprising. Jack rose earlier and I slept later since we didn't have to compromise with a time which worked for us both.

"Sorry to wake you, dear. Your brother is here."

Heavy painful paralysis bit my thighs and upper arms as the smell reached me. Soros was somewhere nearby. We hadn't heard from him in more than two weeks.

"Who?" I asked, hoping to sound sleep bewildered and not terrified.

"RJ, honey," she said through the door. "He says it's urgent."

"'kay, Sheryl. Where's Jason?"

"Probably out back in the garage with Dad," her voice disappeared down the hall toward the front of the house. "They were out before I was up."

That would be more than two hours earlier.

I shuffled to the bathroom to brush my teeth. While I packed my toiletries I sent my sense to the back yard then the front and knelt on the floor as I failed to find Jack.

It was over.

When I trusted my legs to hold me I pulled my duffle from the closet and put my toiletry bag inside and dressed. Soros waited at the front door of the house. He wore a dress uniform, nervously working his hat in his fingers. To me it looked like an act but it was a good enough display of anxiety to fool Sheryl.

"Anna," he exclaimed with seeming relief and held an arm out.

I replied with a friendly 'RJ' but my voice shook like my hands did when I hugged him.

"Can I offer you coffee, Captain Creed?" Sheryl called from the kitchen. It was clear Soros tailored his story to matched the one we gave Jack's parents. I didn't know if the Captain's bars on his collar were legitimate but I was sure the 'Creed' name badge over his pocket wasn't.

"A small cup would be wonderful, Missus Roberts," he answered. "We can't dawdle but I have time for a small one. Black, please."

Soros waited for Sheryl to be in earshot before he spoke again.

"It's what we hoped for, Anna," Soros said. "Talk is we know how you were betrayed. The inquiry needs to confirm some facts with you and Jason."

"He's not here," Sheryl said as she gave Soros a gas station thermal mug. "Take it with you, Jack can't stop bringing them home and the cupboard is full of them. He won't buy a coffee in a paper cup and never has one of these to refill."

Soros nodded.

"Jason can catch up in the car," Soros said. "It's urgent I have you back right away. There's a meeting scheduled for seventeen hundred."

"I'm glad the waiting is over," I said and I meant it. It had been only a matter of time until Soros and Walker figured out I didn't need Jack to live. Once they had Jack, he'd take his last step in as much time as they took to build it.

"Get packed then, love."

I wrote Jack a quick note before sealing it in an envelope marked 'Jason.'

Don't come for me. I don't want you. Anna.

I left it in the middle of the half made bed and finished packing. All I could hope for was to leave before Jack returned and that he wouldn't follow. It was the only thing I could do to save him. I hoped Soros having me would be enough to keep my daughter safe.

At the door, Sheryl held my bag as Soros helped me into my coat.

"I can only imagine how hard it will be to relive it all, honey," Sheryl hugged me and I started to cry. "I'll send Jason along behind you as soon as he gets home. And you have your brother at your side. I'm glad you won't be going through it alone."

She reached around the corner to the table in the living room where the phone sat with a box of tissues and a dish of coloured stones. I expected one tissue but she gave me the box and I laughed.

"It's the least I can do to be there for you," she said.

"I don't think we'll be back for Christmas or settled anywhere else by then," I said. "My love to you, Sheryl, and to Jack. We'll be in touch in the new year."

Soros took my bag from Sheryl as our cue to leave. It felt terrible to lie to her. He held my elbow as we negotiated the steps and the path down to his truck. Sheryl stood in the open door and waved once Soros helped me inside. The door closed behind her as we drove away.

"The truth, Sweet Thing," Soros said. He took the first right we came to and pulled over. "Is this one of your breaks or are you cured? If you say you're cured we will drive straight back. If not we'll wait here for Jack."

"I don't know if I'm completely cured," I answered as I pulled a tissue from the box. I'd let myself feel vulnerable and whole again during our visit with Jack and Sheryl and tears would only weaken the mental armour I needed to put back on. "Jack doesn't need to touch me any more."

"How far apart can you get?"

"I don't know, Mister Soros."

He nodded and pulled out.

Soros bought me breakfast at a drive-through and I ate the tasteless plain food in silence. The truck warmed so I took my coat off and put it on the seat between us with the tissues. I felt a little better. It wasn't much of a barrier but at least its presence offered some protection from him.

He pressed a button on the dash.

"Call Gerald," Soros said and a few seconds later the call rang through.

"RJ," Gerald's voice rumbled through the truck's speakers. Soros turned it down.

"My dear brother, I hope I find you well."

"Of course," Gerald said. "Are you returning alone?"

"Say hello, Sweet Thing," Soros ordered.

"Good morning, Mister Walker," I greeted him as I put my hand on the boys' lines to try and still them. For a moment I wished Jack was there to quiet them with his touch.

"Good morning, Precious," he said. "You'll be happy to hear your room is ready. Good morning, Jack."

"Mister Roberts is missing, my dear brother," Soros explained. "His Missus and I are returning alone as she seems to be cured of her need for him."

"We will send a team then to pick him up," Gerald said and the phone was muffled as he started to give instructions.

"There is no need, Gerald," Soros loudly said and the rustling stopped. "I am quite certain he will return on his own, such is his devotion to his beautiful mate."

There was silence on the other end for a few seconds.

"I will give him some time then," Gerald conceded. "The traitor's life belongs to me and you will not interfere."

"Of course, my brother."

I understood. Jack knew his life was over whether by Gerald's hand in the parking lot behind the house or some other way wherever they caught up to him. He'd return to say good-bye and to break his connection to me before Gerald hung him.

It was the least he could do.

Chapter 15

I heard a knock at the door of the room Jack and I once shared. I spent the last two and a half weeks without him and started to trust he wouldn't return. I missed him. The air still smelled of fresh paint and the carpet had been replaced. The table and chairs had been pushed aside and Soros set himself up a single bed next to mine. He spent his nights in my room for security, he claimed, and I'd become grateful for his presence. More than once he encouraged a drunken Gerald Walker to sleep it off in his own room when he'd come to mine shouting crude amorous sentiments. I took every meal at Gerald's right hand and his attention during the day made his physical interest in me clear.

"Come in, please, Mister Soros," I called. I'd hoped he'd stay away a little longer. It was Camille's first Christmas the next day and I imagined how much Ray and Alina would do to make it special for her. The scene I pictured helped but didn't fill the empty hole in my heart.

"It has been such a busy afternoon," Soros exclaimed as he burst in. "And tonight you shall call me RJ and my brother Gerald and we shall call you Anna."

My jaw dropped as I tried to imagine what could have caused this sudden familiarity. Soros noticed.

"It's Christmas Eve," he threw his arms in the air like it explained everything and nearly lost his grip on the garment bag he held. "Tonight all the rules go out the window. Well, nearly all. No stealing, no killing, no non-mutually consensual sex.

"Otherwise there is dinner and a dance."

Thirty men to three women didn't sound like much of a dance no matter how many first names we'd be using.

"Mister—

"RJ," he corrected.

"RJ," I said. I had a million questions but decided encouraging him to talk about himself was safest. "How has the afternoon been so busy?"

"Well," he started. "After lunch there was decorating and of course all the cooking. We will have company tonight. And the false wall between the dining room and the TV room next to it had to come down to make room for everyone."

I had no idea there was a TV in the house much less an entire room for it. Soros lay the garment bag on the bed and opened it up. He pulled out a pair of red pumps.

"Of course you are attending, Anna," he said as he peeled the bag out of the way and pulled out a strapless red gown. The sequinned satin bodice would just cup my breasts. The skirt consisted of several layers of soft red organza covering the red satin liner. I crossed my shirt covered arms in horror. Christmas Eve had suddenly become all fucked up.

"My dear, unless your tattoos will be stealing, killing or fornicating without permission you will wear the dress. Now hurry please, your date will be here shortly."

I gathered up the dress and took it to the bathroom to change. As usual it fit well, the skirt floated down to my knees and in spite of all the layers it didn't make me look excessively poofy and round. I was surprised Soros wasn't in the room to collect my compliment when I stepped out. Pantyhose with a seam down the back waited on the dresser alongside new cosmetics. Neither would be an easy task.

After another wait I smelled Walker at the door before he knocked. Even though I didn't intentionally read anymore I could still smell them and well enough now to tell them apart. Unlike Soros, however, Walker I would not invite in.

When I opened, he politely bowed his head. He wore an expensive suit with a red puff in the pocket to match my dress and held a clear plastic case with a wrist corsage. It was creepy to think he and Soros had planned my outfit right down to the flowers.

"Hello, Anna," he said.

"Hello, Gerald," I answered. This could only be a bad dream. I half pictured my father at the bottom of the stairs waiting to take our picture as Walker took me to the prom.

"I would enjoy your company tonight," he stated.

"Of course, Gerald," I answered. He smiled in obvious pleasure.

"Your wrist, please."

I held out my left but he shook his head.

"The other, so we may dance without damaging it."

I gave him the other one and he slipped the elastic over my hand and centered the bunch of miniature red and white carnations over the back of my wrist. Then he held his right hand to me, palm up. I took it in my left and he led me to the dining room.

"Perhaps in time you will grow to like being at my right hand," he whispered as we reached the bottom of the last flight of stairs.

"Perhaps, Gerald," I replied, unsure what else to say.

When we arrived, Walker led me to the table. He seated me in my usual chair to his right and I looked around as he took his seat. Soros bustled about with last minute arrangements.

A web of mini coloured lights covered the high ceiling and a mirrored disco ball hung in the middle. The room had indeed doubled in size and the white linen covered tables stood around the perimeter leaving a sizeable dance floor in the middle. The new part of the room held a built-in bar and a stereo and several young men and women in matching black uniforms wandered around the tables pouring champagne.

The biggest surprise was the large number of women. When I saw Gerald watching I lowered my eyes but he put his arm around me.

"I believe you'll recognize them," he pointed and I saw Karen and Debbie waving. I had so much to take in I'd completely missed them and waved back. Karen pointed at me then made a walking motion with her fingers then pointed at herself.

Later, I mouthed and she nodded.

"The other women are hired by the house for the evening," Gerald explained. "If anyone wishes for any more than dance or conversation they will of course negotiate a price and pay the woman directly. They will be seen safely back to town by dawn."

I realized the women were paid entertainment. I was also relieved three pregnant women wouldn't be danced off their feet.

Soros clapped his hands and pointed at the caterer near the stereo. Quiet jazz began to play as the lights dimmed and everyone took their seats. A plate of turkey dinner was placed before me and I waited for Walker's signal to begin eating. In black, the caterers were nearly invisible.

"We will have another party of course for New Years, however it is not a dance," Walker explained as he motioned for his glass to be refilled. "We drink and play cards. Gambling is not normally permitted under this roof."

I nodded like I understood and cared. The hired women sat distributed around the room, two or three to a table and were constantly engaged in conversation. Being alone with Walker like this was just as unsettling as when he was his normal self and I almost wished he'd do a worse job of hiding his dark side. At least I'd know this charade was over.

As the tables were cleared Soros finally relaxed. He hadn't taken much time to eat before disappearing again then returning as the lights came up.

"We have a few minutes, Anna," Walker said. "Why don't you go say hello to your friends?"

"A few minutes before what, Mis... Gerald?"

"The first dance, my dear," he said. "I have a bit of business before we begin."

Debbie and Karen were still smaller than me though they were further along and were excited to hear about my trip to Baltimore and to compare notes about our babies. I filled them in on my two recent visits to Targuer without Jack; one the day Soros picked me up at Jack's parents and the other just the day before. They both liked Targuer. I pushed back thoughts of their motherless sons being raised in Gerald Walker's house and briefly broke down, blaming it on missing Jack while he was, I claimed, away at work.

Gerald gently took my elbow and led me to the middle of the dance floor as the lights went out. After a few seconds of complete darkness *Blue Christmas* began to play as Gerald took me in his arms and started to sway. I concentrated on picking my feet up and putting them down, letting him lead and careful not to trip or step on him. The coloured mini lights came on above as we shuffled about like we were the only people in the room.

"I have a proposal for you, Anna," Gerald whispered in my ear so quietly I could barely hear him over Elvis.

"Yes, Gerald?" I answered. I had a good idea what was coming.

"I will share a secret with you," he spoke. "My son Derek is six months old and I will bring him home soon.

"I cannot offer you another child," he humbly said. "Not without killing you. I have ensured I cannot have another."

I shuddered inside. The last thing I wanted to think about was Walker and reproduction.

"I see," I gave a neutral answer.

"Swear your loyalty to me before your children are born. Be at my right hand, Anna. Be a mother to my son. In return Jack's end will be quick. You won't be harmed again and will want for nothing.

"I will leave you to the others if you decline. Long life and happiness rest with me. I cannot promise how they will care for you."

"I..."

"I will have your answer," he stated. I hadn't paid attention to the song and was sure it was nearly over.

"Gerald," I whispered. I took my hand from his and rested it on his cheek to buy myself a second to think.

"Would you ever trust me at your right hand if I was capable of abandoning my mate so quickly?"

I felt him shake his head.

"Your proposal is well thought out. You know me better than you realize since you've considered how protective I am of my sons. Your power appeals to me and accepting would be the smart decision. I need some time to think. Do you understand?"

The music faded as the disco ball came alive and a million tiny white hot stars lit up all the people I forgot were in the room with us. Gerald turned me to face the main door. He paused to kiss my shoulder and walked away as it flew open.

Chapter 16

Jack stood at Soros' side, well dressed in a shirt and tie.

"Damn it," I muttered as I put my hands on my stomach.

He took two steps in, arms straight, hands in angry fists as the dance floor swelled with people. Something from Madonna I guessed started to loudly play. A woman with long dark hair took Jack's elbow but he gently pushed her away as the crowd swallowed him.

"Jack?" I called, my voice lost. The light from the hall disappeared. I turned as bodies bumped into me and called him again. I lost sight of the door and tried to move in the right direction but people crowded everywhere. I smelled perfume and booze. Fresh cigarette smoke clung to someone's clothes.

Strong arms grabbed me as Jack buried his nose in my throat and carried me clear. As the music built, the crowd pushed more and more and suddenly we were free of them. I banged into a chair as I got my feet under me then he pressed me against the wall, my stomach squeezed against his body and his firm hand as he reasserted his attachment.

I got my chin up and found his mouth as he groaned. His hand dropped down my side then up under my dress grabbing my thigh and pulling my leg up around him. I took a handful of his shirt and let my head fall back as his lips caressed my neck.

"This isn't a woman who doesn't want me," he growled.

"It isn't," I admitted. "You shouldn't have followed me."

"Followed you?" Jack let me go and took half a step back. He wiped off my kiss with the back of his hand. "I got here an hour before you did. I've been chained up in the fucking frozen basement until half an hour ago when they hauled me up to my room to shower and dress and brought me here."

"Oh, Jack," I took his hands as the music changed. "You shouldn't have come."

"You've been sharing my room with RJ," he went on like he hadn't heard me. "What the hell are you doing? Covering your bases? Then you're half making out with Gerald in front of the whole damn house."

In the dim light, I noticed a few heads turn our way.

"Soros has been running Walker off at night when he comes to try and get in bed with me. He sleeps on the cot. It's all the protection I have," I half-shouted. I wasn't doing anything other than what I was told. "And you should have stayed away, Jack. I want to raise these boys and if it has to be here..."

Jack's eyes dropped as he assessed my line. I was sad he didn't trust me but I'd lied when I said I didn't want him.

"I'm sorry, Baby," he said as he held me. "Come upstairs."

We weren't the only couple to wander away for some privacy. A woman's laughter came to us from the other end of the second floor hall as we hurried upstairs and we passed two other couples headed the other way as we came back down. Walker danced with the black haired woman who approached Jack when he arrived and Soros engaged in an animated conversation with Travis.

Jack and I passed by the bar for drinks and found seats. He grabbed one of the caterers and asked for some food. By the time it came Jack had gone to get another drink. Every half hour there was a slower song so Jack and I stood to take advantage of the space on the dance floor and stretch our legs.

Travis and Soros' discussion became even more heated and I watched over Jack's shoulder as Travis stormed out, Soros close behind. The hall light outside the big room had been turned off so there was no blinding flash when the door opened.

Jack only shook his head.

"They're like that," he explained.

"Like what?"

He shrugged. I sighed as the music sped up and Jack took me to our table. He sat me on his leg and I wrapped my arms around his head, gently rubbing my chin on his short hair. Jack's hand alternated between holding my stomach and sipping his beer. I imagined a chill to his skin from two an a half weeks in what he'd described as the dungeon. The music kept playing and after the initial absence of what seemed like half the people who'd been at dinner the room started to fill up. I thought about the hammering which would start outside our window tomorrow or maybe the next day. It didn't matter. Jack's life belonged to Gerald Walker and I had to choose between Walker and the unknown.

When Soros and Travis returned they seemed to have settled their differences. Travis had his arm around Soros as they walked with their heads together and as they waited at the bar I swore I saw Soros kiss him.

"Are they..." I started and trailed off before I could make a fool of myself.

"Are they a couple?" Jack asked. "Sometimes. It's complicated."

"How?" I asked. Either they were a couple or they weren't. They certainly fought like Jack and I did or maybe even worse since they left the room. Jack and I held hands in our corner. He picked up a half full bottle of wine and poured some in his empty glass.

"Did you think that just because Courtesy has so many rules for men and their mates all other relationships are forbidden?" Jack seemed shocked.

"No," I didn't know what else to say. "Well, I hadn't thought about it. Soros and Travis don't seem to be any more than a couple of smelly guys loyal to your father."

"I think I'm embarrassed for you," Jack said. His hand moved up my arm then across my bare shoulders dipping the tips of his fingers into the sequinned rim of my dress.

"Shit," I whispered. "I wasn't surprised who they're with. I was surprised Soros was with anyone at all.

"Now I sound like an asshole," I shrugged and gave up as he nosed the tips of the tattooed flames licking over the edge of my shoulder.

"Promise you won't say a word?"

"This isn't gossip, is it?" I asked, not wanting to hear if it was just rumours.

"No, Baby," Jack answered. "The complete truth as I recall it."

"Okay," I agreed.

Jack pulled on a napkin still wrapped neatly around a set of cutlery. The knife and fork clattered loudly on the table as he handed the cloth to me. "You'll need this. I'll tell you then I need a coffee.

"In the mid eighteen hundreds there were fewer of us than there are now. We hadn't been close to your side of the family in a long time.

"You've seen it happen," Jack quietly continued. I was enraptured already. Jack's East Coast accent in my ear brought with it a soothing sense of belonging after our time with his parents. Any glimpse into the family's past was an honour for me.

"RJ was born female."

"Uh," I stupidly said and turned my head to stare. Jack caught my chin and returned my attention to him before I got caught open-mouth gawking. Soros and Travis had been joined by a couple of women and though they sat close together it was clear they enjoyed the added company.

"Father was cruel. RJ was his youngest son then and would have been better off staying away. We did our best to protect her. Travis in particular seemed most sensitive to her struggle to please Father in spite of Father's prejudice against women."

I wondered since Travis was so much like Wendy and Sig if he could pick up projections from Soros like they did from each other. Her pain might have been something he couldn't tune out.

"They became connected, not unlike you and me. They fell in love and when it was clear she was pregnant we knew there was going to be trouble."

My hand came up over my mouth as I pictured Damian killing her but Jack shook his head, seeming to know what I thought.

"Travis begged us to help: me, Harvey. We stole them away and went west as long as she could travel."

"No, Jack," I cried, needing my napkin already. "Your father didn't kill their son."

"He didn't," Jack said. "He never caught us. We kept going west all the way to the coast with their daughter."

I froze and probed Jack with my eyes, trying to say the questions I couldn't put into words.

"She wasn't a son born female," he explained, softly cupping my head in his hands. "She was a little girl so much like yours. Her line was strong and she was an amazing reader. She could put pictures in our heads of what she wanted, or ideas she had. People thought she was simple because she didn't speak. She didn't have to. She had a mother, father and two uncles raising her who could pick up whatever she had to say."

"Like..." I trailed off, catching myself. Of course, Travis was like Sig and Wendy and his daughter seemed to have inherited the ability to project from him. I desperately hoped she'd grown up and her line had set. "Where is she now?"

"When she was ten," Jack paused and cleared his throat. "She caught a fever and passed away. She loved flowers and anything yellow. And spring and her parents. She was such a little girly girl. It was spring when she died with the fresh sweet air filling her room.

"I need a minute," Jack said. I was so lost in thoughts of Camille and the grand daughter I never knew, I was surprised to look up and see Travis.

"A dance, Anna?" he asked. Something slow was playing.

"Of course, Mister Travis," I answered.

"It's Trent," he told me and I realized I hadn't known his first name.

"Trent," I echoed and took his hand.

As we moved I forgot about the little coloured lights dimming with the music and Travis' aftershave. I thought about a little dark haired girl, slight like her mother, playing in a garden and I imagined Camille with her. Their laughter floated above them into the sky, sharing the sunlight with the warm breeze teasing their hair.

I lifted my head from Travis' shoulder as Jack took my hand to cut in. Tomorrow would be a good day, I thought. I felt cloaked in peace and warmed inside in spite of what the next few days would bring.

Chapter 17

"It looks old."

Jack rolled over and opened his eyes. I turned to the window as he let me look in silence. The heavy notched beams fit together like a puzzle; the smooth wood darkened where the pieces joined by the oils from countless bare hands. Some of the joints had been lashed together by rope. There were no planks yet on the raised floor of the platform but the long timber which would hold the rope was already in place.

Soros and Walker and their men would be at breakfast so the half-finished structure stood silent, not yet a monster; still simply a collection of beams.

"It's relatively quick," Jack said behind me. I'd been lost in thought and hadn't heard him roll out of bed. I rested my hands on either side of the new window's frame as if I could keep the gallows away. His hands covered my stomach as the boys' movement pushed against him.

"Relatively?"

"Some ways shut the brain down faster," he explained. I leaned on him as he kissed the back of my head. "Other times the body suffers for a long time.

"Father had it transported here by ship a long time ago. I don't think there's any wood structure like it anywhere. A few beams haven't aged well and we've replaced the floor joists and planks. The main frame is centuries old."

"A real museum piece."

Jack didn't answer. It was strange to talk about ways of dying and hear the reverent affection in his voice as he talked about The Last Step. Denial and revulsion were the feelings I had for the evil thing in the parking lot.

"I've passed on more ways than I can count," Jack said. "But this is a first. Dying is unpleasant but I don't fear it. I grieve the loves in Jack's life but only until I'm gone. On the other side they'll just be memories like looking through a good friend's photos."

One arm came up around my shoulders and I hooked my hands over it, holding tight.

"I'm sad to leave you; that you'll be alone. I won't know the men these boys will grow to be but I'll meet the men who'll remember them and the woman who remembers you."

"Will they finish it today?"

"Yes," his voice more the soft brush of his lips on my ear than anything my ears could find.

"Will they let you stay with me tonight?"

"Yes," he said again.

Other than the next day being the last of Jack's life, the twenty-seventh of December passed much like the day before. Soros and Walker's men started shouting and working outside the window after breakfast, paused for lunch, and continued until dinner. They could have had it built in half a day but it seemed the tradition of getting the heavy beams in place by hand held fast and the job took two.

Jack chose dinner alone in our room with me for his last meal. There would be no breakfast for him the next morning though the rest of them would be well fed before they ventured out for the big event.

I decided to let Jack break it off with me. The decision had been hard. If I managed to stop Jack from breaking it off so I could try and jump us away I endangered my daughter. If I let him then I could raise his sons without the pain of losing him although if Marie's experience was anything to go by I'd bear a deep hate for him for the rest of my days.

"I'll only be gone an hour," Jack stood and tucked in his shirt. "RJ is going to look after my affairs. We have some things to go over."

I looked away; weak nausea like a small patch of heat seemed to cover my cheeks then my lips.

"Relax, Baby," Jack smiled. "I'll be scared if you and the boys won't be looked after. I need to do this for you."

"Okay, Jack," I said. "I'll have my bath while I wait."

I didn't get up right away. Other than calling 'come in' to the man who collected our dinner dishes, I ignored his presence. When he left, I kept my eyes turned away as I closed the heavy curtains on either side of the bed so I couldn't see the shadowed shape below.

As my bath ran, I felt something brush against the tip of my nose, then my ear and thought I heard the door to our room click shut.

"Jack?" I called as I poked my head out.

Nothing.

With the fan on, I undressed and held the wall so I could kick the bubbles around and test the water. I sunk under, leaned back and turned to my side. As my eyes closed I tried to forget what my life would be like by this time tomorrow. I'd be furious with Jack and heavily sedated to prevent me from rejecting the boys' lines as the trauma of losing him passed. It looked like I'd live to raise the boys if Jack was leaving me his things and it would be up to me whose bedroom I'd be sharing.

When I opened my eyes the bathroom door stuck into the room. I usually closed it so I'd have time to pull on a towel if Soros let himself in when Jack wasn't with me and guessed with everything going on I'd simply forgotten. I reached and gave it a sufficient shove to click the lock when it closed and yelped when it bounced back at me at the same time I heard a surprised grunt. It could only be Travis, invisible and unreadable to me. He was also unreadable to anyone else in the house which meant I was alone with him and nobody else knew.

Water sloshed up over the edge in my hurry to sit and cover up. I expected another proposal like Walker's and kept my eyes lowered, ignoring Travis and hoping his line would demand my attention and reveal his location.

I didn't have to find him. The tub faucet turned on and a towel floated over my chest and shoulders.

"I'm not here to hurt you," his breath said on my cheek though it was completely unnerving to see nobody. I nodded and tried to calm down as I smelled the same aftershave he wore when we danced. The towel moved a little higher on my shoulder. "Sshhh."

Cold ran on my feet so I adjusted the temperature and pushed the water around to even out the heat.

"Don't be scared," Travis said. "I know what Walker told you and I want you to know you have other options."

"No," I whispered as I felt the colour drain from my face.

"Hey," he hissed in my ear. "I haven't asked for you. That's not why I'm here. You've earned the respect of some of us. If you're thinking of accepting Walker's proposition I want you to know there are others who won't ask so much."

"Soros doesn't know you're here, does he?" I quietly asked as I pulled the plug to let some of the water out. "If you're here like this nobody knows."

"That's right. I want you to know if you're deciding about Walker then you're wasting precious time on the wrong decision."

I felt his fingers on my cheek and heard his knee bump the edge of the tub as he adjusted position beside me.

"RJ lost track of your daughter a while ago," Travis said and I jerked upright in surprise. "They're under military protection so he won't get near them."

I felt his hand on my chest over the towel.

"You need to think about the loyalties you feel here; the real connections in your life and not the loyalties of convenience you'll be left with if you fail to act tomorrow."

Travis' hand disappeared and the water turned off. After a few seconds the door closed as he let himself into the hallway. For no good reason at all I believed I could trust him.

Chapter 18

Jack and I spent our last night together awake in each others arms. No sex. No talk. The Last Step waited three floors below. I hadn't returned to the window since the morning when it had been just as quiet outside.

"Are you planning something?" Jack finally asked. He knew damn well I would be. I was also sure he'd try something at the last minute to protect me from the pain of losing him and I'd be just as mad at him whether he succeeded or failed.

"If you promise not to read me when I answer I'll say no," I replied.

"Please don't, Baby. RJ said it would hurt you."

I knew what RJ said. I also knew Sig never told me it would be a problem and he'd have told me first if jumping anywhere would hurt my line more than it already was. The boys stopped pulling at me weeks before and I was well on my way to healed before then.

"I remember," I answered. I didn't lie and if anyone listened to us I didn't give anything away.

I rolled on my back and Jack put his head on my shoulder, his hand on my stomach and I went back to visualizing. The window to the gallows, my arms around Jack. Then to the safest place. Safest place. I didn't know where the safest place would be, but if I disappeared at all I hoped we'd appear there.

Changing position got the babies moving and Jack laughed as he felt them.

Soros had already come in and opened the bedroom window before telling us he would be in the room with me then leaving on some other errand. Gerald's spectators waited outside and with only fifteen minutes to go, their voices rose with excitement.

Jack's fist moved.

If I hadn't been wary he would have connected. He yelled the words he didn't want me as my knees let go. I felt the breeze in my hair as the blow passed just over my head. I turned as I went down and let my weight carry me face first into the dresser, striking harder than I planned. I'd been troubled with how I'd make it look like he hit me and took the opportunity when it came.

Jack stared at me in shock. One of my eyes numbed then sharp pain quickly set in. I was furious with him as I guessed I would be. There was no way I'd let him pass on unconnected and unloved if I couldn't jump us away.

"You son of a bitch, Jack Roberts!" I yelled, putting my hands to my face. I remembered Marie's terrible rage when Keith broke it off. Losing her connection to him infuriated her. Irrationally and uncontrollably. I had no doubt if she could have gotten her hands on him she would have killed him herself.

The door burst open. Soros barged in first, followed close behind by Harvey and another man. Soros was there for me. The other two were there for Jack.

"Awe, Jack," Soros crooned. "Looks like you ripped up your ticket out."

He sounded pleased. It meant he didn't think I'd go anywhere. If I could trust Travis then Soros had no idea I knew my daughter was safe. I realized it was for the better Jack tried to break it off but it didn't make me any less angry at him. Both my eyes watered as my cheek hurt even more. I let Soros put his arms around me as Jack's anger with me filled him. He knew there was nothing he could say about my stunt since we weren't alone in the room.

"He hit me, RJ," I sobbed as I made him work to hold me still. I winced as his thumb brushed the hardening bruise. "The bastard hit me."

I hoped using Soros' first name would prove just how disconnected from Jack I pretended to be. I clung to him like Marie clung to Patrick. The great love she had inside her for Keith had nothing to connect to and once her floodlight lit on Patrick she seemed to anchor herself to him. Fury flew from her at Keith but at least she stopped looking so small and vulnerable.

"Sshhh," Soros said, putting his cheek to mine. His hands moved over my back, one dropping too low as he enjoyed me turning to him for comfort. I glared at Jack over his shoulder as I wrapped my arms around his brother, pressing myself to him.

"You're a pussy, Jack," I spat. "Nothing but a shadow of your father."

I shoved RJ even harder. He stumbled back a couple of steps as I solidly planted a foot on a patch of hardwood and pushed. Jack stood still as a tear left his eye and Harvey had to come help Soros hold me back. The two of them restrained me as Soros tore the collar of my shirt down, exposing my shoulder. His teeth pulled the cap off a syringe he had in his back pocket and he unloaded it in my arm.

His shoulder muffled my shout as I cried out.

"Please, RJ. No," I begged as I connected an elbow with Harvey's chin. His teeth snapped together but his grip didn't even falter. "He's gotta pay for it. Please don't make me sleep. I wanna see him pay!"

My words ended with a growl as I kept pushing, so worried the drug would screw up my attempt to jump.

"Just an appy, Sweet Thing," Soros grunted as I shoved again. "Can't let you get too worked up."

"This place stinks of coward," I yelled as I felt the fight start to leave me.

"Say good-bye, Jack," Soros said as Harvey and the other man took his elbows. "I'll take good care of her. You'll sleep this off in my bed, Sweet Thing. You've been such a good girl."

Jack tried to shake them off but they roughly pulled on him and kept their grip. Jack lifted his chin, holding his head high.

"Get outta my room, Jack," I yelled. My voice hadn't lost any volume though my struggles weakened part from fatigue and some from the shot. "Get out! I would have saved you, Jack. We could have escaped. Now I'm stuck here! Fuck you, Jack. Get out!"

"I won't let you tear your line off for me," he hissed.

Soros laughed as I tried to push through him to get to Jack.

"I'll have you in pieces right here, you bastard," I struggled against Soros' grip but Soros didn't need help to hold me. My body had become sluggish and slow to respond. "I'll kill him here, RJ. He'll take his last step with my hands at his throat."

Jack wouldn't look at me as they pulled him from the room. The door stayed open behind and as soon Soros let me go I stomped over and slammed it. My legs felt like someone else's.

"Bastard hit me, RJ," I furiously muttered, not caring if he answered.

"Bastard... bastard." The little clock beside the bed said there were five minutes to go so I refocused on the safest place as I charged at the window. Soros jumped and got an arm around me so I kept going and made him stop me from casting myself straight out. Harvey and the other man walked behind Jack. He didn't fight. He said he wouldn't.

"Shicken shit Roberts," I bellowed down from the third floor, surprised by the slur. "Big fucking man. When I see you on the other side I'm going to tear you a new one. You won't know what hit you."

Jack glanced up, his face a mix of pain and anger. He only had to admit I hurt myself and Soros would take me from the window so I couldn't see Gerald hang him. He didn't say a word. Maybe part of him dared hope I could pull it off. I stormed past Soros to the dresser and pulled out an armload of Jack's clothes then took them to the window and threw them out.

"You didn't pack your shit." A very small part of me paid attention to my words as I ranted. Most of me pictured my arms around Jack at the gallows below then finding ourselves at the safest place. Soros' building laughter nearly drowned me out. I grabbed another armload. It joined the first on the frozen ground below.

"What's the hold up, Gerald? I thought you ran a tight ship. Where's your fucking watch?"

Jack looked up at me.

His right foot took its last step onto the trapdoor.

Then his left.

Walker looked up and waved then he pulled the noose over Jack's head. Jack was right. They didn't cover it. My hands clutched the window sill as I rocked back and forth. The cold wind blew in and Gerald tightened the knot and positioned it at the side of Jack's neck. I focused as hard as I could, blinking as the icy air made my eyes tear even more and I struggled to see. Gerald spoke but I tuned him out.

"Pull it, Gerald. It's cold and I want to close my window." Cold air hit my bare shoulder. There was laughter below.

"Son of a bitch," I muttered. Safest place, safest place.

"It's time," Soros said between chuckles. He was right behind me. His arms slipped around, hands on my stomach in plain view of Jack. Walker put a hand on the big lever protruding from the floor.

The lever swung away from Walker and the trap door under Jack's feet started to move. My breath froze and I felt Jack in my arms. Soros lost his grip on me at the gallows then I landed on the cold ground, unsure if I landed beneath The Last Step or somewhere else.

Numbed

Chapter 19

"Jack?" I called.

Dense trees came in to focus and I wiped my eyes, avoiding where I hurt. The dresser was a very bad idea and even yelling hurt deep into the bone.

He didn't answer as whatever Soros shot me up with blurred my surroundings. I pushed myself up, fingers digging into hard snow, to look around when something behind me attracted my attention. Nagging and pulling but when I turned there was nothing. Once on my feet, I turned in the trees. I picked up Jack a dozen feet away and staggered to him.

He lay with his back to me, hands still bound behind. I dropped to the ground and leaned over him. He breathed but he could have hit his head. With his arms bound, he couldn't have used them to break his fall, if he was even aware the jump was over. I shook him but he didn't move so I started on the rope. Absently, I reached behind my head and brushed at movement I sensed more than felt. Then I ducked, pushing my shoulders up as high as they would go. I turned and scanned again, back the way I had come. As quickly as it started to wash over me it disappeared.

I kept untying the rope, trying to ignore the ghostly fingers I felt on the back of my neck. It was like Sig and Wendy and Trent Travis when he hid from me but so much stronger and from so many directions at once.

"Jack..." I whispered as the rope came off. He exploded up off the ground grabbing my arms.

"Damn you," he growled in my face. "I am not worth your line. I got selfish and let you do it."

"No, Jack," I pulled an arm free and swatted behind my head as it lolled to the side. "Sig would have told me."

"How could you even think of risking it?"

I ducked and strained to look behind me as Jack held on. He put his hand over my bare shoulder and paused.

"Damn it," he muttered as he traced the small line of blood from the puncture. Then he pulled the torn fabric up as best he could.

My hand went to my face as I struggled to focus on the whispers behind me. As soon as I focused on the most aggressive another emerged as more dominant. I held my free hand to try and block them then waved it under my nose. It felt like cobwebs clinging to my face.

"I'm not letting you die disconnected," I blew air from my mouth trying to keep it out. "And alone."

Jack turned me to him. I was still mad at him for trying to blow our getaway.

"This isn't about me and how I'm going to go," he said, still far too loud.

"Have it your way, princess," I replied. Two of the whispers stood out as closer than the others when I wasn't looking at them. I looked past them and could tell they moved nearer. Sig could be among the ones in the distance but there was no way to know. If he was then the noisy lines with him drowned him out.

"Princess? You don't have an obedient bone in your body. I can't believe you pulled that stunt. And maybe next time you dump us off in the woods in the dead of winter you could pick somewhere it's not below freezing."

Jack leaned around to get a better look at my cheek. I turned, blinking and twitching as I dodged the loudest nudges. He was right. I couldn't tell what was shivering and what was simply my body reacting to the constant bombardment of lines demanding my attention.

"I'm sorry, you're not a princess," I absently said. "You're a Diva. My God there are so many."

"Err," he growled as he ran a finger over my sore cheek.

A man and woman appeared between the trees. When they had my attention, the noise in the distance behind them worsened. The noise from them was minimal. My skin didn't react and all I picked up was a gentle reminder they were there. Nearly invisible among the mental blows from the others. Jack got his arms around me and pulled me to my feet.

"We're gonna talk, Anna," he whispered.

"'kay Jack. Remember when I said Sig is family?"

He didn't say anything. I recognized the silent treatment and we'd talk when he was done pouting.

"I know you can't read him. I can pick them up." I settled on trying to cover my eyes and ears at the same time. The noise filling my head was just as bad though I didn't feel as exposed.

"So many..."

"Jack Roberts? Anna Richards?"

I nodded as Jack held me tighter. The woman spoke.

"Welcome, you're safe here," she said. Then to the man. "Mark, I'll bring them to the house. Run back and call for Anton. Anna will need his help. She's overwhelmed already."

Footsteps disappeared. I closed my eyes.

"I'm Cora," she introduced herself. "You're at my father's house. Can you manage her?"

"Yes," Jack answered. He sounded suspicious. I wondered if her father was the same as Wendy's and if this was Sig's house or if I'd landed us with another part of the family entirely.

"Her clothes are dirty; her face. Did she fall?"

"I don't know. I was still on the ground when she found me."

"Mm," Cora said. "I don't like it when women in her condition fall. We'll check her out. Don't worry, Jack. You won't leave her side."

I felt her hand on my arm. "Come, Little One."

I tried to walk but my legs wouldn't move so I pressed further in to Jack.

"Ah, she is so sensitive to us. We can help her block us out."

"I can't walk, Jack," I whispered. Not only that, I had trouble talking. It wasn't just the cold. It was whatever Soros had given me. My arms and legs stiffened. Jack picked me up. My knees bent just fine over his arm even though I couldn't have willed them to do it.

"Anna?" Cora said. "Stay with us, okay? Anton can help you better if you're awake. Do you know what they gave her, Jack? She projected something about an injection."

"No. They wanted her awake to..." he took a deep breath. To watch, he meant.

"How is he going to help her?" Jack asked instead. He held me tighter and sounded unhappy. He knew I'd just say I couldn't tell him and it looked like he was going to get his own answers from the people I couldn't or wouldn't talk about.

"Anton can numb her sensum. She won't be able to read but at least she won't be overwhelmed by us. It seems we whisper to her even when we're not projecting."

"Oh," Jack said.

Exactly, I thought. She didn't make any sense to me either.

"Sensum?" I mumbled.

"Under your nose," Cora answered.

"Never knew it had a name," Jack said. "You won't hurt her?"

"Anton is the best one here to do it for her. She's a new reader. Her projections are very graphic and visual. Numbing her will stop them. It's very disruptive to us and she probably doesn't want us to see the things she projects."

Jack gave a short sigh. He was thinking. I held my head tighter.

"I can guess what you're trying to understand. All readers in your part of the family project. And all of us. With immaturity the projections are very emotional, visual. Violence, sex. Leak out all over the place. A more mature reader like you projects higher level thoughts. Concepts. Feelings rather than emotions. The images are much less primitive and disturbing. For example you project love for her. But there are also images of what happened this morning before you came here. From your point of view and much less vivid than hers."

"You hear that, Baby?" he whispered. "I'm more mature than you."

"Hrmpf."

I heard a zipper then Cora's warm coat covered me. It helped with the shivering. The noise I picked up from the house made my head hurt so I focused on breathing as a distraction.

"We're nearly there. Her line has been around longer than yours, Jack, but her sensum is just about as new as your sons.'"

"Hear that, Jack? I'm older."

"Jack, your projections are noticeably more mature than hers but not by much. We're going to have to numb you so you can stay here."

"Ugh," Jack sighed.

"I'll take care of you, Jack. Anton is related to her so he'll have an easier time focusing in a way which won't disturb your children."

"Related?" I asked. It was hard to stay part of the conversation.

"Yes."

Cora didn't elaborate.

"Is there any word from my mother?" I asked. Or more like heard my own voice say the question I thought. She should be with Camille and maybe Cora had news of Wendy and the children. Anything to confirm the risk Travis urged me to take.

"Yes, she lives here now but your projections aren't child appropriate or good for her at the moment. She's taken the children to the McDonald's in Billings."

"Who the hell is your mother?" Jack asked.

"Every line has a mother, Jack Roberts," Cora replied. "Even the girls."

Chapter 20

A heavy door opened.

"Anton's coming," a breathless male voice said as Cora pulled her coat from me. "He'll be in your father's study within the half-hour."

I smelled breakfast and heard the sounds of a busy kitchen. Jack shivered as his arms tightened and I opened my eyes to see him watching me. Dark wood trimmed walls covered in heavily patterned old fashioned wallpaper flew by.

"Can I spell you with her, sir?" the male voice asked.

"What?" Jack's teeth chattered. "No, mine."

Cute: Jack's responsibility, Jack's girl.

"Very well," he answered. "I'm Mark. This way, sir."

I tipped my head away from Jack to see Cora's long black hair float around her body as she turned right and led us up a few stairs. A pair of tattooed eyes peeked out between the top of her hip-hugger jeans and the bottom of her lacy blouse. I suspected this house belonged to Sig if Wendy lived here. He either had a taste in the ancient or had been too cheap to redecorate for the past century.

"Put her on that medieval torture device my father calls a chesterfield, please," Cora said as she disappeared through a pair of doors. The room looked like a turn of the century movie set and the chesterfield looked hard as a rock. It was trimmed in wood and I suspected crushed horse hair for padding. I wasn't disappointed. It was as soft as a bus stop bench. At least the arm I leaned against felt sturdy. Cora returned and covered us in a warm blanket.

"Bring me my med bag, Mark, and arrange a quiet room for them on the second floor of the south wing. Anna will need some sleep."

"Yes, Mother," Mark replied and dashed out.

"Cora?"

"Yes, yes," she muttered as she started to examine my bruised face. "That makes Mark your cousin of sorts. May I?"

When I opened my eyes, she held her hand over my chest so I nodded, then I shook my head to try and clear the pressure from the other lines in the house still demanding my attention.

"I'll get a cleaner read of your sons' health, Jack, if you go snoop or something for a minute."

Jack reluctantly stood. He looked overwhelmed. I couldn't blame him. He'd gone from nearly having his neck snapped to my line-mother's side of the family in just a few minutes.

"A little further, handsome," she winked at him before she turned to me. "How are you feeling?"

"Better, I think," I sighed. "Their um, projections seem to have settled down."

"Yes," Cora's eyes seemed to glass over as her fingers started to move over my chest. I held still and tried to relax. "Mark got the word out for everyone to lock their sensums down for a while.

"Oh," she exclaimed as she pulled her hand back. "Smart-alecs. Their lines are absolutely healthy. No worries about them from the fall. They're protective of you. Their lines kick just like their little knees and elbows."

Cora tugged the blanket up over my shoulders and rested her hands on my knees as Mark came in with her bag. He popped an ice pack and held it on my face.

"I'm going to draw some blood for a tox screen though I'm sure whatever they gave you will have worn off by the time I get it back. Come have a seat, Jack."

Jack wound his fingers between mine and waited as Cora quickly took blood and read my blood pressure. My shivering stopped though my cheek still hurt like hell.

"Alright, Jack. You're up," Cora announced and shuffled her knees over so she knelt in front of him. "This is going to feel a little funny but it won't hurt, okay?"

"Do I have a choice?"

"Not if you're staying here with her."

He stared at her for a few seconds before he leaned forward, elbows on his knees. "Okay, what do I do?"

Cora took his face in her hands and lifted her butt off her heels so their noses almost touched.

"Keep your eyes open, Jack," she whispered. "Keep breathing. I want you to read Anna, just see her there. Good."

"Anna, take his hand," she said so I did. Jack squeezed me in alarm. "It's okay, she's right there. You're getting numb, sshhh."

Her thumbs came up to cover his mouth as the minutes passed with nothing but the sound of Jack and Cora's synced breathing.

"Your sensum is quiet," she whispered. "Can you read her?"

Jack shook his head as Cora let him go then turned and wrapped me in his arms. His cheeks were wet as he pushed my hair aside and sought my eyes.

"It's like you're only half here," he whispered.

"Anton's arrived," Cora quietly announced. "Mark, please see them up to their room. I'll be there in a minute with Anton."

"She said I'll sleep," I told Jack as he picked me up.

"And the trip here," he added. "You have to recharge."

Cora turned to listen.

"Two trips, Jack," I whispered, warm and sleepy under the blanket in his arms. "The first to you on the scaffold then here. And travel was harder on me when I was pregnant with Camille... two days sleep. I don't know how long I'll be out with two babies."

"Good to know," Cora interrupted. "Off you go."

Mark led us further down the hall. He didn't offer to carry me again. I remembered stairs and another hall before Jack sat me on a big bed. With the projections around me quieter it was harder to fight the sedative.

The large bedroom was decorated in the same old style as what I'd seen of the rest of the house. The bathroom, Mark pointed out, was added after the original construction and took a six by eight foot bite from one corner on the door side. Opposite the door stood two tall, heavily curtained windows with the bed placed between. The dresser at the foot of the bed backed onto the bathroom wall and a large wooden armchair sat to one side of the bed.

Jack knelt in front of me, hands on my stomach and one of the boys obliged him with a boot.

"I'll find some clothes and things for you," Mark said as he went through the empty sounding dresser drawers.

"Baby," Jack whispered. "That was so stupid. And I'm sick with myself for letting you try it."

"It's okay, Jack. Your brother doesn't have a clue where the children are. They're safe. You said when they're safe we'd make our break for it and we did."

Jack's ears pinked with anger. "How the hell would you know they're safe?"

"Last night," I said. "When you went to see Soros. Mister Travis cloaked himself or whatever it is he does and came and told me."

"What the fuck?" Jack raised his voice. "You trusted Travis?"

"Yes."

I heard Cora talking to a man in the hall, their voices getting louder. Jack didn't seem to notice.

"And Soros only said travel would hurt me so I wouldn't try what I did today," I went on as Jack continued to redden.

"Fuck," Jack said again, quieter this time. He pulled the ice pack from my cheek and softly kissed my half-frozen bruise.

"Jack Roberts." The door burst open. Jack's eyes widened with recognition before he even looked.

"Anton Lee," Jack answered.

When I turned my head, I saw what I first thought was an Asian warrior. Anton Lee wore black from head to toe: jeans, Army boots and T-shirt. His black hair was drawn back.

"God damn, Anton," Jack exclaimed as he landed on his butt, off balance with surprise. He quickly recovered as he got to his feet.

"And you're dressed like a fucking ninja," he went on as he and Anton clasped elbows.

"I only wear what's on top in the dresser my friend and I'm Chinese. Not a fucking ninja," Anton replied though the smile on his face said he was happy to see Jack. "I must say you and your pregnant mate are the last people I expected to drop in here."

Jack was speechless.

"Yes," Anton went on to answer our unasked question. "Cora is my aunt. Anna and I have the same line-mother."

Before I knew it Anton sat beside me on the bed.

"Let's see to you first," he whispered. "My friend Jack and I served together for a decade before I retired. I have some explaining to do."

"Hi, Anton," I nodded. This was the son Wendy spoke of when she came to Paul's compound to see me just after the rape. The thought of Jack running into Wendy now that she was pregnant with his sister worried me. Not only did he not know Wendy was family but his devotion to his sons gave me a good idea how he'd feel about the child he'd see as his daughter.

"Don't worry about that now," Anton said and I realized I'd projected my concern to everyone but Jack who of course couldn't pick it up even if he wasn't numbed. "Mother's introductions are hers to make."

Anton held my face in his hands as Cora held Jack only more gently considering the painful bruise.

"Breathe with me," he whispered and I watched his unblinking eyes. He sped his slower breathing up to match mine and I twitched with surprise at the sudden loss of sensation under my nose, tossing my arms out like a startled newborn. Even though I wasn't actively reading, the little organ was sensitive and alert to everything around it. Jack took my hand and squeezed like I'd done with him.

"How does he numb her?" Jack whispered.

"He needs to reduce the blood flow to her sensum," Cora answered. "Or trick her sensum into doing it to itself more accurately. Makes it sleepy. I could be fairly quick with yours. Not much finesse is required for someone who isn't pregnant.

"There's a link between her sensum and her line and by extension to your sons' lines and their developing sensums. If Anton isn't careful it could be very bad for them."

"Jesus," Jack whispered and his damaged hand tightened around mine.

"Anton is very gifted with this sort of thing," Cora continued, her voice oozing reassurance. "And it doesn't hurt for him to be so closely related. They are very compatible."

Her voice trailed away, masked by a buzzing I felt under my nose like a ringing in my ears and Anton's fingers stroked just above my top lip. The numbness spread and strengthened as I grew drowsier and fought to keep my eyes open.

"Almost there," Anton whispered and before I knew it, he stood a few feet away as Jack held me. "She'll sleep soon. Then we can catch up, Jack. You won't sleep like her. I'll wait for you in the hall as you get her settled."

The door clicked shut behind him. Jack was quiet as he pulled off everything but my panties and put me in the t-shirt he wore beneath the good flannel shirt he chose to wear for his hanging. He helped me to the bathroom before tucking me in and he stroked my cheek until I fell asleep.

Chapter 21

I felt a little too warm when I woke. My stomach rolled and I groaned with nausea.

"Sshhh, Little One," a quiet voice spoke. A woman held me, our feet tangled and my head cozied into the crook of her neck. Her firm belly pressed into mine.

"Wendy," I sighed and regretted speaking as my head pounded. Jack growled behind me.

Damn.

"How long," I whispered and cleared my throat, certain I nearly threw up.

"Three days," she answered. "Don't talk. By the time you slept off Anton's numbing your other sleep hit you before we could get you to eat. That's why you feel so sick. Jack? Gravol."

I felt the bed shift with his weight and tightened my hold on Wendy as the room spun. She gently uncovered my arm as he gave me a shot. He stunk of whiskey, both fresh and stale then he withdrew to where I vaguely remembered a chair. I was glad drunken Jack gave me the shot. The alternative was Wendy moving me to do it.

"We'll let it go to work and try some food. The more you eat the better you'll feel. I know you feel too rough to eat."

"'kay," I managed.

"Don't you have your own room?" Jack muttered. I wondered just how badly the past few days had gone for Jack and Wendy.

"She needs to be watched," Wendy replied. I found my hand on her stomach and felt her little girl move. It was so different from feeling mine on the inside and outside at the same time.

"Fuck."

Liquid sloshed in a bottle.

"Why aren't you with my daughter, Wenns?"

She kissed my cheek and I was able to open my eyes without making the headache or nausea any worse. Her afro had grown and appeared intentionally unruly, rebelling against the air around her head. Brown eyes blinked at me before her warm lips touched my forehead.

"A month after you dropped Dana and me off everything fell apart. Jack's supposedly loyal men had been missing for nearly two weeks and I was so morning sick Ray had me on I.V. fluids. Ray, Dana, and Patrick had their hands full looking after everyone and we had no protection. Ray called in Colonel Iverson and he picked us up. I came home here and the Colonel moved them to a safe house. I know they've been safe for months."

I started to cry with relief and Wendy gently sat beside me. She looked at Jack.

"I'm going to fetch her something to eat."

"You do that," he snapped. "Thief."

"I'm not," she answered and left without another word. The bottle sloshed again and I heard Jack's lips smack just before he put it back down.

"You knew, didn't you?" He half-slurred. "You knew who she was and why she wanted me. You let it happen and you didn't say a fucking word and you let her go and didn't say a fucking word and thought it would be okay to keep it from me."

"Where did you think little girls came from?" I asked and slowly rolled over to face him. When my stomach eased I opened my eyes. I didn't recognize the clothes he wore. His bloodshot eyes glared at me. One hand held a half-full glass and the other held the bottle. The bottle came up again.

"Did you think I'd say no? Is that why you kept it from me?"

"What is your problem, Mister Double Standard?" Wendy demanded as she whisked in with a tray. It contained a sandwich, a small bowl and a glass of what looked like clear juice. "You keep everything from your women and it's not okay for a little magic to happen behind your back.

"And I'm not a thief. Like you were going to use it again after you gave it to me."

"That doesn't mean I don't want her," Jack shouted as the glass slipped to the floor. It bounced and didn't break. His face screwed up with hurt and he looked away.

"We've been through this, Jack." Wendy stayed cool to him. "There's a reason why it's done this way."

Jack paused and looked at her. "*Now* there's a reason?"

I pushed up on one elbow and sipped the juice. My stomach tightened for a moment then thirst overwhelmed me and I took another. The bowl contained simple broth and the smell made my mouth water so I sat up and started on it.

"Take your time, Little One," Wendy instructed as my stomach turned again. Good advice.

"Any man could make the promise to her. If she accepted, she could be bound to someone far too reckless to protect her. In a month or two I'll go where there's no family at all and raise her alone. When the time comes I'll find the man most worthy of her and arrange their introduction."

Jack put his hands on his face and struggled to keep calm. "So then you're just going to take her away?"

"That's how it's done."

I quietly wept into my soup, feeling so much pain for him. Part of him accepted the small chance of seeing his sons grow up but to have no chance to meet his daughter was so much worse.

"You're a bitch, Wendy," he mumbled from behind his hands.

Wendy wiped my tears from my eyes.

"She's not your daughter, Jack," Wendy said. "She's mine. She's your sister."

"You're a bitch," he said again as he gave her the finger and roughly grabbed his crotch. She got up and left. "And you, Anna. I love you but right now I don't like you at all."

He finished the last of his whiskey and staggered to the shower. I was done eating when he came to bed and turned his back to me.

Chapter 22

"It's my Father's dagger," Jack reverently said.

A week and another numbing had passed for us. Anton took a lot longer to numb me the second time. I'd become disoriented as my sense slipped away and threw up with a strange dizziness in my nose and chest; not the usual ears and stomach. Even Cora lost her calmness and there was a lot of whispering between her, Wendy and Anton as I fell asleep. The end result was Anton would only do it once more then I'd have to leave.

There had been more full-on arguments between Jack and Wendy in addition to the constant bickering and half-drunk insults from Jack. He'd kept it quiet at least since Anton grabbed him by the collar and hauled him from the room. There was a thud in the hall as Jack tripped on his intoxicated feet followed by his belligerent replies to Anton's firm reminder to mind his manners in someone else's house. After that he only tried to start trouble with Wendy when nobody else was around and his manners improved in proportion to the reduction in alcohol.

"His blood is still in the guard." Jack's hands rested on the mantle on either side of the ornate dagger. The carved wooden stand appeared as old as the knife itself.

We waited in the study where Cora assessed us when we first arrived. I guessed to finally see Sig but Jack was simply pissed off we had to go where Wendy said so I didn't ask why we had to be here. His father had used the dagger to kill Catherine, the woman I remembered being more than two hundred years earlier. It had since been given to me by Sig to cure Jack's Father. I'd returned it because I didn't feel right keeping it when my job was done.

"Actually, it was my Father's dagger," Sig said from the door.

"Colonel Iverson?" Jack jerked with surprise at the familiar voice. "Are you here to check Anna?"

"It's simply Sig, Jack," he admonished. "And no, my daughters Wendy and Cora are doing a fine job of caring for you both."

Jack glared at me. Another big tidbit of information I left out. Sig was my grandfather and this was his house.

"It wasn't her information to share, Jack," Sig explained. "She had been forbidden to speak of Wendy or me and she's been respectful of our choice in the matter."

Jack rubbed his damaged hand up the side of his face then over top of his head.

"I should have explained my relation to Anna some time ago. I apologize."

Jack nodded.

Sig approached the fireplace and looked at the knife with Jack.

"My father killed her with it years ago," Jack said. "I caught up to him the next day, took his knife and killed him. I left it with his things for the other side but when we returned it was gone."

"The knife has a long history," Sig stepped to the bar and pulled out three glasses. "You know Anna cured your father, Jack. I think I owe the story to you both."

Sig poured whiskey into two of the glasses and yellow juice into the other. He passed one to Jack and gestured for us to join him on the more comfortable seats in front of the fire.

"I think of pineapples when I think of you, Anna," he said. "As soon as I heard you were with us I had the kitchen stocked."

"Thanks," I said as I settled in next to Jack. He needed the drink even though he'd had a glass in his hand almost constantly since I woke in our room. For him the past few days had taken one hurtful turn after another. Sig sipped his and sighed then got up and grabbed the bottle, placing it on the low table before us. It looked like it would be a long story.

"As I said the knife was my father's," Sig started. "It's many centuries old. My father has been gone a long time and the knife came to me."

I wanted so much to know what gone meant but I knew it was either another long story or a life lesson for another time.

"My brother and I were close. I had two daughters and my brother had three sons. All our women are like Wendy and Cora; like the men in your side. Strong lines, strong memories.

"I don't know what made my brother change. It was gradual; so painful for those around him in particular his sons. Eventually we couldn't ignore it. He was insane. Truly dangerous. He murdered a child. My child; a son."

Sig turned his head from us and leaned forward to refill his glass. The short silver hairs at his temples sparkled in the firelight. I curled more tightly into Jack. His father had done the same thing.

"My brother's middle son was very gifted with manipulating lines. We felt our best success curing my brother would be with his youngest son. Since his line wasn't as old it would be easier to do what needed to be done. His younger brother agreed and the second time he was back on the other side we were fortunate. A disgusting home life resulted in a head injury which deeply damaged his personality. My nephew killed him and before his line faded from his body he bound that dangerous personality to it in the hope it would follow him to the other side, making him insane.

"Only a lunatic can sever the line from another," Sig said. It was the same thing Andre, my own insane personality, said to me the night I cured Damian. "But only until the end of their life. A horrible bargain is struck. Curing my brother would have broken the bond between my nephew and his insane past. Failure fuses the connection, making it permanent.

"We're more closely related than you think, children. My middle nephew is Ray Jackson's father, the man Anna knows as Pilot. His younger brother was your father, Jack. The man we made insane was Damian Howard."

"Shit," Jack muttered. "Do you have any idea how much pain he caused before Anna?"

"More than you know, Jack," Sig sighed. "Your father agreed. He thought he could do it, but he failed, leaving them both insane. If he'd succeeded he would have cured my brother and freed himself from his past, becoming sane again.

"So his older brother, Paul's father, agreed. And when the time came, Pilot twisted him to insanity. He succeeded, curing himself by giving my brother the real death. Like cutting off a gangrenous limb."

This time Jack refilled their glasses. The bottle neck rattled on both.

"That left my crazy father," Jack said. "Pilot messed with her and the two of you sent her after Damian."

"Yes. Pilot served in the US Army with you, Andre and your father. He had his eye on Andre and when he died he bound him to Anna's line. Her daughter was an unexpected side effect. As you know she's already mated to Damian's infant son."

Jack coughed hard into his glass. "Father didn't have a son when he was Damian."

"He did," I quietly said. "He got my sister Alina pregnant before I killed him. Her son took to Ray's line after Damian died the real death. If you've read her son you know he's Ray's now."

Jack's arm had been around me and it disappeared; yet another secret laid open to him like the cuts on his body.

"We kept it quiet, Jack," I tried to explain. "He's mated to my daughter and their son will be important. I'm not sure why but Pilot said something to do with healing the family. Alina's son is from all three lines now. Yours, Ray's and Paul's since she's his sister."

I put my empty glass on the table and looked at the knife.

"I can't shed any light on Pilot's prophecy," Sig said. "I'm sorry. Say your question out loud, Little One. You've been projecting it since Camille was born and you deserve to know you're right."

I reached for my empty glass and put it back down.

"When Damian cured your brother, when he died the real death," I said. "Is that what made his sons' lines so different? I mean, Ray and Keith have the same father, so close it's hard to tell them apart, but Pilot and Damian and Paul's father... I thought they called themselves brothers out of convenience since their lines are as different as can be."

Sig smiled at me. "You're a clever girl figuring that out. Once my brother was cured and the essence of his line disappeared from Damian, his brothers, and their descendants. All that was left was their mothers. The same thing will happen with you, Jack, and your brothers. I can read the difference in you already. With your father gone all that will be left in your line on the other side will be your mother."

We sat quietly for a few minutes. Sig opened the top button on his shirt and knelt to see to the fire. Jack remained silent. I wanted to tell him how sorry I was to have kept so much from him but all I'd said was sorry the past few days.

"Jack Roberts," Anton burst in. "All this whiskey and lying around is making you fat, my friend. I have a cord of wood with your name on it 'cause you're starting to look like my sister."

"Yeah, I hear that, Anton Lee," Jack said. He put his half finished drink on the table and stood, scratching his stomach. Jack leaned down and pressed his lips to my forehead without kissing me or meeting my eyes. His mind was already elsewhere. He looked like a man who needed to go smash rounds with an axe. Anton put an arm around his shoulders and walked him out. I heard their boots disappear down the hall.

Sig took Jack's place beside me, holding my hand in his.

"Jack doesn't like secrets," I said.

"He's not upset over what the truth is. He's disappointed he wasn't trusted with it."

"Yeah."

"Don't worry, Little One," Sig reassured me. "Anton will get his mind off things."

I agreed it would be good for Jack for a while, but eventually his thoughts would return to all the things I'd kept from him.

Chapter 23

Precious?

I grabbed for Jack and tried to pull him up sitting. He didn't stir from his deep sleep.

"Jack," I hissed.

"Mm," he said through his nose as he tensed, feeling my panic.

Precious? More insistent.

"Walker's here."

"What?"

Yes, Gerald? I heard my voice.

"Go back to sleep," Jack muttered.

Get me a drink, Precious.

Yes, Gerald.

And get yourself one, Precious.

Thank you, Gerald.

"We're in the bathroom, Jack. I'm in the bathroom with Walker." I shook him as I spoke.

"Then wake up," he said as he rolled away.

"Please come with me. I think the woman in the mirror is here. She's calling your brother Gerald. He told her to get him a drink."

"Then she can get me one. I'll need it to get back to sleep."

"Err," I said as I pushed myself to the edge of the bed.

"Stay put," he insisted. "Tell me what you need."

I didn't answer and went to the bathroom door then put my hand on the old crystal knob. Before I turned it, I quietly pulled it toward me then swung it into the room once the bolt slid free of the frame. She stood in a bathroom similar to Jack's back at his father's house. It looked a lot tidier than Jack and I kept ours; mostly men's toiletries on the counter with the exception of a small basket of woman's things. Things I'd never buy: scented deodorant, perfume and skin cream.

I couldn't see anyone in the room reflected beyond the doorway though I made out the edge of a messy bed.

"Jack, please?"

I put my hand to my chest as the boys' lines became anxious in response to my feelings. There was a glimpse of my naked body in the reflection of Gerald's doorway. Jack paused as he stepped in only briefly looking at the mirror then put his arms around me, calming our children.

"Is she where I think she is?" I whispered.

"Yes," Jack said as she returned to Gerald Walker's bathroom, drink in hand. She took a quick sip and made a face as she swirled it around in her mouth and swallowed. Then some went down the sink. She looked ten years older than me.

"Why is she there?"

Precious? The big fella wants you to stay longer. You'll be going home late.

Thank you, Gerald, she said with nearly sincere enthusiasm as she pulled her trembling lips into her mouth. A tear made its slow trek down her cheek. The last of the amber liquid went down her throat in two swallows then she took a round brush from her basket on the counter and ran it through her hair.

"What did she say," Jack whispered in my ear. I realized I cried along with her.

"He told her she's staying late to sleep with him again," I sniffled. Jack held me tighter as if to protect her. "She's pretending to be happy about it."

She took a couple of deep breaths and put a smile on her face as she noticed Gerald get off the bed.

May I get you another drink, Gerald? She asked.

After, he said as he staggered naked into the bathroom. His long, loose hair covered his shoulders in a tangled grey mane. He turned her around, pressing her into the counter and buried his nose in her neck.

You're delicious, he mumbled into her skin as she tipped her head back. The smile still glued on to her lips. I looked away. I didn't want to see any more.

Thank you, Gerald, she whispered.

From the corner of my eye I saw her reach a hand around the back of his neck; her nails traced parallel red lines down to his shoulder. Gerald growled as a fake flirty laugh good enough to fool him came from her. After a few seconds, he put his hands on her shoulders and pushed her to her knees.

Start me up, Precious, he ordered as Jack pulled me from the room, closing the door behind us.

Gerald was loud and I pressed my hands on my ears as I started to sob. Jack quickly pulled our robes on us.

Cora and Anton stood outside our door when Jack opened it and I almost knocked them over as I tried to escape.

"What the hell is going on?" Cora demanded.

"In the bathroom," I blurted out as I bolted down the hall, Jack close behind.

The direction in which I headed was a dead-end.

Two heavy chairs faced each other by the window at the end of the hall, so Jack guided me there and sat me down before he knelt.

"I'm sorry, Baby. Are you okay?"

I shook my head and leaned forward to hold on to him.

"Can you still hear them?"

"No," I whispered.

"It doesn't always come true, does it?"

"It could," I answered as I thought about Gerald Walker's proposal.

"But not always," he said. He swayed me side to side as I calmed down and tried to force the images out of my head. When I looked toward our room, Cora and Anton were out of sight.

"I bet she was projecting," I said.

"It doesn't matter now, Baby. That was my fault. I'm sorry for what I said about you being his pet."

I sat up a little straighter and put my hands on Jack's cheeks.

"Sometimes she warns me of danger, keeps me out of trouble," I said.

"That's right," he smiled and I gave him a smile in return. Jack's hands came up to my stomach and softly rubbed and the boys moved in response. "Now we know so he won't ever get near you, I promise."

It was only a few minutes until Cora and Anton came out and Jack hurried to meet them at our door. Cora looked angry as she pointed into our room and Jack's arms crossed. It was clear he was firm in his reply and she appeared to back down. Jack relaxed and continued, his hands dropping into the pockets of his borrowed worn robe.

Cora and Anton looked at me as Jack urgently continued. After a moment she offered me a reassuring smile and nodded to him. Anton clapped a hand on Jack's shoulder and left with her.

"Do you think you'll get back to sleep?" he asked as he pulled me to my feet.

"Not yet, I'm hungry."

"Okay, Baby," he laughed with what I'd come to recognize as a heavy load of buried emotion. "Kitchen it is."

Jack pulled out two stools from the bar overhanging the long island. The room was as big as the old kitchen on the main floor of Paul's house back home but the similarities ended there. Where Paul's appliances and counters were old, chipped and mismatched everything in Sig's kitchen gleamed in chrome and granite. The formal dining room through double glass doors looked as old and 'estate' as the rest of the big house and the kitchen was as out of place as red nail polish on a stray dog. Wendy claimed Sig only renovated one room a century and I believed her.

As Jack heated milk in a saucepan, I pulled out a container of pineapple chunks and put them on a plate with a big spoonful of spicy curried seafood sauce. And only because Wendy insisted I help myself to the two items I couldn't get enough of and only as long as I didn't bitch her out for the heartburn her cooking caused. If she hadn't made it clear they were only in the fridge for me I'd have stuck to the warm milk Jack didn't seem to mind cooking for us.

"Why was Cora mad?" I asked as he settled down with two steaming mugs. They smelled of vanilla which I thought complemented the hot curry but Jack eyed my meal and shook his head.

"Un-be-fucking-lievable," he muttered as he rolled his eyes. "Like *I* did something bad by leaving your mirror woman out when they treat *me* like a child they have so many secrets."

I sipped the hot milk to soothe my hotter tongue. Even though Wendy's curry was cold from the fridge it was sixty degrees hotter than the steaming milk.

"I'm sorry, Jack," I whispered. Both for Cora treating him like she did and for him having to deal with her because of my imaginary friend. He dismissively waved like there was no point in me even trying to apologize. "Was she projecting? Is that what made Cora come running?"

"She?" Jack asked. "You mean they. Both of them were. It seems you brought Gerald's future line all the way back here to Montana with yours."

I coughed with surprise. "What did Cora—

"I didn't ask," Jack cut me off. "So don't ask me. You know I wouldn't keep it from you and we're both better off not knowing."

Jack held my hand next to my empty plate.

"It's never going to happen so we don't need to know. I'm taking care of it, I promise."

Chapter 24

"Hey," Jack called. I wriggled my toes at the urgency in his voice and stretched as I decided if I should get up and pee. I grunted as the pillow came out from under my head.

"Yeah, you," he said as his hand smacked the mattress in front of my nose. It had been two days since we saw Gerald in the mirror and Jack had made himself scarce, helping Anton with one chore after another.

"Jack?" I pushed myself up. The bathroom light lit the room. We left the curtains half open and the early dawn sun barely made a dent in the winter darkness outside.

"No shit, Jack," he bit out. "I'm leaving."

"Anton?" I tried. He came in late the night before after helping Anton and a couple of the others clean up a pair of big trees the wind laid across Sig's long driveway. I'd fallen asleep as he showered to warm up and didn't remember him coming to bed.

His tone confused me. It sounded like a case of the four am's after a late night; having to go back into the cold on little sleep. I held a hand up to shield my eyes from the bathroom light and as my eyes adjusted, I stopped. Jack's jaw stuck out as he pulled his lips between his teeth. In that moment he looked like he truly hated me. What I didn't know was why. He let the moment drag on then he roughly pushed his palms over his eyes.

"When Father gave you to me he told me there was something different about you. He dreamed he tried to kill you but you disappeared from the end of his knife. You knew about us, he said. You knew too much. Then he disappeared in February and I assumed he hadn't finished giving you away. He'd have to on the other side. He wouldn't have any of his mates again once it started; he'd be driven by the same urge to shed you that I'd feel to have you.

"No big deal," Jack said. "I was in no hurry for him to have another way to hurt me."

I was quiet. For me his inheritance had been just as unwelcome.

"Then in May I shook your hand and felt it in my skin. You did too. I saw the surprise in your face. I touched you again to be sure. You didn't want me. I saw that." He shrugged.

"That's true," I whispered. "I want you now."

"Shut it," he sniffled and zipped up the small bag on the foot of the bed.

I did. He'd been angry since we escaped for one thing after another and needed to tell me off.

"I told Dana. He said 'you poor bastard, Jack.' He knew Father would use you to control me. Then he said 'at least you'll get lucky even though you won't remember much of it.'

"I laughed. He said you were pretty well put together and I should stop thinking of claiming you as a chore.

"Then you took me to that hotel room and as soon as I got my hands on you I forgot all about Father and the extra responsibility you'd be when we walked out. That hour or two was the most dangerous thing I've ever done. For a man who's been addicted to pretty much everything, tasting Anna was the biggest hit of my life. I remembered every minute and walked out wondering how the hell I was going to get my next dose of you. I was bent over, fucked, screwed, doomed and buggered. Jesus, Anna. I fell in love with the one addiction Courtesy wouldn't let me quit."

"I know, Jack," I tried but he slapped his bag and it bounced off the dresser and landed on the floor.

"Do you have any idea how much I hated you for doing that to me?" His voice rose and I backed up to the headboard. "I didn't ask for it and I was fucking stuck with watching Paul get every fix that should have been mine.

"Do you see where this is going?" He demanded.

I shook my head, refusing to admit it was going anywhere other than apologies and make-up sex.

"So RJ shows up and he can't have you. RJ says you're dead if you and I don't give Father the grandson he can't. I told him you wouldn't do it. You'd never betray Paul but I couldn't let him kill you so I suggested we tell you RJ found Camille and would kill her."

"Liar," I breathed. "You're a liar, Jack."

"Really?" He asked. "I guess you're right but you fell for it and I knocked you up then you fell in love with me and that wasn't voluntary either. The boys' lines pushed hard and you fell in love with me. Yeah, I hated myself for a while for doing that to you. Even with your God damn sobbing for Paul nearly ruining it I got my fix. I got on fucking top of you and rode you until I filled you up. I'd be dead after, whatever, but I got to have you again."

There was a moment of silence as what he said sunk in.

"Camille never was in danger you stupid bitch!" He yelled.

I got my hand on my glass. Water slopped down my arm as I threw, narrowly missing. It shattered in the corner by the dresser, startling me as I started to cry great pregnant angry tears. He was right. I never would have crossed the line with him just to save myself and I despised him for being right.

"Grow up, Anna. I did my job. I lied to you to keep you alive and you act like I violated some sacred trust. There's no sacred trust. It's man and mate. Then I'll be damned if I didn't have to touch you to keep you alive. Fucking Karma.

"But you're a menace. You endangered my sons getting me here and I let you do it. My sons are safer with you out of my life than with you in it. I'm leaving you so you won't do any more stupid-ass shit to save me and good riddance."

"But we're safe here, Jack," I tried, feeling no shame in begging and ignoring the fact our days here were numbered since Anton could only numb me one more time. "Please, Jack. I can forgive you."

Jack heavily sat on the bed.

"And this is why I suffer," he whispered as his anger at me fizzled out. "Point one; my sons are safer if I leave you. Point two; you lied to me about my daughter, sister, whatever. There's a baby girl coming and you kept her from me like her father didn't matter. That's fucking unforgivable, Anna. There's no decency in you at all. Point three; Gerald will catch up to us and you'll spend the rest of your life screwing him for another day with my sons. How does that suit you? I'm still bound to protect you and if you're with me when he comes that's how it's going to go. Point four is on the other side of the door and if you can forgive me for my first lie you won't forgive my second."

"Please, Jack," I whispered.

"Do you remember what happened the night Paul died?"

I froze for just a second before I got to my knees, my hands in fists. There was no need to bring him up.

"When the gun went off you looked away. You fainted like the child you are and I caught you. You didn't hit the ground."

"Fuck you, Jack," I growled. "I tried to save him. I tried."

"Do you know what you didn't see, you coward?"

I swung and as my momentum carried me forward, he caught my fist and grabbed my other hand.

"See?" He demanded over my shriek of protest. "More stupid unthinking child crap. Your line is strong now, Anna. Do you really want to take a chance on breaking it off with me? Risking my sons any more than you already have? You land that right and you might reject my connection and their lines. You want to kill them?"

I shook my head, sobbing, unable to find any other way to hate him than with my fists.

"RJ pulled the gun aside just before Paul pulled the trigger," Jack whispered in my ear. I tried to tear my hands free as I screamed again. He leaned his head aside to avoid my noise. "Then he held you up and told Paul to hit you. To say the words to break it off. I've never seen a man take so much pain avoiding the inevitable but eventually he gave in and broke it off with you."

"Liar, you son of a bitch," I yelled as my voice failed with a squeak and I stopped struggling against his hold.

"I'm the son of a sire, Anna. A real man. One who stopped at nothing to keep his men strong until you killed him and single-handedly tore my family to pieces. I don't care about any fucking cure. It felt good to see Paul end it. That moment I wanted nothing more than to see you both hurt."

I sat back on my heels and watched his face.

"Paul's alive?"

Jack rolled his eyes and pushed me over to the mattress. "You have to be the stupidest woman I've ever taken to bed."

My knees came up and I wrapped my arms protectively around my stomach as I realized what he'd done.

"You shamed me, Jack," I cried. "You made me choose between him and my daughter. Then you took him from me. Gerald's going to find you and I hope the rope is too short and he gets to watch you strangle. Get out, Jack. Get the fuck out."

"Gladly," he shouted as he swept his bag up off the floor. Glass crunched under his shoes as he opened the door.

"Jesus," I whispered as Paul and Jack stood face to face in the hall. Anton and Sig had him, one on each arm. Paul wore a familiar grey shirt, his holsters were empty and he had glasses on. I blinked at the sight of the glasses. He was real. My imagination wouldn't make up a detail like that. As he tried to shake off Sig and Anton, they held him firm.

"You're next on my shit list, Wendy," Jack seethed as she pushed past and came to me. "What'll it be, Paul?" Jack demanded.

Wendy tried to get me sitting and I clung to her, my heart pierced with deep, deep shame. My husband was only a dozen feet away, nose to nose with my lover. I clutched at my chest feeling nothing but my connection to that asshole Jack but in my heart I felt nothing but love for Paul. Jack had destroyed whatever it was I'd felt for him, replacing it with pure black rage.

"My wife's sons are mine to bring up," Paul said, his words measured and calm though he didn't keep control of himself. "Don't come near us."

"Paul," I whispered. The rust coloured paint in the hall faded and I fought to suck in air as Wendy stroked my hair, her hard belly pressed next to mine. Paul looked to me as Jack turned in my direction.

"Bitch," he hissed and stomped off.

The room tilted as Wendy took my weight. Jack didn't say anymore and his boots faded at the top of the stairs. I stared at the side of Paul's head as he watched Jack leave then Sig and Anton let him go.

"Mm," Wendy groaned as Paul stepped in and Anton rubbed his ear against the same invisible fly buzzing around mine. "Anton?"

"Yes, Mother," he answered. "She's projecting again. This has to be the last time. It's too hard on her."

"I know," Wendy whispered.

"Wait," Sig said to Paul as he gently touched his elbow. Paul helplessly looked at Sig then at me.

Anton knelt on the bed and took my face in his palms. "One last time, Anna," he said. "Sshhh, look at me."

I pulled my eyes from Paul and looked into Anton's. He matched his breathing with mine and I felt him under my nose as the humming around me disappeared along with the feel of Wendy's arms and Anton's touch and mercifully, the warring love and anger in my heart.

Chapter 25

Wendy's cool fingertips brushed my hair from my cheek. It would be her, cradling me as I recovered from Anton's final numbing of my sensum.

"Hi, Little One," she whispered, her throat buzzed my forehead with her words. "Relax, you're okay."

Her soft perfume, a mix of musk and citrus was all my nose could read. It had only been a few days since the previous time Anton numbed me and I guessed Jack's leaving was enough to make me blow through it.

"You knew he was alive, Wendy," I said. "You and Sig. You had to know and you didn't tell me. Did you think it was better for me to keep living the lie?"

"No," she kissed the top of my head. "We thought you knew. When you arrived you projected so much shame about going to Jack, about betraying Paul. Your grief was locked down so far you never shared it. We were shocked as well when Jack told you this morning. The whole house felt your grief."

She tugged the heavy blanket up a little further, her legs tangled with mine, stomach to stomach.

"Six months," I sighed, knowing I had to stay calm. "He was dead for six months. Two months ago I asked Jack to be my lover. We had a few months to live and I didn't want to feel so alone any more. I betrayed Paul over and over and he'll never forgive me. The only connection I feel is to Jack. I'd cut it out if I could."

"Do you love Paul?" She asked.

"My love for him never wavered, Wenns."

She nodded, then again and seemed to make a decision.

"When he broke it off something went wrong. We're not sure if it was because you were unconscious and didn't hear the words or if the strength of your line caused it. I think he said the words, severing your connection to him but your strong line held and his connection to you remained intact. I think you refused to let him go. He still feels you, Anns, all the time. He loves you more than ever and he spent the past six months desperate to have his marriage whole. He thought you still felt him because he felt you."

She paused again and turned her head, thinking. I didn't know which was worse: me loving Paul believing him dead or him loving me knowing I was alive and surrendered to Damian Howard's family.

"There is much love between you two. I felt it from you earlier with your grief and shame. If you didn't love him so much you wouldn't feel so bad.

"You must be hungry," she said, working herself upright. "I'll go downstairs and fix you something. As usual you can sit up when you feel like it, okay?"

I nodded and adjusted the feather pillow to take the place of her arm under my head. She still wore the big old robe she'd worn when she barged past Jack to hold me. She kissed my cheek before crossing the floor then I heard the door close quietly behind her.

After a minute I sat and tested my balance. My head stayed steady so I shoved myself over the edge of the bed and got my feet on the floor. The top buttons of Anton's old blue shirt were done up. It was one of the things Anton gathered up for Jack since we'd arrived in Sig's massive wooded back yard with nothing but the clothes on our backs. I'd done up as many as I could but my stomach still stuck out.

"I guess I'll pick up the story where Jack left off," Paul said behind me. I startled and tried to pull my shirt closed over my belly. He occupied the wooden chair on the other side of the bed, hands resting on its wide arms. I pushed my knee around and turned to face him as I pulled the blanket up. He wore the same clothes as he had earlier. A little more grey hair than I remembered. Behind the plain brown frames of his glasses, his green eyes sparkled and he looked as rugged and handsome as ever. I pressed my lips shut in embarrassment over my missing tooth. He used to love to make me smile but now it was just one more thing to be ashamed of.

"Paul," I whispered then pressed on my stomach to stop a little knee from coming out. As soon as I could I hid my hand, upset I'd drawn attention to even more of my shame.

"Hi, Sugar," he answered automatically as he sighed. Although he always greeted me with those words they didn't sound fake or forced. I was still his Sugar and it pained me even more. As hard as our first words together were going to be one of us had to break the ice and it looked like he waited for the okay from me.

"Come," I said, holding out my hand and needing to touch him. Paul sat on the other side of the bed. "More."

He moved closer, stopping within reach then he took my left hand and fingered my wedding ring. Paul turned my hand over and touched the scars, nearly invisible in places but twisted and rough on the base of my thumb. I put my other hand on his cheek. He hadn't shaved in a couple of days and his whiskers still felt rough and a little sharp.

"Let me see," he said, dropping his eyes to my mouth. I shook my head and looked away. "Please, you don't need to hide anything from me."

His fingers brushed my lips, coaxing them open. Paul's smile fell a bit when he saw the gap in my upper teeth.

"If Walker knocked out more then Jack wouldn't have had to trim off so much of his fingers," I explained.

"Oh, Sugar," Paul whispered. He moved closer and I let him get his arms around me. "I'm so sorry."

"You've got nothing to be sorry for, Paul."

"No?" he asked. "That's so Anna."

"Maybe," I answered. "Is Camille here?"

"Ray bought Alina a house in San Diego. I split my time between her there and the compound."

"You've seen her?" I exclaimed. There was light at the end of my horrible tunnel if it was safe for Paul to be with her. "Take me."

Paul cupped my cheeks in his hands, seeming happier. I leaned my mouth to his, touching his nose and he didn't pull away. He let me kiss him, keeping his lips closed but not hesitating to kiss me back.

"Sig explained your bargain after Soros took you. Our children would be left alone and I had to promise to stay away from Howard's compound as long as his family's children were there. Sig says Soros is keeping an eye on Walker and his men. He made the same promise I did."

"Okay?" I asked.

"Not yet."

One of the boys squirmed and I sat up straighter, holding my hand on my stomach again and tensed as I felt Paul's hand there with mine.

"You have nothing to be sorry for, Sugar," he whispered in my ear. "What you did protected all the children, theirs and ours. I know you feel terrible. I know you don't feel our connection like I do. I want you to know they're your sons too, not just his. They're part of my wife and they'll have everything they need. I forgive you for needing Jack while they held you. You survived, okay?"

I let my head fall to his shoulder as the door opened. His easy forgiveness should have stunned me but I was limp inside and would have told him bullshit if I wasn't trying so hard to stay calm.

"I'm so sorry to intrude," Wendy said. "She needs something in her stomach. Breaking through Anton's numbing and then his redoing it is hard on her. If she gets weak with hunger she'll be sick."

"I'll make sure she eats, Wendy," Paul said.

She put a tray down on the bed beside us then shrugged a bag off her shoulder.

"You know you can't stay here much longer, right?" she asked. "I packed some things for you; clothes and stuff until you get a chance to shop."

"I have a bunch of maternity clothes at home, Wenns," I said as I took the lid off the plate to see what she had for me and wasn't surprised to see the bland assortment she guaranteed wouldn't cause heartburn like the curry. So far she'd been right. There was oatmeal with brown sugar, a hard boiled egg and an apple. A little pot of camomile tea for now and a container of cut up veggies for later.

"I thought so," she answered as she passed Paul a cup of coffee. "But you can't get through a three day drive naked so this should help."

"Three days?"

"Cora won't clear you to fly or be cramped up in the truck for more than six hours a day."

"Okay," I conceded. That meant eighteen hours a day in a hotel feeling awkward with Paul.

I started on the oatmeal even though I wasn't hungry. She was right, if I got weak with hunger I'd have a hard time getting anything down. Wendy rested a hand on Paul's shoulder as she kissed the top of my head and I looked up, offering her a weak smile.

"There's my Little One," she whispered, her fingers briefly on my cheek before she left us alone. I found a lump in the oats and used my tongue to push it between my front teeth.

"After I," Paul stopped and ran a hand over his face before he continued. "When they took you in the house Steele put the boots to me. I remember hearing you scream my name and a truck leaving. When I woke up it was nearly noon and I was still on the lawn. All the hoses from the truck were in pieces on the ground with me and I could barely see.

"This one," he gestured at his left eye. "Needs help now. I've needed glasses for a few years anyway. My arm was fractured and a few ribs. I got in the house and looked for you but you were gone. Your clothes and Jack's mixed together on his bathroom floor. I still felt you but I knew part of what you'd told me was true. You'd been with him again."

The teapot rattled as I put it down and Paul reached for my hands to steady them. He took the tray to the dresser and sat close.

"I still had my phone so I tried calling you but it rang in another room so I got hold of Sig. He said to stay put. He'd seen you the day before and was still in the area. I couldn't go anywhere anyway with the truck in pieces and a broken arm."

"I'm so sorry," I whispered. Somehow I'd saved him that night but he'd been hurt so bad and lost so much.

"Four and a half months later," he went on like a briefing back home at the compound, just the facts, concise and clear. "We got word you were one night into a four night stay in Hartford. Not just you but the other two women as well. We got the A.T.F. in with us and moved on their compound with weapons warrants. From the hill across the field we saw a God damn gallows and two dead men on the ground beside it. They were stringing up a third. We moved in but they hung him and shot another as they split up and fled. The A.T.F. made a couple of arrests but they had their escapes well planned."

"I didn't know the other women were at the hotel," I said as I struggled to avoid thinking about the men I'd helped sentence to death. It was gunfire I overheard when Soros called to send us to Baltimore, not hammering. "Soros sent us to Baltimore for a few weeks."

"I went through the house and found your room," he went on. "There'd been a hell of an explosion behind the house and the windows were boarded up. I looked in the mirror you used and I could smell you when I lay in the broken glass on your bed.

"Two days later the other women were brought back so we stopped our surveillance and left. The house was off limits again and we lost track of you. Early yesterday, Sig called and said I needed to drop everything and come here. He didn't say why until I arrived late last night."

The mirror topping the big old dresser reflected a couple I didn't know any more. They looked comfortable enough together, his arm around her and head turned to the side like he'd be welcome to kiss her if he wanted to. But her fingers knotted together as they tried to cover her bare pregnant stomach. He looked like he wanted to comfort her and soothe away all her hurt and she looked desperate to be anywhere else.

"When I woke up they told me you were dead. I was mated to Jack."

It was all I could say. Jack didn't matter anymore. Jack was over.

Chapter 26

I excused myself for a shower so I could get away from Paul's hovering and dress in private. Wendy gave me a pair of maternity pants and a loose short sleeved top. I felt naked with my arms bare after six months of keeping them carefully covered in comparison with the relief I felt no longer displaying my stomach.

Wendy promised an early dinner and invited us to meet in the dining room. She apologized to Paul for asking him to take so much on faith when he arrived and told him he'd meet more of the family through the evening.

Anton waited outside when we arrived. He shook Paul's hand and led us in.

"Paul," Anton said. "It's good to see you again."

"Is everyone here family?" Paul asked, getting right to the point. His mind needed to know how everything fit together.

"Indeed we are, my friend," Anton said. "Anna's mother has given me permission to speak of her to fill in the gaps for you unless you wish to, Anna."

Paul looked at me and I shrugged. For a moment I pictured Jack's reaction to all the secrecy on this side of the family and hesitated. My hand went to my chest as I became anxious.

"Stop it," Anton nudged my foot. I turned to him. "You aren't fully numbed. I'm watching you for any sign you're pushing through it again."

I crossed my arms and frowned.

"Don't worry," he laughed. "I'm the only one who can pick up your projections. I can't numb you again and if it wears off you're right out the door."

Paul rubbed my shoulder.

"Wendy is my line mother, Paul," I started. "When she came to the compound months ago one reason was to be with Jack. The baby she carries is his line sister; biologically his daughter but in the grand scheme of family, his sister."

"Okay," Paul said as his eyes widened.

"Wendy is also my line mother," Anton continued as he guided Paul and I toward our seats. "My Father sticks to Europe and I spend time there as well. You caught me on my way to the airport when you appeared here, Anna. Mother doesn't have much use for him. She prefers what she considers the more noble work of ensuring the survival of the family. My Father prefers his tulips.

"And Sig is Wendy's Father," he added. "You already knew Sig is family."

"Which makes Sig your grandfather?" Paul asked.

"Yes," Anton answered as he kicked my foot again. "Stop it, Anna."

"I wasn't," I protested but maybe I was. Wendy's laughter filled the hall outside and she burst in, followed by Cora, Mark and Sig. I half listened as Anton explained the rest of my immediate family and received another nudge from him. Cora and Mark introduced themselves then Mark disappeared to help serve dinner.

My mood darkened as dinner went on. I ignored the talk around me and preferred to be angry with Jack for ruining things with Paul. I caught Anton glaring at me so I switched to thinking about the bargain protecting the children. The bargain which betrayed my husband. It didn't seem like a good deal at all. I loved my little boys and hating the bargain meant hating them. I just couldn't do it. The next time I caught Anton giving me the eye for getting worked up I concentrated on forming a solid picture of me sticking my tongue out at him. He snorted around his glass.

Paul moved closer as we moved to Sig's study; his hip against mine and his arm over my shoulder. He still smelled like the forest. Like the shade and cool water or mint. Even in the summer his soft, soothing darkness about him brought me calmness. Jack, on the other hand, reminded me of salt and the sea storms back home on Vancouver Island. It was summer when we'd met and in the winter the scent of his skin warmed me like the sun did.

I felt another boot from Anton when I sunk into an image of screaming at Jack as I threw an axe at the back of his head as he receded down the hall.

"Seriously, Anna?" Anton asked. "How old are you really?"

"Shut up, Anton," I muttered but his chiding sufficiently distracted me.

"Seriously, you two?" Wendy broke in. I hadn't imagined her pulling patriarch on us though if anyone had the right to parent us it was her. "Keep it up and you're both going to your rooms."

"Hah," I snapped at Anton. He pursed his lips. My nostrils flared with the impression my smug outburst didn't please him and guessed his monitoring my projections left me open to his.

"That it did," he muttered.

I turned my attention back to Paul to try and settle down. If bickering with Anton removed my numbing Paul and I would be on the road. I couldn't understand why we argued anyway. Anton had only helped me since I'd arrived.

Paul's hand came up and pressed my head to his shoulder. He forgives me, I thought. But for how long? Anton should have let Paul go after Jack, I decided, and glared at Anton this time. He was already scowling at me.

"What?" I demanded. "And you better not be broadcasting every thought of mine to anyone else."

He scoffed. "The children have less childish thought tantrums than you."

"Hey," Wendy snapped.

Paul started to laugh at us but Sig's serious expression shut him up.

"Anton," she said. "Perhaps there is a gentler way to help your sister."

I had been right. Anton was out of line and Wendy called him on it. His arms crossed and he looked sideways at her before offering me a forced smile. I pictured Anton over Wendy's knee for provoking me and met his eyes, staring him down. First he pressed his lips together. Then he pulled them into his mouth. Then Anton burst out laughing.

Wendy quirked an eyebrow at him then giggled.

"I've never used corporal punishment, Little One," she said then pointed at Anton. "Though I must admit Anton has tempted me."

Anton stood and offered refills as Sig began to speak explaining what finally pushed Jack into leaving.

"Excuse me," I said and looked at Anton. "I need to step out. It sounds like you have business and I think my sensum will feel better if I miss out."

I slipped out the door before anyone could answer and stopped, unsure which way to go once it closed behind me. My room smelled of Jack and his stale whiskey. I dreaded the thought of Paul joining me and didn't want to spend another night there alone either. I took a deep breath and imagined alternate sleeping arrangements. With Paul, it didn't matter. Just somewhere other than the room Jack and I shared.

"You got it, Anna," Anton shouted from behind the door.

Wendy found me alone in the kitchen a while later. I'd helped myself to a bowl of vanilla ice cream but hadn't tasted it. I decided to put it back in the freezer before it melted or anyone caught me with it. It made me sad to think how timid I'd become, afraid to eat in my family's own kitchen even though they'd told me dozens of times to help myself. Since I was numbed I needed to eat often and not just after waking up. Any hunger made me feel sick.

"My Little One," she whispered as she took the stool next to mine and pointed at my bowl. "That kind of night?"

"Am I the only one who realizes I got dumped today?"

She laughed and stopped herself then turned her head as if looking for something. "Paul is looking for you. Cora will suggest he try your room and you don't want to eat this to get over being dumped."

Wendy dropped the full bowl in the sink and went to one of the freezers, reaching in until she was shoulder deep in the icy fog pouring from it.

"This is what you're after. Don't tell Cora about it. She'll have it eaten by dawn."

I agreed and she pulled out two spoons. Chocolate and vanilla ice cream, ribbons of caramel and mini caramel chocolates filled the plastic tub.

"It's perfect, Wenns, thanks."

We ate in silence for a while.

"Why..." I paused, thinking of the ten year old boy they called 'the children.' "Why didn't my projections bother you when you first got pregnant or was it having both of us here? Cora said you had to leave with the children when we arrived."

"Mm," Wendy swallowed and pointed her spoon in the air like she needed it to speak. "I was never bothered by you, Jack or Patrick after you dropped me off. Or even the three of you together. The content of your projections needs censoring with children here, that's a given."

She paused and looked past me.

"Paul's decided you're not in your room. They've avoided him because he's gonna ask someone where you are. He figures we can all read each other and he's right. Anton's going to tell him you're here with me."

It was like having my own personal spy network. Their ability to focus and communicate with their projections was impressive compared to mine.

"Anyway," she said. "You can pick us up when we're quiet and it seems to add to your own volume no matter how silent we try and be. That's how your projections didn't bother me. As long as I kept mine to a minimum you didn't get too loud and there was only one of me. There are more than twenty of us here. We overwhelm you and it seems you have to project all that energy from yourself making you very loud.

"It was like you held my ears and shouted 'listen, listen.' The others said the same thing."

"Like feedback?"

"Mm," she nodded around another mouthful.

"What did I do to make Anton angry?" I asked as I put my spoon down.

"You didn't, Little One. Anton is very fond of you."

I shook my head, not understanding.

"It's not just seeing what you send. He feels your moods. Right now your emotions are in a very dark and angry place and he has to work hard to keep his cool with everyone as he rides out your feelings."

I pictured a big red heart and tried to add an image of me kissing Anton's cheek since I understood what a difficult task he'd taken on for me. My own head was a hard enough place to be in and he was stuck in it with me. After a moment something invisible, soft and warm brushed my cheek and I touched my fingers to it. Then I felt the idea Paul approached the kitchen.

Wendy smiled.

"Wenns," I said. "I don't know whether to be more ashamed or angry with myself. Jack did his job. I don't know why I was stupid enough to expect anything different from him."

"You don't have to decide now, Little One," she lowered her voice as Paul came in. "Give your past a chance. When the boys are born you'll find Jack's connection reflects your real feelings for him."

South-West

Chapter 27

Avoiding Paul for the drive home hadn't been as difficult as I'd thought. After we left Sig's, we drove south-west toward California. Paul made small talk and seemed relaxed and comfortable with me in the passenger seat although the great weight he carried wasn't far away. He hadn't left it behind. He'd merely put it down to rest his arms.

I imagined his disappointment with me. He'd expected to find a woman perhaps only ashamed of something she'd done six months in the past and not his wife mated with another man. A woman who grieved her husband's death and tried to get her life back with someone else, brief as it would have been. A woman who had her future taken from her for a second time and found herself trying to fit in to the past.

My emotional burden felt ever present, dragging me to my pit of guilt every time I began to enjoy being with him. Though he wanted and deserved happiness with his wife, it felt like only a matter of time before the honeymoon wore off and the word 'unforgivable' began to crop up every time he thought about me.

When we weren't talking about everything but us and our marriage, the roads were bad and he tuned me out to keep us on the pavement.

Idaho Falls offered us a warm room. Paul checked us in then excused himself for a walk to get a feel for the neighbourhood, leaving me a handgun. He switched to thinking like a soldier; looking at me but seeing everything around me instead. A feel for the neighbourhood meant cataloguing everything from fences he could get me over or under, yards he could drive through if we needed an alternate route and if it came down to it, defensible positions away from civilians if there was any serious shit from Walker or Soros and he needed the two guns under his coat.

I was grateful for some time where I didn't have to worry he'd call me out for the cheating wife I was and opted for a bath before dozing on the couch. At least there wasn't room for Paul to curl up with me there. Anton had put me in his own room the night before to keep an eye on me, he claimed. He'd dragged in a sofa for himself.

The bathroom fan hummed when I woke and Paul slept on the bed. He left me a sandwich and half a salad. The two empty coffee cups in the garbage didn't seem to hamper his ability to snore. He'd showered and changed his clothes; his glasses neatly folded on the bedside table with his guns.

After dinner, we watched TV together on the couch as he drank more coffee. Once I turned in, he disappeared outside. I woke every time the door opened as he divided his time between peering past the nearly closed curtains and stalking the neighbourhood. At dawn I realized I must have finally given in to real sleep since Paul lay in the bed with me, dressed down to his boxers. The last I remembered, he stepped out for yet another patrol.

His cool skin hadn't been against me very long though he breathed soft and deep already. I kept my eyes closed and thought about the strength of my mated connection and after a moment I could ignore who it was to. Paul's hand slid from his hip and brushed against my skin so I took it and rested it on mine as I focused on good familiar memories and the scent of winter which accompanied him in from watch.

Paul's lips smacked as he swallowed and reached further around me, holding my stomach. My muscles tensed and gentle movement rippled the skin beneath his fingers, reminding me I couldn't be Paul's no matter how I deluded myself. Married to Paul I couldn't be Jack's and mated to Jack I couldn't honestly accept intimacy with my husband. At least for a very long time.

I moved his hand behind me and pushed myself up to sit. Paul's guns lay on his side of the bed and he'd moved the one for me to my table. I sighed and reached for the bottle of water beside it. As I put it to my lips, a menacing hiss erupted behind me. Paul grabbed me around the shoulders and before I knew it he had me in the corner, his hand sealing my mouth shut. The hiss turned into a deep throaty growl with each of his quick short breaths. At the end of his arm, my handgun tracked back and forth between the door and the window.

"Paul," I mumbled behind his palm as I got my hands up to try and peel it away.

"Sshhh, don't move," he ordered. His voice was dark, terrifying. It was a tone he'd never taken with me.

"Don't. Move."

I took a deep breath through my nose and tried to relax. He'd heard something I didn't and in spite of my pounding heart and sudden need for the bathroom I complied. The boys didn't. My terror stirred them up and I tried to be at least brave enough to sooth them by rubbing my chest. Our bare legs stuck out before us.

"Sshhh," Paul said again. He uncovered my mouth and pushed me to the floor, covering me with his body, his dampening chest in my face as he peered around the foot of the bed. I turned to my side to ease his weight on my stomach.

"Don't move, Stevens," he whispered. Stevens? Shit. I craned my neck up. The gun pointed at the wall and Paul's eyes were barely open. God damn, he was armed and asleep. "Jackson's just a few hundred yards behind us. You'll be fine."

Ray Jackson was the only Jackson I could think of. I vaguely remembered Stevens from when I'd first arrived at Paul's compound. He wasn't family, I recalled. A smallish man with a limp. I had the impression it was from a somewhat recent (at the time) mission. That at least let me place what Paul relived.

"Captain," I whispered. Paul had been a Captain then. He pulled back to hide behind the bed and put a hand on my cheek. Paul glanced at me.

"Captain Richards," I said a little more strongly. Paul had to put the gun down which wasn't likely if he believed he defended a wounded man.

"Yeah?" he whispered, head turning, still scanning.

"What do you see?"

"Three," Paul answered.

"I only see one."

"Yeah, one," he agreed after a minute. I didn't have a clue what I was doing but at least if he was open to suggestion I could try and change the ending of his fantasy.

"He's leaving," I tried. Paul pushed himself up on his left elbow and cradled my head in his arm. The gun moved urgently to the left and I watched his finger slip into the trigger guard.

"No, he isn't."

"You're holding me like a baby, Richards," my voice shook as I watched his finger. "I'll never live this down."

"That's right," Paul answered. No inflection to his voice at all.

"Major," I tried. He needed to come back to the present.

"Yeah?" he answered. I took a tight breath.

"Kiss me, Major," I demanded. I tossed something completely incongruous with his memory in to the mix and hoped it would bring him back to the hotel room and away from wherever he'd been with Stevens.

"That's what your girl said to me," Paul said with the shut the hell up tone. "Before I bent her over your bunk."

"Major, please," I pleaded. "Look at me."

Paul took a look around the imaginary battle zone. I watched his pulse pound in his neck as a path of sweat thickened with the passage of another drop past his ear. His chin dropped as he pulled further back behind the bed. His eyes met mine, blank and barely focused.

"Look at me," I tried again, more softly than before. "Kiss me."

"I..." Paul's brow furrowed as he tried to look up again, seeking the unreal scene in his head. "What?"

The gun slowly lowered as his senses returned.

"Sshhh, Paul," I soothed. "It's Anna. We're okay."

"Anna?" he swallowed. "Sugar?"

"Yeah. It's Sugar."

"Okay," he said and rolled off me, breathing heavily at my side. "Okay."

I didn't move, unsure how awake he was. He put the gun down by his head and rubbed his hands across his temples before pulling them away to see the sweat they'd collected.

"Did I hurt you?" He asked.

"No, I'm fine." I sat beside him and leaned my head against the bed. He rolled away from me so I picked the gun up. The safety was off so I put it back on before putting it up on the table. My now empty water bottle was on the floor beside me so I put it up as well.

"You talked me down?" He asked.

"Yes."

"Thank you," he sighed. "I'm so sorry, Sugar. The last really bad one Denis one-punched me out cold."

Instead of answering I put my hand on his shoulder. Denis had been dead for nearly a year so it had been a long time.

"Did I scare you?" Paul asked. His eyes focused on the frozen pavement ahead. We hadn't talked as we packed and took breakfast in the small diner near the motel lobby. I thought he'd want to know what happened but he hadn't asked.

"Yes."

"Shit. I'm sorry, Sugar."

"I wasn't scared of you," I explained as I tried to ease his conscience. "I was scared you'd shoot and hurt someone in another room."

I offered him my hand and he gave me a tight smile and took it.

"That's why Camille lives with Ray for now," he said. "I've had some really bad dreams and was scared one would escalate like this morning. The bargain you made protects them so I secure my guns in his basement when I'm there. Alina would raise hell if she knew I brought them in the house."

Paul gave me a gentle squeeze just as I was about to pull away. I felt dirty and didn't want it rubbing off on my daughter's father.

"I feel," he tried and I waited. "I've put so much pressure on myself to protect you. It's overwhelming. I'll get better rest, I promise. It won't happen again."

"Maybe I should drive?" I suggested. Fatigue wore him down. At least I'd rested a little more than he had.

"You have no ID," he snapped.

"So?" I challenged. "Just because I didn't make an extra stop for my wallet when I pulled Jack from the gallows doesn't mean I'm useless."

Paul's hand stiffened in mine and he jammed it under his thigh as I crossed my arms and stared out my window. I thought of Jack and the pain I'd live with when his brothers caught up with him and wondered if I shouldn't have turned my back when the lever swung and the floor moved beneath him. At least I'd be somewhere I understood. I couldn't think of a place I deserved to be more than Gerald Walker's house.

Chapter 28

Other than favouring greens over browns, our room in Elko was nearly the same as the one in Idaho Falls. Paul apologized for being short with me and again for the incident during the night before, following through on his promise to make his assessment of the neighbourhood quick and get a nap. I slept on the blankets while he slept under them and we spent the evening the same as before: diner dinner and TV.

I thought more and more about returning to the compound with him. Or not. When I asked if we could get Camille on the way home Paul flat out told me no and walked out for his first evening patrol. I couldn't imagine what he looked for. He couldn't read Walker and Soros' men anyway so I suspected his forays were simply to give me some space. Or to give himself some breathing room.

His bad dream stuck with me. I couldn't live with myself if he shot someone in a deluded attempt to look after his wife. Jack was gone and I wasn't reconnecting to Paul. Wendy said to give the past a chance and I had.

The past didn't stand a chance.

Rock hard tightness in my abdomen took my breath and I sat on the bed. After a minute it muted to a simmer but then heated up, consuming everything in its path as it bore its way up into my chest before sharpening again. Then stomach pain burned my skin as I cramped up and I cried out, falling sideways to the pillow.

Even laying on my side I felt a hard lump where there shouldn't be one. The pain in my chest was anxiety from the boys, it couldn't be anything else. They were stressed and I was sure the lump had something to do with it. It wasn't huge but it also shouldn't be there.

I got on my feet, gasping for air and looked at the phone across the room then the door. Paul had his cell and would be back soon but he'd only been gone a few minutes and I was sure if I made it out and yelled he'd come find me.

My boots sat by the door and I clung to the knob as I struggled to balance on one foot at a time to put them on. Two steps and I stepped on the second floor balcony looking down at the truck through the metal railing running fifty feet in either direction to the stairs. My coat waited on the other side of the locked door. The pressure in my belly didn't worsen though the knot of pain in my chest throbbed with each breath I took. 'Something is wrong, Mom,' they seemed to say. I rubbed the bulge, unsure which baby I soothed as I made my way along to the closest stairs.

"Paul?" I shouted. Pain surged down my left arm in response to my alarm so I shut up and sent my sense out. He moved south at a good speed already a block away. Damn it. At the pace I moved he'd be back by the time I got to the truck.

Paul disappeared from my range as I neared the top of the stairs so I stopped looking for him. I needed all my attention to stagger down without falling. Near the bottom of the flight the bulge shifted, pointing straight out ahead of me and I cried out for Paul again as I doubled over to keep my skin from tearing.

Six first floor rooms. That was all I had to do, walk past six first floor rooms doubled over and clinging to the flimsy plastic tables and chairs outside each. I could do it, I thought. Paul would be back by then if he wasn't already running from our empty room to find me. After all my thoughts of running off, I wanted him when in trouble. Not the asshole Jack Roberts.

I looked up to see a man letting himself into a room down the other end of the building. He couldn't help me. Part of me thought I should call for help but I kept quiet.

Finally at the truck, I looked up to see our door closed. I hung on the passenger side mirror and tried the handle. It came up with an unsatisfying click. I let it go and sunk to the ground, having gone as far as I could.

"Anna!"

Paul's shout startled me and I looked up to see him gripping the railing above in both hands. It only took a moment for him to spot me on the frozen pavement beside the truck.

"Jesus," he cursed. "Don't move, Sugar."

I weakly nodded, frozen beyond reason. The rocky surface under me had been below zero for weeks. Paul's feet thumped along the balcony, echoing below before the high pitched clatter of him slipping down the stairs. I held my breath until his quieter boot falls reached me.

"Something's wrong," I whispered, one hand clutched my boys and the other rubbed at their scared lines. "They're stuck."

"Okay," Paul unlocked the truck and picked me up, putting me in it. He didn't bother with my seatbelt until he'd climbed in the driver's side and reached across me for it.

"They're scared," I breathed. "Hurts."

Paul nodded as he tossed the big truck into reverse and backed us out. He braked hard and we skidded backward as he put it in drive and stepped on the gas. We pulled right onto the main road, barely slowing as he dialled his cell.

"Ray," he said after a minute. "We need to talk."

He waited as I guessed Ray made sure Alina couldn't hear.

"I've recovered Anna. She's with me and I need a hospital. I don't know Elko."

After half a minute Paul gave the name of the hotel then did a U-turn and sped up in the other direction.

He slowed for a red and kept going as we passed a sign showing the way to the hospital.

"Love to Camille from both of us, Ray. I'll fill you in when we know what's what."

"Where's it hurt, Sugar?" Paul asked as his phone went into his pocket.

"Here," I breathed as I put my hands over their lines. "They're scared, I think. I feel it as pain."

"Alright."

We turned into the hospital parking lot, following the signs to Emergency. I took Paul's hand and put it over the bulge.

"I think he's stuck sideways and they're distressed," I whispered as he took his hand off to put the truck into park.

"Wait," Paul ordered. He locked himself down. He put too much on himself the past few days and taking me to the hospital made him withdraw further. Function only, falling back on automatic responses before the feelings became too much.

I could only watch and remembered when I was the buffer; the one thing he could cling to when there was real shit in his life.

As Paul got my feet on the ground someone yelled for him.

"Major Richards?" It was a man in a lab coat pushing a wheelchair, the tails of his coat flapping along behind him. "We got a call you were bringing someone in."

I couldn't straighten up very much but it was enough for him to see my stomach.

"Labour and delivery?" he asked. "I was led to believe it was an injury."

"Twins," Paul said and helped me sit. "She's not in labour."

Paul told him I thought one of the boys was stuck sideways and I was quite uncomfortable as they wheeled me into the bright and noisy lobby. I imagined Alina working in a place like this and wished she'd come around the corner and look after me.

"How many weeks, Missus Richards?"

"Twenty-eight," I breathed. The more stressed the boys became the more my chest hurt. I pressed both hands there and Paul added his. I knew he didn't do so well when I needed something he couldn't help with. "Hurts."

"I need you to relax," the doctor said as he felt my stomach. He nodded to the nurse. "Get obstetrics. Little guy needs a hand getting his head down.

"Were they both breech or just this one?"

Damn, I didn't know. They could have been playing basketball in there and Targuer wouldn't have said a word.

"Just one," I lied. He nodded like it was the answer he expected.

Paul excused himself while they checked me out. By the time he returned his guns were gone. I was on fluids and the obstetrician and emergency doctors were trying to get me to stay flat long enough to help. Paul took my hands in one of his and rested the other on my sweaty forehead.

"Try and relax, Anna," one of them resorted to my first name.

"Relax," Paul echoed in my ear. I wrapped my arms around his head and let my legs go limp. The doctors were quick and as I let out a yelp, it was over. My stomach felt normal but the pain in my chest spiked. I cried on his shoulder as they checked the boys were head down and listened to their hearts.

"I'm admitting your wife tonight, Major," the obstetrician said. "Both babies have elevated heart rates. They'll go back to normal but I think your wife will feel better if we keep an eye on her for a few hours."

Paul agreed.

Chapter 29

Settled in my room, I waited as Paul excused himself to check in with Ray. I felt more ashamed than ever. Ray would never be angry with me but I could imagine Paul's embarrassment with sharing my news. He slept sitting up in my room, listening to the monitors scratch the boys' heartbeats onto paper.

After I was discharged, I talked Paul in to driving us the full ten hours to the compound in spite of Cora's limits on travel. Both nights alone had been disasters. We stopped every couple of hours to stretch our legs but otherwise we kept our thoughts to ourselves.

It was dark when we reached the compound gate. The last time I'd been there Soros waited to greet us and Jack turned the car around and we fled. The drive there with Jack had been long and unpleasant on account of our constant bickering. I should have known then I rubbed him the wrong way but asking him to be my lover ultimately exposed his lies and freed me.

Paul spoke casually to a guard I didn't know, his tone light and he laughed like he was happy to be home but he shut down again as soon as the window was up.

"Paul?"

"Mm?"

"I'm sorry," I tried apologizing again. He only shook his head.

As we took the corner onto the main road, Paul turned off the headlights and stopped at the second cabin on the right, Two East.

"We're here," he said.

"Where?" I stared into the dark and couldn't see the house.

"Here," his door slammed and he walked around the front of the truck, lit briefly by the flashing park lights.

"What about the house?" I demanded as soon as my door opened.

"I can't stay there anymore," he looked down as he held my hand and I moved closer to the edge of the seat.

"I'm sorry, Paul," I said again. I understood why he couldn't stay there without his wife and daughter. Alone. More than once I'd argued with him about keeping the carpet clean for Camille and imagined all the dirty boots marking it up as our apartment was repurposed for whatever else. He chewed the corner of his mouth and helped me down.

"Anna!"

I looked up the road to see someone running full out toward us. Paul took his glasses off and rubbed his tired eyes.

"Josh?"

Paul stepped aside as his little brother nearly knocked me off my feet.

"Oh, Jesus," Joshua gasped as he got me in a bear hug. I stuck my butt out so my stomach wasn't squished. He held my face in his hands. His tears shone in the dim light but his smile was a mile wide. I couldn't help but smile back until I felt Paul's arm around my waist. "When the Colonel called Paul I hoped it was news about you but he left before I could ask."

"It's me, Josh," I whispered.

Paul tightened his hold on me. "I didn't know Sig had her until I got there. She'd been there a while. He had to keep it quiet so nothing else would be compromised. Called me as soon as he could."

"Yeah, wow," Joshua whispered as he got an arm between Paul and me to hug me again. This time he stopped short as he noticed my belly. "Paul?"

"Yeah, Josh," Paul answered. He sounded tired, too tired to explain to Joshua.

"Congratulations, big brother," Joshua exclaimed. "Damn I didn't know, I mean kidnapped and pregnant I mean... shit!"

Joshua crushed us together and I realized he was the only one who'd see me the way I saw myself. I needed someone to call me out. Not for the bargain but for being so stupid for not seeing through Jack Roberts before it was too late. Joshua would never know about the bargain so having him lose it with me for being with Jack again under any circumstances would have to be enough.

"Twin boys, Josh," I said as I held my head high hoping to look arrogant. "But they're not Paul's."

Paul turned to get his shoulder between Joshua and me. Joshua's shocked look was a good start.

"The assault," he whispered like he could fall apart. The word 'twin' had gone right by him. All he heard was 'not Paul's.'

"Oh, man. Whatever you two need. That's gotta be tough," he stammered as his eyes bounced back and forth between Paul and me. His pain for us was obvious.

"It wasn't the rape, Josh," I challenged. "The boys are Jack Roberts.'"

"Son of a *bitch*," Joshua yelled and rubbed his hands on his face like my words dirtied him. "Dear God."

"I went to him, Joshua. It was my choice," I hissed then I shook free of Paul and slammed my palm into Joshua's shoulder as hard as I could. My wrist flexed with complaint but I didn't care. I'd talked Joshua out of being suspicious of Jack and me once and now he looked like a fool and I'd hit him. In an instant his eyes went from smoulder to closer to out of control than I'd ever seen either Paul or Joshua. Or any man for that matter. I'd turned his strong feelings for me into something ugly.

"Stand down, Josh," Paul warned as he shoved his way between us.

"Say it, big brother," I dared Joshua. "I don't want there to be any misunderstandings."

"Stinking whore," he breathed. Joshua turned his shoulder to Paul and got his fists up. I didn't see that coming. Joshua wanted to find out if Paul thought my honour was worth anything at all.

"Back off, Lieutenant," Paul ordered. "We don't judge. She did what she had to and came home alive."

"Dirty slut," Joshua spat. He was so angry with Paul for sticking up for me he was past listening. "Fucking easy lying bitch. I wouldn't have screwed Jack Roberts no matter what they did to me!"

"Screw you, Josh!" I goaded like I didn't give a shit what he thought.

Joshua didn't go for me. He went for Paul but Paul was faster, pushing me back a step as he charged, tackling his younger brother. I cried out, unable to tell which was which. Fists flew though it seemed more a wrestling match; each seeking dominance while avoiding leaving any visible marks to give away their confrontation.

The first fight I'd ever seen was between Kenny and his older brother. I'd run away screaming and hid from them for weeks in spite of the fact they laughed together within the hour. I wanted to run from this too but instead I begged them to stop.

Joshua squeezed out from under Paul and jumped on him and though Paul nearly rolled out of harm's way he groaned, exhaling under his brother's partial weight. Paul pulled himself clear and swung his foot around, catching Joshua in the ribs and sending him rolling.

Both were quickly on their feet, shoulders locked, each desperate to kick the feet out from under the other to get the advantage. Paul feinted a kick while allowing Joshua to push him backward. While Joshua's attention was on their feet, Paul leveraged himself against Joshua's shoulder, twisting him until his own weight collapsed him face down in the snow.

Paul was on him before he could roll off his stomach. This wasn't a movie fight or anything the military trained them for where the goal was to defeat the opponent. They fought without any real intent to injure.

Paul knew just how to effectively hold Joshua down without hurting him. I realized they weren't fighting against each other. They struggled together seeking something more important.

Unanimity.

Unanimity and reaffirmation of family.

"You're a fucking fool, Paul," Joshua grunted.

Paul straddled Joshua and picked him up by his shoulders and slammed him back on the ground. Joshua had his hands out and wasn't hurt. Both men sounded exhausted.

"She survived, Josh," Paul panted. "My wife survived six months of hell and came home to me."

Joshua shuddered with a sigh of consent. I leaned heavily on the side of the truck.

"And those boys are hers. I love my wife and I love her sons. They are as welcome in my life as my own daughter."

Joshua made a half-hearted attempt to push Paul off before Paul rolled away on his own, lying on his back on the frozen road next to his prone brother.

"Don't you dare speak to her like that again, Josh," Paul warned though the fight was clearly gone from him as well. "Your little sister is the bravest person you'll ever meet."

Paul turned his head to me and I curled up, sobbing on the ground. Nobody came out to see the fight or stop it and I was grateful. I wasn't proud of my role but a round with each other seemed to be something they both needed.

"I'm sorry," I whispered to them both. "So, so, sorry."

Paul crawled over and held me while I cried. Joshua knelt, his back to us before standing up and walking away.

Chapter 30

"You know how Jack and I learned we could spend a bit of time apart?"

Paul undressed for bed. He'd excused himself to catch up on everything he'd missed during the past few days while I took a bath but now he was back.

"No, Sugar," he said, still drained from the fight I started between him and his brother.

"I took a bun," I said, cupping my palms together like I held one. "We'd been there three months and allowed to eat with the other two women for a few weeks. That night Mister Davis and Mister Carter ate with us. I hadn't met them and both were back from a couple of runs on this place. I didn't know the extra buns were for them. Usually one of the men served us but that night was different because Davis and Carter were there."

"Mm hm," Paul nodded and disappeared into the bathroom, leaving the door half open.

"I started to stick my thumbs in it to tear it in half," I loudly continued so Paul would hear me over the running water. "But Carter made a sound so I glanced at him. Just from the look on his face I knew I was in trouble. The other women didn't notice, they were yakking on about Karen's ultrasound but Jack and I did. I didn't eat it."

Paul stepped out of the bathroom in nothing but his boxers. I moved a little closer to my edge of the bed as he turned out the light.

"We'd been back in our room about half an hour when Soros came in with Carter and Harvey. They grabbed Jack and tried to pull him away and I begged for them not to and I was so sorry about the bun but they knocked me down and did anyway. I stayed on the floor, expecting the pain to start but it didn't so I started counting. I made it to two hundred before his sons started demanding him then I did scream. I screamed until I passed out."

"I'm sorry, Sugar," he said.

"I woke up in the bed with Jack's hand up in my shirt to calm the boys," I said. "He had three freshly sewn up cuts high on his right thigh near the track marks. I never took another thing which hadn't been put in front of me."

I turned my back to him, deciding how badly I wanted to be left alone. At least in the hotel room he was up half the night. Then the hospital. The whole trip was surreal. What seemed to be the marital bed was something I wasn't ready for.

"Look," he said as he tried to curl up behind me, his hand on my hip as his lips brushed my ear. Cinnamony toothpaste made my stomach roll with nausea. Lingering morning sickness made sure cinnamon and I still didn't get along. "Whatever you need to talk about I'm here, okay?"

"I can't do this, Paul," I blurted out as I pushed myself up and got on my feet.

"Do what?"

"Pretend I didn't spend half a year cheating on you."

"Anna," he said. Blankets rustled as he sat. "Is that what it felt like at the time?"

"No," I whispered.

"Then listen, please? I told you and I told Joshua. We don't judge what a person does to survive. We don't and I mean it. Joshua understands with the men and he will with you."

"That's such crap," I muttered.

"Pardon?"

I decided to go up to the house and sleep in our old room. This wasn't our bed and I didn't care what the rest of the house was used for. I wanted to be near Camille's things and not a couple of hundred feet away. My coat hung in the closet at the foot of the bed so I got it out and pulled it on.

"I could believe those words from you to a buddy but not from you to your wife."

My night table went over, striking the wall so hard I felt it where I leaned on the other side of the cabin.

"I love you, Sugar," Paul evenly said. "I forgive you. I want to be everything you need."

"I don't doubt your love or your forgiveness. But how could you give me anything I need when I don't even know myself?"

"We'll figure it out together," he said. I heard the mattress as he stood and stopped just in front of me. "Take your coat off. If this is too soon I'll give you your space."

He reached for the coat and pushed it off my shoulders and I let him slide it down my arms. It softly landed on the floor next to me, tipping sideways against my leg.

"So that's it?" I asked. "We're all good now?"

Paul reached past and lean against the wall. I didn't turn, hoping to avoid the cinnamon.

"No," he answered. "We're a long way from good."

I let my head tip to the side and rest against his arm. He sighed and put his other hand on my shoulder.

"My wife has been a P.O.W. for six months. I found out a few days ago she'd been lied to, believed me dead and has been sleeping with the father of her twins. I figure she fell in love with him because I get the distinct impression she wants to keep her distance from me. I'm grown-up enough to understand why all that happened but she doubts my commitment to her and our marriage.

"Do you agree? Is that about what I have to work with?"

"I don't doubt, Paul," I whispered. "I don't deserve."

"Just... honesty. Please, Sugar? We're a long way apart right now."

I nodded. He didn't move.

"Did you forgive yourself?" I asked.

"For not saving you when I had the chance?"

"No," I answered. It was cards on the table time. We had more to work out than Jack and me. "When Denis called you to say I'd gone home. Last February after I took off. Was it after the third time you slept with her or before the fourth?"

Silence.

"Marie told me when Jack and I dropped off Dana and Wendy with the children. I forgave you both right away. I'd run out on you and threatened to kill her. Either I'd be crazy forever or sane with no memory of her or you or me when I got to the other side. I told her I loved you both because I was comforted by everything you did to get me through the inheritance. I decided to be a grown-up about you and your second."

"Okay," he said.

"Then she said you went back to her the next night and again two nights later. So was it after the third time or before the fourth that you came to me. I've been up front with you. You're not going anywhere with Marie unresolved."

Paul dropped his arm then went to the desk chair and pulled his jeans on.

"Is it none of your mere mate's business oh great male patriarch?" I asked, voice laden in angry sarcasm. "I understood how Jack couldn't let go. I believe your new attachment to her lingered for a time too. Are you ready to accept my forgiveness?"

Paul pulled his flannel shirt over his shoulders and started on the buttons.

"Before the fourth," he said.

"It took a long time to forgive you, Paul. All I could think was if anyone found out it was unforgivable. They would take you away from Camille and me. I took Jack to Reno. Thought about using him to get back at you but instead I ran off. I picked up a stranger and promised him sex if he got me drunk because a self-destructive fight would cool me down enough to talk to you about it. Jack found me beating the guy up in an alley and I never got the chance to talk to you until now.

"I didn't go to Jack to get back at you."

"I know," Paul said. He pulled his coat on.

"Please can I go to the house with you?" I sniffed.

I felt him shake his head as he got his arms around me.

"Am I just trading one cell for another?" I demanded. My aggravation irritated the boys and I rubbed my hand on my chest to soothe them. It was clear this cabin was my place now. "You don't have her locked in the next cell do you? Or in the house?"

Paul let me go.

"I'm not afraid of being locked up!" I shouted as he walked out, slamming the door.

I ran into the bathroom and grabbed the red tube then yanked the door open and threw it at Paul's back. He was at the end of the walk, turning right to the house. The throw went bad and it landed at his feet. He glanced down at it and kept going.

"I'm not afraid," I yelled again.

The door of the cabin across the road opened up and a man stepped out, lit briefly from behind before his door closed.

"But I'm afraid to be alone," I whispered, afraid the man overheard. Paul walked away, hidden in a few seconds by the dark and the trees between my cabin and the road. I turned my head, hoping to see him through the snow laden low branches.

"Commander?" I jumped when I saw the man was closer. "It's Doctor Flood. Let's go inside, you're shivering."

"Yes, Doctor Flood," I answered and stepped in though I strained to see Paul. I kept my sense to myself, comforted with ignorance when it came to who was around me. The cabin was as cold inside as it had been outside, still only lit by the glow from the wood stove. The desk light came on and I stood uselessly near the door as Flood checked the fire and added a small piece of wood. I didn't realize how comfortable I was with Paul until confronted by a stranger in my strange room. Paul made the room feel safe in spite of how much I wanted to crawl away and hide from him.

"I received your medical file from Colonel Iverson yesterday morning. I was going to see you tomorrow to make sure I have all the details of your care and get some baseline stats on your health. I didn't expect you to arrive until then," he explained. Snow melted in his short salt and pepper hair and he ran his hand over it presumably to control where the melt ran then he dried his glasses on a tissue from the desk. "But I heard your raised voice and thought I'd at least check in with you now."

"You heard?" I asked. The last thing I wanted was to draw attention to myself. It was silly to think since nobody ran out to Paul and Joshua's fight it meant nobody heard. Anyone who'd heard the preamble would have had the respect to realize it was private.

Flood gestured. His arm indicated the entire compound. "I heard."

"Yes, Doctor Flood," I answered. His forehead lined with what looked to be concern. I tried to relax my crossed arms but found myself scratching at my chest so I grabbed my elbows again.

"Russell," he reminded. "It's Russell."

"I..." I paused, entirely uncomfortable addressing the man without using a title. "I'm sorry I disturbed you. Tomorrow is fine. I'm tired from travelling and spent last night in the hospital and need my rest please."

Flood raised his eyebrows.

"Baby B isn't breech anymore," I said, wheeling my hands around. "Cramping so Paul took me in. We got there late so they kept me overnight."

"Ah, is this good news?"

"I don't understand Doctor... Russell," I answered. Of course it was good he wasn't breech though it was early enough he could still change his mind.

"I meant the pregnancy. Paul didn't mention your condition until he called me from the safe house where he picked you up. Is it a result of the assault?"

I shook my head.

"Good news then," he smiled.

"We've got some things to work out," I trailed off before I dropped my eyes. "Lieutenant Roberts is their father."

"Your companion the past few months," he stated. I nodded and chewed my bottom lip. "I understand he's back in the field."

"There's no future for me there," I said. "He made that clear. Not that I ever thought there was but I thought he'd have some interest in them."

I gulped air and Flood guided me to the bed to sit. He rolled the desk chair over and sat facing me.

"I stressed to Colonel Iverson how important it was for you and Lieutenant Roberts to return together. Coming home can be hard enough but I understand now why he said you'd come home alone. I understand if you're worried about him."

I let out a rude laugh. "Nobody needs to look out for him. That man only looks out for himself."

"Anna," Flood took one of my hands and held it, rolling the chair a little closer. "I've spent many of my years helping soldiers return from the field, whatever the circumstances of their service. I understand the confusion, things which were so familiar and comforting become frightening. I understand you had to be someone else to survive there, perhaps for so long you've forgotten how to be anyone else. Guilt maybe for wanting to go back or protect your captors even though they no longer have any hold over you.

"Your body is back and I know it feels like your mind is still trying to find its way home. I'm your guide through your emotional recovery. As long as I'm doing you some good and you're physically well you'll remain in my care, okay?"

"Okay," I agreed. He didn't know a thing; so caught up in the isolation of the compound, the military. I sighed and nodded again.

"But not tomorrow," he said. "Rest and settle in. I'll get your file from last night and bother you as little as possible in the morning. Expect to see me more the day after. Your recovery is between you and me, Anna. Unless there is danger to you or someone else, anything we talk about remains private."

I thanked Flood after he adjusted the wood stove one last time and locked the door behind him. The snow stopped falling and I peeked past the curtain and watched him as he made his way across the road, along the walk to his cabin and disappeared through his door.

"I don't know what you can do for me, Doctor Flood," I said out loud. "Your world isn't full of men who think nothing of taking a finger or a hand."

I pushed the chair back to Paul's computer. There was no password on it. I didn't expect one. Paul still considered the compound secure enough it didn't need one. He never kept anything confidential on it anyway. I retrieved Wendy's email address from my coat pocket and went to gmail and created one for myself. Just a brief message to let her know I was in the compound and about the hospital. That I'd provoked Joshua and Paul into a fist fight before I pissed Paul off and he walked out of the cabin. That he wouldn't let me in the house. I sent it and found my toiletry bag and Anton's old blue shirt which I put on before I brushed my teeth with the peppermint toothpaste she'd packed for me. Then I sent her a second quick note to say cinnamon made me sick and to thank her for the little bottle of her perfume she'd put in my bag. I told her I loved her.

When I looked around the room, nothing looked familiar. I stepped around the bed where the night table and lamp still lay on the floor. Flood hadn't seen them or I supposed they'd be righted. It was bad enough I was stuck in here, insulted by someone else's order. I didn't look too closely at what was on the hangers and pulled off a shirt. I held it to my nose and inhaled before I dropped it on the ground. Then another and another. Before I knew it I shouted with each one I pulled free and threw behind me.

I shook as I caught my breath then went in the bathroom and starting with the shower curtain, I went to work.

Chapter 31

Paul's muffled alarm clock woke me from its spot under the mattress. I'd only pushed it half off the bed while I protested my living conditions the night before because there wasn't enough floor space for the whole thing. The two front windows on either side of the door were bare. One set of curtains had obediently came off its bar but the other held on, taking the bar with it. The alarm meant it was five am. I left it buzzing, too sore from my prison riot to pull the mattress up and look for it. When I got to the bathroom I realized I could have just unplugged it. Unrolled toilet paper and broken plastic shower curtain rings littered the floor. The curtain itself was heaped behind the open bathroom door. I washed up and brushed my teeth as I decided what my next move would be. I was certain someone would be by to either bring me breakfast or take me to the house by five forty-five. A tray of something made cold and rubbery by the long walk from the house was most likely.

I stepped from the bathroom and surveyed the damage in the light cast by the computer monitor. All the drawers in the dresser had been emptied as had the ones in the desk. I left the computer intact since I still needed it. Paul had several pictures of a much bigger Camille than I remembered and I slept with them on the part of the mattress resting on the floor.

The room still felt a little warm but the wood stove was cool enough to touch. I let it be as I dressed, keeping Anton's shirt on and pulling up the pants I wore for the past three days. They needed a wash but everything else was in my bag under the mattress. My boots waited on the rubber tray by the door so I made my way over and slipped my bare feet in. Then my coat which I had the sense to toss in the same direction as my boots.

Joshua and another man went down the main road lit by what passed for a streetlight. The bare bulb in a metal cage hung from a branch. I couldn't remember if it received power from this cabin or the one beside it. Joshua looked in my direction so I stepped back although the darkness inside kept me out of sight. I gave them a minute to move further along before I slipped out, leaving the door wide open. The cabin would be quite unliveable by the time Paul tried to put me back in considering the cold and the mess. I'd do the same thing to the next one when my arms and back stopped aching.

When I got to the road, I turned north and trudged through the deeper snow keeping as far to the side as I could. Only one other streetlight illuminated the road to the house and the porch lights were usually sufficient to light the little intersection where the road formed a T leading to the warehouses and the garage at either end. Nothing lit the porch this morning. I hustled under the second light.

"Anna?" Paul called from behind me. I ignored him and kept going, peering into the dark to make out the shape of the house but I couldn't. Even with the porch light off, the common room, dining room and apartment windows shouldn't be dark.

"Anna, wait," Paul tried but I sped up. Before I knew it I stumbled on the first step. My hand took the railing in the dark and found snow. It wobbled under my grip as I forced my bare fingers through frozen snow and grabbed on. Paul's boot steps weren't far behind as I found a stair under the snow and took another step. There shouldn't be any snow on the steps or the handrail. I stopped, picking up a hint of wet smoke smell.

"Damn it," he muttered as he took my elbow. "Step down. It's not safe."

Snow covered the branches in the distance. No house sat between me and the forested back yard.

"Where's my house, Paul?" My voice shook and I started to cry. "Where's my God damned house?"

I let him lead me down the two steps I'd taken and he turned me to him, tipping my face up to his and putting his lips on my forehead.

"Where's my house?" I shouted, getting my hand in my coat and clutching at the front of Anton's shirt as I wailed. Paul held me tight, one hand around my back as far as he could considering my big stomach. The other held my head to his shoulder.

"After they took you I was in the hospital for a few days," he fit in between my loud sobs. "Ross had everyone back here by the time I came home. Soros and his men lit the house up before they left. We're lucky it was all we lost. The explosions when the armory went up knocked the last of it flat."

"But I just wanted Camille," I gasped, trying to keep my noise down. "Camille..."

"I know, Sugar," he whispered as he pulled me away. "It's all gone."

I understood why he couldn't live there anymore. I'd thought memories of Camille and me kept him away. Memories were all he had left.

Joshua silently joined us under the second street light, his arm around me with Paul's and a hand under my elbow. The deep snow on the side of the road hadn't been slippery but the ploughed part was. I cried into my hand as they led me back to the cabin. Joshua let me go and he stepped into the black room.

"Damn it," he muttered as he stumbled on the mattress and then a chair thudded over. "What happened in here?"

Paul's flashlight came on and scanned the room, illuminating his brother straightening his coat.

"It was like this when I woke up," I said. I took a couple of steady breaths before I started weeping again. Paul sighed as Joshua pushed the mattress up onto the box spring.

"Josh, can you get the fire going?"

Joshua turned his flashlight on and got down to the floor to find the firewood I'd thrown around. Paul let me go and straightened the bottom sheet before he pulled the rest of the bedding in to place. He put the pictures back on his desk and turned the monitor back on.

"Wendy sent you a message."

I took my boots off though I kept my coat on as I sat on the bed.

"What did she say?" I asked. His wooden chair made my back hurt just looking at it.

"Little One, you're welcome for the perfume," Paul read. "Remember everyone loves you, Wendy."

"Why's she call you Little One?" Joshua asked. He sounded hesitant to speak to me after what he'd called me the night before.

"She thinks she's taller," I said.

"She is," he said. I quietly growled and wiped my eyes on my sleeve.

"Does your back hurt?" Paul asked.

"No," I snapped, surprised by how sullen and hurt I sounded. I slipped my legs under the blanket and covered the gap in the front of Anton's shirt before I took my jacket off and pulled the blanket up to my chin.

Joshua was satisfied with the fire and by then Paul had the table and lamp standing. When the light came on, the rest of my devastation was apparent. Clothes and drawers covered the floor and the towel rack from the bathroom was jammed through the drywall beside the bathroom door and into the closet. Joshua looked in the bathroom as Paul started to collect his clothes.

"You're gonna need toilet paper, shampoo and maybe toothpaste, Paul," Joshua said. "I can't see it."

Yeah, I'd made a right mess with the shampoo as well, all over the small window, the mirror, toilet, tub and counters. I avoided the floor because a pregnant woman didn't want to slip although I'd left plenty of other obstacles.

"Jesus, Anna," Paul said, exasperated. His first comment on what I'd done to his room.

"You had coffee, Paul?" Joshua asked. Paul looked at the ceiling as he shook his head. "I'll get us both one and grab the supplies you need, give you a hand putting this back together."

Joshua glanced at me as he carefully walked to the door. I looked away and turned my head in the direction of the house. My lips curled, encouraging a high pitched whine from my throat and a fresh batch of tears.

"Why are you acting like a child?" Paul asked. I shook my head as he pulled his coat off and sat on the bed beside me.

"I just wanted to go home," I sobbed.

He didn't say anything. I let him come closer and hold on. He didn't smell like cinnamon this morning.

"How could you keep that from me?" I demanded. "How could you live here so close to that?"

"That," he replied. His voice broke. "That is all I had left of you. When I didn't have to go out in the field I was back and forth between that and Camille. God, Anna. I look at her and I see you. Just as willful and beautiful. Everything you are, so much like you.

"I wasn't ready to hurt you any more. I see how much pain you carry and I wasn't sure I had enough left last night to get you through seeing it."

Paul cradled me to him and I pushed my chest to his, pressing our lines as close together as I could. I wouldn't take any comfort from it since my connection to him was gone but he would. Instead, I concentrated on my feelings for him as he relaxed with a small shiver.

"This is going to sound terrible," he whispered. "But I forgot."

"Pardon?"

"Marie," he answered after a moment. He was so damn private about his past lives I realized this may be personal to him as well even though he'd never hesitated to explain things to me or talk about other men's seconds. "After I went back to you I simply forgot. I didn't think about her at all until Jack showed up then I came home and you'd already left with Ray and the women. Even then, as long as she had what she needed she was nothing more than Keith's widow. I'm bound to you, Sugar, to our daughter. Marie and Adam are important if they need something but otherwise she's nothing."

"It was like that with Jack," I said. "Unless someone brought it up he was nothing more than an ally. I considered him a friend at least; sometimes more a brother like Ray or Josh than anything else. I felt so ashamed if anyone brought up the inheritance."

We sat close for a while until there was a quiet knock at the door. I sat up straighter as Joshua let himself in. Paul and I watched each others eyes and I heard the familiar sound of heavy tools shifting in the toolbox as Joshua put it on the floor by the desk.

"Here, Paul," he said as he stepped from the bathroom and passed Paul his coffee. "Sorry, I'll come back later and help sort this place out. I'm sorry I upset you, Anna."

"Josh, wait," I said and he paused. I dropped my eyes and watched Paul pop open the top of his travel mug and put it to his lips. "The night they caught Jack and me was so bad, Josh."

I held my scarred palm to him.

"This was from the stove," I said and waited until he took it. He ran his thumb over the deepest scars and glanced at Paul before letting it go. "Jack was cut up. They said we'd be dead in the morning. Executions at dawn or some unimaginative shit. I was so scared. We were both in so much pain. We were shut in a room together.

"This happened," I said as I stared at my belly. "But they didn't kill us. Paul came for me a few days later. There was a gunshot. Jack said he saw Paul's body when they took us away. They all said he was dead. I trusted Jack. I believed him. But he lied to me like they did. After four months locked away together I thought I loved him and went to his bed again.

"Anna, you don't have to say this," Joshua said but his voice ground rough with emotion and I shook my head, cutting him off. Paul took my hand.

"When we got away he couldn't leave me fast enough. Nobody was more ashamed or surprised than me a few days ago to see Paul alive.

"I never wanted to hurt him."

"Paul is right, Little Sister," Joshua said and kissed my cheek. "They're yours."

He made a hasty retreat out the door. A burst of cold fresh air took his place with us in the cabin. Paul sipped his coffee and we waited for the room to warm.

"I want to stay here alone," I said. "Or put me in another cabin if you want. I love my husband with all my heart but every minute I stay connected to that son of a bitch is another minute of betrayal and I don't belong in his room right now."

Paul cupped his palm around my cheek and brought his lips close, trying to turn me to him.

"Anna, please?" He asked. "You know I don't see it like that."

I pressed my cheek to his hand and turned away.

"You've been hurt enough," I said. I put my hands on the mattress behind me and leaned on them to take the pressure off my back. "I need some more sleep."

Paul got up and put his mug on the desk. When he turned around I already had my head on the pillow. He offered me a small picture of Camille in a pink shirt with a lace collar. Wavy brown hair in a pony-tail like a fountain spouted from the top of her head. There was a profile of a reddish-brown haired little boy next to her, judging by the blue and red striped shirt, the back of his head and the edge of his ear. I'd noticed the boy the night before.

"Camille and Julian," I said, hoping Alina and Ray hadn't changed their minds about his name.

"Anthony," Paul said. I looked at him in surprise thinking they had. "Dana and Virtue named him after you, or as close as they could to naming a little boy Anna. Everyone loves you, Sugar, even your husband."

I smiled for a moment in spite of how much worse it made me feel for him then I wrapped my arms around the picture and closed my eyes.

Chapter 32

I woke to a quiet knock on the door. The bed shifted as Paul stood to answer it and the hollow thud of boots stomping the big front step entered unbidden. I'd fallen asleep to the quiet noises the hangers made as Paul re-hung his clothes. The room was bright in spite of the wood panelling which afflicted the top floor of the house before we put in the apartment. Before it all burnt up while I knocked on Jack's bedroom door to fulfill my deal with Soros. Paul hadn't put the curtains back up to spare me the noise of the drill.

"Major," Flood said. "Good morning."

"Hey, Doc," Paul answered.

"I didn't see you at breakfast and hoped to catch your wife with an empty stomach."

"Sure thing, Russell, but she's still sleeping."

"I'm awake," I cheerfully called, hoping not to stir things up any more than I already had. Flood eyed the bare windows as I sat. I remembered he wanted to see me about medical stuff today which seemed harmless enough. "If you want me to pee in anything now's a good time."

My stomach rumbled as I stood and I tightened my muscles to try and keep it quiet.

"How are you feeling today, Anna?"

"I'm well thank you, Doctor Flood," I answered and saw his brows push together just a bit.

"It's Russell," he corrected me as he had the night before.

"I'm aware," I said and held out my hand. He returned my stare for a moment before glancing at Paul and handing me a specimen bottle. "I'll leave it on the counter."

Once I filled it in the bathroom, I started the shower. The curtain had been hung up and I'd slept through the room being cleaned. Folded towels sat on the counter. I peeked out the door.

"Paul, can you toss me in something to wear from my bag please?"

I didn't wait for an answer and stepped in the shower. Once I dried and dressed, I stepped out. Paul sat on the bed and Flood occupied the chair. I'd hoped he'd give up and leave but he stuck around and had other plans. A bottle of orange soda waited on the desk.

"I had the three hour glucose weeks ago," I complained. "It's fine."

"I understand Colonel Iverson had a local physician assess you," Flood said. "I have those records but no routine screening."

That sounded like Cora. More concerned with any repercussions from the fall. She said the health of the boys' lines spoke more than anything else regarding how they were doing and was satisfied with my word I received regular care. She didn't insist on redoing everything.

"I was transported regularly to an obstetrician," I explained.

Flood pulled out his pen ready and held it over an open file on Paul's desk. "Name?"

Name indeed. I crossed my arms and shut up.

"Are you concerned you or Lieutenant Roberts may be in further danger if you provide his name?"

"No," I answered but I was. Cold stress built and I absently scratched at my chest above the buttons on my shirt. Flood noticed so I held my hand still.

"Paul told me Roberts was injured if you stepped out of line."

"I... no, that's not really true, Doctor Flood." Scratch, scratch. Not quite true. I never stepped out of line but ignorance of the rules was certainly no excuse. I tried to give Paul a stern look but only conveyed fear. He told out of concern without understanding how naked I would feel and how unlikely I was to share anything else with him.

"Perhaps I misunderstood. Look, Anna. You have a choice. If you won't tell me the name of the doctor you were seeing then I need to fill in the gaps in your care."

Scratch, scratch, scratch. My skin stung and I knew I scratched too hard but couldn't stop. I looked at the bottle then at Paul.

"What do I do?"

I felt trapped between betraying Doctor Targuer and inconveniencing Doctor Flood. Both men who'd been introduced to me by title.

"Drink," Paul said as he pulled my hand from my chest. There was fresh blood under my nails so he led me to the bathroom. I breathed through my nose far too quickly and heard myself whimpering as dizziness set in. "Sshhh, okay?"

I closed my eyes and tried to calm down. Water ran and I felt a cold cloth on my scratched skin. Paul put my left hand over top. "Hold that, Sugar."

Paul washed my bloody fingers. Concern shaped his brow as he dried my hand. As soon as he let it go, I put it over top of the other one. There was a hiss as Flood cracked the soda bottle and poured it in a glass. Paul sat me at the desk and Flood took my arm.

"You remember how this works? I take some now, you drink it up then I keep drawing more over the next few hours."

"Yes, Doctor Flood," I whispered as Paul nodded in reassurance. When he was done I drank down the sickly sweet soda, instantly sorry I'd brushed my teeth after my shower. Flood set a timer and left it on the desk.

"Alright, Anna. You said last night Baby B isn't breech anymore so I'm guessing you had some scans?"

I nodded. Targuer had done them all himself.

"Any other concerns?"

I shook my head.

Flood went on with questions about their milestones. When I heard their hearts and felt them move. Paul stood near the bathroom door at first but as Flood continued, he sat near me then next to me, a hand around my waist then the other on my stomach. Shame and comfort fought, neither taking charge though both got stronger.

After Flood's first reminder his name was Russell he didn't remind me again and I continued to call him Doctor Flood. He pulled his chair closer when he put enough ink in my file and took my left hand, examining the burns without comment then he asked to see my tooth, or where it had been. He took the cloth from my chest and looked underneath it. Red smears marked its whiteness.

"A lot of scarring around the new ones," he observed. "Any idea why you've been doing this?"

I wondered what I should tell him. In truth, I tried to make a hole to let the pain out but it sounded more psychological than physical and wasn't such a bad idea but I didn't want Flood moving right in to examining my head. Telling him the boys' lines tore at mine when Jack wasn't touching me until I started screwing him wasn't such a bright idea either and would push Flood into my mental state even faster.

"Coping," I said.

"A couple appear to have been sutured."

"Yes, Doctor Flood."

He drew more blood with a promise to be back in half an hour and a second promise he'd be all done in time for me to join everyone for lunch. Paul dabbed at the cuts one last time, still sitting much too close.

"Coping?" he asked.

"What else could I tell him?" I shrugged.

"Sig explained why you hurt," he said. "But not why you don't hurt anymore."

I rubbed the heels of my palms over my eyes and settled for holding my mouth shut with one hand. He ran his fingers over the backs of mine then softly pulled my hand away. "Please tell me why," he whispered.

"The truth will never hurt you," I said and he nodded.

"You can live with the truth they're not yours," I continued. "I'm so sorry I lied to you the night I thought you died. Soros said if I could make you leave you'd be spared but you wouldn't go. Nothing happened when we got Dana. It was a few nights before you came to Jack's. The night they caught up to us like I told your brother."

He nodded again.

"You can be so damn thick and stubborn, Paul," I laughed trying to avoid his question with humour. He smiled as his eyes kept asking. "Every time I slept with Jack it cured me a bit more. When they found out I didn't need him anymore they hung him. Jack tried to break it off just before they took him away but I dodged and bashed my cheek on the dresser and pretended to flip out. When they dropped the floor, I grabbed him and took him away. I was hoping for somewhere safe and it turned out to be with Sig.

"If I hadn't asked him to be my lover we'd still be there, stuck together."

Paul looked down, not because he couldn't look at me but because he watched his hand on my stomach. It bounced once, then again.

Chapter 33

I replied to Wendy while Paul re-hung the curtains; told her everything. It was much easier to unload through a machine to her than it would ever be to tell Flood. And I didn't have to filter anything with Wendy like I did with Paul, Flood or anyone else. She knew exactly who and what I was and what I'd been through better than anyone other than me. I'd co-operate with Flood as much as my mood allowed and say what was needed to stay here. I didn't like the sound of 'remaining in his care' and didn't want to think about where he'd put me if he thought I wasn't doing well.

Paul hauled my laundry and the bedding out as I hit send, promising he'd have it all back to me by the end of the day. The sleeve of Anton's shirt waved sadly from the bottom of the armload as it disappeared out the door. It wasn't so much that it belonged to Anton which made me attached to it. The thin light blue flannel had become Jack's in a way and I wasn't sure if I needed it because I somehow won it from that asshole or if it was simply because other than the boys, it was all of him I had left. The first reason made me feel strong and victorious. The second co-dependent and weak.

Flood took blood twice more as I waited for lunch. I'd become used to boredom during the long months at Jack's Father's; finding simple satisfaction in peace and stillness and not getting anyone hurt. Flood promised an Army assigned obstetrician in Sacramento in a few days and Paul promised a bookstore when I timidly asked if there was anything to read. He said one of the men had an e-reader and offered to get me one so I could buy whatever I wanted without two hours of driving. I accepted because it sounded like he wanted me to have it to spare the driving more than he wanted me to choose.

"We've taken over two cabins for meals and a control room," Paul explained as he closed the cabin door behind us on the way to lunch. With Paul in this one there were three fewer for his men to share. At the end of the walk he paused.

"Lieutenant Wells," he called. "Welcome back, Kelly. How was work?"

"Kelly?" I asked as I turned.

"You mean Tucson and Santa Fe," she mumbled and to my astonishment, Ross kissed her. Then she said something that sounded like Denver as she waved.

"I didn't catch that last part," Paul tried not to laugh.

"Who is that?"

"Kelly Myers," Paul whispered. "She's a flight attendant. Ross found her a couple of months ago on our way back from the A.T.F. raid in Connecticut."

"Jesus, Paul. Do they need a rating of some sort?"

"Only if they don't keep the carrying on inside his cabin," he laughed as Ross grabbed her butt and let her go.

"Denver," she said and her eyes widened a bit at the sight of me.

Paul got his arm around my shoulder and she smiled, perfectly framing her chin and cheeks in the neat dark brown bob around her face. Found her, Paul said. Not met. And she was his age, mid-thirties, not mine or younger like the other women.

"She's family?" I asked.

"You tell me."

"Anna," Ross called as he sped up, dragging Kelly with him. "I heard you're back."

"May I read her?" I asked Paul as I smiled properly and waved to Ross.

"Of course," Paul answered like it was obvious so I let my sense out. She was family alright, connected to Ross both by their lines and the firm hold he had on her as they made their way across the icy road.

"You're nervous," Paul whispered into my hair as he pulled me a little closer. I resisted and made him move toward me. Visions of another fist fight came as I wondered what Ross had heard about Jack and me and if I'd given him reason to hate me again. Before I knew it though Ross had his arms around me, knocking Paul's free. I heard Kelly greet Paul and over Ross' shoulder I saw them hug.

"Paul told me everything," Ross whispered. I gratefully nodded and started to tear up again. "Anna, I want you to meet my girl, Kelly Myers."

"Paul's Anna," she exclaimed as she took my hand. "All I've seen are pictures and heard are stories."

"Nice to meet you, Miss Myers," I answered.

"Miss?" she laughed as Paul and Ross shook hands. "The only thing that would make me happier is if you carded me. It's nothing but Kelly."

"Okay, Kelly."

"I met your daughter a month ago when we were in Sacramento," she went on. "A-dorable. And my goodness but you're huge. Congratulations, Paul. I had no idea."

"Not Paul's," I stammered, madly blushing. He tried to get hold of me again but I shrugged him off not wanting to drag him into my private shame.

"Oh," Kelly looked as mortified as I felt inside. "Shit, now I've stepped in it with my old fashioned assumptions."

"It's okay, Kell," Ross reassured her. "Paul and Anna aren't planning a cover-up."

"I'm sorry," she said. "It's just you look ready to pop and only gone half a year so..."

"No, it's," I tried. "Twin boys."

"Ah," she said. "Count on me to say the wrong thing. Disaster mouth."

She laughed but Ross rolled his eyes and shrugged behind her where she couldn't see. Paul chuckled and I let him take my elbow.

"You know, Kelly?" I offered. "The more you talk, the more I like you." In spite of the lurching in my stomach as I placed my worry for Karen and Debbie on her I realized she was just a subordinate and she was safe here and I simply liked her. And her running mouth kept the attention off me.

"Really?" she deflated with relief. "Are you sure you're not related to your sister's man Ray? He said the same thing when I asked which of the grandfathers their boy took after because he doesn't look a thing like either of them."

I winced as she carried on.

"Your sister said she was pregnant with him before they met and they laughed it off but wow, I really could have embarrassed myself."

Disaster mouth, Ross' silent lips said. I ignored him and tried to explain about being away.

"I was—

"Wait," she held a palm to me and looked at the sky. Her other hand went on her stomach. I followed her gaze way up to try and see what she spotted. Her stomach rumbled as her eyebrows frowned and she pushed her lips from one side to the other.

"Is this going to be a long story because I haven't eaten since like three this morning or maybe yesterday. Not sure."

"Well, yes," I answered.

"Perfect. You sit with me," she said as she dragged me along, lowering her voice and putting her mouth to my ear. "I'm so grateful for some girl company 'cause nice as these guys are this place reeks of stuffy old boys' club like wandering into the pilot's lounge."

I kept my eye on the icy snow ruts. Paul took my hand and Ross got an arm around her.

"I know about twins," she said as Paul opened the door and led me inside. Kelly pulled me away to a deserted end of one of the two long tables and took my coat. I looked around and took inventory of faces: new and familiar. Absent.

"My girls are grown. I got a rough start myself. I hooked up with an older boy when I was fifteen. My folks were strung out most of the time and life at home sucked and Terry seemed like a good catch. His parents owned a trucking company with nearly thirty employees and their clean life was night and day different from mine but they liked me and didn't care where I was from. He was three years older and had a job. Or I thought he did, he was selling dope all over Portland."

Paul put plates down in front of us and went with Ross to sit with Joshua and Lieutenant Wight. I wasn't sure how Ross would feel about Kelly going on about her ex.

"Next thing I know I'm too sick for school and my folks are raising shit 'cause they think I'm drinking. Terry actually got a job when he found out I was pregnant but it was hard to keep away from his old gang. I moved in to his parents' basement with him. Two girls. I made it to twenty-nine weeks when I started haemorrhaging and they rushed me to the hospital. Couldn't pick up their heartbeats and I was close to not making it."

She shrugged and paused for breath and a few bites.

"I woke up from the C-section just fine and took my girls home two months later. Terry felt a lot of pressure to do better for us than working as an apprentice mechanic for his Dad so he started up dealing again. They were four months old when he was gunned down."

"Oh no," I exclaimed. I pictured her with a helpful or not ex on the other end and not picking up the pieces as a sixteen year old widow.

"Oh yeah," she answered. "But his parents have been great. They raised the girls and finished raising me until I could look after them myself. Got me through college. I never moved out of their basement and they take care of them when I'm out of town working. Without them I was headed down the same dark path that claimed my folks."

We ate for a few minutes, listening to the chat around us. I sighed and leaned my head on her shoulder after filling up far too fast in spite of not getting breakfast. She leaned her head on mine for a moment and I straightened up then she waved at Ross.

"So what's your long story?" she asked. "Paul just said you weren't here and he didn't know when you were coming home."

I glanced at Paul. He seemed lost in thought though the officers kept talking around him.

"I was in the field with one of Paul's Lieutenants," I started. "Everything went wrong so fast and I was isolated from them and was raped."

"Oh no," she whispered and looked at my stomach.

"I don't remember much after but I lost it and hurt some people," I pointed a finger like a gun and pulled it like a trigger. She whitened as I explained. "Sniper. Jack and I went into hiding. Stupid thing to be on the run when you've got history with the guy. I was hurt, scared. I just needed comfort and found it with Jack because Paul was off on assignment somewhere. He's their father. We were caught by the group we had the altercation with. Got away a couple of weeks ago and Jack decided he'd be happier without me."

"Shithead," Kelly muttered.

"Paul knows. He's still just glad to have me home but I really messed up."

She pushed her hair back behind her ears and we both looked at Paul. He watched us so I concentrated on my empty plate.

"Well, he doesn't seem the type to let you go no matter what you did. It's written all over him."

"Yeah," I admitted.

"Just makes you feel worse though."

I looked at her in surprise.

"Hey," she brightened. "You want to hear how I met Ross and got famous?"

Chapter 34

We moved to the cabin which served as the new common room. It looked almost identical to the old one except it wasn't across the hall from the kitchen. It was across the road. Maps of everything from the compound grounds to all of Northern California were aligned on the walls along with clipboards holding fans of well worn pages. The radios on the desk were new. The old ones and everything else in the house were either burned up or unusable.

"I swapped watch with Paul," Ross winked at Kelly. "I'll be around all night but I have to cover his watch now."

Kelly giggled as I groaned inside. That meant Paul would be around this afternoon instead of tonight when he wouldn't be in my cabin anyway. Ross took the semi-automatic from one of the last men on watch and hustled out to the gate. Paul took one of the big chairs by the sofa Kelly and I occupied.

"So?" I asked. I wasn't really dying to hear but the famous part had me curious.

"Well," she started. "I work for one of the big airlines out of Los Angeles. Mostly commuter flights: up, down, never too far from home or gone too long. With the girls starting college in September I've been taking all the overtime and extra work they'll throw my way and Dad... Terry's Dad had been laid up for a while with his back and had a surgery date coming. I hoped the extra cash would help us through while I took some time off to help out plus go toward school. Even if they go somewhere local I know Mom and Dad can't swing college for two. Economy, fuel prices: the trucking business has been hit pretty hard."

"So I got this long run of flights two months ago and we're taking off from LaGuardia on a trip straight home to LAX and one of the other flight attendants tells me one of the passengers came on board smelling a little boozy but acting real sober. We kept an eye on him. He ordered a couple more drinks and stayed on good behaviour so I didn't think anything of it. Found out after he was slipping the people around him cash to order him drinks."

She took a sip of water and pulled slippers out from under the couch before putting them on and stretching her long legs out on the table.

"Anyway," she continued. "I'm securing the galley for landing and all of a sudden he's got a handful right up under my skirt and his other feeling up the front of my shirt. Well on his way to performance level right up against my ass if you know what I mean."

"Oh my God," I exclaimed, horrified for her.

"Did I mention I used to be a cop?" she asked. I shook my head. "Yeah, university for law enforcement then eight years on the force before one too many close calls got me in the air. My crew mates always defer to me if there's a problem especially if we don't have a Marshall onboard which we didn't that flight and at that moment LAX was our closest place to put down in an emergency.

"I was out from under him in half a second and the fool is half humping the fridge before he realizes I'd moved. I'd yelled of course part in surprise and part to look bigger."

Paul laughed, his eyes closed.

"The curtains were open to the galley and the cabin's gone quiet but I don't notice. This drunken suit got his hands on me and I flip to red zone. I'm thinking about my jerk supervisor who won't give me time off to take care of Dad because I won't date him and how if I pop this guy instead of sweet talking him back into his seat I could get fired and have some time with the folks and the girls and maybe just go to college with them and get a job closer to Mom and Dad since they're getting up there. Whether I coax the drunk back to his seat or put him down I just know my sup is going to find a reason to say I made the wrong call."

"I yell. 'You son of a bitch! Why you got your hands on me?' but he laughs and calls me a slut and thinks I've been leaning too far over when I serve him apparently asking for it even though I served the other aisle.

"I decide to send him home bruised up and he can explain to his wife why he got knocked around in my galley. Then this quiet voice behind me says 'Hey, pal. Let's take a seat.'"

She did a perfect imitation of Ross right down to the eyebrow which meant you weren't going to be asked twice. I held my stomach still and squeezed my knees together as I started to laugh.

"So now some guy is going to take away my vacation," she exclaimed. "So I said, 'Hey Captain Budzinsky. Take your seat and let me do my God damn job' and I clobber the pervert as hard as I could straight in the face. He goes down like a sack of stones and I broke three bones in my hand. Then I spin around to run off the interloper and I'm face-to-face with Ross and Paul who are stopping half a dozen other passengers from getting the idiot on the floor 'cause everyone wants to be an airline hero these days. There's applause filling the cabin and tears filling my eyes 'cause my hand hurts like hell.

"I asked if they wanted one too and Ross gives me this 'No thank you, ma'am' but Paul's laughing at him and hauls him back to his seat. I get my hand iced and the other two flight attendants get the drunk cuffed in a row of his own as we begin our priority descent. He wakes up and keeps his yap shut. I figure I'll be fired on the way off the plane and I'm so close to Don't-Give-a-Shits-Ville I slip Ross my phone number on the way to buckle in to land.

"I never give my number to passengers or anyone. I was sick about it after. Not because I was worried he'd call but because I was worried he wouldn't.

"So we get the passengers off in LA and I get hauled into the supervisor's office while I'm running a mental inventory of everything I'll have to clean out. He gets out his phone and tells me to look at it. It's a shaky video of me and the horny drunk including the groping right up to me running off Ross and Paul. He said it was all over the internet already and they were afraid to fire me because of the public back-lash."

There were tears in my eyes I laughed so hard. Kelly perched straight up on her cushion reliving her victory. Paul didn't move as he snored.

"I got my vacation," she gasped, sticking her hands up in triumph. "Helped Dad out since I couldn't work with my busted hand. I was even on CNN for about twenty seconds. So there you go. Meeting Ross made me famous."

"That's amazing," I told her, impressed.

"Ah, it's nice to tell someone who didn't see the video." She lowered her voice when she noticed Paul sleeping. "By the time I got home it had been on the news and the girls were all over their kick ass mom. I told Dad I gave one of the men my number 'cause I tell him everything. He starts to get a little pissed and I know he doesn't approve. Knew he wouldn't but I told him anyway. He asks me to repeat myself so I do then he puts his hands on his hips and makes a stern face." She posed to demonstrate. "He says 'so you have two big level headed Army boys backing you up and you can keep them in line and you didn't give them both your number?'"

"How'd he know they're Army?" I giggled.

"Not sure," she shrugged. "Well, I am. Dad's ex-Army and he can just tell the way the career guys carry themselves. But I didn't know Ross' name then. A few days later I get home from getting my hand re-casted 'cause the swelling's gone down and Dad's on the phone. Mom's tight lipped and Dad sneaks down to his office. All she'll say is he's been on the phone for an hour and a half. I peek through the door and he's stuffing a picture of me in my police uniform through the fax machine and bragging about my stellar service record and my kids. He catches me watching and shoves the phone in my face. 'It's Captain Budzinsky,' he says as he walks out leaving me with the phone."

She turned sideways to face me and leaned her head on the side of the couch. Her knee piled up on mine and she didn't move it.

"He took me out for dinner that night," she said. "My family shoved me out the door. I didn't think I'd have anything left to say about myself after Dad finished with him but I did. I didn't make it home until the next morning and I've been back and forth between there and here ever since."

"So here, home and work?" I asked and she looked weary, her excitement with her story spent.

"I want Ross," she said. "And my family and I have to work. I can't just work less and Ross comes to Los Angeles as much as he can which helps but I miss my girls when I'm here and him when I'm there."

"I'm sure it'll sort itself out," I tried to reassure her, understanding how she felt being so far away from her daughters.

"After Dad's surgery one of the x-rays found a lump in his lung," she wiped her eyes on the back of her hand. "They raised two sets of kids and now this. You'd think in a trucking family Mom would drive but she doesn't. I have to quit my job to take care of them but he's not going back to work until the chemo's done even then he's sixty-five."

We listened to the wood stove crackle and watched Paul sleep for a while. Kelly slipped out for a bit and came back with a thermos of tea and a couple of mugs and we blew on the decaf chai until it was cool enough to drink. Paul still hadn't moved. I didn't remember him sleeping much the past two days with the hospital and wherever he spent the last night. Joshua's cramped cabin, I guessed.

"Do you love him?" Kelly asked.

"Of course," I answered, looking at Paul.

"No, Jack."

I opened my mouth but stopped short of speaking when I looked at her. She seemed lost in her own thoughts.

Chapter 35

I woke slumped over on Paul. He'd moved behind me and Kelly had gone to help Ross with dinner. I recalled some giggling and discussion with Ross whether we were awake or not until Paul mumbled we were. Kelly apologized and they left. Now Paul took little strands of my hair and slowly ran his fingers along, moving them a bit at a time behind my shoulder.

"Sshhh," he said when he felt me tense. My head rested on his arm and I reached out and fixed his folded up cuff, smoothing it out. He lifted it so I could ease the twist in the sleeve from sliding down the back of the couch. I realized it was a different type of connection which gave us the small familiar intimacy of adjusting his sleeve, the kind of old fashioned connection shared by the regular couples in the world which only came with love and time. When he'd cleared my shoulder he rested his hand and waited for me to relax before he moved up my neck. He loosened the knots at the top and made his way down.

"You carry so much stress right now."

I sighed in agreement as my tension eased.

"It's not as easy to work out of you as it used to be," Paul added as his fingers started their way down the middle of my back. "Why do you still scratch yourself? Is it really coping or is something else going on?"

"When I'm worried their lines still pull. They don't tear me anymore but their anxiety can be uncomfortable."

Paul's hand slid up, his thumb found tight muscle and his touch softened it.

"Sugar, if we're going to find our way back to each other we need some ground rules. I don't believe either one of us was ready to be together again like this."

"No," I agreed. His breathing changed a little and I knew he wanted to be closer but instead he kept massaging my back. I still felt like I heard and saw a ghost.

"Do you love Jack?"

I felt myself grow cold having to name my feelings for Jack, especially to Paul.

"I thought I did," I whispered as my hand came up, fingers curled to attack my skin again. I realized the boys weren't anxious at all and I did it anyway. Paul's hand slid under mine, taking my nails in his knuckles and I immediately backed off before I could hurt him. I forced my fingers to straighten and rest on top of his.

"What do you mean?"

"He did his job, Paul. He said he loved me and acted like he loved me. But I was just a God damn burden he unloaded as soon as he could."

Paul moved around to face me. He took my hands and held them on my lap.

"That's not really what I want you to think about," he whispered then he waited for me to meet his eyes. "Do you still have feelings for him?"

"Is that your question or Doctor Flood's?" I asked. Paul looked hurt for a moment, pushing his lips together as I realized I was twisting his relaxed fingers.

"It doesn't matter either way to Russell," Paul said, not quite able to hide the edge of his emotion. "What matters to him is how clear your feelings are to you. I know Jack turned on you when you thought he was all you had and if I've learned anything the past six months I've learned you don't turn off your love for someone when they're brutally taken from you.

"I need to hear your answer."

I glanced at him only briefly before I gave him a tiny nod and looked away. My feelings were so mixed.

"Do you want a divorce?"

"No!" I gasped as I grabbed on to Paul. "No, no, no, no, no. How could you say that?"

"Are you sure," he asked, quiet tenderness in his voice as he let me cling to him.

"Please, Paul. I'm sure," I moaned as I held on.

"Okay then. I'm sorry to ask. As long as you don't want a divorce I'm not leaving my cabin and neither is my wife. I don't expect sex or any kind of intimacy. I just want to be close to you, understand?"

I relaxed and Paul kissed my forehead.

"I don't want you to shy away from me, please? If I want an arm around you or to hold your hand it's because I love you. If you want to do the same I'm not taking it as a sign you want more unless we've talked about it first," he said as he put his hand on his chest. "My connection to you is almost overwhelming, being near again. I understand you don't feel me like I feel you but if we're agreed upon our physical relationship we won't have that conflict getting in the way of anything else."

"Okay, Paul," I agreed. He was right. Being clear about physical expectations was a huge relief but after he'd told Flood Jack got hurt if I caused a problem the rule would be silence about things like that as well. And I wondered how much coaching Flood had given him.

I lay down on the couch for a while as Paul dealt with paperwork and other business at the oversized desk. The three o'clock watch change had come and gone while we napped so we had the room to ourselves. My eyes briefly opened at the snap of a lock as Paul opened the arms cabinet and inventoried the handguns, a daily Day Officer task I remembered from before everything went wrong. Done entirely in the armory before Jack, part in the common room after. Paul noticed me watching him as he locked it back up.

"I have something for you," he smiled. I pushed myself up as he joined me then he pulled a new phone from his pocket. "It's one of those smart phones."

He tapped one of the buttons on its smooth glass front, then another and rows and rows of small pictures appeared. He chose the first. "It's all the pictures I've taken since I got Camille back. There's some movies, too. Like you're turning pages."

He swept his finger across and sleeping Camille in a car seat turned into another then one of her in a highchair at a restaurant. She hadn't been old enough for one the last time I'd held her. Ray sat next to her holding up little Julian as Alina was frozen mid-pose pulling a puffy winter coat off him.

"I thought you could call Alina sometime."

"Maybe," I said as I changed the picture again. "Thank you."

"You're welcome. Put whatever you want on it, okay?"

"Sure, Paul," I murmured, lost in pictures of everyone I'd missed and somewhat aware of Paul's amused chuckle. I paused on one picture: Marie and a blonde little infant. Patrick's arm around her suggested more closeness than expected from her dead husband's best friend. I looked at Paul for an explanation.

"His name is Adam," Paul said. "The family made an exception for his sake. With the possibility of being responsible for my mate's three children a fourth would have been too much. Three is unheard of. Ross, Ray and Dana unanimously granted an exception for Patrick to care for her and to excuse me from her care this time. Patrick is going back to Edmonton with her and the baby as her boyfriend."

"How do you feel about that?" I asked, selfishly pleased.

Paul shrugged. "Like I said, unless they need something she's only Keith's widow."

I wished I could still feel that same detachment from Jack.

"—inner!" Kelly interrupted. The door popped open as Paul nudged the phone for me to keep going. "Hey, Anna. You're awake. I made sure you have bland enchiladas, spice 'em up as you want. I wasn't sure how much of that kind of food you could take."

"What kind of animal does bland come from?" I asked and she laughed.

"It's like a cow," she mused. "Only cuter but they got a real mean streak so you don't feel bad about eating them."

The Charm

Chapter 36

My new obstetrician was nice.

She hummed to herself and took her time showing us everything about the boys since Flood didn't have Targuer's scan results. Paul held my hand like he had with Camille's ultrasound.

Kelly and Ross tagged along to shop for her girls while Paul and I went in. That meant 'the guys' had to take night watch. I'd been home a few weeks and didn't mind Paul around as I had at first. He kept his promise to go slow which was fine with me. I was still hard on myself and hid my guilt with bitchiness he took with varying degrees of grace. In spite of our lighter conversations and seeking happy common ground in memories from the past, we fought more and more the longer he avoided going to see Camille. We didn't talk about it but 'the trip' was always there; a big stumbling block for our reunion.

My new psychiatrist had his work cut out for him. Flood decided he wasn't qualified to deal with self-mutilation in a patient and farmed my head out to a military approved shrink in Sacramento. I decided I did just fine emailing Wendy and getting to know Kelly and was close to having enough of his talks. The only thing which kept me going to see him was his opinion I wasn't yet ready for rejection from Camille. He felt bonding with her again would take time and until I had a solid foundation of support, a visit with her guaranteed setbacks for me.

Today Paul and I drove alone to Sacramento. Ross was Day Officer and Kelly was up in the sky somewhere. It was better like that. The psychiatrist visits usually set me in a bad mood.

"Have you spoken with your sister?" He asked. The doc was big on Alina. If I didn't know better I'd have thought he wanted an introduction.

I shook my head. Paul spoke to Ray in my presence but that was as close as I got. I looked around the masculine office and tried to appear bored. He set his notepad on his desk and put his pen down beside it.

"She's asked to speak with you?"

I shrugged.

"Before you go, we'll talk about some strategies to help you break the ice with Alina. I want you to call her before I see you next. From what you've told me, you sound very close. Do you think you can't trust her?"

"I trust her," I said.

"Good," he smiled. "You haven't told me much about your mother."

The change of subject startled me though it was part of his tactics. I didn't trust him so I acted uncooperative and suspected he wanted to get me off balance.

"Which one?"

His mouth opened part way and he paused as I caught him off guard.

"Do you mean my mother who passed away when I was a teen or Wendy, my best friend who fills that hole for me?"

He shrugged like I had. My temper flared and I put my hands under my knees before I could smack him.

"Your biological mother," he said but his voice rose at the word mother so it sounded like he asked. I realized I admitted to having a hole.

I thought about the loving and protective man my father was before she died and the pain he lived with to be the same man after. She was the greatest love of his life. He'd have given her his heart to keep his wife and daughters together. My heart softened for him as I put Paul in his place. Paul would have traded himself for me and still would. There was a time I thought Jack had it in him to do the same.

"Was it an accident which took her from you?"

I shook my head. I was years past crying for her though in so many ways her loss still made me sad.

"It was a genetic heart defect," I allowed. It was safe to talk about her. She'd been gone too long to have anything to do with what my life had become. "At first it was little things before she was diagnosed. We'd go to the rink in the winter and she'd have to sit down long before the rest of us were ready to go then she'd lay on the couch as Dad made dinner. By March she stayed home and we went without her."

"And when she found out she was going to leave you?" He prompted.

"They didn't keep it from us if that's what you're asking." I slid down in my seat to remove the pressure on the backs of my legs as I leaned to the side.

He shrugged again.

"Dad took time off work. We knew she didn't have long. He did everything he could to make sure she could spend whatever energy she had every day on Alina and me. At night she cried when she thought we couldn't hear."

"It was painful for her?"

"Maybe," I answered. "Well, physically I don't know. She never let on it was painful. I think the hardest part was leaving us behind. Her heart was broken in more ways than one."

He scribbled on his paper for a few minutes.

"Genetic?"

"Yes," I answered. That's what I said.

"Have you inherited it?"

I felt my head twitch like I wanted to make sure the thought couldn't stick to me.

"Mm," he nodded. "You've told me you want to see your daughter more than anything. Could putting her in your shoes be what's holding you back from working with me?"

"No," I whispered even though I saw how plausible it could be. This was his M.O.; planting ideas in my head to think about later.

"Something to consider. You said you thought your husband dead when you were taken."

He was aggressive with me today and I felt myself winding up inside. I put my hand on my chest. He closely watched so I was careful not to scratch.

"I wasn't looking but I heard the gun," I defensively said. He rattled me so I kept going. "Told me he was dead. Jack told me."

"Paul left you didn't he? Like your mother?"

"Fuck you," I whispered. I'd admitted to having one hole in me and he'd moved on to lining it up with the others and connecting them.

The doc remained impassive.

"Then your babies' father."

I looked out his window. Everything was grey outside.

"Go ahead," I coldly said. Today's meeting was over. "You can write 'abandonment issues' in my file if it isn't already there."

"It would be understandable for you to worry Camille could do the same thing. Or even you to her."

He didn't move and watched to see what I'd do next.

I sent my sense out to the waiting room and Paul wasn't there so I scanned down the hall and found him where I believed the men's room was.

"I need a break," I said, wanting to throw up the feelings he'd found for me. "I have to pee, I'm sorry."

The doctor gestured toward the door. I quickly stood and made my way through the waiting room. My coat hung on the hook so I grabbed it and stepped out into the hall. Instead of going right to the restrooms I pushed the elevator button and rode down to the main floor. Then out toward home.

Paul disappeared from my range, still in the men's room, as I made my way down the sidewalk. It felt good to be on my own, simply putting one foot in front of the other. I made progress all by myself even if it was by running out on the doctor. As usual, he'd been a step ahead of me and I didn't like it.

All I needed was to be near my daughter again. I'd faced leaving her behind, in fact I'd done it. I'd said good-bye to her in a North Dakota hotel room and walked away before I led trouble to her.

My feet stopped and another pedestrian bumped me from behind. I could still bring trouble to her. Was that why I stubbornly insisted I get my way without listening to anyone? Was I trusting Paul and the doctor to keep me away so I could avoid dealing with Jack's role in my life?

I had all the patience in the world for her when it came to getting to know each other. I felt like I knew the little girl in the pictures; the sound of her voice and her laugh. The way she cried. I wasn't a fool. I knew she didn't know me the same way but she would. I was the Mom and she was the baby. It was my job to wait for her.

My phone buzzed in my pocket after only a few blocks.

"Hi, Paul."

"Where are you, Sugar?"

"Walking home," I answered, looking back over my shoulder to make sure nobody was going to turn right into my backside.

"Alright," he sounded tired. "I'll rebook you for next week."

"Whatever."

Paul sighed and hung up. I made it another three blocks before he pulled over, double parking so he could run around and lift me in. As we left the city he held his arm to me so I slid over and he put it around my shoulder.

"Rough visit?"

"I thought he was supposed to help me feel better."

Paul held his tongue. He knew as well as I did I only made things hard on myself.

Chapter 37

"I'm heading out for a few days," Paul whispered as we drove through the final turns before the gate. He wound his fingers between mine as he picked my hand up and kissed it. "Nothing to worry about, Sugar."

"Really?" I didn't believe him. Paul would see Camille and the only chance I'd have of going with him was if I stowed away in the back of the truck. He waved at Ross as we passed through the gate.

"We have an opportunity in Connecticut," he sighed. "A big one. I need a day or two of prep before I get everyone together. I can't clear out the compound until the last minute. They'll know something's up."

"What about me?" I demanded. "You're just leaving me here alone?"

"You won't be here alone."

We stopped in front of our cabin to see Joshua and Flood waiting. I groaned. Flood was here for his usual debrief from my visit with the psychiatrist though I usually got a chance to at least take my boots off. Joshua would fill Paul in on anything he missed while we were gone.

"Let me guess, I'll have the cheerleaders," I pointed at Joshua and Flood. "Why the hell do I have to run the gauntlet just to get in my fucking front door?"

Paul's eyes flashed, disapproving of my language so I popped my door open and without waiting for help, grabbed the seatbelt and handle and slid myself out. It was fine for him to swear when he was pissed off. Apparently it wasn't fine for me to have a short temper.

"Josh," Paul said and pointed at our cabin. They disappeared together.

Flood smiled at me and held his arm out toward the common room.

"Hello, Doctor Flood," I tried to look cheerful.

"Afternoon, Anna," he replied before taking my elbow to escort me across the slippery road. "It's Russell."

"I'm aware."

And so our little dance started.

"Supposed to clear up the next few days," he said. A couple of blue patches interrupted the high cloud. Even the small amount of extra light coming through made me feel better. It would all be black above in a few hours.

"Yes," I agreed. Giving Flood the feeling of common ground with me would get our chat over faster. He held the door and led me to the sofa. He took the chair.

"Anything you'd like to share from your session today?" Even though he'd sent me to a professional he was still a counsellor.

"It went great," I exclaimed, hoping to get out and see Paul before he left. I felt nervous for him going east to take on Walker and Soros. "I think I had a real breakthrough."

"Indeed?"

"Mm," I nodded, listening out front for any hint of Paul leaving.

"Well?" He cocked an eyebrow.

"He decided I have abandonment issues and I walked out."

Flood pressed his lips together. I crossed my arms, disappointed with myself for giving the outward appearance of closing off.

"He thinks I'm worried Camille abandoned me. Won't take me back," I struggled, hugging myself tighter so I wouldn't scratch. "But I expect that," my voice broke. "I mean, I'm her mom. I can be there for her as she gets to know me again."

Flood put a hand over his mouth and rubbed his knuckles over his top lip.

"You have a strategy then to help you through reconnecting with her?"

"I don't need one," I hissed but my hands trembled so I laced my fingers together to keep them still. Flood moved beside me on the couch. I fidgeted inside and knew I wasn't keeping him from seeing it on the outside.

"I've been through hell, Russell," I admitted, only registering I'd said his name after I'd done it. "Every day I'd do it again for her to wake up in a safe warm bed surrounded by people who love her. Her father would too and nobody corners him to see how his head is."

"Are you so sure about that?" Paul said. He stood just inside the door. "You've seen how my head is; the compromises I've made for her."

Now I saw what was going on: the shrink pushing me so hard today, Flood wanting to speak to me before I could even go pee. Paul might have a big assignment coming up but the days of prep involved a visit with Camille in San Diego.

I pushed myself up and stood, bravely facing their decision.

"What's the word, Russ?" Paul asked.

Flood shook his head.

"No, Paul. Please," I braced my legs against the sofa behind me. Flood took a few steps toward the desk. "You know what I've done. I'll never hurt her or fail her..."

"I'm sorry, Sugar," Paul whispered, discretely wiping his eyes.

Before I knew it I picked up the end of the coffee table and hurled it out of my way. It struck Flood and the desk simultaneously as I charged the door to try and get to the truck. I heard a woman scream as the door burst open before me and Joshua stepped in.

I struggled but it didn't take much for two trained soldiers to restrain a hysterical pregnant woman. My knees buckled as Paul and Joshua eased me to the floor. The screaming quieted to shuddering wet sobs. Joshua knelt behind me and I leaned on him. Flood winced as he rubbed his shoulder.

"Sugar?" Paul whispered, his fingers under my chin tipped my face to his. He pulled a tissue from somewhere and wiped my eyes though he wasn't holding his tears in very well either.

"Is this the woman you want getting to know your daughter? She's thrown furniture and hurt someone she'd never hurt. Something she'd never do if she let herself find a place for the past."

I looked at Flood again as my hand slipped over my mouth. Joshua's arm crept around my shoulders, hugging me from behind.

"I love you, Sugar," Paul whispered, pulling my hand aside to kiss me. "Camille loves you. I know you love her. She's happy and healthy and you deserve to be as well.

"Yes, I'm going to see her. Then I promise we're finishing things in Connecticut. Make a deal with me, Sugar?"

"Yes," I whispered. I forgot about Joshua and Flood and saw nothing ahead but me and Paul and the future. Paul took my hands and put them on his cheeks.

"Don't slip back into yourself from this. Hold on. Be brave. Face yourself. You're the only one who'll really know when you find peace inside. I promise I'll come home and I won't go see her without you again."

"I will," I agreed. "I love you."

"I love you, Sugar," he whispered, kissing me one last time before he left.

Once the truck drove off Joshua helped me up and took me to sit on the big sofa. I told Flood I was sorry over and over as Joshua iced the nasty bruise on his collar bone. Then with my promise to get some rest, he sent me to my cabin before driving Flood into Redding for x-rays.

I curled up in bed and phoned my sister. We talked until she put Julian to bed then I talked to Ray. Hearing Paul come in and greet Camille was too much so I hung up and turned my phone off.

Chapter 38

Nineteen days passed since Paul left.

Sixteen since he broke the first part of his promise. He called to say he was leaving San Diego and to tell Joshua he'd be home at nineteen hundred. Joshua said it meant the mission was on and within half an hour most of the men were gone.

Fifteen days since the men returned. Sig flew back with Joshua to tell me Paul never arrived and the mission was off. Paul disappeared before he left San Diego.

I kept my promise, to face myself. I'd become less resentful of Jack's connection to me. At least I connected to something. I didn't kid myself. It was only a matter of time before his brothers caught him or he didn't get away with some stupid move against them. At least for the time being I wasn't alone. Maybe when I lost it there would be a way to regain my stolen connection to Paul. As long as it was to Jack I kept looking for a way to accept it.

Four days passed since my last visit with the psychiatrist. For three straight visits I talked about Jack, the other man in my life. It was tough. The complicated family ties and connections were nothing he'd understand so I made due with analogies.

I agreed with the doc. There was no completely shutting Jack out. If by some miracle he avoided his brothers for years I'd always feel his pull. My feelings for him had been strong and our harsh breakup left them unresolved. In any event, I'd see him in my boys every day.

Jack's presence with me was certainly easier to accept without Paul around though I desperately missed my husband. I wished my mated connection was to Paul so I'd know if he were alive or dead.

With an obstetrician appointment in Sacramento in a few hours I didn't bother stoking the stove. Even if I wasn't going out I wouldn't have touched it anyway. Joshua had taken to looking after it. He seemed to feel a real need to look after me in his brother's place and I needed to let him.

Wendy had stuffed a couple of disposable razors in a tropical print zippered bag along with baby powder scented deodorant, Ivory soap, peppermint toothpaste, nail clippers, cotton swabs and a handful of pads just in case the boys became too much for my squashed insides. She even tried to give me an electric toothbrush but I politely passed and accepted a regular one. The fruity smell of the shampoo and conditioner she gave me didn't fade as the day went on. There was even a little bottle of her perfume which I tried once in an effort to pretend she was close but it didn't smell the same on me.

Once the fan was on, I half closed the bathroom door and started filling the tub with water hotter than I could stand. The air seemed to suck the heat from it as soon as it left the faucet. I sat on the toilet lid and dug around for the things I'd need and put them on the edge of the tub. I suppose I could have unpacked but every minute here still felt temporary so it didn't make much sense.

I was clumsy putting the little bag back on the counter. It slipped from my fingers as it fell, my other hand swatted it in an effort to catch it. Everything flew out including the vinyl covered cardboard from the bottom which helped it keep its shape. As I picked up the bag, several sheets of paper folded into quarters fell out, flipping once just before they landed on the mat. I'd been here a month and a half, in and out of the bag every day and I hadn't noticed them before.

Instead of stepping in the bath I turned it off and returned to the room. I wrapped up in the comforter on the bed and put the pages out in front of me. When I unfolded them, I faced a sketch of my stomach sticking out from the blue shirt I wore the night Jack left, my hand resting loosely upon it. My left I since I didn't sleep well in any position other than on my right and from the presence of my wedding ring. Jack's left hand on my swollen belly next to mine. I knew it was his from the missing fingers.

My heart seemed to stop for a second as his connection to me surged, renewing itself. Distance and time had reduced it to a fraction of what it once was. Guilt quickly followed and I turned to make sure nobody looked in the windows.

I put the coloured sketch aside. Beneath it, the second sheet was a collection of smaller pencil drawings. Another of my hand. One of my sleeping face. They seemed to have been drawn in a hurry. The lines went go too far in places and some were too dark as if to say 'her chin is here, not that other line' unlike the care taken with the drawing of the blue shirt. I moved it aside to find a note in Jack's tight boxy print.

Anna, You sleep so soundly in this place. I don't think I've slept at all. Doesn't matter how drunk I get. I think it's your conscience. Clear and honest unlike mine. I've done something terrible to you. I lied. I want you to know I did it for all the right reasons. I don't know if I'd do it all again but it's done. I want you to know I love you more than anything. I insisted I get a chance to say good-bye. I hear their footsteps outside the door. It's time to wake you up and make you hate me. If I fit in any small corner of your heart after today, please hold me there. I love you, Baby. Jack.

I ran my fingers over his printing then placed my hand over the sketch of his on me. He'd sat there that night while I slept. I imagined the dim light as Jack sat beside me, drawing. He'd pushed aside his feelings for me to do his job again. After lying to keep me alive he got ready to lie again to set things right. The story about connecting to Jack sparing me the pain of Paul's death was just that.

A story.

But it was the only way I'd accept being connected to Jack instead of Paul.

He'd lied again to protect me from my vision of Gerald Walker though the exposure of his lie about Paul's death was inevitable once we'd escaped from the big house in Connecticut.

His love for me had been real.

I knew in my heart he would never allow us to have a future. He stole me to protect me and gave me back when the job was over.

I dressed in the same clothes Joshua picked out for me the day before and tucked the pages in my pocket.

As I opened the curtains to peek outside to see if the cold brought anything white with it, I heard a knock and let the curtains fall shut. After half a minute there was another knock so I opened up.

"Hey," Joshua said. His hands were stuffed deep in his pockets and his breath glowed in the morning sun. No heat rushed out the door to greet him. "Can I come in for a second?"

He hadn't slept well. As Paul's number one, he'd been in charge for the past nineteen days; a task he had no trouble with in the past but he'd been left looking after me in addition to everything else.

"Yeah, Josh," I welcomed him in.

"That tea you and Kelly like," he mumbled as he shoved a mug in my hands on the way to the wood stove.

"Josh?" I tried. He sounded more down than usual.

"No word, Little Sister," he said. Orange light flared around him as the fresh firewood caught. "I talked to the Colonel already this morning. Nothing from his phone, the bank. Nothing."

Joshua straightened up and reached in his coat. He watched me for a moment before pulling his hand out.

"Listen, Ross helped me dig around in the wreckage of the house. I mean those things are built tough," He brightened as he went on. "Shit, the papers inside weren't even brown."

"What are you talking about, Josh?"

"Oh," he reached back in his coat and pulled out a couple of jewellery boxes. I recognized both. "The safe, Anna. We found the safe and your necklace and ring."

My hands trembled so Joshua opened them.

"They're perfect," he quietly said. "Here."

I teared up as I lifted my hair. Joshua strung my diamond on the chain and locked the clasp behind my neck.

"I know it doesn't mean the same coming from me."

"Thank you," I whispered as I got my arms around him.

"Look, Little Sister," Joshua said as he let me go. His hands wrung as he spoke. "I just want you to know if we don't hear anything I'm here for you and Camille and your boys. Whatever you need."

I ran my fingers over the smooth chain and held my engagement ring for the first time in months.

"Joshua?" I cupped his cheek in my hands as I spoke. "I'm scared too, Josh. I miss him too."

The day brought me priceless memories of both Paul and Jack.

Chapter 39

I fidgeted at the desk in the new common room. The room stayed as warm as the old one so I hung my coat over the back of the chair.

My phone stood on edge in front of me and I picked it up, rolling it onto its top. Thunk. Then again, wheeling it along in place like the square peg I felt like, marking time as I adjusted as Flood assured me I would. Thunk, thunk. I'd come to trust the psychiatrist and Flood somewhat when it came to Jack but there was so much more to my time in Connecticut I hadn't trusted to anyone here.

I was lost in thought about Jack's letter, undecided if I felt furious with him for lying to protect me yet again or daring to believe it was okay to love him for putting me first even though he was gone. Then the renewed shame of living under Paul's roof and harbouring those thoughts.

I jumped when my phone rang, making it skitter across the desk and into the monitor before I wrapped both hands around it and pulled it close to muffle the shrill sound. With Paul so far overdue it could only be him.

"Hello?" I answered. The silent line stayed open. I heard rustling and nothing else for nearly a minute. "Please say something."

Paul would if it was him, so it wasn't.

"I found your letter this morning," I whispered, looking behind me. There was no sign of the truck in front of the cabin and I would have at least a few seconds warning when Joshua pulled up.

"I know why you did it... said those things," I said. "It worked, Jack. You broke my heart and kept me away but I'm not so mad because I see you broke yours too."

"Baby," he murmured, his shaky breathing got a little louder.

"You were right. I'm all those things you said. There was love, two little boys, but being bound together like that brought out some of the worst things we had inside us. I still love you but you're right. I'm no good for you or our children when we're together. I'm not sure there's a place for me here but I'll stay out of trouble and take care of them. Maybe you can forgive me some day.

"I'm okay. Paul's doing everything he can to take care of me but I won't let him close. I keep trying to make the men here treat me like your brothers did. I can handle that at least. I get so scared when they try and talk me out of my shell. I act like they want me to but sometimes I want to go back to your Father's. It was bad I know but at least I knew the score. Flood knows we leaned on each other hard and I'm still trying to protect you by following your brothers' rules."

I knew I was running out of time to talk but I kept going, to keep him near me as long as I could.

"Damn it, Jack," I let out a shaky laugh. "If I can't trick someone in to telling me which shirt to wear I keep my coat on at the table so they can't see I'm wearing Anton's blue one."

"You need to listen to the Doc, Baby," Jack finally spoke and I nodded as I let loose tears. "Jack isn't coming for Anna. Not today, not ever. Jack is dead. I can't stay on the run forever sparing you that pain. They're close on my heels, all the time. They'll have me soon."

"I know," I whispered.

"Tell Wendy I'm sorry for the things I said. I've had a lot of time to think and I'm proud I was chosen to have a sister. I hope seeing her find her mate is a memory I'll have someday."

"Jack, I have to go in a second," I interrupted as I heard the truck coming.

"I know. Listen, Baby," he said. "Gerald has Paul a mile away from me. He's not going to live out the day but if I get there soon I can get him out while it's just the two of them in the house. Soros is coming and I need to do it fast. I have no right to you but at least the man who does will come home tonight.

"Promise me you'll stay put and wait for him," Jack's voice broke. "Promise—

The line went dead.

The truck's idle changed as Joshua pushed the shifter into park and I rifled through the desk drawers. For what, I didn't know. A sign. Anything to tell me if I should promise or not.

Then I saw them. The handcuffs from the night Captain Taggart tried to take me to Soros. I slipped them in my pocket as the door opened.

"Ready, Little Sister?" Joshua asked.

"Yeah, Josh," I answered, feeling light with easy purpose for the first time in a very long time.

I wasn't going to promise.

"Alright," Joshua said. "Arm over my shoulder."

He'd opened the passenger door and I stood near the opening. My arm went up and around his neck as his left went behind me and his right scooped my snow boot covered feet from the ground. He took a step forward and put me on the seat. I turned enough to knock my boots together and clear the treads before Joshua passed me the buckle.

"I'd say you're still light as a feather," he said as he leaned back and popped his spine.

"Maybe like a horse-feather," I finished, gently calling him on his kind fib.

He laughed and closed my door as he went around behind the truck.

"I hope you don't mind if I feed you in town," he said as he climbed in. "More snow coming. It'll slow us down. I won't rush us back for lunch."

"Nothing spicy. I don't want to look down my throat and see flames." I wouldn't survive Wendy's curry now like I had before. Everything burned.

"Gotcha."

Joshua put it in gear and took his foot off the brake, letting the automatic's idle roll us without spinning the tires. I kept my hand in my right pocket, thoughtfully fingering the bit of chain between the cuffs. Joshua had to want to leave the truck with the keys in it. Not an easy thing to make happen. He was like Paul when it came to the keys and the truck. I'd have to make him think something else was far more important.

"Anna?"

I looked to my left in surprise, unaware we'd stopped.

"I'll let you know if there's any word from Paul," Ross said. Joshua leaned back so Ross could see me. "Whether he's on his way or needs help. If he needs help we'll be on the road first then we'll call you, okay?"

"Thanks, Ross," I smiled. "I appreciate it."

"Your kid brother will take good care of you."

"Kid?" Joshua demanded. "We'll see who makes Captain first, Wells, we need one around here."

Ross punched his shoulder, barely pulling his hand out as the window came up and I waved. They meant well but Paul was only minutes away for me, maybe hours for them. Time Paul didn't have. Or Jack for that matter. Jack would be in over his head with Gerald and I figured he'd go in after Paul in an effort to make things right before his brothers finished him off.

Joshua picked up his mug for a drink before he relaxed and stuffed it between his thighs to save the reach to the cup holder. I waited through the end of the news on the radio then the sports and weather which he turned up to hear. I looked up through my window at the grey clouds. No new flakes yet but you didn't have to grow up out here to sense when it was coming.

The best way to manipulate Joshua was with the truth, make him feel protective of me. If I caught him up emotionally he'd be more likely to react without thinking to whatever urgent situation I had yet to come up with.

"Josh?"

"Yeah, Anna," he answered. His foot eased up on the gas as a steep turn took us down hill.

"I thought maybe I could talk a bit. You don't have to say anything, just listen. Doc Flood and the shrink gave me some psych homework and if you could think about something else while I run my mouth I can say I did it."

He laughed. "You mean sign off on it so you look good?"

"Something like that," I whispered. Even though I used my real homework to play him I was still hesitant to talk.

"Sure, what do you want to talk about?"

"Well, I want to see Camille but he thinks I'm not ready. He's full of it but I have to do what he says. He thinks I still mostly relate to the person I was when they had me. He says I need to start reconnecting; building a bridge between my family and the situation I was in with Jack so when Camille doesn't recognize me I'm able to accept support to get through it."

Joshua picked up his coffee and we watched a couple of flakes appear ahead of us.

"It's not like you to procrastinate, Little Sister," he said between sips, urging me to start.

I went on like he hadn't spoken. "He asked me if I remember what it's like to trust someone and I don't. The last person I trusted abandoned me, Josh. Before that Paul died. It took eight years and finding Paul to be able to trust again after losing my mother. Then I lost him."

"Nobody here is going to abandon you," he said. The sky hopefully lightened as I thought about where to start before it darkened again.

"I had some people killed, Josh," I said. His brows raised and I looked away. He kept his eyes on the road. "They're like a cult: corporal punishment, strict rules. Jack turned on them you know, by coming to us. My tooth, that was a hard right. I tried to get in the way when they went after him. They took off two of his fingers one knuckle at a time. I tore the new skin off my hand getting his belt around his arm as they did it."

"Oh, Jesus. Anna," he whispered. "I had no idea."

"Nothing for it now," I shrugged. "I saw a man take a gun from the armoury without permission. There were rules about that. It was stealing. I thought if I told I could make things a little easier for Jack and me; prove to them we could be trusted. They took the man's hand off with an axe for the theft before he confessed he was going to use it to assassinate one of the leaders. It was treason for him and his friends. I didn't know what the penalty was for theft and it was bad enough I had to live with that, but four men were hung because of what I started."

"That was when Paul ran the raid on the place. We just missed you by a couple of days," Joshua's mug rattled as he put it in the holder on the dash then he shoved his hand under his thigh to still it and drove with a tight grip of his left.

"I don't know, Joshua," I admitted. "I wanted to be there when they hung them. Right up front. Maybe I'm not the kind of woman who's ready to be around Camille."

He shut down more than I hoped. I expected his protective side to jump in with reassurance but with a few sentences I pushed him farther. He drove, speechless and angrier than the night Paul brought me home to the compound. I needed to direct him towards impulsive reactions to look after me and away from planning the extra rounds he needed to finish Damian's men after intentionally sinking a couple in painful non-life threatening places.

"You're right of course, Josh," I said, pretending I didn't notice his mood. I'd have felt a lot better about him being behind the wheel if he wasn't so close to red line. "I didn't go there on purpose or make their rules or make the man steal the rifle."

Joshua's temper peaked for the next dozen or so miles.

"Please don't think badly of me," I tried. He took his hand from under his leg and turned off the radio then ran it over top of his head like Paul would.

"No, Little Sister, I don't," he sighed as he gave me a tight smile. I turned to look out my window.

By the time we reached the outskirts of Sacramento, Joshua cooled down and appeared wrapped in his own thoughts though he kept looking at me with concern. Worry lines on his forehead told me he was still shaken. I remembered how hard he was on himself for not being there when I was raped. Rubbing his nose in those feelings and his helplessness with my situation in Connecticut just so I could do it to him again made me into someone I truly despised.

Snow steadily fell when Jack's mated connection to me disappeared for nearly a second. Not long though an empty eternity for me. I cried out and clutched my chest as the moment wore on causing Joshua to reach for me and swerve on the road.

"Hey?" Joshua asked as I started to breathe again.

"Fine," I murmured but I wasn't. Was this how it started? I rubbed the boys' panicked lines as I assessed our connection. There was no doubt it returned but it didn't feel right. It tried too hard to stay connected only it was weak. Like when my father busted me for putting too much water back in the liquor bottles back in my teenage drinking days. It made more but it was too weak.

"Maybe," I swallowed, more like a loud gulp as Joshua looked at me. When I shifted in my seat I felt the weight of the handcuffs move against my leg and noticed a long chain linked fence coming up ahead on our right.

"I'm going to be sick, Josh," I pointed my face at the roof like I tried to keep it down. "Pull over!"

Joshua did. If the roads were dry our skid would have made noise. As it was we were jarred as the front right hit the sidewalk. My door opened and I crossed the shoulder to the fence before Joshua had it in park. I leaned over, resting my head on the top rail and waited until I heard his door slam. The engine continued to run, telling me he left the keys inside so I clicked one end of the handcuffs to the fence and readied the other.

"Hey," Joshua said as his hand rested on my back. I coughed and panted like I had trouble and reached my left hand for his. He took it without thinking so I pulled it under me and as the other end clicked tight around his wrist I backed away.

"What the?" He said, puzzled. I took a couple more steps until I was certain I was out of reach.

"I'm sorry, Josh," I whispered.

"What's going on?" He looked at the cuffs and tugged his wrist testing them.

"Jack called me just before we left," I said and saw pain in his eyes. "He knows where Paul is. I'm going to get him."

"Bullshit, Anna," he said, pulling harder. "If you know where my brother is you tell me. I'll deal with it."

"No, Josh."

Snow melted on his blonde hair and ran down his face.

"You're going back to him," he accused. "You gave up on my brother and you're running back to Jack. Paul never gave up on you."

"No," I raised my voice. "I'm bringing Paul home."

I doubted I could but I would damn well try. More than likely I'd wind up going home with Gerald; widowed and in pain from losing Jack but I had to try. If I did nothing it would happen anyway. My men would be dead and all I'd have left was surrender to Gerald Walker to protect my children.

"Anna," Joshua shouted. He thrashed against the fence, his bare hand turned white in the tight cuff and the metal shook. "God damn you, Anna. Get back here."

I heard his humiliation. Humiliation he felt for his brother and for himself by letting me run off to my old lover.

"Don't do this," he cried and I stopped, hand on the back of the truck. "Please. I'm not going to watch your family break into pieces again when there's something I can do to stop it.

"Please, Anna. I'm not stupid. I know things go on I'm left out of; the whispering and silence with my brother. He's up to something and so are you and I'm not letting him die or you walk away to Jack without a fair shot at keeping you with my brother."

A car approached and Joshua put his hand on the fence rail to hide the cuff. It passed without slowing.

"It's bad enough Paul's in trouble. I'm not risking you."

"This isn't some bullshit clearance issue. He's my brother."

Joshua kicked at the fence to emphasize 'bullshit' and 'issue.' My eyes momentarily closed as I double checked my connection to Jack.

"You were there when Denis died at your house weren't you?" His voice dropped as he spoke. "The file was sealed but I heard things, did some snooping through Paul's paperwork before he gave it to the Colonel. Hours before you showed up in the compound with him stinking of fire and jet fuel from the plane crash that burned down your house. The clothes you wore were hidden in the trash and it took weeks to get around to burning them with everyone working on your apartment. Plenty of time for me to find them, plenty of privacy to look."

"No, Joshua," I answered but I knew my face said it wasn't the truth.

"And after you ran out on him for two months he filled up in Michigan only sixty minutes before his truck was checked into the compound.

"I've heard the whispers: lines, Courtesy, family. Organized crime or something? You've both been lying on your reports to the Colonel but you got way to sloppy. Don't shut me out, Little Sister. Isn't whatever shit you have going on important enough for Paul to have every chance? You need me and you can't deny it. I don't care about the rest of it. My niece needs her dad, I need my brother and you need your husband."

I walked half way to him, slipping in the snow. Joshua jerked toward me to help only to be stopped by the chain. He'd be a ghost to Walker, invisible and would be the only man he wouldn't be able to use the charm on. Since everything in the vehicle would make it, Joshua shouldn't be a problem. He needed to be part of my next move.

"No questions, Josh," I ordered. "I drive. You listen. It's my show and if you don't do it my way it's going to be a one way trip."

Joshua's eyes narrowed as his grip on the fence tightened but he nodded in concession. I wasn't completely certain he'd do it my way but I couldn't afford to leave him behind.

"How do I get you off the fence?"

Of all the things on Joshua's keychain, it held a useless piece of bent metal which easily removed the cuffs. He was silent as he lifted me into the driver's seat. I started it up and he got in. The front wheels were still cranked to the right and the rears spun and caught, driving us up against the sidewalk before I straightened out the steering.

The road was worse than I thought. I appreciated Joshua's driving for making the trip as smooth as it was. I hadn't driven since before Jack and I were caught by Soros. My lack of practice didn't help. I had only half the speed I needed and barely kept it on the pavement.

My attention wandered as I reached over my left shoulder for my seatbelt and the truck slid sideways. I eased up on the gas and regained control as I snapped the buckle closed and pushed the lap belt down under my stomach.

"At first I thought Paul was in trouble," Joshua flatly said as he stared straight ahead. "Like Major Howard. Wasn't ever clear how he went bad but Paul seemed next in line for it. Howard's men were the same way: Roberts, Soros, Walker. Then when Roberts turned up with you I knew you were mixed up in it."

The urgency I felt was nearly overwhelming. I knew I needed it to focus and tried to use it but every time Jack's connection to me faltered the building pressure I felt for the jump weakened. If I could ever get the pressure where I needed it, I hoped Joshua would listen and close his eyes.

"It's a small bunch of us, Josh," I started, imitating his emotionless tone. "We're into the same shit as Howard though not really by choice."

"Fuck," Joshua muttered. "Whatever you're getting me into better be damn well worth it."

Then he threw his head back. I shook my head, feeling my temper rise. He'd delayed me and insisted on coming and *I* was getting *him* into something? But then if he came with me he could be sure he ran Jack off. His reasons for sitting next to me in the truck at that moment were as complex as mine for bringing him along.

"Whatever, sorry," he added. "If we get Paul out it's worth it."

I gave up on the jump for the moment since I could still time our arrival back to before Jack went in after Paul. The two of them could sort it out; Jack creating the distraction while Joshua went in unread and dealt with Walker. Quick and clean, I hoped.

"I remember the day I met Paul," I said over the rolling tires on the frozen pavement. "My mother arranged our introduction."

"Your mother passed a decade ago."

"Allison Creed did," I choked, surprised by my reaction to saying the words. "The woman who introduced me to him did so eight hundred years ago, I figure from the clothes and technology. The language. I don't really know for sure. Eastern Europe, I think."

Joshua considered as I tried to focus in on Jack.

"Like you've had past life regression?" He asked but he didn't sound serious.

"Maybe," I shrugged. "Paul remembers too, far better than I do. A lot of them do; come together again and again carrying their memories from one life to the next. Damian Howard is one of them: his men, Jack, a lot of Paul's men. Paul and I have been together over and over; had children like Camille who will remember their past lives as well as he does.

"I know it sounds crazy, Josh."

I pushed the truck a little harder though thinking about Paul my focus shifted to him.

"Sure does," Joshua said.

I concentrated again on my sons and their father. We'd get to Paul in time and the last thing I needed was to turn up with Paul at Walker's side without Jack's help.

"There's been a feud going on for hundreds of years between Howard's side and Paul's. Walker is Howard's son from long ago like Camille is Paul's daughter.

"Damian Howard is dead. We take out Walker when we get Paul then hunt down Soros. We'll have peace at least for a while."

Joshua crossed his arms. "We get my brother then you get real professional help, Anna. Whatever they put you through messed your head up even more than I thought."

"Sure, Josh," I agreed. "Just do what I say or we won't get there."

"That's what I agreed to."

Maybe all he agreed to. I couldn't blame him. He grasped at logical reasons for the turns his day had taken.

"When I say so, close your eyes," I said.

I tried to recall how long it had been since I first felt Jack disconnect so I could aim at least that far back. It had to have been at least half an hour I guessed as I sped up, I focused on him. I knew if I could get there before he made his move on his brother, he'd take Joshua but he wouldn't let me help.

I wasn't prepared to take no for an answer.

Jack's connection stuttered only once and I tuned out Joshua's alarm with my driving as I quickly regained the pressure I'd lost. I knew I needed more speed and once I had the pressure I stomped on the accelerator. I had to get to Jack before Jack got to Walker.

"Close your eyes, Joshua."

The truck surged around a gentle turn and we nearly made it. Joshua grabbed the wheel as the left rear caught the gravel on the wrong side of the road. I focused on preparing for the jump then Joshua's hand on mine reminded me how wrong it was to put him in danger.

I closed my eyes then thought how stupid it was to bring someone in from outside the family and how I had to keep Joshua alive for his parents and for Camille. The truck tipped too far as Joshua crushed my hands between his and the wheel and I thought, *Jack*.

Chapter 40

Winter bit.

I hugged myself tighter, keeping my eyes shut against the stinging snow pelting me from every direction. Jack's mated connection to me still felt watery and I knew something was wrong. I hadn't even made it back far enough to stop whatever disrupted it though I suspected a catastrophic wound. I didn't feel pain yet so he lived.

"Joshua?" I called and heard no answer. Either he'd appeared out of earshot or stared into the distance, caught in those moments of travel as his mind caught up.

When I opened my eyes, I lay on the ground. An upright wooden fence post appeared horizontal. The truck ran but it suffered with an ungodly rattle like every metal panel hung loose though I couldn't be sure. At least it wasn't dead though a high pitched hiss from somewhere inside told me it might not run for long. As my eyes shut, I remembered thinking how much I loved my brother-in-law for suspending his judgment and being at my side then everything went sideways.

I turned to my back and winced at pain in my left shoulder and lower lip. I'd rolled the truck as I jumped, escaping serious injury only because I'd appeared here before it went all the way over.

There was nothing but frozen corn stalks as far as I could see. I scanned with my sense, reading nobody family within my range but I knew which way to go to find them.

At the top of the wooden post, a new mailbox with a freshly painted name on it told me all I needed.

Pilot.

I knew where we'd face Gerald Walker. I'd been here in the heat of summer fourteen months earlier for me; seventy or so years earlier for its former owner.

The farmhouse a mile away once belonged to Ray's father Pilot; Sig's nephew, the man who'd tinkered with both his brothers and with me in order to inflict 'the cure' on two men who'd gone insane.

I rolled toward my front so I could use my right to push up and off my left shoulder then I grabbed the post and pulled myself to my feet. I tugged my zipper up and spotted the truck to my right. The entire left side was heavily damaged as was part of the roof. The black canopy hung half off and cracks webbed the dark windows.

Joshua's legs stuck out beside the rear wheel. He'd appeared prone as I had. Always landed on my feet when I jumped and I guessed the rolling truck put us down.

"Josh?" I called as I rounded the rear of the truck to get to him. Eyes half open, jaw slack; he lay on his side nearly beneath the bumper. I leaned on the truck for balance as I got to my knees.

"Hey," I called as I patted his cheek. He didn't even blink. "Joshua?"

No response. I'd been aware it was over for two minutes at least. I spread my knees to get down further, leaned over and put my cheek to his mouth as my fingers dug at the side of his throat.

No breathing, no pulse.

"Joshua!" I screamed as I pushed him on his back. His head turned away from me as limp and dead as I could ever imagine. I buried my face in his chest and cried then smacked my head on the bumper as I got upright and tried to pull it together enough to remember 'what to do.'

Three minutes maybe? Soon there would be no point in doing anything. I couldn't do CPR under the truck. As high as it was there wasn't enough room so I pulled on his arm but the ice and snow on the dirt road gave me no traction and I fell on him.

I kept shouting his name as I bent one of his knees up and used it to lever him over to his side then onto his stomach. For a moment I entertained the idea of doing compressions on his back but abandoned it as I pulled his other knee out to his side. Using it to roll him was even harder. Sweat broke out inside my coat as I crawled to his head. I tipped it back and sealed my mouth around his. It wasn't as hard as I thought it would be after I remembered to pinch his nose. His chest obediently rose and fell and I forced another breath in.

Joshua's coat already hung open so I found the spot on his chest and piled the heels of my palms on it.

"Don't you *dare* fuck this up, Anna," I muttered at my hysterical reflection in the chrome before my eyes. "You did this to him and don't you dare fuck it up."

I pumped as hard as I could, knees nearly coming up off the snow. Five then five then five before I filled his lungs and filled his lungs and five.

"You should have left him on the fence you stupid bitch," I yelled at the woman in the bumper. Five and five. "One day you're going to learn to say no!"

And breathe and breathe.

"And then you won't do this shit," five, "to the people you love," five, "don't fuck this up!"

And five and breathe—

Vile wetness filled my mouth as Joshua's stomach emptied and he gagged so I grabbed his knee and rolled him again.

You're so damned lucky, Anna, I thought. And so is Joshua you stupid, stupid woman.

I spat then adrenaline sent my own vomit free to wash his from me. Joshua blinked and coughed as he threw up again and took a shaky breath on his own. We gasped together on the ground and as my adrenaline faded, pain returned to my shoulder made even worse by the violent compressions I laid on him. Blood from my split lip covered his cheek.

"Josh?"

His hand clutched at his chest and he coughed in obvious pain.

"Your heart stopped," I leaned on him, crying. "You stopped breathing. I was so scared."

"Jesus," he whispered. "You pack a punch."

I smiled and wiped tears from his cheek.

"Yeah," I admitted.

"You might have broke a rib."

"I'm sorry. I rolled the truck," I shuddered as Jack weakened inside me before holding strong again.

"Okay."

I brushed a hand over his head and felt a big lump.

"Do you hurt anywhere else?"

"Just my chest."

Joshua pushed himself sitting then onto his knees before helping me up. We staggered together to the driver's side but the door wouldn't open. That side of the truck had taken the brunt of the roll. The windshield shattered as had the window in the door.

"Where are we?" Joshua asked.

"Nebraska."

"Okay."

Three minutes without air and the blow to his head. I felt sick inside, worrying about the permanent damage I may have caused.

"Paul's in a farmhouse about a mile away," I whispered as I helped Joshua in the rear passenger door. I climbed in the front and slid across, panting by the time I got there. My left hand pressed firmly on my stomach, keeping the shoulder still. It functioned, though not without increased complaint. I relaxed and rested a hand on the boys' lines to read what I already knew. They seemed calm, unstressed by the accident and I was fortunate only my shoulder and head hit anything before the jump. In the mirror I could see my split lip and a growing lump on my forehead.

"Here," Joshua whispered. I turned and he held a gun to me, butt first. "One each."

I took it and watched with dismay as his head fell against the glass. Maybe, I hoped, he just needed rest. He coughed then grunted as he got his arm around his ribs again.

"Something's moving in there," he whispered. "Is that normal?"

"I don't know, Josh."

Internal injuries, I thought.

But his colour looked good. Maybe it was normal after CPR.

Jack flickered inside me again as I shifted it into gear and turned right into Pilot's driveway, shedding the canopy as the truck tilted around the corner.

When Jack connected his sensum to mine I sneezed, confirming at least he wasn't dead. I rounded the last bend in the drive and Pilot's house came into sight.

Oh, shit, I sent to Jack without thinking. He responded with alarm. Knowing I was at Pilot's and actually seeing the house before me were two different things. It had been updated with new windows and a new porch but the barn behind was gone. Walker's truck sat out front next to an older car I didn't recognize. Keeping Joshua's truck straight had been a struggle. The left front fender ground against the tire and even if it hadn't, the front end felt misaligned.

This is Pilot's house, I sent to Jack. *I've been here before.*

Go, Baby, Jack sent. *Please. There is nothing but death here.*

Not if I can help it.

Jesus, get the fuck out of here!

I read pain in his message and anger with me. If he hadn't phoned first, Walker's hurting him would have been just as effective in getting me to come even without knowing Paul was here with them.

Don't treat me like a child ever again, Jack Roberts, I replied. *I'm offering myself.* I had no choice now the truck was totalled unless I could get Walker's keys. *If he doesn't go for it I'm going to crush him, Jack. I have Joshua's gun and I'm going to crush him.*

I sharply turned so the back of the truck pointed toward the house. Unless someone came around and looked nobody would know Joshua was there. Bringing a ghost, someone who wasn't family, was hopefully the last thing they'd suspect.

I checked Joshua's gun before putting it in my pocket. He breathed okay and I leaned over the back of my seat and pulled him over on his side in case he threw up again. He didn't stir.

I found his phone in his pocket and called Sig, hoping he'd pick up.

"You have reached the confidential voicemail of Colonel Sigmund Iverson…"

Joshua breathed easily then his lungs hitched once while he paused to swallow and I waited for the beep.

"Sig, Lieutenant Richards and I have tracked the Major to Pilot's. Joshua is unconscious and I'm not waiting for help."

When I killed the engine it died with a final solid crunch.

I had no intention of leaving and in any case, the truck wasn't moving. It was probably the stupidest thing I'd ever done. So stupid that any other day self-preservation should have won out.

Today stubbornness trumped self-preservation.

Paul says go home, Jack tried but even his voice in my head weakened. *Go to your daughter.*

I'm sure he does, Jack. But I'm not. I'm going to get you both out and first chance I get I'm going to slit Walker's throat and take our sons and leave.

Baby, Jack tried.

I ignored him.

The wide front porch spread before me. The stairs had been replaced with the rest of it maybe a decade or two earlier and the paint looked new. I imagined the warm gold light of summer though winter cast everything in cold white. A rumbling motor in the rear of the house gave the only outward sign of occupation.

Before I reached the stairs, a muffled gunshot sounded from deep inside the house. I staggered the rest of the way, clutching my knee as I sat and cried out. The shot hadn't hit me or I'd be on the ground though I felt much of it. Jack's pain echoed inside me.

Walker says to hurry up.

Damn him, Jack. I will when my knee works again. I tested it, straightening it out but the joint felt wrong. *I'll betray him in the most disgusting way I can think of.*

I want you to leave.

One way or another, I will, I sent as I stood. Pain crept into my thigh but the joint held even though it still felt ripped up. *This can't go on. If I walk away now I won't have you or Paul to protect me. I'll be his no matter what I do. We have to stop it today.*

Damn you, Jack weakly sent and our connection stuttered.

I love you, Jack. I love my husband. I sent as I started up the stairs. *That doesn't make me bad. If I save you both I'll be alone. I could never choose. If I fail I'll be alone. That choice has been made for me.*

Jack stayed silent. The rumbling grew once I reached the porch. I felt it in my feet. To the left was the spot where I sat with Pilot. I imagined us there in the heat, sweat still running from me. There was no sweat now. The dry air tore the moisture from my skin.

Another shout came as I pushed the front door open. The smell of roasting chicken welcomed me. A long hall led to the kitchen and a big living room opened to the right. New furnishings sat on the old hardwood floor.

As I stepped in, Walker appeared in the kitchen at the end of the hall.

"Hello, Gerald," I answered with as much unruffled bravery as I could, hoping my open familiarity with him would be welcome.

"Precious," he warmly smiled. My feet stalled and I waited as he approached, pulling bloody blue latex gloves from his hands and turning them inside out before opening his jacket. His cheeks were pink from the cold basement air. My lungs tightened as his line entered me, not for control though I felt its heavy presence inserted in my chest flirting as he explored.

"Precious," he whispered, his line taking gentle hold of mine. I felt no pain or pressure. The contact felt intimate though it was something Jack and Paul had never done with me. My cheeks involuntarily warmed as my body responded to his sexual advance. "Wait here."

He stepped through one of the two doors on my left and I heard water running. When he returned, he held a warm wet face cloth and wiped around my eyes. I winced as he cleaned the bump on my forehead.

"Sshhh," he soothed as he kissed it and went on to clean the blood from my chin. "What have you done?"

"I lost control of the truck, Gerald," I tried his name again. "It rolled as I jumped here and I hit my head."

"Mm," he murmured, holding my cheek in his hand as his lips traced across my cheek bone. His head turned to the truck.

"I sense you near your poor truck as well. RJ said travel would ruin your line," he said in an 'I told you so' kind of way.

"Yes, Gerald," I agreed. Perhaps RJ was right and I'd only gotten lucky saving Jack from the gallows. My attention had been on too many things when I jumped with Joshua. If I'd done anything bad to my line it was my own fault.

"I know what you're afraid of," Walker whispered as the caress of his line strengthened in me for a moment. It still didn't hurt but I felt horribly discomfited as if he groped me with his own hands.

"A little something to slow you down, Precious," his voice rumbled, rough with lust. "And give me a chance to get ready. Let's see if you can save them.

"Join us," he ordered and turned on his heel. I watched his long grey braid sway down the centre of his back as he disappeared from sight. A door creaked and I read him as he descended then doubled back in my direction toward the front of the house.

Though he was gone his line lingered. I turned and rested my head against the wall as I trembled, sick with myself for physically giving in to his interest in me. For a moment I forgot about the egotistical drunk who banged on the door to Jack's room to explicitly describe how he'd like to spend the night with me until Soros ran him off.

As I gained control of myself I scanned downstairs. Paul, Jack and Walker somewhere nearly below my feet and when I scanned the truck I read what Walker noticed; a hint of myself, there briefly then gone.

I passed the two doors on my left as I made my way to the kitchen.

The stove light showed me a big black roaster full of chicken, I guessed, and the table was set for several people. Jack had said Soros was coming.

I took a couple of paper towels from the roll on the counter to blow my nose then cupped a mouthful of water from the tap to rinse the taste of vomit away.

A cry of pain came from the floor below. Lights dimmed as the rumbling stuttered and through the back door I saw the cause. Two heavy generators sat on the back porch. One belched smoke as it hesitated and caught, dimming the lights a second time.

Paul, Jack sent. I crumpled into one of the chairs and broke down. I could get the old car going and flee leaving Joshua behind. Take my boys as far away from Camille and San Diego as possible. Hope for the best until Walker found me. No part of that plan made sense. I could never promise her safety as long as Walker lived. I could only keep Walker close if I couldn't kill him here. She was more important than any of us. Get help for Jack, Paul and Joshua if I could.

Tell him I'm coming.

The basement creaked open allowing a dank cold draft out across the floor and around my legs.

Chapter 41

An absolute absence of light and sound filled the stairwell. I opened the door enough to let some light in and could tell there were no stairs, only a steeply sloped roof sharply sinking down into an undulating floor at the same level as my feet. There was no light switch inside so I reached around to the kitchen wall and felt one.

When I pushed it up, water splashed my feet and I shrieked, backing up into the porch door.

Black water filled the stairwell to the top step. The surface shivered with the vibration of the generators behind me and lapped up onto the kitchen floor.

A man's scream reached me from deep below as the surface surged like something huge rolled just below and steam rose from the top of the bulge. I cried out again, paralyzed with fear as the black wave broke over the top step and spread gallons over the linoleum floor; water so black it obscured the white and blue design until it spread all the way across the room to the stove.

Baby?

Black water, Jack, I sent. *The stairs are full of black water.*

It's not real, he reassured me but as I watched, it stilled until only the vibration remained. I smelled it and heard the sucking noises it made under the soles of my boots. I remembered Colliery Dam and the hold on my leg. I could still smell the foul deep water on my skin when I finally made it home.

So real, I sent. *There's something in it. The monster is there under the water.*

You're right, Baby, Jack angrily sent. *You'll never make it down here. The monster is real, you brought it here and if you don't lead it away it will drown Paul and me.*

Yes, I agreed, backing up. In my heart I knew it couldn't be but I'd seen the thing under the water with my own eyes and knew Jack was right.

It's your fault, he yelled inside my head.

Another gunshot from below and I grabbed my already aching shoulder as I dropped to my knees by the counter. Cold water soaked through my pants.

Jack?

There was no answer.

"Jack?" I yelled as I got my feet under me but he was no help. He was alive down below so there was no way the basement could be full of water. And I'd heard Walker go down the steps only a few minutes earlier.

I took a step closer and watched the deceptively still surface. The wetness on my pants chilled me in spite of the oven-warmed room and I kept going though I breathed far too fast.

"You're not really there," I whispered as I took another step toward the stairs. "You never were."

It rumbled in reply, becoming so disturbed fist sized balls of water leaped up nearly a foot before crashing back to the surface like it demanded to know why I would talk to something which didn't exist. I wasn't so sure why I would. Walker's line shifted gently in me again and I realized his words filled the stairs with water. That didn't make it any less real.

"I saw Jack swim in the pool and you didn't touch my sister when she went in looking for you." I found a small amount of courage as my breathing slowed but I pulled out Joshua's gun and held it before me anyway as if I expected the monster to jump out and take a round.

This time the water didn't rumble. It splashed all the way up one side of the stairwell then the other. Small drops sizzled on the bare bulb over my head. The bulge came for me through the tumult and I took careful one-handed aim. I only had a couple of seconds and as I squeezed the trigger, the water calmed, barely washing up into the kitchen.

"Run, you son of a bitch," I said but I shook. I hoped the monster was gone and I still had to deal with the water.

I pocketed Joshua's gun and leaned flat against the wall to my right then clutched the railing on my left. I put a foot in the water before I had the chance to think about what I was doing. The water stayed still as I took another step and another.

"See? Gone, gone, gone," I gloated but my nose wrinkled with the stink of decomposition stirred by my feet. The stairs seemed less solid and as I picked up my boots it wasn't just the weight of the water which made each step harder than the last. The muck beneath held them down in a silty vacuum.

I drew in a sharp breath as the cold hit my belly and I felt my stomach tighten. My sons were within the monster's reach if it returned.

Another step and it did. A writhing ball of murk hit me from behind, collapsing my knees. I slipped, clinging to the railing as my butt landed in the mud. My shoulder tore under my skin. Water splashed up on my cheeks as the light dimmed with another bang from the porch.

My feet found purchase but even with the small amount of help my left arm provided, my clothes were so waterlogged I couldn't get anymore than my shoulders clear. I gagged with the stink of what I'd stirred up on the bottom as I decided my only chance was to go down and get to Paul and Jack straight ahead, thirty feet away.

I took a deep breath, let go of the railing and let the monster pull me under.

A single bare bulb ten feet away lit the hall, its walls covered in cobwebbed seafoam green paint. My arm was still up and I grabbed at my coat, astonished I wasn't wet at all. The walls were dry and the light shone above the top step.

It's your dream, Baby.

I stopped in my tracks, boots scratching at the dirty floor. Jack sounded weaker than before as though communicating to me like this was too much.

Jack, Paul and Walker were in the room down the hall. From where I stood I could smell blood and the scent of Walker's dinner which followed me downstairs.

No.

I started walking, refusing to believe. The pain and pressure above, thunder and lightening from the generators. Going to Paul and Jack could kill them. Going to Walker, the storm which met me above and sacrificing myself to save them. My near death experience said I wouldn't survive Walker either. Surrounded by frozen corn.

Coincidences only.

The cold dirty water took the place of the rising ice in my dream and was a sufficient enough incongruity for me to have some hope to hold close.

Even if it was the dream, no clue would save everyone as Jack once suggested. I'd leave with Walker and the rest wouldn't leave at all.

Laboured breathing came to me from the door to the right at the very end of the hall. As I neared, Walker stepped into the doorway. I imagined we were almost underneath the generators though they weren't as loud since I'd gotten turned around and was near the front of the house. Only their vibration in the air.

"Precious, you are a brave girl," Gerald softly said. "Richards was lured so easily. We leaked the women would be away. He couldn't resist the chance to foul my home again. Then these men insisted you wouldn't come. I disagreed so Jack helped me call you."

By taking a bullet from you, I thought. He'd been badly injured before I arrived. The second shot was just to get me the rest of the way into the house.

The third down the stairs. My cowardice before the water hurt him.

"Get out," Paul moaned from inside.

When I took another step, Walker shifted his weight to reveal a man's legs on the ground. One knee torn and bloodied by the bullet I heard from outside. It was Jack's, his damaged hand rested next to it.

Dear God, Jack. Your leg.

Don't look, Baby. Walk away.

"Gerald," I whispered. My fingers took his braid and I ran them down his back. Over his shoulder, I saw Paul. He appeared seated since he was much lower than me, his face badly bruised, both lips deeply split and an eye swollen shut. His head shook as he glared at me, furious with my stupidity. As long as I didn't look too closely at him or at Jack I could pull this off. I'd seen the woman in the mirror do it. It looked like she'd pulled it off with Walker night after night for at least a decade.

I covered my mouth and plugged my nose to keep from sobbing as my other hand reached for the side of Walker's head. The rumble above stuttered, lights flickering in response to my physical contact with Gerald Walker.

"Precious, my dear," he contentedly murmured as he turned his head and rubbed his rough cheek against my palm.

"I didn't come for them, Gerald," I said, taking his cold ear in my warm hand and caressing it with my thumb. "Though your message gave me an opportunity I couldn't pass up. I knew of no other way to find you."

He didn't know I could travel to a person.

"Indeed," he said. "And why did you want to find me after you so rudely fled my home?"

"I had to be sure, as you have to be sure of me."

Damn you, Jack sent.

If I don't pull this off we're all damned. I'm in too far to back out.

A wet cough followed by a moan reached me. It sounded like Jack but I'd never seen either of them in such bad shape so I couldn't be certain.

"And what are you so sure of now that you would come to me?"

"Look at them, Gerald," I whispered. "Powerless, weak. You singlehandedly broke them both. They abandoned me. What do they care? Paul's daughter is safe. These boys will grow up. I've been their property for too long and it's time I decided how I'm going to live the rest of my life."

"These boys deserve better."

"On that point we are completely agreed, Precious."

I rested my hands on his shoulders, my forehead in the center of his back. Jack coughed again as his breathing grew more laboured. It was him this time, I was sure.

"And why me," he asked, suddenly turning. "I'm certain you've had other offers."

I took his chin in my hand and pulled him with me across the hall, away from the smell of blood and the possibility I'd see inside. A drop of blood marked his glasses and another soiled his coat. Considering the amount I inhaled it was obvious he was careful to keep clean. My stomach lurched with the idea he could be so well practiced and meticulous with whatever he'd done to Paul.

"Some asked a lot less of me; stay home, be good," I gestured with my head at the men in the room behind him. "But they offer a lot less in return, do they not?"

Walker laughed. "On that point, we also agree."

"It's never been in my nature to stay home and be good."

"Go, Anna," Paul grunted, his voice rising to squeak with pain. I heard movement in the room and imagined him struggling.

"You are most intriguing," Walker whispered as he came at me from the side, his lips brushing my neck as his erection kneaded my hip. Then he kissed the bruise on my forehead. His line tangled with mine again and I bit my cut lip in an effort to resist my body's response. One hand unzipped my coat. Fortunately, the pocket containing the gun was on the other side. "But I'm sure even my generous offer comes with a price. If you only sought my protection you would have gone to Connecticut, not waited until your mate lay dying in the next room. I somehow doubt this body interests you as much as yours interests me."

I swallowed, tensing as his teeth grazed my neck and he bit more than gently.

"Look at me, Gerald. No man's body interests me now," I slowly ran my hand down his side, closer to my pocket.

Do it, Baby, Jack sent. *If you're going to shoot him fucking do it.*

Not yet. He's suspicious.

Walker was hesitant, questioning me and I didn't think I'd get away with any sudden move for the gun.

"I still read your little lost line, Precious," he whispered. "It seeks you."

"Yes," I answered as his line rubbed against mine. My hand let go of the gun, wanting to pull him closer and I willed it to grab it again. I wasn't prepared for this type of insidious control from him. I'd expected brute force crushing, not irresistible foreplay.

"When it finds you I shall set it," he reassured me. "It won't do for it to be incomplete."

I read it above, somewhere between the porch and the truck.

"Thank you, Gerald," I said as I understood what I'd done to myself.

What the hell did you do? Jack sent, angry with me again. *RJ was right you'd tear your goddamn line.*

I lost focus, Jack, I explained. *I rolled the truck but I'm not hurt too bad. I think a piece of my line came off.*

"Idiot," Jack's voice broke into a wet gurgle from the other room.

The lights went out as I looked at the bare bulb in the room holding Jack and Paul. For a moment lightning trailed left across my retina then the lights came on with a bang above as the generators started back up.

"I feel Jack's connection to me sliding away already," I gulped, shaken by the momentary blackness. "Like it's trying too hard. It'll burn itself off quickly when he dies."

"True," Walker whispered. His hand went into my coat and ran over my breast and to my stomach. "They are two glorious heirs to my Father's legacy. Loyalty and honesty are rewarded in my home. Should their mother continue to show me both I will be at her service as long as I'm able. Name your price."

"Gerald," I spoke slowly hoping to sound confident and honest. "Leave my daughter alone. Let Paul leave. I will promise myself to you as your loyal mate. I'll accept you as mine. When Jack passes we'll make the promise to each other. Take me to bed and take my pain away."

Walker turned to face me, giving my stomach some room. His hand rested gently on my sore shoulder as if he could feel my injury.

"You shall have your own house, built on my Father's land. In that house you will raise these boys and my son," he pulled me in, speaking wetly in my ear. "And I shall come to your bed whenever I desire you and of course when you feel the same need. You may also join me in the house as there is no shortage of caregivers in Father's home."

"You are most generous. Thank you, Gerald," I said. Privacy and a place of isolation would be a true gift.

"You have asked me for three things. One you shall have. Unfortunately you have asked me for two things you will not receive. One because I cannot and the other because I will not."

"How?" I asked, unable to hide the tremor in my voice. My left hand grabbed his shirt, pulling him closer while my right wrapped around the handle of Joshua's gun, seating it perfectly in my palm. I'd get one shot and I needed every chance I could take to make it count.

"Gerald could never take the pain of Jack's death from Anna. He's hurt her and her line would never accept his," he breathed as he pressed me into the wall, helping my reluctant knees keep me up. His thumb dug into my shoulder and I cried out as he found the most painful spot. "And I would never spare your mates. How loyal and honest would you be as long as even one of them waited in the wings?"

I tried to draw the gun from my pocket but pain lanced up my arm and through the rest of my body. Intense pressure in my chest built as Walker's line ground into mine, holding it still. Without any orders from him all I could do was freeze as coldness spread up into my lips.

"I'm going to get you both out and the first chance I get I'm going to slit Walker's throat and take our sons and leave," Walker's voice tore through me like thunder as he quoted the words I'd sent to Jack.

"No," Jack cried out from the other room before his voice failed in a series of moans and coughs.

"I have Joshua's gun and I'm going to crush him." Walker went on. "You've done nothing to show me honesty, Precious. Though it may not be too late.

"Walk with me," he ordered and took my elbows, forcing me to turn then he shoved me ahead of him into his abattoir.

Chapter 42

As I complied, Walker's hold on my line loosened but the sight of Jack and Paul was too much for me to concentrate enough to split mine; to hide and protect a part of it to use over top of Walker's to take control of him.

I came to a stop as soon as Walker stopped pushing and closed my eyes though I'd already seen too much. Jack lay on the ground, his stomach and shoulder soaked with blood like his knee. He coughed once and fresh blood wept down his side. I imagined the near frozen concrete beneath him turned the pool solid.

Nails held Paul to his chair.

Beside him, the metal pins I dreamed lay out on a mesh table. The two pins missing from the leather case ran through Paul's shoulders and into the wood behind him. He couldn't slump without more pain and if he passed out, the agony would bring him 'round.

Rusty farm equipment from every era hung on the wall behind Paul; eight-foot long two-man saws, axes and hammers. Even a heavy spool of barbed wire sat in the corner by Jack. So many pieces of metal I didn't recognize, some with freshly sharpened edges and others still covered in blood only slightly different in colour from the rust.

"You see," Walker hissed in my ear. "These gentlemen hesitated a moment too long and lost their chance to try and control me, just as you did, Precious. Now they are in too much pain. It takes a healthy line to control another.

"I've tired of them, however," he continued. "Look at Richard's left hand."

I complied, eyes popping open. It had been zip tied to the metal grate, each finger immobilized by its own tie and a piece of metal shoved under his ring finger. Next to it lay a chisel and wooden hammer. The plastic tie holding the finger down kept it from bleeding at the missing tip.

"Please," I barely whispered. The pain of speaking without permission prevented me from saying any more. A drop of blood fell through the grate to the cement floor before exploding with its tiny impact.

"Please what, Precious?" Walker asked. Paul reddened. His one eye narrowed as he got angrier. A bubble of blood burst from his nose.

"Please let me do it, Mister Walker?" He suggested. "Please let me end it with him to prove myself to you? You may speak."

"I promise, Mister Walker," I whispered. "I promise I'll come with you, just let them go."

"Hurry it up, you bastard," Paul growled. "Just don't hurt her."

Walker wrapped his arms around me as I stood still, unable to move.

"You're only sincere when you beg, Precious."

"Please, Mister Walker," I tried. "Please let them go."

I stood to Paul's right, facing him and Walker moved to my left then took my chin forcing me to look at him.

"Words, Precious," he sadly shook his head then he nodded. "Actions."

"You're coming with me regardless of what you do next. Whether you live past the end of your pregnancy depends on how willing you are to prove yourself."

Then he laughed nearly to the point of tears. His glasses steamed up in the chill so he took them off and cleaned them on a soft cloth from his pocket. Jack twitched on the floor and Paul cursed.

"Actually, I'll make sure you prove yourself to me anyway. You don't have a choice. You will be good when we go home or I will hunt down your daughter. RJ's sentimental reasoning won't stop me from seeking out his very young sister.

"She will grow up to appreciate me," his eyes wrinkled with obvious pleasure and Paul's legs struggled against their bonds, causing Walker's pins to dig in. "And when you're no longer able to fill my father's home with strong sons she will take your place."

"I'll be so good," I promised, sickened with the thought of my Camille sharing my fate. "I swear, Paul. He'll never have her."

But when I turned to Paul, his eyes rolled up and in spite of the pain of the pins he passed out. The shining stainless steel bore his weight.

"I swear," I whispered again then cried out as the room went black and silent. We waited through a pop and a bang from the silent generators above.

"You shall not move, Precious." Walker sighed in frustration. A flashlight came on and I listened to his steps disappear down the hall then up the stairs.

"Jack," I whispered. A low moan from Paul came in reply but nothing from Jack. I knew now Walker could listen in when Jack and I were connected. This was the only chance I had to reassure him.

"I can do this, Jack," I whispered. "I can win. You know I can."

There was still no reply as one of the generators above sparked to life. The bulb dimly flickered as it came on and I could see my breath again. I could also see Jack in the periphery of my vision: unmoving and silent. With Walker's distance the hold of his line weakened, not enough to move but enough for me to put my line in pieces to protect the boys and challenge him.

First I let my sense sink into my chest to understand his hold on me. Jack had made the connection to my sensum so I was free to read. I split off a piece and carefully wrapped the boys' lines in it, pushing them as far away from my own as I could. I'd keep my line between Walker and theirs. Then I took more than half of what was left and pushed it aside, near the boys for when the time came. I'd fight Walker's charm over my line, forcing him to bring all of his in to control me then I'd snap mine over his and crush him long enough to put bullets in his head until he let me go. It wasn't complicated or fancy but it would work.

It had to.

Jack? I tried. Walker would hear but just sending his name would be harmless. There was a bang as the second generator started up. The light above Paul grew far too bright. With a pop, the one in the green hall exploded just before the one in the room went back to normal.

"I can do this, Jack," I whispered again.

"No," Jack whispered then coughed once. Walker's unhurried boots made their way down, crunching the broken bulb even finer as he passed through the hall.

"Ah, Precious," he said like he was surprised to find me in the room. He smelled of chicken and gasoline and cleaned his hands on a wet wipe as he took his place beside me. "Jack isn't answering? Let's see which one of them lasts the longest. It will be up to you of course.

"It's a mystery to me why RJ let Richards live months ago. Perhaps he couldn't bring himself to murder his line-mother's mate. Certainly convincing you he had was effective in making you obedient so I forgave his embarrassing display of weakness. I doubt you would have been very good at all if you knew he wasn't dead."

Paul's head came up with a shout as he became conscious and looked around assessing the situation for any small thing he could use to his advantage. It wouldn't matter what he spotted. He was as immobilized in the chair as I was on my feet.

Walker stepped away and dropped the wipe in the garbage.

"We have company coming, Precious," he said. "Your son RJ and his men. I'm certain they will be as pleased to see you as I. Now show me what you have in your pocket."

I knew where Walker wanted this to go; forcing me to shoot Paul as Jack died so there would be nobody left to save me and no reason for me to save myself. It would be a miracle if Joshua stayed hidden in the truck long enough for Sig to send help. The only thing I would have left to live for was keeping Walker from Camille. I wanted to fight him now but nothing would make me fight harder than resisting pulling the trigger on my husband.

My hand sunk into my pocket on its own and came up, holding Joshua's gun pointed at the ceiling. Even in the coat the metal had grown cold and I knew I could lose control of my fingers if I held it too long. I hoped the agonizing minute it would take to get Walker's line in me wouldn't be so long my trembling hand accidentally pulled the trigger.

"Ah, Joshua's gun," Walker exclaimed. "I wonder what talk there will be; suspicion of your husband's brother giving you his weapon for the deed. Your hands have been all over it, Precious. People will think they were all over him too."

Let's do this, I thought. Walker's fingers caressed mine on the handle as he pulled me back a step and extended my arm. The gun rested only inches from Paul's head.

"Shoot him," Walker simply said and before I could get a breath the pain crushed. First my finger which I kept out of the guard and flat against the barrel. Then my chest like something sharp swelled inside me, taking up every available corner. The boys' lines struggled in their safe cocoon, panicked, and my left hand came up inside my coat. My nails dug in an attempt to create an opening for Walker's burning pressure.

As I continued to resist, Walker wrapped his arms around me, holding me up.

"Shoot, Precious," he said again and again the intensity of his assault increased. Walker's breathing shuddered in my ear with effort as the generators upstairs stuttered again. One sped up, rattling its weight against the porch and the light pulsed in time.

Only a few seconds passed but already my skin slicked with my own blood, making it difficult for my nails to catch and cut me further. As I struggled to concentrate and read how much of his line was in me, my resistance slipped and my finger curled, tracing along the barrel of the gun until my nail hooked on the guard. There I fought to keep it, having found nearly all of Walker's line wrapped around mine.

The reserve I'd held snapped shut over his and the pain left me as suddenly as it had come. With a shout I turned, sliding my finger in the guard and over the trigger. Walker stood frozen in place.

"Don't breathe," I ordered and he stopped. The coldness of the room found its way up inside my sleeve.

"You won't hurt us again," I growled as Walker remained impassive and immobile. "Your delightful father died the real death at my hands nearly a year ago and when I see you on the other side you can just bet you'll be a whole lot nicer. Right now his stink still comes off you in waves."

Walker's eyes glanced at the hallway behind me and his nostrils flared. I delayed pulling the trigger long enough to send my sense behind me and found the piece of my line drifting near the stairs. If it found me quickly I'd try and use it against Walker but it would have to be very quickly. Our agonizing yet brief battle was nearly over.

I cupped my gun hand in my left though the shoulder drooped and sighted one glass lens covered eye along the top of the barrel. He resisted, drawing a breath and my heart rate shot up as I fought to contain him, not realizing the simple act of contracting my finger muscles was as much a challenge for my concentration as it had been when I tried not to pull the trigger. He was unbelievably strong beneath my line; practiced and experienced and I'd only done this once as a lesson from Paul. It was possible the damage the boys had done months earlier also worked in Walker's favour and I couldn't discount how much of my line was in the hall.

The corners of Walker's lips came up as he exhaled, his teeth grinding as his hand came up and pushed the gun aside. It discharged past his head and in that moment my concentration disappeared and he was inside me again, crushing. The throbbing light just over my head drove the pain even deeper and my crippled line ached in time.

"Do you think you're the only brilliant reader who has a backup plan?" He sweetly asked. "Not many have figured out how much less can pull it off and I certainly didn't expect it from you. If I hadn't kept part of my line safe out of habit you may have had me."

I prayed each agonizing breath I took was my last. The only reserve I had left shielded the boys who even now fought against it as they tried to protect me. I wouldn't let them go, soft and immature as their lines were, instinct told me it would kill them and it wouldn't be enough to be any challenge to Walker.

"Shoot him," Walker breathed easier as he pushed the gun at Paul. My finger was still on the trigger. I could feel it there under the tiny muscle which would pull it and end his life. Paul closed his unswollen eye and turned away as I continued to resist.

"Don't fight any more, Sugar," Paul whispered. "You fought better than Jack and I did."

He cursed under his breath as I started to cry, knowing it was over.

"I'm proud of you," he moaned. "I love you. You've suffered too much for me. Close your eyes and end this. Get on with protecting Camille."

"No, Paul," I said then I nearly roared, venting my pain with my mouth as I eased up on the trigger but Walker's heavy breathing told me how hard he worked for control, our lines in constricting layers in my chest. Even though he had the upper hand, part of his line was sandwiched inside me somewhere and experienced the pressure of the layers above.

My finger tightened, ever so slowly as the last of my strength gave out.

"I love you, Paul," I whispered as my eyes fell shut. "I'm so sorry—

"Don't move," Joshua shouted behind us. Walker grabbed my gun and pushed it up at the ceiling. He moved, putting me between him and the door. Paul's eye opened in alarm as he strained to see past me.

"Well, well, well, the little blonde Lieutenant with a line that smells of Precious. How on earth did you grant this little boy a line, my dear? And an exact copy of yours to boot?"

Walker took a handful of hair from the side of my head and turned me around. The bump on Joshua's head had bled down his neck and my blood still coated his cheek.

Walker's left hand held mine and the gun. I knew what happened but not how. I'd been touching Joshua when we jumped. The jump itself killed him, stopping his heart. What triggered the jump to make a copy of mine and give it to him was a question for Sig if I ever saw him again.

Joshua leaned in the doorway, his handgun in one hand though pointed aside now with Walker hiding behind me. His other grabbed at his chest.

"It moves, doesn't it?" Walker hissed. "Trying to set? I've seen it happen enough to know you're running out of time."

"Joshua," Paul whispered. "Get Anna out of here."

"Done and done, big brother," Joshua answered.

"No, Paul," I said. "He can't go. It's true."

"Alas, my dear woman will have my line as soon as I let go to control yours," Walker said. "Put your gun down, little Richards. I'll set your line before I kill you."

"You're a fucking lunatic, Walker," Joshua replied. I realized he didn't care about the gun on him or understand what I'd done. There was no gun on me or Paul so Joshua didn't feel at a disadvantage.

"You weaken, *Joshua,*" Walker sympathetically said. "The longer it struggles to set the weaker you become: paralysis, unconsciousness, coma, and eventually death.

"As long as you aren't dead it's not too late."

Joshua's gun wavered and I wished him unconscious like he'd been in the truck. Unconscious before he could kill Walker. Whatever I'd done to Joshua I hadn't read it because his new line smelled just like mine. If Paul and Jack weren't in good enough shape to set it he was screwed. I didn't know how to do it.

"What did you do to my brother, Sugar?" Paul whispered.

Joshua's stomach heaved and though nothing came up, he wiped his mouth on the back of his hand. He cleared his throat and pushed the gun at Walker but his knees started to bend and he leaned against the door frame for support before standing on his own again.

"I was touching him for the jump," I struggled to answer. Reasons why it could have happened tumbled through my mind though all were plain supposition. "Walker says he has a line, a copy of mine."

"He can't resist," Paul went on with obvious effort. "He *must* set it. If I wasn't tied down I'd be there doing it. Let me go so he can set my brother's—

Walker pulled me aside and knocked Paul's head sideways with a right that should have broken a board. Paul had been silenced but his message hadn't. Paul would come back on the other side. If I fought Walker too long then Joshua wouldn't. All Paul saw now was his little brother as a child as precious as Camille.

Joshua's response to the blow his brother took was quick, uncontrolled, and rash considering I was in his bullet's path.

His gun went off with a flash. I felt the spray of concrete from the wall behind us at the same time the room went momentarily black and Walker fell away to my right. I went the other way, landing on Paul before sliding to the floor as the lights came back up.

I realized I was free of his control but rather than turn my gun on Walker like I'd wanted to do only a moment before I went to him. Joshua sized him up for another wild shot. Walker's hand clutched the back of his leg and he kicked with the other as he came toward me.

"*Joshua!*" I screamed but his grey eyes barely registered he heard. He shuffled a step, clearly having difficulty with his left side. His right hand held his gun but he couldn't get his left hand up enough to grasp his chest. Instead he'd taken a fist full of his coat and clung.

"Whudu do tooma *brudder!*" He shouted from the right side of his mouth as he tried to get his right leg up for another step. The left side of his face sagged, eye drooping. His left leg gave way as he fell against the wall.

Joshua's right eye closed tight for a moment like he had something in it before his gun zoomed in on Walker. My left arm was still too useless to bear my weight as I tried to get to him and my knuckles scraped the cement while I crawled the last couple of feet with my gun in my fist.

I backed into Walker and held my hands up.

"Joshua," I cried again.

"Traitor," Joshua bellowed, less than clearly. I wasn't sure if it was meant for Walker or for me but the gun went off again missing us by several feet.

Shoot Josh, Jack sent and I looked at him in astonishment. Walker moved closer behind me. *My shoulder, look where he hit me.*

"No, Jack," I answered but I knew I wouldn't have a choice. Joshua shuddered as he took another shot, the round going wide to our other side.

Do it, Jack sent. *It'll be clean, survivable.*

Joshua adjusted his aim again and this time he wasn't going to miss. His right arm stayed steady and his eyesight cleared.

I took the shot one-handed, landing it right where Jack said.

Joshua fell back as my round passed through his right shoulder an instant before he pulled the trigger. His bullet hit above our heads. Through a haze of falling cement dust I watched Joshua hit the wall and slide down, leaving a red smear marking his path.

"Gerald," I breathed.

"No," Walker said, his voice barely betraying the pain he should be in. "Richards might *need* to set it but I do not."

"Please," I begged.

I knew I was drained, the fight all but gone from me. I tried to pull my line apart but even the small piece which embraced my sons during the battle with Walker felt limp and fused with the rest of it.

Walker simply laughed as I felt his line in me. Not for control this time. It was simply there like it had been upstairs.

"Hello, Gerald!"

Company had arrived.

Walker's wicked grin spread and I kicked away from him, smacking my dropped gun along beside me until I got to Joshua and took his. By the time Soros and Travis stepped in I had both.

"RJ," Walker smiled. "Get Precious and me to the truck."

"No," Soros and I said at the same time. I took a step toward the wall behind me and put Joshua's gun in my pocket then held the other ready.

"We're done here," Walker said. "Get me up."

"Please, Mister Soros." I said and pointed at Joshua.

Soros' nostrils flared as he studied Joshua and Travis grabbed his elbow to shove him in Joshua's direction. They felt the urge Paul spoke of.

"Yes," Soros said. I trained my gun on Walker before he could interfere and hopefully as an incentive for Soros to not change his mind like Walker had.

"Not another step," Walker growled and Soros and Travis stopped in their tracks. Joshua opened his eyes once and focused on me before he said something I couldn't make out. They closed as the floor shook beneath my feet.

"Do it," I yelled. Soros turned to me, his feet still rooted to the ground. My own feet were suddenly wet and cold and I looked down to see black water welling up beneath them. It spread as Walker's deep laughter filled the frozen chamber in advance of the water's stench.

As I watched it spread, lapping at Walker, Joshua and Jack on the floor before it swelled over them in waves far too high considering it was only a few inches deep. It surged up the walls like the room itself tilted from side to side, draining out past Soros and into the hall before flooding back in. The lights went black, several seconds at a time before flashing on far too bright.

When I looked back at Walker, what remained above the water was gone, replaced by a black bulge. It moved, hugging the walls, dodging Soros and Travis before swallowing Joshua up and moving on. By the time it reached Jack the water completely covered them even when the room was tipped toward the hall.

"Jack?" I cried as I turned my head wildly from side to side, trying to catch a glimpse of either him or Joshua floating in the waves. Paul was still out cold but the water reached his waist as it continued to boil up around me.

It's not real, Jack sent.

Bullshit, I answered as I staggered to my right. The water was deep enough to push me around though it didn't move Soros and Travis. Travis covered his ears with his hands, bleeding from the nose, before burying his face in Soros' shoulder.

The mountain of water roughly hit me from behind as the monster below passed and I took a shot. The bulge it carried flattened and reappeared across the room. I sighted it—

Don't, Jack sent and I pulled my finger from the trigger just before I shot again. *You're aimed at me.*

The bulge froze and waited. I tried to send my sense out but found nothing. Walker's hallucination affected all my senses.

There's nothing there, he told me.

The lump boiled straight up and burst and as the water deepened then it charged me. I waited until it was almost within reach before I shot again. The empty gun clicked and I tossed it aside before pulling Joshua's from my pocket. The wave hit and threw me back into the wall, hitting my head with a crack.

As I blinked, the monster circled. I couldn't tell the difference between the flashing bulb overhead and the stars in my eyes from impacting the wall.

Jack?

Walker hasn't moved.

If he hadn't the wave sure did. It was the distraction, taunting me to shoot at Jack and Joshua, spending my rounds in fear. I shook as the cold climbed higher, icy and thickening with each passing moment.

"Where are you, Gerald!?" I called.

The only answer was the moving water, more and more frantic, disorienting me. I glimpsed Soros and aimed where I hoped Walker lay, so near where Paul should be. The room went black and I couldn't be sure at all, then the monster hit driving me sideways into the wall again and throwing my aim off.

What Walker didn't count on was the frame of reference I had with a solid surface at my shoulder. In the black of the room, I closed my eyes and took careful aim. I had no idea how many rounds Joshua's gun had but I'd to make each count.

Aim? I asked.

Higher, Jack answered, his voice not much more than a whisper over the crashing waves around me. I took a single shot as the monster pushed me forward. My coat dragged down the cement as I fell to my knees, chin barely above the maelstrom. Even with the wall on one side, the water circled, faster and faster.

Moving, behind Paul, Jack sent so I shuffled forward on my knees. If Walker was out of my line of sight then I was out of his. I opened my eyes and saw nothing. I hoped Walker was so distracted with holding Soros and Travis immobile and driving my hallucination that he wasn't paying attention to Jack and me. The water churned around but the bulb stayed dark.

Now! Now! Now! Jack's distant words reached me and I pulled the trigger as the frigid water appeared over my hand, my gun, and my face. Two tight shots as it slopped in my mouth and down my throat.

Again, lower! Jack sent. I inhaled blackness as it entered my ears and burned my eyes. *Yes!*

Two more deafening shots challenged the darkness then it faded to nothing but the soft idle from the generators and the electric hum of the bulb over Paul's head.

Chapter 43

"Easy," a man's voice came to my ringing ears as I clung to Joshua's gun. My finger wouldn't relax on the trigger and I couldn't take my eyes off Walker as he lay flat, toppled over behind Paul's chair. "Easy."

"Don't talk, Jack," I knew I shouted though my voice sounded faint to my ears. I turned and saw Soros on the other end of Joshua's gun.

I'm not, Baby, he sent. *It's over.*

My eyes went to Walker as I shuffled on my knees the last few feet. Walker's legs twitched as his hands grabbed at what was left of his neck. The massive flow of blood from the round taking his life slowed, his hands stilled and his face relaxed. His eyes unfocused at the ceiling.

My left hand protectively took Paul's cold one as I turned to find Soros closer, only a few feet from us. I risked a glance at Jack. His chest still rose and fell. Joshua was the same. He stared at me, his eyes empty, for only a moment before he drifted off again.

"Back away," I gasped at Soros, now my only hope for Joshua.

Soros raised his hands and complied though one hand held his handgun. The smell of spent powder mixed with the stink of Gerald Walker's blood in a dark cloud around us. My frozen hand shook, palm still buzzing from the explosions which sent bullets from the gun and my left shoulder ached as I got my arm further around Paul.

"Put it down," I whispered and Soros slowly dropped and placed it on the floor.

"Kill him, Sugar," Paul whispered beside me. I felt his chest heave with effort and could only guess how much pain the vibration of his voice added to the nails through his shoulders. "I'll help Joshua and we'll get out of here."

I adjusted the grip on Joshua's handgun as Soros silently watched me. No living scent of Damian Howard remained anywhere in the house and in its absence I struggled to find the emotions I needed to pull the trigger. As I read Soros more deeply I found no loyalty to his father in him at all. Only to me. It had to be a trick. Soros changing loyalties was too good to be true.

"Do it," Paul tried. "Remember what he did to us, how he took you from me."

I shifted to the side to shield more of Paul with my body as I heard another set of boots on the stairs. The third man was unrecognizable to me as well. No loyalty to Damian either.

"I will, Paul," I answered as I tried to picture what he went through the night Soros stole me from him. He was Gerald Walker's brother after all and only minutes before Gerald nearly made me shoot my husband.

"Jack?" I said.

Baby.

"Who's coming?"

Harvey, Jack answered as Harvey stepped into the doorway and stopped at the sight of the carnage within.

"Do it do it!" Paul demanded.

"Please," Soros whispered. One hand came up like a stop sign. "Please listen, then I have to help the Lieutenant. Your husband is in no shape to help anyone. He's in too much pain to focus. He'd do more harm than good."

I had no choice but to do as he asked. My line was too tired to fight and I couldn't take them both with the gun.

"Get in here, Mister Harvey," I ordered. "Gun on the floor."

"We have a chance," Paul continued to plead. "You can get them, Sugar. You're a good shot."

Harvey kept his eyes on me as he came in and slowly removed his gun from under his coat then he lifted it and turned to show me there was nothing down the back of his pants. Travis put his down as well before he reached behind Soros and relieved him of his second gun. Both went on the floor.

"That night at Jack's," Soros started as he took a step toward Joshua. I shook my head and took a step toward him and he stopped. "I'd have been satisfied with Richards' death. A simple threat to Jack would keep you in line if your husband was dead.

"Then I asked you to choose which single life I would spare. I expected you would do the sensible thing and ask for Jack to protect your sons and the bargain to keep your daughter safe.

"I spared your husband because you asked for your daughter. Your request shielded her protectors as well as her. I couldn't take Richards' life without breaking my promise to your daughter.

"Then Christmas Eve," Soros whispered as he nervously looked at Joshua. "You saw Trent and me fight. I know you did. He'd had enough of lying to you but I clung to the lies to keep you in my life. I couldn't have you as my mate and I still couldn't let you go.

"He said I'm as stubborn as my mother."

Jack? I asked. I need his help.

I'll tell you the moment the truth fails him, Jack sent and disconnected from me to read his brother.

"I watched every day you survived Father's house. Every day you spent protecting your daughter. Trent said there was a time I had that devotion from you and it didn't matter who your mates are."

"You would always be my mother."

"It's bullshit," Paul whispered. "Don't do this, Sugar. Don't go back to them. I'm sorry I failed. Please, Sugar. Finish this."

"No, Paul," I answered as he fought his bonds again, shouting out with frustration. Jack would say if Soros was dishonest which meant Paul could do nothing for his brother.

"Jack said he'd break it off with you the night before he took his last step. I had the sedative ready to protect the twins. But you just weren't mad enough and I knew he hadn't done it. As furious as Gerald would be with Jack's escape I was relieved you were finally safe."

Travis moved closer to Soros as I listened and though he didn't stand in front of him, his presence was clearly protective.

"Please, Sugar," Paul started to cry and me with him. After he'd been through so much the indignity of his tears was more than I could bear.

"Forgive me," Soros whispered as Travis stepped forward, his hand up like Soros' had been.

"You trusted me once, Anna," Travis said. "You risked everything to get away because you trusted me."

He's right, Jack reconnected. *I've been working with Soros since I left you. I couldn't wait for them or Paul would be dead. I used my life to try and buy him some time. Forgive me.*

"I forgive you," I looked at RJ as I said it even though the words were meant for both him and Jack. "I forgive you."

But the gun wouldn't come down. I'd fought too hard and my terrified muscles wouldn't move. Paul went silent, his head slumped as far forward as his bonds would allow. There was no way for me to tell if he was unconscious or broken-hearted.

"I forgive," I sighed as Trent stepped forward and took the gun, tipping it to the roof before prying my numb hand from it.

"Jack doesn't have much time," RJ said as he came to me. "Neither does Lieutenant Richards."

Without hesitation he embraced me, holding me up as I cried on his shoulder. "I don't need to check your husband's line to know he'll survive if we leave for the hospital soon.

"Harv?" RJ gestured to Paul as he led me to Jack, still propped up against the cold cement wall. "Truck."

I got a knee under Jack to support his back and without moving him I wrapped my arms around his head. He was as cold and silent as the frozen cement beneath us. There was still life in him though not very much at all.

Paul swore and struggled, demanding he be freed to see to his brother. Trent tried to hold his head but Paul thrashed as much as he could. He finally got his hands on Paul's head and within a few seconds Paul, went limp and his breathing eased.

"How long can you keep him under?" RJ asked.

"Long enough," Trent answered but he slurred, deeply focused on Paul. I imagined he manipulated his line like Walker had with me to force the nightmare of the water into my mind and to trigger sexual attraction to him as a means of ensuring my obedience. "Until we get him to the hospital for sure. We're fortunate his line is weakened or we wouldn't have long."

Harvey took a set of relatively rust free clippers from the wall and cut the plastic ties binding Paul's hands then a larger pair pulled the metal pins from the wood. They dropped to the ground with a loud clang.

I stroked Jack's cheek as Harvey grunted, picked Paul up and shuffled him from the room. Travis kept his hands on Paul's skin.

"Travis is able to keep him unconscious," RJ whispered. "I'll have to go with them just in case. If Paul wakes up he'll hurt himself more trying to fight them. And in case Joshua wakes up. Once his line is set he could recover quickly in spite of his injuries."

RJ knelt beside Joshua, quickly checking his shoulder and his pulse before holding his right palm over his chest.

"It's a strange honour," he whispered. "Setting the line of my own mother. So very strange."

I watched Joshua, expecting a dramatic jolt like from a defibrillator but there was nothing. He looked peaceful and after only a few minutes RJ pulled his hand back.

"Amazing," he breathed. "When it set, all that was you disappeared from it. He's completely unique, like the men who just show up and don't appear related to anyone. It's like his line created its own scent as soon as it was secured."

I nodded. It was all too much to think about. Paul and Joshua would live and for now that was enough.

"Can you carry Jack?"

"No," Jack breathed and shrunk in my arms with the effort. His connection to me stuttered again like the generators above had before reasserting itself.

"I can't move him, Mother," RJ said. "He's hurt too badly. It would only cause him more pain and he wouldn't make it to the truck."

"No, RJ," I whispered. "Please, we can't leave him."

RJ watched as I tightened my hold on Jack.

"His line knows when the end is near," RJ said. Gone was the flamboyant arrogance of the man I met months earlier. It had been replaced with compassion and soft sensitivity.

You felt it when he first shot me. I did too, Jack sent. *My line knew right away it was time.*

"Ask Jack for permission to read it."

I took Jack's damaged hand and pulled it over his body, resting it on my stomach. "I don't know how."

RJ held my right hand over Jack's chest, his overtop.

"May we?" I whispered, scared of the truth I would find. If I could carry Jack myself I'd ignore RJ's warning and take him to the truck.

"Yes," Jack whispered.

"I'll teach you like a child," RJ hurried to explain. His urgency with this task alarmed me and spoke to how little time Jack had. "I will read him. You'll feel my energy pass through your hand. Let yours flow. Just follow me and I will guide you.

"Your instinct will be to fix it, connect it. Don't. You'll knock it free. Don't interfere with my energy at all. After, you'll read my line so you know the difference."

"Okay," I shivered. Jack's cold blood underneath me was like ice.

At first I felt nothing. Then a faint tingling at the back of my hand followed by stronger vibration in my palm. My vision blurred as my involuntary release of energy joined with RJ's and I *saw*.

Jack's line filled nearly my whole field of vision and I startled at its nearness. It was blue like the energy I'd once been able to cast from my hand and it flowed past but I didn't understand how I was aware of any movement.

Jack shuddered and a crack opened along its length exposing a rotten blackness then a piece of blue peeled away exposing even more.

The blackness wasn't anything unhealthy. It was pure absence where parts of his line were already gone.

"Dear God," I murmured. "Fix him, RJ. You must know how. Set it like a child's."

"There's nothing I can do, Mother," RJ answered as the room coalesced around us. He rubbed my hand between his to warm it.

"We're ready," Harvey said behind RJ. Fresh snow dusted his shoulders and hair. He dragged in an electric heater and plugged it in near me as he continued to talk. "Travis has Richards quiet but the time it will take getting to the hospital in the worsening conditions will push him to his limit."

RJ quickly held my right hand up, palm over his chest.

"Copy what I did," RJ said. "Don't be alarmed at the sight of your energy. Don't hesitate. Work with purpose or my line will lash back. Withdraw when you're finished.

"Just look long enough to see how a healthy line looks."

"Yes," I looked into RJ's eyes.

"Do it. You have my permission."

Again it took a moment for the tingling to start then as my energy flowed, blue light ran from my palm and into his chest. I gasped with surprise but kept going, letting it strengthen.

"Blue," I said.

"That's your energy," RJ whispered as I faced his line, a beautiful shimmering blue, uncracked and not damaged like Jack's had been. In places it was so bright the colour changed to a pearly pink as my brain tried to understand what it saw. "Nobody can see it but you."

I was still looking into RJ's eyes when his line disappeared from my sight. Jack's fingers moved on my stomach, feeling his sons as I started to cry.

RJ kissed my cheek and stood then he took off his coat and covered us. He helped Harvey pick Joshua up.

"I'll be back for you in a few hours, I promise."

Chapter 44

Jack didn't speak though we remained connected through my sensum. He passed the point of shivering in the cold and I tried to keep mine to a minimum because every time it got bad his connection to me faded a little more. The little heater helped but the cold concrete around us took every bit of warmth it provided.

"Jack," I whispered. His head tipped of its own accord and I kissed him. I didn't mind the sticky blood on his mouth. It helped him kiss me since he'd become so incredibly weak.

"I love you," I said. He couldn't keep his hand on my stomach on his own any more so I held it there. "I'm not ashamed of us or sorry. Please don't leave me thinking you're unforgiven or unloved."

One of the boys kicked and I put Jack's hand in the right place to feel it.

Thank you, Baby, he sent, barely a whisper over the rattling in his throat. *I called to reassure you and had to go in alone. RJ was delayed and I couldn't wait. I thought I'd use your trick and get him out but I couldn't split my line like you. If you came I'd have Paul out and I could redeem myself in your eyes before I said good-bye properly.*

For good, I nodded, knowing what he meant.

My God, Baby, he said. *You were so strong. I'm so proud of you.*

"If RJ hadn't come I'd be leaving with Walker," I whispered as I tilted my head at the body.

Doesn't matter now.

"Suppose not," I answered as I kissed his cold lips again.

I'm leaving, Jack sent and my warm tears ran onto his cheeks. I pressed my top lip to his so he could hold on to my sensum as long as he could. I could only be brave for him now and save my grief for later. He hurt enough and I didn't want him to leave with guilt.

I read his line and found no shortage of faults upon its surface which I could latch on to and see through his eyes.

Jack exhaled cold air on my lips once, then again.

Tanned hands hold the wheel; dark hair climbs bare arms. Below them, a pair of knobby knees and bare feet in sandals. The dials and lights on the dash are nothing I've seen before though I know their meanings.

The passage of time hasn't changed cars much.

My head turns to my passenger, Camille. Her long dark hair toward me as she looks out her window and her hand absently rubs her pregnant stomach. She turns to me, tears running down her face. They sparkle in the dawn sun streaming in. She looks at me like she listens then she nods as we pull over.

I held my breath and press my lips to Jack's. He hadn't drawn another and I think I feel his tighten against mine... just barely.

She's out before I am, striding to the front door. I get out but linger beside the car.

The house is big: two stories and a wide porch. The street is clean and well kept. It's painted a terracotta colour with white trim and empty flower baskets. It feels like fall in Southern California.

The door opens and four people emerge as one onto the porch. An older man and woman. Anna and Paul. His hair is nearly white and his rimless glasses don't disguise his face. Still fit and handsome. Anna smiles at her daughter, showing a full set of teeth before her face becomes troubled and she looks at me.

She clings to Paul, eyes on Camille but her hand clasps the front of her shirt and pain fills her face. The two young men are a bit taller than Paul. Both blonde and muscular: a mix of Jack and my father John. One runs down the steps to meet her and the other stares at me, holding his mother. She speaks to him and shoves him down the stairs then I can read her lips.

"That's not Jack," she says and turns away, disappearing into the darkness of the house...

The image starts to lose colour, the concrete basement walls gave the vision the time-worn patina of an old photo. His line began to fade from him as my own line started to feel picked at, like pulling off a scab which wasn't ready to let go. The looseness in his chest was readable even without Soros' lesson. I cradled it with my sense as gently as I could. It's as light as a child's line. The boys' lines in my chest stilled as if afraid to hurt me any further. Another shallow breath as pain like heartburn started to grow. The image flickered out as I pull Jack closer and got the vision back.

Camille glances to where Anna stood, worry on her face then she takes her brothers' elbows, one in each hand and leads them to me down the walk...

Then it's gone.

"Jack," I whispered then I kissed him again.

California

Chapter 45

Incredible warmth touched my cheek before sliding down to my neck then my shoulder. My skin chilled even more when it moved to a new spot on my cheek so it could have been there for a while. I would have startled if I wasn't frozen solid to the ground.

"Anna," RJ softly said. "Hey."

"Hurts, RJ," I whispered, tightening my arms around Jack to make sure he hadn't fallen over while I dozed. The encroaching pain as his connection slipped away left me exhausted. I felt Jack try and pull away and when I opened my eyes, RJ pulled him from me. "Are we putting him in the car?"

"What's left belongs to his parents. The part that made him family is gone."

I looked in RJ's red eyes. A single tear escaped before he blinked it away.

"I liked Jack," he said.

Walker's body still slumped where it had fallen. I was glad his neck or what was left of it was out of sight. RJ eased Jack over onto his other side.

"Come on, Anna," he said. He tried to pull me up but my joints wouldn't unlock. I cried out as the movement seared the pain inside. RJ squatted down and forced my arm up around his shoulders then he lifted me from the ground.

"Don't move me," I yelled. The pain sharpened so quickly I shuddered as my vision grew dark. My head sagged to the side as RJ held me like a child. He held his breath until my eyes opened. I was grateful for his complete stillness.

Trent stood near, watching my face.

"Her pain is terrible, RJ." Trent's hand went to his chest as his brow furrowed. He looked at RJ.

"She can't stay here," RJ said and Trent agreed.

I buried my face in his shoulder as he turned sideways, taking us up stairs and through the back door. When I walked in a few hours earlier it seemed to take so much longer.

Harvey stood by the truck. The engine ran and as soon as he opened the rear door, Trent climbed in and helped RJ lift me inside. They quickly stripped off RJ's coat and mine and my boots so they wouldn't hold the cold to my skin and closed the doors. RJ stayed in the back with me and Trent sat up front with Harvey and drove us out. The truck I came in disappeared out of sight.

"Sig knows where they are," RJ whispered. He held me in his lap, keeping me still. "The nature of their injuries is under military jurisdiction and they won't have any trouble from the police."

Rows and rows of short corn stalks passed on either side as Trent negotiated the snow hidden ruts, speeding up to get us over the little rise then onto the main road. I shivered, setting off a groan as the movement made the pain worsen.

"The first few weeks will be the hardest," RJ said. I nodded and relaxed against him. "You'll be tired, let yourself sleep through the worst of it. Trent and I will keep you safe. You won't be up to looking after yourself."

"Where are you taking me?"

"Wherever you want."

I thought for a few minutes, unable to decide.

"I don't know, RJ."

"Trent, make for Jack's, please."

Trent didn't answer but I caught his nod in the corner of my eye.

I woke curled on the rear truck seat, my head on RJ's leg. It would only be a brief respite from the worst of the pain which peaked just after dusk. I'd shrieked until I passed out. RJ slept against the door and Harvey was behind the wheel while Trent slept up front.

RJ's phone rang, startling him. The past few hours taught me to keep still and quiet. He took it from his shirt pocket and checked the number on the front before he answered.

"Soros," he said.

"Good evening, Sig." RJ listened as he rested his hand on my shoulder. "Although her strength is admirable she shouldn't have had to suffer so."

He held the phone to my ear.

"Don't speak, Little One," Sig said. "Just listen. I'm so very sorry you're paying the price again for peace.

"Jack has been recovered. I'm on my way to inform his parents. RJ told me about your visit with them and I'll be sure to maintain the story you gave so don't worry.

"Thank you," I whispered setting off a tremor in my line. The pain of loss was so different from the boys tearing with anxiety. That pain came as vibration like tearing a piece of meat or pressure like the tension of a wound spring. It was so tangible I pictured it inside. Movement push in heat and my line spasmed around itself trying to close the painful gap and keep the burning out. The boys' lines continued to be still as if they knew their movement would only make my suffering worse.

"I've spoken to the doctor. Paul and Joshua are out of surgery and resting. The hospital is my second stop later tonight.

"RJ told me what happened with your brother-in-law and we will be sure he has support as he learns about the family."

I didn't try responding. My skin still prickled with sweat from thanking him the first time.

"My love to you, Little One," he said. "I'll see you again. Trent and RJ will be with you as long as you need them. Rest. Now let me speak with RJ."

I risked moving my eyes to look at RJ and he put the phone back to his own ear. As he listened he pushed a stray hair from my cheek.

"We're taking Anna to Jack's house. It's hers now. I'll make sure it's handled as quickly as possible."

The vibration of the truck wheels on the road calmed me and I closed my eyes, picturing two blonde little boys in Jack's sun filled back yard. In my vision they chased their older sister as they accused each other of 'cheating' at hide and seek since they could all read each other.

"It's okay you loved him," RJ whispered. Somehow I rolled over and used his leg for a pillow. Dawn light welcomed the end of my first long night without Jack. "Make sure his sons know you loved their father."

Chapter 46

The first few weeks after Jack passed blurred waking pain and sleep, vague memories of civilized meals with RJ and Trent back to back with them gently restraining me, bruised and scratched as I raged. Always patient and kind, sometimes Trent would hold me up in bed while RJ coaxed me to eat.

They talked of Paul and I heard Ray's name and Alina's. Jack.

I never woke up alone and usually with both of them nearby.

A clear and lucid memory of sitting bundled on a rusty old porch swing which hadn't been there the last time I was at Jack's. Trent held my hand and we watched fat flakes of snow fall and obscure the walk. He smoked on the downwind side of me and passed me a thermal mug of fruity tea from time to time. We waited for RJ to return from a trip to town and I rested my head on Trent's shoulder and thanked him. He gently pushed with his feet and started us swinging as I fell to sleep.

Bright sunlight filled the room when I woke feeling normal for the first time in weeks. Normal plus the heavy burning in my chest which seemed to be a gift considering how much worse it had been. I gave myself a minute to see if this scene would also fade as I found myself somewhere else but it didn't so I shoved myself upright and wriggled my toes before placing them on the floor. On the table sat a glass of water coated inside with air bubbles starting small about half way up and larger near the surface. I sipped, listening to them pop and rejoin the air in the room clearing a small U shaped patch on the far side. It tasted stale and I imagined dust on my top lip but I felt thirsty so it was good.

My afternoon nap consisted of being corralled into the guest room and told to sleep. I might have dropped a couple of F-bombs at lunch when I spilled, more in frustration with myself than anything else, before I caught myself eyeing RJ with momentary fear. He used his napkin to clean up and said he was relieved nobody had my plate in their lap. Trent laughed. I was getting used to this new RJ who insisted we serve ourselves at the stove. He said I'd still only wear what he told me. He wasn't surprised. He'd been an asshole he reminded me and had a plan to get me functioning better. I asked for a hint and he smiled and shook his head.

I dreamed I sat in the corner of a big log cabin. Deer heads covered the walls and the furniture didn't appear much different than the trees from which the pieces were made. Jack and Zeus played cards. Zeus had nearly all the chips and Jack wore his white eagle hat and cowboy boots. He'd added a black scarf to his white shirt and grubby jeans. Zeus wore red and yellow Hawaiian shorts and a shark tooth necklace missing the tooth. Zeus' neatly folded yellow t-shirt sat atop his chips. It looked like he'd lost it to Jack and won it back at some point. Jack teased him about the tooth.

"Really, Jack?" Zeus laughed as another round of cards flew from his hands. "Do you see any sharks around here?"

"Put in, old man," Jack replied as he tossed in a few chips from his dwindling pile. "We'll see who's going home first."

Zeus screwed up his face then with a small pop, a tooth appeared at the end of the leather thong around his neck.

"Really?" Jack laughed as Zeus dropped chips on the pile. "The fucking thing's fake!"

Zeus pointed a finger at Jack's chips and with a flash, they disappeared before reappearing a few inches away. "Seems whoever dreamed me up made sure I can only conjure plastic."

I giggled and Jack glanced at me, putting a finger to his lips. Two more men appeared from the shadows and took two of the remaining seats. Zeus zapped them in with more chips and placed a final pile in front of the empty fifth chair. Then he made five hollowed out pineapples appear.

"Pineapple juice," Zeus muttered when he put it to his lips. "Our host has very little imagination, Jack. You think you can do something about it?"

"She's pregnant, buddy," Jack answered as the others plopped chips in the centre of the table. "If she can't drink then you can't either."

"Whatever."

Jack sighed and looked at the small pile in front of him. Then stood and came to me, taking my hands and pulling me up onto my feet. He held me close and I wrapped my arms around his shoulders as he kissed me, swaying us back and forth. One of his hands came up and cradled my cheek as his lips worked their way along my jaw to my ear. I grabbed his belt and tugged him in tighter, as close as we'd been before I got big.

I let go in alarm and put my hands on my flat stomach.

"It's your dream, Baby, not theirs. They're back at my house."

"Okay," I understood.

"You've had such a rough time," he breathed down my neck and kissed the scarred skin in the V of my shirt, making me melty inside. "RJ's taken good care of you but he can't stay with you any more. Father's house is a mess with him and Gerald gone and he has to go back. He has the other women safe. Carter and Davis are his men. Karen's baby is coming now and they'll be fine."

I wondered how he knew and remembered I was dreaming. Even so, I felt reassured.

"You in this hand, Jack?"

"Fold," he answered.

"I thought it was just an end of life experience then the other side," I said.

Jack took a step back. He pulled his hat off with one hand and rubbed the top of his brush cut with the other. He looked puzzled.

"Yeah," he said. "I can stay here and keep an eye on you until I'm out of chips and that's just a couple of hands away the way Zeus' luck is running. This is the longest damn card game I've ever seen. But then, yeah, the other side. I didn't think I'd see you again. I'm glad you're here."

Jack grabbed my butt and picked me up. I wrapped my legs around his hips as he carried me up a narrow flight of stairs I hadn't noticed even though I'd been sitting on the bottom one. He pulled me up a little higher and I buried my face in his neck.

"I need you to do something for me, Baby," Jack whispered.

"Anything," I promised.

"First you're gonna get off RJ's left tit and start thinking for your self. He's making all your decisions while you wallow in self pity. My boys won't last long with a mom who can't decide who to feed first."

I glared at Jack as he grunted, lowering us to the floor. We knelt facing each other. I kept my hands on his shoulders as the room darkened.

"Second, get your life back," he continued. "You're going to have a long one. I'm gonna be back on the other side soon, I think. So many have died this past year it has to be enough to shift the balance and send us waiting ones across. I'm going to finish up my game and before I know it I'll be looking into the eyes of some pretty young woman and thinking about getting up in her shirt for a sleepy top up as she bathes my baby ass in the kitchen sink. I'll have the sense to keep quiet about what I am and when I roll through puberty again I'll start getting the urge to find more men like me.

"I need you to send them home," he whispered in my ear and as the room fell dark his voice faded, repeating the same numbers over and over. I grabbed his shirt tight to hold on but the fabric shrunk from my grip as his skin grew cold, smooth and hard.

"Jack?" I shouted out, finding myself kneeling before his open closet, my hands on his safe. Inside, it held Jack's journal of his past lives and the one he'd started for me. When we put them away months ago a glimpse showed me a stack of similar old books nearly six inches high stacked on top of old boxes and other things.

"Anna," RJ called from Jack's bedroom door. I turned, gripping the cold metal even harder. "Until you can see your feet you get a hand to hold on the stairs."

"Jack said to send them home," I said as I purposelessly spun the dial around and around.

"Jack never gave anyone the numbers," RJ said. He pushed my hair behind my ear. "I have to haul it to the truck and put it in his room at Father's."

"Send them home," I repeated, stooping in the failing daylight to see the print on the dials. Jack's voice echoed in my head as I turned left and right and with a final soft thunk I felt in my fingertips more than I heard, it unlocked and I pulled it open.

Chapter 47

Two days later I went to Sacramento for my last doctor appointment. RJ and Trent waited in the truck while I listened to the most outlandish proposal I'd ever heard.

"I've planned an amniocentesis next week. If their lungs are favourable I'll book you in for a C-section the following Monday, if you don't deliver on your own before then."

He stood, indicating he was finished but I stayed in my seat as I decided this would be the last time I'd ever see him.

"So what's in it for the boys?" I asked. Ray wouldn't have planned something so stupid because he knew taking them before their lines descended from me to them would kill them. Of course there was no way for this doctor to know about lines and baby boys since he wasn't family which put me in the position of either agreeing and not showing up or refusing and making a scene.

"Well," he slowly said as if I didn't understand. "If their lungs aren't ready then delivering them early would be very bad. The amniocentesis will tell us if they're mature. They're better off inside you until then."

Of course they were better off inside me.

"However, you're thirty-five weeks and they're big, more than six pounds each, and will only become a bigger drain on your health the longer the pregnancy lasts."

Checkmate, his look said.

Bullshit.

"I see," I mused. "Then I shall see you next week."

"Of course," he smugly smiled as he thought he got his way.

I told the receptionist I'd call later in the week once I knew if I could get a ride into town on Wednesday or Thursday. They were less likely to notice I hadn't shown up if the appointment book didn't have my name in it. I shrugged my coat on and made my way out the front door and around the rear to the parking lot; six spots on the left and six on the right. Before I approached RJ and the truck, I took the house key he'd given me earlier and walked around the doctor's car in the first spot on the left.

I had to press firmly but I managed a deep scratch down the passenger side and up the driver's before I went to the fourth spot on the left to meet RJ.

"C-section?" RJ laughed.

"Uh huh." I opened the passenger door. "Can I get a boost?"

I didn't know what it was about these men and their trucks but I couldn't get in without a lift.

"Nope."

I closed the door most of the way and crossed my arms, puzzled.

231

"You brought a ladder?"

"No, Anna," he smiled. "We're not going back with you."

"So you're lifting me in? You know I'll be stranded once I get home and fall out."

Trent tapped the window and waved good-bye as RJ took my elbows and sighed.

"I need to get back to Connecticut," he said. "You seem to have sorted yourself out since you opened the safe. There's a new baby to look out for and another coming. Carter and Davis are my men. They took the women from the house when Gerald died and had an out-of-state doctor deliver Karen's baby. They're not going back. You are going home."

He turned me to face the other row of vehicles and I saw a little pink booted foot sticking out from under the elbow of a tall dark haired man. Even with his back to me, I knew him.

"Paul," I whispered as RJ steadied me.

Paul turned. He smiled as little green eyes on Camille's face peeked around his shoulder. She looked even more like me than ever.

"Who is it?" Paul asked and pointed. Camille wrinkled her nose.

"My Mama," her little voice squeaked. I slapped my hands on my mouth with surprise and felt warm tears start.

"Go on," RJ said. "We won't go until you say it's okay."

I took a couple of quick steps then glanced down to make sure my path was clear. Paul adjusted her on his hip as I realized I still had my mouth covered.

"Hello, Sweetie," I whispered. As I reached them, Camille leaned away from Paul and into my waiting arms.

"My Mama," she announced again as I tried to find a way to hold her close which didn't involve squishing my stomach. I beamed at Paul to see him as moved as I was by her response. Camille touched my tears with her fingers.

"Owie," her mouth puckered into an O as she pushed her brows together with concern.

I wiped my cheeks with my free hand.

"Better?" I asked.

Camille smiled.

"I show her pictures every night," Paul whispered.

"Thank you," I said as I pushed back her fake fur trimmed hood and kissed the top of her head.

"We had a strange visit from Sig last night. He came out about being family. You could have heard a pin drop then he spoke to Ray alone. Within minutes Ray gave me an hour to pack and kicked us out with nothing more than a phone number."

Paul tilted his head at RJ. He was obviously uncomfortable with RJ's presence so near his wife and daughter. "He suggested you might be able to put us up and to meet you here today."

I looked over at RJ. Trent had stepped out of the truck and stood beside him, his arm around his waist and RJ's over his shoulder.

"Of course, Paul," I answered. "And Joshua?"

The last time I'd seen Paul's younger brother he was unconscious and bloodied from a bullet I'd put through him.

"He's recovering," Paul gently pinched at Camille's nose making her laugh. "He remembers you shot him. He goes back and forth from we're all nuts to thinking it's all neat. He bought a place in Nevada and is going to live on his own for a while. I think it'll be good for him."

"I killed him, Paul," I said. "When I rolled the truck all I wanted was to protect him forever but he was dead when we appeared. Then I shot him to save his life again."

"He'll forgive you," Paul leaned past our daughter and warmly kissed my cheek. "Sig doesn't have a clue how you gave him a line and has spoken to every relation he can think of. Your explanation is better than anything he's come up with."

"My Mama," Camille squeaked again and I looked to see her arm pointed across the parking lot.

"I'm the head of RJ's line now," I said. "He smells like me."

"Sig explained all of that, too. About his brother and Damian and my father," Paul said as he nudged me in RJ's direction. "Camille, go meet your brother."

I looked at Paul in surprise. RJ had caused nearly as much pain as Damian.

"Go," he urged though he looked like he wanted to grab Camille and run the other way. "If you say he's trustworthy, I believe you."

I carried her, slowly at first, but her obvious excitement bouncing in my arms sped me up before I could drop her. Her little nose wrinkled as her head snapped back and forth between RJ and me.

"My Mama," she said again when we got close. She tucked her head by my neck and held her hand out to RJ.

"Hello, Little One," he whispered. Trent held RJ tighter as RJ took her hand in his. "She's beautiful, Anna. So much like my daughter..." his voice trailed off as he blinked back tears. Trent kissed his cheek and wiped his own eyes.

I realized his lost child had been my grand-daughter and was sad I didn't remember her.

"I've never hurt a child," he whispered. "Always did everything I could to keep my brother and father away. Take good care of her."

"Will I see you again?"

"On the other side, Mother," he said. "If not sooner."

Chapter 48

I woke in the big main floor guest bedroom I claimed when RJ and Trent brought me home to Jack's. A little knee pushed my stomach and Camille's arm came up around it as she buried her nose in my chest to read her brothers.

"My baby," she said and I laughed, pulling her close. Paul had the other end of her monitor up in his room so she'd been up during the night and he'd tucked her in with me. Her crib was across the hall with two empty ones ready for 'her baby.'

"Banana?" I asked.

"'kay," she answered. For a thirteen month old her language skills were ahead of the game like everything else with her. Paul said she'd walked at ten months and by twelve it was two word sentences.

"Alright," I said as I pushed myself up sitting beside her. I held her hands as she shimmied over the edge and hurried to her room. As I stood, I swayed side to side to work the stiffness out of my lower back. Unlike the grinding agony with Camille I only had minimal pain in spite of the fifteen pounds of baby already in front of me. At the door, I paused as tightness worked its way low around my stomach unlike the all over tightness of my evening Braxton-Hicks. Camille stomped in a circle in the hall waving a clean diaper so I took a deep breath and followed her into her room for a change.

The rhythmic soft thud of Paul's feet on his treadmill in the bedroom over the kitchen sped up as Camille and I went to my bathroom for a tooth brushing. In the kitchen, I put her in the highchair for the promised sliced banana and watched the stragglers from the night's snowfall as I made coffee for Paul. Then a sippy-cup of milk and a handful of Cheerios for Camille as slow wetness trickled down my legs and my back ached again.

I pressed my knees together, certain I'd peed and as my hips shifted another push of fluid coincided with a much firmer cramp around my middle.

"Paul?" I called but the thud thud overhead continued, slowing, but he obviously didn't hear me. I waited for the flow to stop before I grabbed a towel to sit on and a bowl of yogurt for Camille and me to share. After only a couple of bites, I surrendered the bowl to her and let her slap the surface with her spoon. She was a tidy eater, most of the time.

"Paul?" I tried again when the treadmill stopped and Camille glared at me. She wasn't supposed to shout and her look said I had some nerve doing it myself.

"Sorry," I said as I picked up the phone from the table and dialled four-one-one and asked for J Roberts in Baltimore. I confirmed the street since there were several matching names to choose from and the operator put me through.

"Sheryl?" I said as the shower upstairs started. Paul would be quick since Camille was an early riser like him. This phone call made my line ache badly with memories of Jack and I rubbed through my shirt to try and calm the pain.

"It's Anna, Jason's girl."

"Oh dear, Anna," she exclaimed. "My goodness, are you alright?"

"I'm okay, Sheryl," I said as I stood. Camille pointed at the other half of her banana; arm in the right direction and finger pointing up. She gave up on the spoon and lost interest in the cereal. "I'm so sorry I didn't make it to the service. I really struggled the first few weeks and wasn't able to travel. I'm home now at his house in California."

"I understand," she said as Camille sighed with satisfaction at another plate of banana. "When your brother picked you up I never got a chance to thank you for making him come home."

"I loved Jason," I said as I leaked again. "Please hear me out. I'm sorry. He wasn't my husband. I'm married and have a little girl. Jason and I had a past and something bad happened to me in the field and we found ourselves together. The boys are your son's but I wasn't his wife."

She was silent but only for a moment like she waited to be sure I was finished. "I know, honey. When your brother came for you Jason told us. Jack was angry with him, ruining a marriage but he's come to understand you young folks can have complicated lives. Jason's death hit him hard, but he's more worried about you now.

"Jason said you were raped on a mission with him and when you returned your husband was in the field and things happened he couldn't undo. All he wanted was for you to be safe and happy. He and his father agreed you and the twins were more important than anything. He wasn't sure what sort of place he'd have in your life and his heart was set on respecting your decision between you and your husband."

"Thanks, Sheryl," I started to sob and she waited for me to take a breath around the knot in my chest. Camille picked at her cereal, her banana gone. "My water broke this morning and I wanted you to know the boys are coming soon."

Paul put a hand on my shoulder and took the phone as my voice failed. I rested my head on his shoulder as I started to ache again.

"Missus Roberts?" he asked. "I'm Paul Richards, Anna's husband."

He listened for a moment before continuing.

"I served with your son for many years. He was a good soldier and better friend. I've come to understand what happened between him and Anna and it's not keeping us apart."

Paul paused and smiled although Sheryl couldn't see. "He and I were injured in the same incident. Anna was with him when he passed. I wanted you to know he wasn't alone.

"I appreciate that, Sheryl," Paul said. "What happened between her and your son isn't going to be hidden and you're right. For us to move forward we need to accept it. I'm here for Anna and whatever she needs. Your grandsons are as well loved as my daughter regardless of what my wife and I are able to put back together."

Paul's hand came down and felt the hardness of my stomach as I sighed through more cramping, then he tipped my chin up and rested his cheek on my forehead.

"Her water broke and we have an hour drive to the hospital in Sacramento. I have a few calls to make as I get us out the door.

"I'll call you later when there's news. She won't be travelling anywhere for a while but our daughter and I have settled in here to help out. We'd like you to come out west and see us. Come meet your grandsons and our daughter. I think it would help us all if we got to know each other sooner rather than later."

Paul sat me down and unbuckled Camille before one-arming her out of the highchair. She took off down the hall, brown hair waving along behind her. He spoke to Sheryl only another minute before hanging up and calling Ray to meet us at the hospital to take Camille as he went after her.

I carefully stood and felt no new leakage so I tossed the towel onto the floor and stood on it, shuffling my feet along the path of drops from the counter to the highchair.

"Are you okay for a minute?" Paul asked. I looked up to see him standing in the doorway.

"Yes," I gave him a quick smile since for the moment at least I felt fairly good.

"I have to get the snow off the truck and check the chains, warm it up," he said then went on talking betraying his nervousness. "Get our bags out there and dress Camille. Are you okay dressing yourself or do you need a hand?"

"Camille?" I called. "Wanna see your baby?"

A shriek of affirmation came from down the hallway. Seeing my bare stomach while I dressed was seeing her baby and would keep her busy while Paul stepped outside. Paul laughed and Camille followed as I went to my room.

Paul's truck rumbled to life outside my bathroom in its spot next to Jack's old sedan, parked where we left it nine months earlier. The car belonged to me like everything else and my breath hitched when I realized the image of Jack and his sons fixing it up wouldn't come to be. Camille kissed my stomach and chatted to her baby. She'd be surprised to see there were two.

We waited on the couch for Paul and Camille climbed over me for a book but I didn't get far in to it before my stomach tightened again.

"Alright, Miss Missy," Paul announced as he stomped his boots on the mat, head stuck in the front door. "Ready to go?"

"I'm stuck," I said. Like a turtle on its back. There was no way out of the soft couch without tipping on my side and trying to roll off. Before I could, Paul was on his knees before me. A little path of tread shaped snow chunks followed him.

"Sugar," he whispered, his hands on my stomach. "Are you hurting?"

"Just my line," I said, certain there would be plenty of other hurting as the day wore on.

"Look, I meant what I said to Jack's mother," he started. "You know me. I can live with the truth. I won't pretend I'm someone I'm not."

Camille pushed the book aside and squeezed between us and up into her dad's open coat.

"Do you remember what we promised each other when we were married?" He asked. I sat up a little straighter and said I did. "Do you think we've both lived up to our vows?"

I started to nod but then shook my head and looked away. Paul caught my cheek and wouldn't let me.

"You're right," he admitted. "When it came right down to it we both chose family first. I asked for Marie because it was the right thing to do. Nothing would make me more protective of her and her son than being freshly bound to her. I never would have done it otherwise. I had to choose to do it over my promise to you. You did the same thing for our daughter. You turned your back on me to make sure our child would be safe. I know nothing else would have driven you to Jack. And you only became close with him again because they made me break it off and you believed me dead.

"Neither one of us is blameless in what's become of our marriage even though our grownup reasons were sound. You were a bigger grownup about Marie than I was about Jack. She said you comforted her when she confessed to you in spite of the pain it obviously caused. All I wanted was to kill him. I didn't stop to think there was a grownup reason you did it. I still thought of you as a simple mate like her until the night I came here and it became clear you're not. I'm so sorry."

I put a hand on his smooth cheek and Camille put her hand on mine then she reached further and tugged off his glasses. They disappeared deep inside his coat. We watched each other for a few minutes until another round of aching passed.

Camille's quiet snore came from inside Paul's coat. She must have had him up for a while if she napped so early. I reached in and recovered his glasses before he could stand up and drop them. The truck kept rumbling in front of the house.

"Come, Sugar."

Chapter 49

Baby A announced himself with a wild cry just before midnight. Paul stayed at my side as Baby B was quietly delivered the next day, just ten minutes later. His silence was made even more pronounced by his older brother's wailing as he was pinched and poked, remaining still. Though his colour remained good, I couldn't make out the whispers of the doctors and nurses. They packed him up and rolled him away to intensive care even as they connected miles of tubes. I desperately squeezed Paul's hand as they left before I turned as far as I could toward him, pulling him close as I buried my face in his chest.

I heard Baby A behind Paul and looked at him, scared to bits he was being taken too only to see a nurse bringing my little boy to me.

"Your younger one is in the I.C.U.," she soothed as the head of my bed came up. Paul put his hands on the crying bundle as she passed him to me. "Do you want to hold him first, Dad, or be with his brother?"

"He wants to do both," I said, desperately wanting him to be in two places at once as long as I couldn't. Paul pushed the flannel blanket back from his little red face and held him close for a moment before I took him. I kissed Paul before he kissed the boy then a nurse led him away. Another nurse wedged a pillow under my elbow as I aimed and latched him on. Within seconds the room quieted with the exception of my loud sobs. She passed me some tissue and I did my best to stifle it as I nervously watched the door. After ten long minutes she took my blood pressure again and I straightened his little blue hat before I moved him to the other side. Tears still ran but my crying stopped.

"Mrs. Richards?" I looked up to see a tiny grey haired woman come to the bed. She wore two watches: one on her wrist and the other hung upside down from a small chain attached to her 'Betty' name tag. "I'm Doctor Carr from the I.C.U. All is well my dear."

She smiled and rubbed A's back as she pushed up on her toes to rest her bottom on the edge of my bed.

"Bradley has no fever, nothing in his lungs. His heart sounds good. We're running every expensive test we can of course but he looks like my old grand-dad did after his second plate of Sunday dinner."

I digested what she said as she kept talking. He was okay. I stroked the older baby's cheek as I tried to remember how much Bradley looked like him before he'd been whisked away down the hall; pink face and a fuzz of straw blonde hair, Camille's nose in profile.

"Bradley?" I asked. My heart sank. The old dear came to reassure the wrong mom. I hadn't named them. Up until half an hour earlier I still believed I'd never live to do it.

"Yes," she said.

"Your husband said their father passed away recently," she continued without any judgement in her voice. At her age I guessed she'd heard it all. "Bradley and Jason for this little fellow, after their father. He said 'no argument, Sugar.'"

I burst out laughing as I covered my mouth. Jason's puffy grey-blue eyes lazily opened and closed, followed by a little snore.

"Up on your shoulder," she said. Of course she was right and somewhere between exhaustion and worry I consented. Jason remained quiet for only a minute until he seemed to deflate with a little poof of air then the wailing wound up again.

"Goodness, if he's been carrying on like this for nine months no wonder his brother needs his sleep."

I agreed and she lowered my bed and helped me tuck him in.

Paul's hand on my cheek woke me and he was all smiles when I opened my eyes. I'd rolled over back and forth with Jason keeping him connected as much as I could to keep the noise down. Paul had been in and out trying to calm Jason with walking and rocking and a bottle eventually so I could get a bit of sleep or watch his brother in the I.C.U. but I was all he wanted.

"Bradley's awake," he whispered. "They've disconnected everything. He'll be with you soon."

I reached over Jason for Paul's stubbly cheek and tried to smooth away the last of the worry from his forehead. His voice roughened with the long night. The nurse had swooped the curtains open in my private room as the sun came up.

"Jack should have been here," I said. "He wanted them so much."

"I can't decide if they look more like Jack or your father. I wouldn't have hurt him, Sugar. That night at his house I went there to kill him. I would have then but not after. Even if it meant you choosing him. I never could have caused you the pain of his death. He didn't deserve to suffer like that."

Paul rubbed his eyes to hide the emotion on his face.

"It's right to name them after him," he went on. "He's their father. I want to be their Dad, Sugar. More than anything. I want to stay by your side however we turn out."

Then he leaned back in his chair to wait for my answer.

"Mister Richards?" I whispered.

"Yeah, Missus Richards?"

"I couldn't love you more even if I felt you here," I said, rubbing my chest near Jason's quiet cheek. "Be my husband, Paul. Whatever you need to be my husband is yours."

Paul sighed once through his nose then again as he nodded.

"Thank you," he whispered. "This last month watching you and Camille fall in love with each other again has been so good. Most nights I've gone to my bed upstairs thinking it's all I'll ever need but some nights I've just felt so alone and I wanted to go to you but I didn't know what you really wanted."

A quiet squawk came from the hall and Jason's eyes opened wide. Then he started to sniff as another bassinet was rolled in. Paul stood and squeezed my hand as Doctor Carr appeared behind Bradley.

"Here's mom," she said.

"Ready?" Paul asked. He picked up Jason who immediately started to cry as Carr passed Bradley to me. I fussed for a few minutes getting him started on his first feeding. Paul tucked Jason in behind his brother, quieting him and there was a little 'da da da da' from the hall.

Paul laughed.

"How does she know where he is, Ray?" Alina's voice came to us.

"She's as smart as you, Sweetie," Ray answered. "And you know where we're going."

Alina harrumphed.

"No, Mimi," Camille firmly said.

"Mimi?" I asked as Doctor Carr slipped out.

"She calls Julian Mimi."

Camille faced forward on Alina's hip. Her arms and legs pumped as she tried to run through the air to her dad. As Ray brought Julian in Julian's eyes went wide as he looked at me and the boys. He looked so much like Damian even though his line was all Ray.

"Ah," Julian shrieked.

"Mimi NO," Camille yelled and Alina put her down. She ran to Paul but squirmed out of his arms, squishing her brothers and starting another round of wailing.

"No, Mimi. My baby!"

I hadn't seen Ray or Alina in nine months, not since a few days before the boys were conceived. Ray looked older, finally earning a bit of grey on his temples but Alina clomped along in heels and a skirt just as made up and beautiful as ever. As they pulled Camille off the boys, Alina took Camille's place smothering me.

Nearly an hour and a half passed before peace descended on my room. The boys slept nose to nose in Jason's bassinet and Paul dozed in a chair. Ray took Camille for a walk so Julian could sleep curled up on his mom. His nose twitched every time her hair tickled it.

"He's a good looking boy," I said and she brushed her lips on his forehead.

"Yes," she answered. "I know how much he looks like his father and I'm okay with that. His father was a nightmare but Julian is as cute as they come."

She looked at my boys and then at me. "Ray and I tried for another for a while. Having Camille with us so much and the others. The house is so full. Plus we're both working again, shifts and stuff. We have so much now we kind of lost interest."

I laughed.

"I can't thank you enough, Sweetie," I said. "For taking Paul and Camille in."

"Ray said after the rape you ran off."

So that was the story. I sighed and went with it, as close to the truth as I could.

"I did. I couldn't be with her and there was trouble at home so I couldn't go there. Paul isn't their father but I figure you guessed that."

She nodded, her long earrings swung with the movement. All it would take was one good pull from a chubby little hand and she'd go to studs. Maybe it already happened and she was too stubborn to swap.

"It wasn't the rape," I went on. "Jack was there when I couldn't go home and the boys are his. Jack and I had some history and I fell back on it for support when I couldn't be with Paul. When I found out I was pregnant I was so much more ashamed."

She looked pained and glanced at Paul.

"He knows. Damian was killed, Sweetie," I said, intentionally mixing up the facts. "Jack was shot, Paul and Josh were hurt. They took Paul and Josh to the hospital but they couldn't move Jack without speeding up his end. I was with him when he died."

Alina carefully picked up her little boy and cuddled him between us in my bed.

Epilogue

Camille's shriek stood my hair on end. Ray said if we didn't make a big deal about it she'd lose interest but it was easier said than done. His three-year-old's scream couldn't break glass. Julian only screamed when Camille grabbed his ears and tried to stuff her nose up his to read him.

"Paul?" I called, attempting to sound unruffled. It was my turn to get her ready for bed; no point in both of us being unable to hear if one of the kids was up during the night.

I held the toothbrush to her and she opened up, freeing a scream. When I pulled it away her pink lips snapped shut, filling the bathroom with silence. I checked the windows behind me expecting to see cracks. Then the picture frames. Paul had covered nearly all the walls in the house with pictures of the children, particularly Camille during the months I'd missed. Although it was almost dark the brightly lit room gave the illusion of blackness hiding the truck parked a few feet outside. Paul and I shared what had been Jack's guest bedroom on the main floor. I was in the adjoining bathroom trying to get Camille ready for bed. The kids shared the large bedroom across the hall from ours until the previous weekend when we moved them all upstairs, giving Paul an office on the main floor.

"Paul?" I tried again. So much for not making a big deal. I kept the toothbrush out of sight and Camille stayed quiet as her toes reached for the taps.

"I need Pony, please," I tried, even louder. Ray said nothing about bribes.

"Hands kinda full, Sugar," he answered. No doubt. Jason would be half undressed before Paul had Bradley in his pyjama bottoms. I tried the brush again with the same result as Paul shuffled into the doorway behind me, a blonde two year old clutching each leg riding his feet backwards. A brown bear, a Christmas gift from Grandma Sheryl, flew past and landed in the other sink.

"Thank you," I called out as I passed the bear to Camille.

"PONY!" she cried out then she opened up silently and I got the brush in. She let me get it around every nook and cranny. Her eyes nearly crossed as she grunted like she had toothpaste coating her kidneys before she leaned over and spat.

"I'm having a word with your Uncle Joshua about little girls," I muttered, feeling a strange sense of familiarity with this scene like getting goose bumps on my temples.

I'd found her and Joshua leaning over the front porch rail just a week earlier. Camille claimed Joshua saw a rabbit, a red one in fact, but I suspected a gobbing lesson.

"Close your eyes," I said as I put Pony to her nose. Camille squished her lips up looking very much like her father. "Who is it?"

"Reading Mommy!" she squeaked. I laughed at the mix-up game though the odd feeling persisted and my eyes were briefly drawn to the mirror. I put my nose to hers and she tried again. "Reading... Pony!"

She tipped over sideways, laughing as I found a clear memory of Jack and me watching this exchange from the other side of the glass. A thrust of sharp pain like an evil hiccup surged into the right side of my chest and I grimaced at my reflection as I tried to contain the discomfort with my palm. Memories only made the pain worse so I focused on Camille, sitting her up and putting our noses together.

"Reading clean teeth," I announced and returned her smile. She was obviously pleased with my declaration even though she hadn't made it easy. I helped her from the counter and she held my hand, skipping along beside me down the hall to the living room with Pony dangling beside her. Paul got the book up just before she pounced onto his lap and I scooped up Jason and curled in next to them. He didn't miss a word as his other arm reached around Bradley pulling the nearly sleeping boy closer.

After Yates the pirate fish recovered the ship's wheel and sailed his pirate friends to safety, Paul carried Bradley upstairs and I followed behind with Camille and Jason. No night owl awards for little Bradley. He'd been the first to regularly sleep through the night, even before

Camille. Camille's new room was the same colour blue as her brothers,' her choice. They shared Jack's old room and Camille had the little one I used when Soros caught up to Jack and me years earlier. We left the hall light on and their doors part way open and made our escape downstairs to restore some order to the house before we turned in.

The phone rang as I loaded the last of the dinner dishes in the dishwasher. Paul abandoned the cloth he used to wipe the table and took the handset down the hall. I heard him greet Sig and my stomach soured. He'd apologetically called Paul up four times in the past two years. Each absence was harder than the last for me. Paul knew it. It wasn't only looking after three toddlers alone; without feeling our mated connection I suffered without the constant reassurance he was okay. The last time I pulled up stakes and took the kids to Alina and Ray's in San Diego. Ray resigned just after Julian was born and he and my sister both worked for the same hospital. She was still in Emergency and Ray found a home in the children's wing.

I read Paul behind me as I finished rinsing out the cloth; the running water masked the sound of his footsteps then his hands rested on my shoulders as his lips nuzzled my neck. A gentle nudge of pressure in my chest got my attention as I hung the cloth over the faucet and pulled down the handle, shutting off the flow.

"It's working," I murmured.

"Yeah?" he whispered as his warm lips moved up to graze the tender spot behind my ear, making me shiver. "Oh yeah."

"Mm hm."

The first time it worked was a shock. I hadn't thought much about the building pressure in my chest, figuring it to be a combination of sex, too little sleep, and too much coffee but then in the moments of release Paul clutched his chest, gasping the name Agnes. I'd held him tight as the pressure in me ballooned like when Agnes first connected to him and when it burst I felt our connection for the first time in well over a year. I called him Dammo, expecting the heavily private silence I received from Paul anytime past lives came up and as I revelled in my restored link I told him of the memory Wendy helped me find.

He listened and then in the dark, barely whispering, Paul told me how Dammo felt when he first connected to Agnes. How inadequate Dammo felt to bear the responsibility of having a mate, his panic when he sent Agnes away. The courage Dammo found in himself as he laid out a soft place for her to sleep in the clearing before he went to take her from her mother. Within hours my connection to Paul faded and the pain of losing Jack took hold again. I was devastated but Paul said it was a miracle for me to feel our connection again, even for a short while, and I had several times since.

"I need to talk to you," he whispered. I read the top floor and sensed the kids in their rooms.

"Is this a going away thing?"

"No," he answered as he pulled me out of the kitchen toward our room, catching the light switch with his hand on the way by. "It's an 'it can wait' thing."

We never wasted our few hours of full connection sleeping. There would be another round of intimacy before it wore off and we usually talked until then, our chests and lines pressed close.

"I need your help making a decision, Sugar," Paul said as he tucked my head under his chin.

"Of course," I answered as I reached around his waist and held on.

"I kept serving so long for a number of reasons. One to keep an eye on Josh; as long as he stayed in I felt responsible for him. He idolized his big brother growing up and as long as he wanted to be there with me I wasn't going to move on. It's different with him becoming family but he's still my mother's son and in her eyes it's my job to take care of him even at his age.

"I guess the other reason was I really don't have anything else I know how to do.

"Then I found you and we had Camille and now the boys. Nobody is more proud to have a house full of kids than I am."

"I know," I said. It was never a secret who their father was and Paul told everyone who would listen how proud he was to be their Dad.

"Josh took a position as a civilian instructor and resigned his commission. I suspect there's a woman involved," Paul said. I waited a minute for him to keep going as I put my hand on his chest and leaned back to look at him. "I wrote my resignation letter this afternoon. The past week I've had a couple of meetings at the Sacramento Police Department. I'd be a new recruit. Law enforcement is a big change from what I've been doing for so long but the work interests me a lot.

"Every time Sig calls now I see your heart break even when it's only to say hello. I can't leave you again and honestly it's a million times safer."

"I know it's a tough decision for you, Paul," I said. "Starting over like that; but what are your options in the military? Promotion, relocation? You know we'd go wherever your career took you but I think it would take you away from leading in the field. Maybe you're concerned you'd miss the saddle too much?"

"That's not it," he sighed. "I'd miss getting my hands dirty."

I brushed my nose on his chin then kissed his throat as he tugged me tighter.

"What about you? You want to go back to taking pictures of bikers?"

I vehemently shook my head. "I spent too much time away from Camille already. I'm not leaving her again. My life is full here. There's nothing I want more than to enjoy living it."

"I feel the same way," he said.

"I remember the first time I saw you in uniform," I whispered. "I said you looked cute but you looked so damn good. You winked at me and then were out of the room before you could see me blush or catch me leering."

"I see," he replied as he rolled me to my back and settled his weight on me. I hooked a foot behind his knee.

"If you joined the Sacramento Police I'd get to see you in uniform every day?"

"Yes," he laughed as his head fell to the pillow next to mine. "Just when I thought I knew you I find you're easily taken with a man in uniform."

"Your wife can be as shallow as they come, Paul," I answered as we started to warm up again. "I think we've decided... I'll give Sig your letter myself."

Thank you for reading Deadly Redemptions. Writing it has been an amazing experience and sharing it with others has made that experience even better. Other readers would love to hear your thoughts on this book (or any others you have enjoyed!) Please take a moment to visit the online store from which you downloaded it and share your thoughts. Your support helps small publishers and independent writers continue to provide great and original stories!

Thank you.

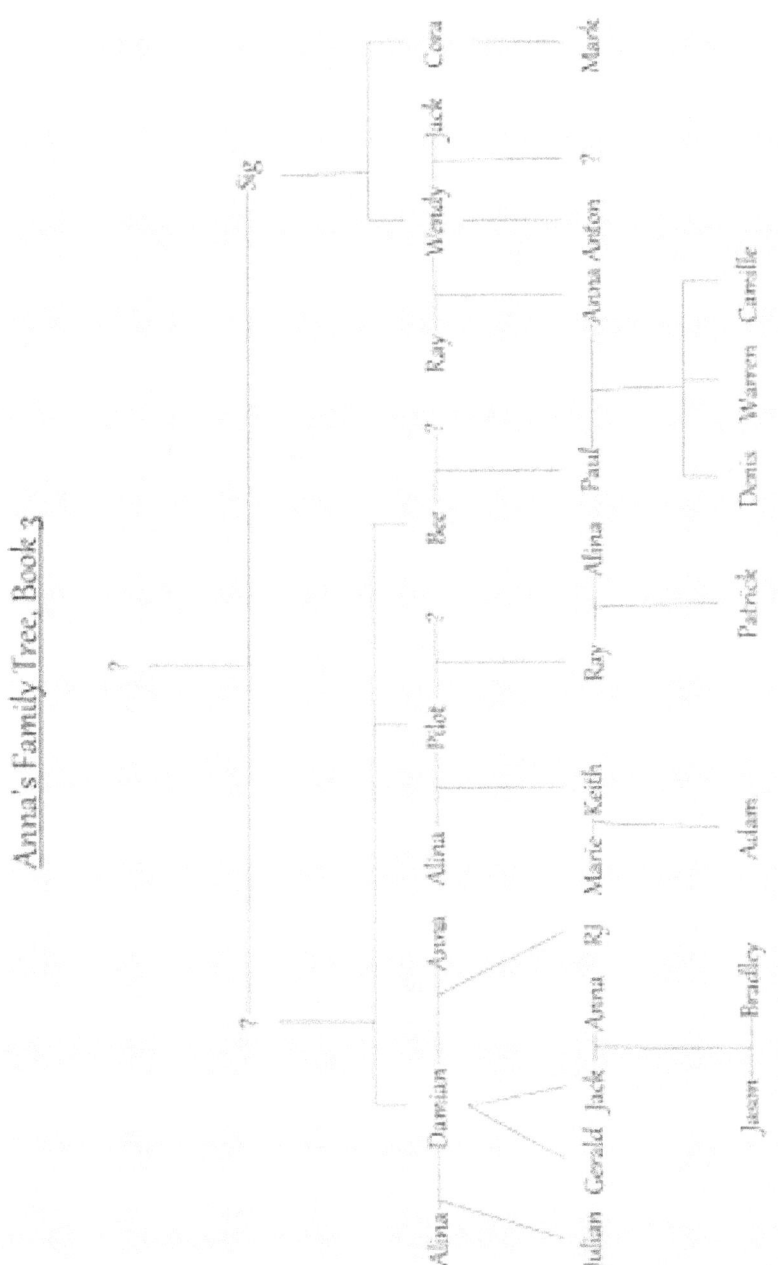

Anna's Family Tree, Book 3

www.ingramcontent.com/pod-product-compliance
Lightning Source LLC
Chambersburg PA
CBHW071256250626
47159CB00004B/1215